Distance

Becomes

Sky

~~~~~~~~~~~~~~~~~

Distance

Becomes

Sky

~~~~~~~~~~~~~~~~

~~

RACHEL DUTTON OLDS

HEART SEED PRESS

All characters in this book are imaginary, and any resemblance to any actual people, places, or projects is unintentional and coincidental. Some of the science is imaginary too, but the Earth skills are very real.

Heart Seed Press
www.acircleisdrawn.org
email: robert.rachel@acircleisdrawn.org

ISBN 978-0-983-1945-1-4

Book design by Robert and Rachel Olds.
Cover illustration © 1995 by Rachel Dutton Olds.

Dedicated to all Earth peoples and to all those who are choosing to return to a life blended with our First Mother, and to all the rocks and waters and plant and animal kin who share this beautiful Earth with us.

Cold wind. A faint dampness in the air. Tundra skies, mountain high. A hint of the sea in the mineral smell of the bare grey rocks, in the wind echoing silence in the stones. The mountain speaking in sea tones, sea smells today. Time thinning, vaporous, tentative. Like the day moon fading above her, and the porous chalk bone clouds melting into the clear blue sky. Time no longer keeping future and past apart. Nothing to prevent her current now from dissolving into both of them. This season, this time still holding her here, would be her last.

She was old. Frost color on her muzzle, threaded through her grizzled fur. Cloud wisps of memories in her eyes. A small notch in the edge of an ear, another memory, torn from long ago when she fought the big tawny-shouldered male to defend her cubs. She and he standing tall, roaring, growling, facing each other. He twice her size, she growing larger and larger as she roared, mother fierce in her greatness. Her teats showing proud through her fur. They cuffed each other as she grew, and then he backed down, leaving only that small notch in her towering form, a token of his dignity denied. Oh how she could roar and shake when she was full of life, full of mothering. The younger males gathering to her, growing stronger in their fullness too, challenging each other over her.

Young and full of her own life then, sloe-eyed, pleasured, looking coyly over her shoulder as the male mounted her. Nuzzled her neck. Entered her. Long in his heat. The two of them together. Bear flesh clasping bear flesh. Longly, tightly, rhythmically. Locked together like mountains for eons of rock sloped high peaked time, seas rising and falling again, leveling the mountains in their sea tides. The future pulsing into her, meeting a future already prepared, waiting, born within her, her mother's memories and her mother's mothers' before. Seed essence of bear meeting sea wild mystery, ancient with bear kind. Sloe eyed tall roaring teat hanging mother eggs greeting sea tossed wanderers, welcoming them home, memories weaving together, waiting, intertwined, to weave new livingness of the gathered dreams of their kind. Sea spent, she and he part. The notched ear one not even a memory for him. Except to step aside impartially, impersonally, giving way to her overpowering motherness, when she wanted the salmon place where the waters plunging parted just so around the rock and she could snag the quick silver rainbowed fish as they leaped. Except for that, she would not be a memory for him, only a memory to be, for those of his seed who rode to harbor on their mutual heat.

She would remember for both he and she instead, how she had been with him, water parting, catching quick swimming bear seed fish, adding to the other memories living cellular, secure, in each mothersea egg

2

mystery carried cell to cell in their passage through time. Warmth of blood and fur. Cave dark, moist breathing in blind darkness. Her own blind darkness as a small cub, breathing in her mother's breath. Her own breath as a mother, surrounding her cubs in their newborn darkness, cubs suckling on her breathing presence as much as on her milk. Warm tides of mother breathing reaching back through long lines of bear kind. Salmon catching, water splashing, deep digging, root eating, ground squirrel eating, insect eating, larva eating, carrion eating, berry, nut, and green shoot eating futures pulsing in tiny drops of memory. Ever curious, testing spring of sapling, taste of leaf, of air, testing rotted log and gravely earth, raking claws casually through each, dirt churning, rock flying, grass clod eating, tender bulb eating, rock and earth eating, ant and grub eating, the wanderers. Bears crossing mountains, rivers, meadows, sand shoals, sea thinned mud flats, leaving their wide strong flatfooted tracks stepping in each other's footsteps pressed in waiting earth braiding side to side, stepping in their own and each other's tracks in the same way each time, weaving familiar paths through the middle of their discovering. Careful, fearless, wide roaming, confident bear essence dissolving in seas of memory. Egg seed essence of new lives waiting until she, sheltering them in her body enters earth, sleeps deep beyond sleep and dream, and they germinate and grow inside her sheltered in her winter sleep. Yes, she would remember how she had been with him, water parting, catching quick swimming bear seed fish.

She looked up at the sky. Sifting the tundra sea air with her breath, seeing the sky with mountain eyes.

Seeing someday far away, on another mountain in another land and another time, one of her line of daughters' daughters' daughters would perhaps remember this one moment, this one memory out of all the others, carried on the sea passions of their kind. A daughter moving through the gates of timeless memory as freely as the bear seed eggs moved through the gates of her sea tides. Remembering not her, the bear as she stands here today looking at the sky, but what she sees, just now, in the sky above her mountain. A long salmon shape fish scaled vaporous cloud. Four long thin vaporous cloud rays slanting side by side above it bursting out of the fish, like claw marks on the sky, each ringed with a soft edged rainbow band of color, luminous and pale, part of the ephemeral circle around the sun. Rainbow clawed bear catching cloud fish in the sky. Sun eyed bear within the halo of the sun.

4

"I'm sorry, Sir, no one is allowed in to see her," the man guarding the entrance to Medical repeated, his lips flat, thin, barely moving. He was not sorry. He had been expecting them, recognized them on sight, almost as soon as the sensors did. Their ID profiles loading automatically to his CID, the corneal implant device. He had watched their approach down the long corridor through a screen of their public and private data streaming on the CID, letters and numbers falling across his eyes like geometric rain, or regiments of tiny spiders.

"She is my wife. I am Linn Brenner, and this is our son Kai. Why can't we see her?" Linn kept his gestures restrained and his voice mild, as he tried to deal with the man blocking their way. The guard would already know their names, would already know everything about them. He had said it anyway, determined to engage on a human level. In the harsh light of the hallway, the man's eyes looked like holes in a mask. Remote. Impersonal. They didn't offer much hope.

"Regulations." The guard knew the name all right, and he could read between the lines too, drew his own conclusions. Just as the chief had done. His orders were clear. Keep them out. Brenner was one of the academic hot shots, a maverick, creative type, research, worked over in SA, Systems Analysis. More than enough to justify the orders. The guard set his weight firmly in front of the door. "New regulations," he added for emphasis. This was ISEC business now, Internal Security Executive Committee. Let Brenner analyze that.

"What regulations?"

"She has been placed in quarantine." Their files finished playing on the CID. The thin lines monitoring their vital signs continued to show on VSIC, the vital signs composite index. He studied the father and son directly. Both tall, the father taller, the son catching up soon. Unruly hair, both of them. Something the guard disapproved of. Personally disapproved of. There weren't any regulations about hair, but setting a good example was important for morale. Theirs was a bit long over the eyes, and any moment one of them would be brushing it aside with the casual, almost intimate gesture people with hair like that had. He found it distasteful.

"Quarantine? Why?"

"We cannot risk a potentially lethal virus spreading to the rest of the Lab."

"She wasn't sick this morning. She's one of the healthiest people here."

"Recent medical tests show she may have been carrying it dormant all these years."

"What medical tests?"

"Her records are classified." The guard did not like being questioned. And he did not like having to look up at the tall man and his tall son while answering.

6

"Classified? She is my wife. I have a right to see her records. I have a right to see her."

"Quarantine is under ISEC jurisdiction. Her records are now classified." He watched them. Their frustration was beginning to show, on their faces and in their vital signs. The father was careful to keep it in check, good control. The guard approved of that. The boy not yet careful enough. Good material though, if he had proper training.

Kai had been quiet while his father tried to reason with the guard. Now he broke in, his tone insistent, taut, with a slight quaver beginning to rise in a voice still navigating his coming of age into manhood. "Why can't we see her?"

The guard had readied himself when he saw a surge in the boy's VSCI lines just before Kai spoke. He put all the force he had been prepared to use physically into his words instead. "You will have to leave, now. I will be informing the chief of ISEC about our conversation and your concern in this matter." Informing him about which aspects of their conversation and concern was not exactly clear, but certainly implied. He didn't think they would miss the warning.

"Thank you. Come on then, Kai. Let's go." Linn stepped between Kai and the guard, put his arm around the boy's shoulders, and steered him away. He kept his arm protectively around him as they moved down the long hallway. The pressure of his arm on his son's shoulders was as much to steady himself as to reassure Kai. Dangerous to provoke the ISEC people.

Faces floated into view again, like pale fish, or stones in deep water coming in and out of focus, always there, always deep, and she was falling toward them as they sank farther away and then returned. She could no longer remember who she was or why she was here. The faces wanted something from her, answers, words, words they wanted her to say. Her mouth refused to shape the words they wanted to hear. Those words would not be true. She waited, falling, sinking, while they tried to reach her.

The fever gripped her again. They must have bio-synched the mind drug with a flu virus, dangerous to use a combination like that, she should warn them, the cellular cascade.... She faded out, turning inward, seeking refuge. The glowing heat of the fever helped her resist, not by opposing force with force, not through the battle of wills they were trying to provoke, but simply because she was no longer there, no longer bound by identity, or time, or place. She had melted away, into vapor, into mist, incandescent, evanescent, expanding bits of light circling, dissolving, no one to defend, no one left to inhabit fear. The disorientation they had induced to increase her suffering provided sanctuary instead. Letting go into an unknown vastness, molten, glowing with the heat of light, was perhaps what they themselves most feared. They had propelled her there for torment, and she went home to the light instead. In her homeward turning a simple radiance, welcoming and plain, opened to her and rescued her from the confusion of the mind drug. She remained on a small island in that bright inward sea, sifting translucent strands of memory, brightness and distance protecting her each time they tried to pull her back.

More shadowy faces above her, trying to come closer, shouting through the hollow tunnel of space between them, their voices echoing. She remembered now, being summoned to the ISEC office, the chief of internal security pretending it was merely a minor infraction he wanted to question her for. The pompous ass. As if we even needed an internal security officer. For what? We were all internal security here. Everything hinged on everyone doing their part, everyone knowing what was going on. A separate policing function had seemed ludicrous and grotesque as well as superfluous when it was first considered. There were those of us, and vocal too, who could see the potential for abuse. The bureaucrats had prevailed. Just for coordination, and to mediate any conflicts that were sure to arise they said, already postulating a future us and them, already polarized, wanting to be sure they did not lose control. So much for consensus and mutual respect. And that must be one of the reasons she was here.

9

Voices echoing again down the long hollow distance. They were so adamant that she recant. Re-cant, -cant, -cant, -cant, can't, can't, can't, canto, cantar. And the singing too. They must have heard her even though she had tried to find a secret place. There were a few, those blind spots. Here and there, a forgotten corner in the angle of a buttress or a turn in a hallway that was out of range of the sensor fields. She had sung so softly, sung only a small song, as one would sing to a small child or a lover, a delicate song, full of tenderness and beauty, like the softly breathing wings of a butterfly. Her love of beauty, unquantifiable, unpredictable, along with the singing, she added that to the list of her presumably undesirable qualities, as she faded back into the private distance of memory, incandescent, without form.

Surfacing again. Edges, and shadows. The room dark. A bright bubble of light in front of her. Hard to see, it hurt her eyes. More faces, in the bubble this time. Linn and Kai. They were trapped in there, just as she was trapped in here. A monitor screen, grainy image flickering. A surveillance tape, a replay. Or were Linn and Kai out there now, trying to reach her? A longing to be with them, to hold them, touch them, lurched out of her, stretching her, tearing her, before she could pull it back. She couldn't leave the safety of the inner brightness. The other faces, shadowed now behind her in the darkened room, were trying to lure her out, into the bubble, into a different brightness, hard, cold, exposed. She couldn't go to Linn and Kai, not with the other faces lurking so near, waiting to prey on her.

10

Another face in the bubble, confronting Linn and Kai, the face of the man blocking their way. His features sharp and cold, like the light in the bubble. Bands of data shouldering across the bottom of the screen. Names and ID files. Assessment summaries. Systems analyst. Research. Level 4 clearance. A rough voice beside her. Harsh. "Yeah, Brenner. Hot shot. Maverick. Creative type." Another voice repeating sarcastically, "Hot shot, maverick, we'll see." Coarse jagged laughter. She wondered for a moment what the laughter would look like on VSCI. The VSCI lines for Linn and Kai were wavering, hard for her to focus on them. Some flatter curves, Linn was good at keeping calm, but some lines spiking when he spoke with the guard, and when the guard rebuffed him. Kai's lines rising and falling like an echo of his father's. Kai almost as tall as Linn. Same engaging shyness about his height, same confident ease that had nothing to do with being tall, even with his adolescent body still going two ways at once as well as up. Same hair. Familiar hair. She longed to brush it from their eyes, to look into, not at those eyes, and tell them to go away, to get out of the danger here.

A voice-over from the bubble, the one the guard is hearing on his auditory implant. "She is being detained, just tell them quarantine." Her own voice, soundless with the cry she cannot let herself give out loud. *NO!!!!!* Linn and Kai were leaving. She wanted them to stay, she wanted them to get away. She wanted to never lose sight of them again. She wanted to keep them safe. *No safety here.* She wanted to will them away down the long corridor, shrinking smaller and smaller, farther and farther, until they were safe. They wouldn't go away.

They were still there, up close in the bubble. A surge in Kai's vital signs, the guard bracing. *Be careful Kai.* She watched, helpless, as the scene played out on the bright screen. She tried to look away. Into the darkness of the room shadowy around her. Hands from behind her forcing her head back toward the screen, forcing her to watch. Slapping her face when she closed her eyes. Linn so confident and at ease in other ways. An easy generosity about the range of his mind. Faces turning her head, shaking her, forcing her attention back to the screen. Voices in the room with her. "Yeah, academic, hot shot, a maverick." They said that before. Replay. Replay. "Level 4 clearance. High up." "Not for long." Laughter. Another voice. "This is ISEC business now, not research." *Be careful Linn.* The chorus again, voices sharp like evil crickets. "Creative type." "Yeah, maverick. Well this is ISEC business...." *Shut up! Shut up! Shut UP! Shut.... shut.... shut..... shut.... up.*

They must have eased up on the drug. She was coming back into focus, lying bound on a table or some sort of gurney. Her body unfamiliar, condensing around her, growing heavy, with the dry land feeling of weight no longer floating, returning to painful gravity. The bubble screen was gone. She was in the reclamation area now. Through a gap between the faces suspended above her, she could see the shining steel ring framing a darkness she knew was there. Everyone knew it was there, few had seen it, but the space beyond the circular rim was the size of an adult human body, they all knew. A space only for those who had passed on, not for the living. Were they still trying to break her, before they disposed of her, had they already decided that they would?

She remembered other faces, absent but still floating free in memory. The unexpected deaths, usually among colleagues in whose presence you felt a certain subtle vividness, an opening into possibility, a little breathing room in this ultimately claustrophobic space they had all volunteered to live within and had pledged not to leave. It had been easier in the beginning, the project filled with hope and a sense of discovery and contribution, before the Last War and the Wasting that followed it, before the desolation of the Earth, before there was nowhere to leave to, even if you wanted to leave. Before the equipment had begun to break down, before improvising repairs with what they had on hand had lost the feeling of resourcefulness and became desperation instead.

Reclaim had been designed into the system from the start, modeled after the space burial ports on the early transport ships, but in the closed biosphere they had here nothing leaves, nothing comes in or out. Here reclaim was a way to not waste that which was already given, and likely to be given infrequently at best, as long as everyone remained in good health. Which was, after all, one of the objectives of the project. Mutual health. Once. She was surprised they were using reclaim, expensive process, used more energy than it recovered. Unless some of the bio trace minerals could be found nowhere else. She had seen the reports. There were shortages in some key trace minerals needed for the food crops, the same minerals now sequestered in the bodies of all of us. The shortages had been expected but not for a much longer time. And no one had expected to be out

13

here so long without possibility of relief, at the mercy of miscalculation or worse. If hard choices were to be made, it was a matter for the whole group to decide, not imposed by the ISEC chief and his privileged inner guard.

People had noticed, slowly. Some challenged, some talked quietly. Most kept their thoughts to themselves, and at worst, some sought the protection that collusion with security presumably bought. Everyone had become withdrawn, many afraid. It added to the burden of their physical isolation, along with the lack of comtrans. Not that the communication transceivers were down, they were still working fine, that kind of equipment was apparently not so vulnerable after all, compared to the fragile bio web, compared to the frail human mind. The ISEC chief had pulled more than a few others to him in their fear. Divide and conquer, divide and rule. Why in some people did the human flower refuse to leave the bud, so obstinately and with great effort refuse to bloom? A poet, read somewhere far away, in another life.

Whatever of her that had coalesced in the shadowed space of the reclamation room, accompanied by an oddly busy clarity, seeking here and there like a small hand held flashlight determined to find some coherence in whatever came into its gaze, began to melt away. They must have given her more of the drug again. She receded into the safety of the inner brightness. Perhaps they had only wanted her to see what they were going to do so they could feed on her fear, rather than trying to control her. Had cruelty, even more than security, become their prize, had they gone that far? The hybrid fever had not let her surface long enough for them to work on her in that way. They had almost broken her, almost. The flickering images of Linn and Kai they showed her had pulled at her, wrenched her apart, but the fever had pulled her back even then. Linn and Kai had gotten away. They disappeared down the long hallway. She had watched them leave, somehow she was sure of that. And just as surely she kept them with her in her heart, sheltered in her love within the protective brightness. She kept them, sheltered, wordless, imageless, unnamed, just love itself, hidden safely in her heart on the inner island where the drug and the faces could never go.

Darkness closed in, enfolding her in a kindness beyond light at the brink of complete dissolve. Within the darkness, a warmth kindled from the expanse of her love, a warmth that remained unseen by the unseeing faces as her still living body was slid into the reclamation tube.

Clanking, cold, metallic, far away, latches clicked, levers pulled, a rubbery thump followed by hollow sounds. Sliding, rolling, toward the hollow sounds, a sudden change in air pressure, and an unfamiliar smell, long forgotten, minerals steeped in moisture, like desert air after a rain. A brief swirl of tiny flickering lights, pinpoints in the darkness, then cold, bone cold with the weight of mountains falling through cold darkness, through bottomless depths, rich saline smell of wet earth embracing her within the darkness, then absence, beyond depth.

Faces, faintly seen as if by starlight, faces of tall figures wrapped in soft shadows, silent, touching her with gentle

15

hands. Air crisp and cold as nights remembered from long ago, merging back into compounded memory, spiraling out of time, hands lifting her carefully, carrying one part of her away while the rest dissolves.

McPhearson rubbed his eyes wearily. Too early in the morning to be tired, long day ahead. How had he come to this, an old school field biologist now tethered to a desk, a reluctant bureaucrat trying to survive? He sighed. The sound of his unguarded exhale startled him, brought him back to the job he was trying to evade. He searched through the papers piled in shaggy stacks in front of him, their disarray pointedly at odds with the smooth grey metal surface under them. He set aside a few more pages for ink recov, and wondered as he fingered the flat pages, how many times he had handled the same sheets before, each time bearing different directives, different urgencies, their surfaces wiped clean of memory each time. Working from paper copy was all he had left of his old school self, a self he barely knew anymore, erased more slowly but just as surely by the same necessity. In response, the printer on the side counter clicked and whirred into life. More directives, another issue demanding his attention. The screen of his computer glowered accusingly. Whatever they had just sent on the fax was waiting for him on the screen too, if he had

17

looked. He sighed again, then rubbed his left shoulder gently and grimaced to suggest physical cause for his sighing if anyone was monitoring the sensors. Definitely not going to be a good day.

He found the form he was looking for. The one that needed his signature, logical enough to be dealt with on paper this time. EQUIPMENT AUTHORIZATION FOR SHORT RECON HOVER FLIGHT. INTERNAL SECURITY MISSION. PRIORITY LEVEL URGENT. First flight in decades. Of course it's urgent. Everything is urgent here these days, and since when is an outside mission under ISEC jurisdiction anyway? PILOT LINCOLN BRENNER. This was the hard part, the reason he had been putting off signing the requisition. Linn was the only one of us with any hope of remembering how to fly the damn thing, but McPhearson didn't trust the sons of bitches over at ISEC. They had their own hidden priorities. They hadn't given Linn much choice, hadn't given McPhearson much choice either. That brought on another sigh, this time out of frustration, rather than, what? Better not go there. Frustration bad enough. Hauling the hover out of storage, scavenging parts for it, parts that had been scavenged from the hover in the first place after more essential equipment began to fail. A shell game. All that had taken time away from other repairs demanded just as urgently. A rock and a hard place, grinding against each other.

He looked out the open door of his small office toward the source of the directives, straight across the main footbridge that spanned the vast interior space of the central dome of Lab 7. Only a few people out already, getting an early start on their workday. How did these people maintain their zeal? More likely finishing something left undone the day before, as he was. He could see the office of the ISEC chief, directly across from him over the wide walkway. The door was shut, was always shut, even when the chief was in. The closed door had a presence as disturbing as it was eloquent, whether the chief was in or not. Poignant, ironic, the geometry of this place, their two offices facing each other across the dome, the footbridge connecting opposite sides of the hemispheric space. Open door and practical logistics on one end, and behind the shut door on the other end, the nebulous, secretive, increasingly intrusive functions of internal security. ISEC had commandeered a row of offices on either side of the chief. Balance of powers decidedly lopsided now. McPhearson felt the oppressive heaviness emanating from the ISEC block almost as a physical weight. The soaring space of the dome pulling inward from that weight no longer felt grand and inspiring, but claustrophobic instead.

More people on the walkway and the balconies now, coming and going from living quarters to offices and workstations. The morning rush hour. A familiar murmur of hushed voices and careful steps. Blurred echoes, cautious ghosts of moments ago, reflecting from the hard plass and steel dome shell above them. He turned the metal nameplate on his desk around to face himself like another ghost, to remind him of who he was supposed to be here. E R McPhearson, External Security Operations. He had insisted on "operations" instead of "office" in his title, hoping to keep from getting caught behind the desk. Hadn't worked. Rest of the title wasn't right either. Once the outside sensors failed after the solar storms, no external anymore. Nothing left to monitor out there anyway. It was just us and the equipment inside, and his teams had been relegated to fixing whatever broke. Operational Repair. OR, as in surgery, always feels like surgery here these days. His first initials could stand for Emergency Room instead of the names he never used. Emergency surgery. Despite the wary, muted tone of the murmur outside his door, it carried an acknowledgement of the same uneasy discord, the same unquiet urgency he and his crews dealt with every day.

He turned his thoughts to his friend Linn. Sad about Linn's wife. Tragic. The suddenness of her mysterious illness, the quarantine, her unexpected death. Two years now, and hard for Linn to complete his grieving with so many unanswered questions. Hard on their boy Kai too. Hadn't seen much of him since her death. Heard he had been assigned to the training dome, fast track academic studies, immersion method. He hoped the kid was doing okay. Young people are resilient, but some wounds go deep, very deep, at any age. The loss of his wife had shaken Linn, shaken McPhearson too. They went back a long way, the three of them, all the way back to their days in graduate work at the academy. They had been quite a team. Linn, tall, thin, a bit awkward with his height, dipping his head like a long necked bird, kinetic, unpretentious and direct, with an engaging ready smile, an enthusiast, a born explorer, a born questioner. Miri, Miriam, quick like Linn and just as playful, shorter, earthier, with a generous heart, a "givey person" another friend once said, spirited, loyal, a pint size momma bear. The two of them were already so thoroughly bonded together when McPhearson first met them in one of his field classes that they had welcomed his friendship as if they were one person. Apparently they had seen, from their stereoscopic vantage point, a McPhearson beyond the intentionally nondescript persona he cultivated. His pale freckled ancestral skin perpetually red from being outdoors in the sun, round face, medium build, pale hair already thinning even then, he had been the straight man, the secret agent, keeping the playful range of his own mind carefully undercover except with his friends. The freedom fighters, the three of them had called themselves. Long conversations late at night, how to stop the tide of statistical analysis threatening to overwhelm the still presumably living life sciences, how to keep the heart of what they loved alive.

And how with all of that, had they ended up here? The lure of pioneering work, the challenge, the dare. Can a group of humans really live together in a totally enclosed self-contained bio system? Could they create a viable, nurturing, cohesive social process within that closed space, one that was flexible and vibrant enough to continue through several generations, through the hundred years or more that long distance space travel required. Worth a try. Miri was the one who said, *If it's going to work, they need people like us. What's the point of sending a bunch of number crunchers out to other worlds? What about the music of the spheres, they'll need someone who can listen, and delight.* He missed them, Miri's definitive absence, and Linn's withdrawal into himself. McPhearson missed himself too, so distant from his earlier years. He missed the dreams of what could be. Another sigh, and for a moment he was beyond caring what the surveillance sensors might or might not be making of it, then he picked up a pen and added his signature to the requisition form. He looked at the scrawl of his own name loping across the bottom of the page. Maybe not emergency room, maybe hospice care instead.

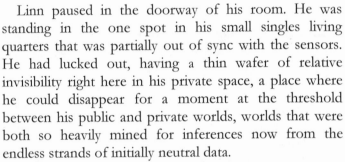

Linn paused in the doorway of his room. He was standing in the one spot in his small singles living quarters that was partially out of sync with the sensors. He had lucked out, having a thin wafer of relative invisibility right here in his private space, a place where he could disappear for a moment at the threshold between his public and private worlds, worlds that were both so heavily mined for inferences now from the endless strands of initially neutral data.

Nights were the hardest for Linn. Suppressing the natural range of his mind. He hadn't slept well last night, most nights. Too much wanting to surface, too much that had to be held back. He used to welcome wakeful hours in the night. After going back and forth at the edge of sleep chewing over the same thoughts again and again, his ruminating mind would settle, spacious, free of outer and inner scrutiny. He used to enjoy allowing his thoughts and feelings to come and go in that open space, allowing deeper clearer perception to arise, unlike the vacant protective transparency he had to cultivate now. Often Miri would be awake then too, roaming the same restless shoreline between sleep and sleeplessness, between daytime and nighttime mind. They both did some of their best work then. They spoke little, it was enough to wander the same shore together. He winced as if from physical pain, and shied away. Another reason the nights were so dangerous for him, so full of remembering. The omnipresent sensors now reading even the secret metabolism of memories and dreams.

How the hell had they ended up here. Tracing back, to the beginning. Finding the announcement about the project in a journal. Researchers needed for simulated space travel. Wide variety of fields. Prestigious project. Science frontier. Long term, your whole life. They had been undecided at first, he and Miri and McPhe. Looking up references, reviewing all available material on space travel. Not the cryo-suspension pods of the early space adventure films, but the real voyages, real people awake and living in real time as they catapulted through decades of space in rehearsal for the generations and centuries required to reach far distances, far even to the imagination. No one knowing if their real time would turn out to be foreshortened, and they would find themselves barely aging after all before their return. Sometimes sci-fi was way ahead of the game. Flights cancelled abruptly. Program mysteriously aborted. No more launches. No explanations. Data from the missions classified.

After they were involved in the project, they found out only that the first missions had failed due to "human dynamics." Covered a big range. Apparently the first teams had not been able to get along. Not well enough for it to last. Tough call if you're in it together for life.

The way things were going at Lab 7 now, those first crews had his sympathy.

New land-based project set up to research functional composition of crews for space travel and colonization. Long term dynamics of small communities, evolving social structures. In situations as close to actual space voyage as they could get. Total containment. Same skills and personnel, same biosphere responsibilities as on the ships, same risks. Personality profiles, data shields, subject A, subject B. Questions of optimal levels of diversity, and a big question for a science mission, whether to include some aspects of the arts. Each of the eight labs in the Human Habitation Project, the Hab Labs, would have a different mix.

Once we were "launched," each Lab would be on its own. Adrift in "space." No weekends, no time off. No sabbaticals. No spacesuits for strolling through the surrounding wilderness. Sealed in. No windows. Outside repairs, if any, handled by remote. Ironically now with the whole Earth ravaged back to lifeless barren rock by nuclear, chemical, and bio weaponry in the last great War to end all wars, the off limits world outside had become more like an inhospitable world in deep space than the project designers would ever have imagined. Except, he thought grimly, in a way we did, collectively as a species, entrained by our prevailing cultures willingly turning our home planet into an alien earth by the way we treated it, as if it was not alive. The war had just been the last gasp of a dying culture trying to live on a dead earth.

Which brought him back to the day at hand, the hover flight, and the uneasy feeling that he might not be coming back, a feeling complicated by the ever present need to not let it show, to not let anything show. Not many people left to say goodbye to if he dared. McPhearson, he would be seeing him on his way over to the hover deck. Kai, he was cloistered over in the academic training dome. No way to engineer a chance meeting, no way to see him casually on his way to transport, might as well be quarantined. He winced again, the analogy had hit too hard. He cautioned himself away from where his thoughts were leading him. Better take a different tack, turbulence ahead. They had been keeping Kai away from him for quite a while now. Afraid Linn would influence the boy in ways they did not approve, ways his mother might have done.... turbulence there too, always there.... He veered away more decisively from the disturbing weight of sadness he could not afford to acknowledge even here in the doorway, and took a deep breath that would certainly show on the room air monitors. Invisible breather now revealed, he stepped out from the protection of relative anonymity, reemerged into the sensor fields, shut the door firmly on the room and his sadness, and headed for the garden terraces and the upper walkway.

The balcony corridor outside his room was empty. Still early in the day, but light already seeping through the plass panes of the dome skin. Molecular louvers in the outer layer would be at high translucence to make the most of what was presumably autumn light outside. The inner layer of the dome glowing with the same pale blue milky hues by day from the biolumen transfer no matter what time of year. Linn climbed the two flights of stairs that led from his level to the garden areas on top of the living quarters. A hushed dawn feeling, plants growing peacefully on their own. For now at least, until the crop techs came on duty. The plants were as monitored as the rest of us. He took a long breath, seeking a bit of extra oxygen in the air lingering around the plants, the daily gift of their tidal breathing. Finding it laced as always with greenhouse mineral smells of growing substrate, amendments, hoses, metal frames, and chemicals. Half garden half mechanics bay. He shook his head in rueful irony and inhaled again, concentrating on the oxygen. For all they knew these plants here with their ordered rows and ordered genetic codes were the last green plants on the Earth. If they had only known for sure, if they had foreseen the unthinkable future, they could have included so much more.... But the lean functionality of a space voyage, pretend or otherwise, may have prevailed even then. He sighed and looked around. Nothing superfluous. No redwoods, sequoias, Jeffery pines, no banyan trees.... all sadly gone beyond recall. This was all that was left of the great outdoors. He looked up toward the soaring arc of the dome, his geodesic mountaintop. His eyes traced the narrow zigzag service stairs that led to the catwalk crossing that high space and down again on the other side, the route of his daily pilgrimage.

The metal frame of the stairs clung to the inner wall of the dome shell as it rose curving inward to the top of its arc. As he climbed the sweep of the dome with the stairs, his thoughts and feelings began pressing up from inside, no longer wary, all crowding against each other wanting to get out like eager birds longing to fly. Gradually, step by step, stair by stair, he set them free. Pausing on the small landings between the switchbacks that marked his passage, he rose with the high curve of the shell until he was looking down at the vast hollow interior of the dome as he climbed, as if he too had taken wing.

Very few sensors for human signs up this far. Very few humans ever came up here either. Sensors in this area were mostly for mechanical operations, monitoring the dome itself. Repair crews wore personal safety devices when they worked up here. Not that the PSD would protect you from falling, just give more data as you fell. Field data. Like the whole project now. Hard science in free fall.

For Linn, data opened other doors. When he was young, he had seen an archived documentary about research satellites, the first ones turned toward the Earth to record the complex rhythms of the planet itself. Herself. After the documentary he was never sure which pronoun to use, the planet was always alive for him after that. He had fallen in love with the sheer beauty and scale of the patterns unfolding, a living breathing interconnected biosphere. Data, statistics, beauty. The links were there, between intricate measureable patterns and the poetry of life. Even though those vast cycles were all gone now, the whole living web of global systems already slowing down before they sealed the Labs, for Linn the patterns of life were still here, their dynamics just expressed on a smaller scale. The capacity for even the smallest life to assert its unpredictability still enthralled and captivated him.

His childhood epiphany had determined his chosen field, systems dynamics. He had been, he was, very good at it. His secret was simply to look for the patterns that made any system integral, an organic rightness that was, for him, beautiful. For him, beauty was not a static state, an ideal. Like the Earth, beauty lived and breathed. And so, his alternative views largely unnoticed at first, he had ended up in the closed world of the Lab, a quiet champion of unpredictability and flow in a precisely metered world, in the domain of people clinging ever more desperately to a supposed order, wanting chaos to perform on cue, wanting the big picture to hold still.

For Linn, systems coordination invoked the fluidity inherent in patterns that make things whole, but the Lab wanted more. Equilibrium as certainty, the holy grail. The big secret, the dynamics of the interconnecting interacting parts of any living process were always changing. Fleeting moments of stability and balance purely illusory. Like our characteristic bipedal human gait, a series of minute adjustments, falling and recovering again and again in fast time lapse. A triumph of skill and mastery. You could see it in the face of a young one learning this precarious art, the difficulty and the joy. His young son's face when at last Kai could steer himself across a room on his own two feet. And Linn's aging mother, going the other way, struggling with Parkinson's, born too soon, before the cure, trapped in a tunnel closing around her, her stuttering steps growing more faltering as the disease progressed. Why, once we learned to walk, did we so readily forget the philosophical implications of our biology, why did we demand certainties and stability. Because sometimes the changes hurt. The same hurt that drove him to reach for the secure handhold of observation, the astute observer's view. To steady himself. To distance himself, even now, from the memories of the determined eyes of his son and the tired eyes of his mother, for whom the same steps held challenges, steps forever in his heart. They would forgive him, he knew. Because even as memories they understood he was where they were too. Struggling for balance, falling forward and backward at the same time. Memory was omnidirectional. So was love.

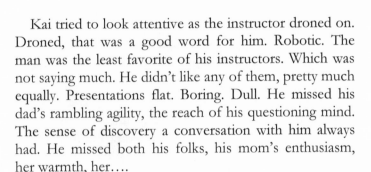

Kai tried to look attentive as the instructor droned on. Droned, that was a good word for him. Robotic. The man was the least favorite of his instructors. Which was not saying much. He didn't like any of them, pretty much equally. Presentations flat. Boring. Dull. He missed his dad's rambling agility, the reach of his questioning mind. The sense of discovery a conversation with him always had. He missed both his folks, his mom's enthusiasm, her warmth, her....

"Cadet Brenner?"

"Yes, Sir."

"I presume you are still with us?" The instructor's voice had barely shifted in tone, but the emphasis and the threat were there.

"Yes, Sir." Add potentially dangerous to robotic. His thoughts about his folks had not been neutral enough, apparently they had started to show. Usually he was better at double streaming. Kai composed himself and picked up where the instructor had left off. It was all in the text anyway, the section they had been assigned for last night's homework. "Although the first officially

31

acknowledged Psy Ops were conducted primarily as overseas operations as extensions of activities initiated during the major wars of the first half of the twentieth century, domestic applications, while technically interdicted, were also increasingly...."

"Thank you, Cadet." The instructor cut in sharply. "I believe I was giving the lecture this morning."

It irked them, how he could appear to be daydreaming, as they called it, and still follow whatever was being said. Challenged them, which was worse. He had not been daydreaming, in fact he had been thinking, even more suspect in the context of the rote education they were programming into the cadets. Students. Where did they get the cadet thing anyway, who needs paramilitary on a science station? He had started out innocently enough, phrasing the geodesic patterns of the training dome, tracing the lines radiating from each hub of the tension members. Remembering his dad talking about the ancient circle and star arrangement of the five elements in Chinese medicine. How tinkering with one part shifted energy in the next element along the lines, changes multiplying, spreading out from each succeeding point, rebounding, returning eventually to affect the initiating point. Linn had been explaining systems theory then, but as always any topic ranged outward, inward, from its starting point. Radiating, like the metal supports holding the plass sky over our heads, interconnecting a whole greater than its parts. *A harmony,* his dad would have said, *an intrinsic beauty to the wholeness of things.* Kai turned himself away from the memory and concentrated on the dome again.

The training dome was smaller than the big main dome that had been his home since his birth. He might as well be a million miles away now, connected only by an off-limits underground tunnel. Cloistered with other Lab offspring born here as he was. The Lab Rats, they called themselves in rare moments of unguarded solidarity. Imprisoned, basically, for the immersion program. Histories of the world outside, a world that no longer existed, even in present tense. This class was his least favorite. Early dawn, before early breakfast. They took the cloister thing seriously and kept us to a monastic routine. Medieval. A two hour class every morning devoted to catechism and "prayer." He groaned inwardly, invisibly, in comic relief, but it wasn't even funny. They took this class very seriously, used an early Department of Defense manual for Psy Ops as one of the texts. Like a Bible. So blind in their allegiance, so sure of themselves, not even considering it might, duh? make one of us think. It certainly didn't inspire trust in the other subjects they were force feeding us, doctrinal views of the events leading up to the War and the Wasting, and the supposed cultural and scientific factors driving the choices that had led to the devastation.

He may not trust the analysis they presented, but he did accept what the outcome had been. The barrenness outside was real. The isolation inside was real. It made the futility of learning all of this even greater. He wondered what a history of the Lab would be like. A true history. How a group of civilian researchers sealed inside a biosphere for simulated space travel went off the beam and got lost in inner instead of outer space. Obsessed with security and surveillance. At the End of Time.

33

Don't forget that. His folks had dealt with the destruction of the outer world and the growing desperation at the Lab in a different way. *All the more need for kindness and openness,* his mom would say, *to make sure we don't turn our hearts to wastelands too, inside here.*

This was about the same place where the instructor would try to catch him out. Kai steered himself back to the patterns of the dome. The day must be growing brighter outside. The shadow of the adjacent garden dome would still be covering the east side of the training hemisphere. Soon it would begin to slip down, sliding steadily across the curved surface, photoreceptors in the outer layer of the plass transferring more and more light energy to the inner biolumen layer. He could imagine the edge of the shadow moving, pane by pane, hub by hub, season by season outside. Inside, seasons pretty much abstract, just small changes in the glow of the biolight. But he noticed, and he remembered the changes, his private calendar.

The plass panes to one side of the hub he was watching glowed more brightly now. He imagined the shadow moving slowly as if it had weight and substance. The instructor's voice came into focus, casting its temporary weight across his thoughts like the imaginary shadow. "Unified perception is implemented most effectively by…." He knew that one. Isolate and saturate. The whole class knew that one. Every day. It was not lost on any of them that the immersion program was a form of Psy Ops. He made another effort to look attentive. The instructor was beginning to approach the close of the session. Kai could tell by subtle changes in the man's monotone delivery, otherwise so expressionless. Where did all the emotion in people like that go? Projected onto the rest of us. To fuel their fears and paranoia. Action and reaction. *Meeting themselves in us,* his mom would say. He turned his thoughts carefully away, like the rebound. Like the tension holding the layers of plass sky overhead. The massive shell that kept the outside out and the inside in. Worked for people as well as architecture. Inside isolated but alive for now. He watched the instructor. The routine that signaled he was coming to the conclusion of the lecture had started. The man's hand reaching for his glass of water. Pausing while he took a sip. Setting the glass down precisely where it had sat all through the lecture. Resuming his presentation. Raising one hand theatrically, self-consciously, for emphasis at a crucial point. This was the big cue. Orchestra ready. Coming to the stirring finale, the homily to inspire us for the day. Ideal society, our responsibilities, and all that. Kai continued to wait. He had learned not to move before the man gave the actual signal to dismiss the class. They had all learned. Whatever else he felt or thought about his fellow classmates, he knew they were pacing out the script too. Getting ready to close their terminals, rise from their desks as one body, and stand at attention with a crisp "Sir!" in unison as the instructor left.

Linn was almost to the top of the stairs. He looked out over the high interior of the dome, savoring the deepening space. His thoughts and feelings, reassured by the familiar cadence of his steps, continuing to well up and cascade from him as he climbed. He felt lighter, freer, with their release, one with the expansive heights, one with the curving plass pane sky. Was there a rapture of the heights to match the rapture of the deep? He paused on the narrow landing before the last switchback and glanced down at the miniature world below. More people on the lower levels. Mostly crop techs, beginning to move out through the planting beds and tanks on the dome floor, checking gauges, printouts, and occasionally the plants. Simulated space travel, by the data, by the books. He sighed. Biology was supposed to be a life science. Where had we allowed so many numbers in, to dominate our interactions with our first love, the natural world? Here it was again. The old ongoing wound. How to reconstitute the poetry out of the data fields. Beauty. Inescapable beauty. Links between data and living processes. Beauty woven through the patterns of life itself, or reduced to numbers. Organic living patterns or formulae. Vast phytoplankton blooms, swirling, evanescent, anchoring all life, or rows and rows of predictable conveniently engineered crops with terminator genes. We see what we expect to see. Perception, point of view. The fragile freedom that rides on the wings of a butterfly. Strange attractors, fractal curves gliding toward each other over and over in oblique symmetry, never the same way each time. Convergence points. There was a wholeness of the mind too, no longer distanced or at war with the senses or itself, a way home, he knew, it was already there, if only we could accept it.

"Spiritual intelligence," "self transcendence," some of the early researchers in consciousness and brain function had called it. Very specific. Not in the vaunted frontal lobes of so-called higher thought, religious maybe, but not spiritual. Not in the left parietal lobe, domain of symbolic functioning through language and numbers, activated by counting, numbering, and numerical ordering. Spiritual none of these. Spiritual activated instead spatially. Through hand eye coordination, as in drawing, hand connecting with the eyes, fingers tracking what the eyes see, and ongoingly through moving in space, as in dancing, running, walking, the ongoing shifting relating of our bodies with the space around us, experienced directly by the right parietal lobe, not visualized or monitored by the frontal mind. Direct spatial perception and response as a doorway to belonging, connecting with our place in the harmony of the universe. Transcendence, without the overtones of oblivion and erasure. Transcendence as relation, connection, belonging, coming home outside the self. Miri, talking about space travel, what weightlessness might feel like. *Perhaps they will meet up with God out there*, she had said quietly. Not joking or laughing, no teasing laughter in her eyes. He had looked at her, puzzling it out. She waited, he got it, the possibility, orienting with no fixed up or down, moving omnidirectionally, animating the right parietal lobe, the doorway, portal to belonging to a greater beyondness in all directions at once, Miri smiling gently, her smile spreading to her eyes....

He smiled at the memory. Safer to remember her now. He could allow himself that up here. The sadness he tried so hard to keep away at other times was not only from his loss, but also from the need to distance himself even from his memories of her, his joy in her livingness. The two of them together, the unexpected turns her mind would take. A sleepless night, cloaked in blankets, feigning sleep in the artificial dimness of the night lit Lab when they were first here. Lights everywhere at night, marking monitors, entrances, stair steps. Nights darker now with the cutbacks on energy. Brighter then, in so very many ways. *So many lights here,* she had whispered, *why are they so afraid of the dark? Too real?* His answering whisper, *their darkness is not like ours, theirs has scarier things lurking in it,* and Miri's soft reply. *Yes.* And she would press her body into his and they would begin their rolling dance, kneading themselves into each other. To make sure there would be no room between them for the demons of others to populate. Moving in space, moving in the space of their own belonging. He wished she was here. He let the memory linger, then let it fade and disperse, not trying to turn it away, letting bright particles of memory drift and fall instead, blessing the interior morning air below with unfamiliar joy, like alien dew, as he climbed the last flight of the stairs.

He reached the catwalk near the top of the dome. The high curve of the plass sky lifting close above him, the steady weight of gravity pulling downward toward the hollow space below. He loved being up here. Like flying. The curve and lift and pull, the tension and the ease, the sky bridge riding delicately the balance point between, suspended between worlds.

He took a deep breath and let it out slowly, offering all his thoughts and his memories into the slow exhale, and started across the narrow skyway. Lifting his hands from the guardrail, walking slowly arms outspread. Letting his eyes melt into peripheral vision, allowing everything to flow into his eyes as a whole, his surroundings merging into another kind of slow movement seamless with his own. He walked blending with the pearlescent curve of space all around him, blending with the morning light. The daytime glow already growing stronger on the east side across the walkway, with a focus that would move steadily through the day until it reached the west, and he would be walking into it again on his way back from work. His private ritual, following the far away sun toward another kind of sun, the spacious surrendering brightness for which he had no name, his provisional freedom measured out by the time it took to cross the fragile bridge.

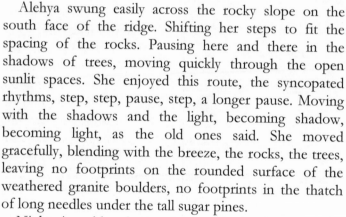

Alehya swung easily across the rocky slope on the south face of the ridge. Shifting her steps to fit the spacing of the rocks. Pausing here and there in the shadows of trees, moving quickly through the open sunlit spaces. She enjoyed this route, the syncopated rhythms, step, step, pause, step, a longer pause. Moving with the shadows and the light, becoming shadow, becoming light, as the old ones said. She moved gracefully, blending with the breeze, the rocks, the trees, leaving no footprints on the rounded surface of the weathered granite boulders, no footprints in the thatch of long needles under the tall sugar pines.

Night air, cold and crisp, lingered under the trees. The open spaces were already warm, and the morning sun felt good on her skin. Gentle greens of young new plants growing everywhere between the rocks in small pockets of meadowlands. Mats of tiny pairs of seed leaves held close to the sheltering Earth, mustard's children, and wild radish, wild carrot, and winter cress. Young grasses pushing up like green fur through blond and grey strands of older grasses dried by summer suns. A rich season now, in the land. Harvest and renewal together. Autumn rains and autumn suns bringing on the greening of new life, while the People gathered ripening acorns and manzanita berries and the last blackberries that had dried on the bramble canes in the same suns that bleached the summer grass.

She carried a few baskets for gathering and small pouches for herbal seeds. Medicine trail work today, along with gathering. Collecting seeds that were ripe. Checking to see how far the families of healing herbs had spread in this year's growing, to say hello and offer thanks. And to tuck a few seeds here and there in places they might also like to grow. The time of seeds scattering, after a few rains, when many seeds naturally began to fall, looking for moist earth to nurture them. And so the People helped the seeds to spread then too, with our simple prayers, and our joy, and our thankfulness, to add to the rain's blessings. *May the plant people grow strong and full, each growing in their own ways. May our relatives the plants have enough to share the generosity of their life with us when we might have need of their aid.* The mugwort people along this part of the trail had spread farther down the slope. She paused to linger for a while, to feel the bond of friendship she always felt with them, a gentle hello, a warm glow, reaching out to her heart. Their bearded grey green leaves already curling and browning with the waning of their year, the pale rosy glow of their inner light and friendly warmth still strong. *Thank you, my friends.*

Her route meandered diagonally up the steepening slope toward the top of the ridge. She paused in the shadow of a sugar pine a little way from the top. A dense stand of manzanita bushes crowned the ridge up ahead on this side. Above the manzanita she could see the tops of tall cedars, pines, and firs growing lower down on the north side of the ridge on the other side. Through a gap in the ridgeline just past the manzanita, she could see wave after wave of hills and ridges covered in green forest turning to the hazy blues of distance, and beyond, far on the horizon, the white peaks of the big mountain and his sister already cloaked in winter snow. Her eyes drifted back to the nearer ridge and down to the narrow valley below her. Here and there the last yellow gold of the oaks and maples lingered in their crowns. Many of their leaves had already fallen, a quick wind would bring the rest down.

Movements in the manzanita on the ridge, flashes of color, blue as the bluest autumn skies, teased at the corners of her eyes. Bright birds like bits of sky fluttered in and out of the softer blue grey greens of the manzanita, then disappeared back into the leaves again. Birds busy harvesting the miniature apple berries. Pale red browns of berries, redder purple browns of curving trunks, blues of birds, of leaves, of sky, and of the distances beyond. Beauty everywhere. Beauty moving, flying, fluttering, blending, dissolving into distance, and growing, greening, ripening from the Earth close below, beauty all around her, beauty arising effortlessly, offering itself as life. The steady grace of the moment lengthened. She settled herself within the shadow of the tree, embraced by the beauty of the day, to wait until the birds finished grazing and moved on.

Linn reached the far side of the skyway and stopped for a moment. Drifting gently in the temporary softness enfolding his senses. Not quite an afterglow of the elusive grace he sought, yet most days there was a tentative beginning, blending outward, inward, trusting, toward a grace that was always there, he was sure of it, even though unseen. And today especially, with the hover flight up ahead and other memories pressing from within, these brief moments of trust would be as close as he could get.

Finally he focused his eyes and looked down from his high perch. Much busier below. The cautious murmur floating up from people on the lower walkways carried a familiar undertone, strained and wary. The tension seemed to increase as people approached the ISEC offices and lessened a bit as they passed by the closed door of the security chief, safely this time at least. At the other end of the long main bridge, the door to McPhearson's office was already open. Always was, when he was in. *Office of Insecurity,* McPhe used to explain with a grin, *I need to see what's outside.* Linn missed his

43

friend's irreverent wit, his easy humor. He missed the Phearless One. We were all so shielded and careful now.

He let his breath out forcefully all at once, inviting heaviness, sinking out of the relative weightlessness of the heights. Resigned to reentry, he started down the narrow stairs, an inverse mirror of his climb up the other side. Flight of stairs. Fall of stairs. Ascent and dissent, descent and assent, upward toward the freedom of the heights, downward in collusion with the fall. His daily exercise in symmetry and counterpoint. Terrain of his thoughts different coming down, reorienting to the gravity and density of the insular small world of the Lab below. Solidifying, of necessity, his perceptions again.

A ghost of a body memory rising to the surface. Taking a bath as a child before water had become so scarce that everyone was rationed. Opening the drain and lying back in the hot water, submerging as much of his body as he could, half floating, feeling the weight of his body returning, pressing more and more against the smooth surface of the tub as the water drained away. Now he felt himself growing heavier in just that way, as the world of the Lab grew larger and larger with his descent and the not quite brightness drained away. He let his thoughts drift where they would, unwilling to watch them sink and congeal. Listening to the sing song rhythms of his feet echoing on the metal stairs, the same number of steps each time, phrased in familiar rhythms with a swirling turn on the small landings between each successive switch back. Ta Da!

He finally tuned in reluctantly his thoughts as he neared the bottom of the stairs, only to find them busily immersed in a cadence of their own talking to themselves. "…. with all of that, here at the Lab, where are we? Stuck on the edge of high tech eternity, at the mercy of increasing scrutiny from sensors insuring our security…." He tried to halt them in midstream, then let them go plunging on ahead. Too late to push away. His propensity for rhyme and even measure, remnants of archaic speech, had showed up again. He had noticed through the years, how unexpectedly the cadence and texture of his thoughts could begin to shift. Not only on the stairs. In other situations too. Whether in the service of the thoughts or from another need, older, once revered, he was never sure what triggered it. Hard to shake free sometimes. Played havoc with the tone of scientific discourse he had to maintain in his research work. Courting the muse of inspiration while guarding against archaic poetry. Ancient holy speech. Mnemonic tongue. Shipwrecked on the shore of techno speak.

He reached the terrace gardens again after his long descent. Icarus returned. Back to flat Earth. Time to sober up. He made a determined effort to redirect his vocabulary. He galloped down the three flights of the main stairs to the lower level, ka clop, ka clop, ka clop, his feet moving in their own stubbornly syncopated rhythm, his body still dancing to the outlaw cadence of his submerging thoughts. You can lead a horse to water. At least Linn wasn't the only one. McPhearson had his own forbidden mode of verbal expression to indulge or restrain, for him it was comedy. Linn wished they didn't have to be so careful now. He wished a lot of things.

McPhearson looked up as Linn came through the door. No polite pause or knock required. They knew each other that well. They both smiled warmly, for a moment naturally unguarded from their long friendship, before they caught themselves. McPhearson recovered first, looked away, and shuffled a few papers on his desk. Linn saddened but grateful for the cue. Made it easier to put on the sensor show.

"Hi, you doin' okay?" McPhearson was asking him. Which McPhearson, the one uncomfortable behind a desk, practicing his congenial but managerial put them at their ease manner, or the one who was his friend, who knew him well after all these years and was just as concerned about the upcoming hover flight as Linn was, or the one who could not be acknowledged by either of them, the one feeling the strain and weariness of just about everything at the Lab and fed up with the whole damn thing too. Probably all of them.

"Fine, I guess, considering…" Linn added a brief grin, which could be read as either ironic or genuine, to keep the tone appropriately complex.

"Tough assignment for you, but you're the best we've got." Praise or more irony, they were both riding on ambiguity here. Their friendly repartee hobbled, tethered to a difficult more wary beast.

"Yeah, I know." his voice drifting off.

"Any questions?" It was definitely the business as usual McPhearson who asked this time, to pull him back, covering for the guy who was his friend, very aware of the possible motives for sending him out like this.

"No, not really." Not ones he could voice at any rate, and certainly not ones McPhe should answer out loud. Not that Linn would want him to. Their layered caution as much for each other's safety as their own.

"Guess there will be time for questions at the field prep over in tech."

"Sure."

"Well, take care now."

"You too."

They both let it drift. Sensors seeing, hearing, evaluating what? Not much. Two men carefully masking whatever may or may not have been said. McPhearson was sure, as Linn must also be, that the sensor fields for this conversation would all be closely examined. Finally he handed him the paper. "Here's the R7-10 form."

"Thanks."

"Guess it will just turn up on my desk again anyway." He shrugged his shoulders and gestured at the untidy piles in front of him, thinking sadly of the things they could have said but did not dare.

Here's the keys.

Thanks, I'll try to remember where I parked it.

Hey, Wouldn't want anyone stealing off in one of these things.

No joy riding.

Be sure to get the pumpkin back by midnight.

All very much off limits now, might risk being understood.

They shook hands, made brief eye contact. A glimmer of the old warmth, the familiarity, the bantering ease. They broke away before a real goodbye could take hold and their sadness could begin to show.

Linn headed for the transport bay, gathering himself for the next round. He took the lift to the lower level junction, the cavernous service hub underneath the main dome, crowded at this time of day with tech crews coming and going, guiding repair carts filled with tools and broken or resurrected equipment. McPhearson's domain, except he never got to be part of it anymore, stuck with coordination. Neither of us had seen it coming, the bureaucratic potential lurking in our chosen fields. He shook his head. Wide tunnels led out like spokes of a wheel to the other four domes. Kai was somewhere down one of those tunnels. Don't even go there with your mind he told himself. Hard enough to say a non-goodbye like that with McPhe. He was definitely weary of the caution so necessary now. Especially with the hover flight approaching, he needed a different kind of vigilance. He needed to be very clear. He needed, he realized, fresh air. Literally and in metaphor. He needed, impossibly, to be cloaked and clear at the same time. Jump or dive. He could not afford to belly slam.

Next stop, the hover pad in the mechanics bay, current location of his dilemma, and with any luck, the cure. The mechanic techs were generally an independent lot. They worked with hardware, with tools and machines, with physical things that had limits, quirks of their own, things that wouldn't let you bullshit them. Kept the techs honest, more grounded. Gave them more plain common sense. Just as the bio sciences once had, at least for him. He liked the techs. Straight forward. Not much chance for him to be in their sector anymore, not since the Lab had been sealed after the shake down year, and flying had been limited to sky walks on the narrow bridge and to memory. Until today.

Finally, on the long walk through the tunnel to the mechanics dome and the hover bay, Linn allowed himself to consider his sudden assignment, building a pattern out of fragments, too many variables, too many what ifs, too much that could be inferred by the sensor fields to consider it before. Any quickening of his vital signs would make sense to the monitors now, might even be expected. Finally the script might relate to what was going on inside. He went over what he knew so far. Contact presumably lost with the last of the other labs still transmitting in our range years ago. Lab 6 had been the last. Now suddenly the situation was urgent enough that ISEC wanted to send someone, was willing to breach the bio seal. Linn could guess why they had requested him specifically for this mission. For a lot of reasons beside his flying experience. Most of them not good. At least for him. And why he was going anyway. But not why they wanted him to go to 6. What was so urgent that they were willing to risk contamination, risk introducing unknown variables into the data fields? The hover flight deck had been designed to contain and remedy any anomalies that may be introduced by outside work before the Lab was sealed, anomalies introduced under normal conditions. But there was a very different world out there now, and we had never had to deal with that. What was happening at the other Lab that concerned them so much? He was careful with his thoughts. Even the tunnel was not safe. Wait until he was out of here and in the air, wait for the larger movement to reveal itself.

He was surprised to see the head tech, Kendra Williams, in the central repair bay instead of over at the launch pad where he had expected her. She saw him too, and waved him enthusiastically over to her workstation.

"Hey, good to see you." Her smile was warm and genuine, one of the few people at the Lab who still refused to hide a smile like that. Safer over here, away from the epicenter of so-called security. He realized he had missed seeing that kind of smile. McPhe should figure out a way to get over here more often. He needed to see that smile as much as Linn did.

"Hey, good to see you too."

She wiped her forehead with the back of her hand, and pushed unsuccessfully at a few curling strands of red hair that were spilling out from under her cap. "How have you been? Haven't seen you around for quite a while. You've been making yourself pretty scarce." She stopped before she intruded any further, before she trespassed on his private loss. Damn, she might have already said too much. She was surprised by how worn he looked. Carrying a big load inside.

"Hard to get away. Had to cook up a real emergency before they'd let me over here." He laughed, but she could see the strain. She missed his easy smile. She hadn't known him well, but everyone in the mechanics bay knew him on sight, and liked him. He was a good person to work with. The last two years had been hard on him.

"Well don't stay away so long next time. Maybe we can find something a little less dire to get you over here. We're pretty good at fixing things you know." She paused. "You've been missed."

"Thanks." Linn didn't know what else to say. Caught off guard by her good-natured openness.

"And hey, if you get back early from the flight, maybe you and I could find something around here for you to do with that extra time?" She waved one hand around the crowded work bay. They both laughed, and this time it wasn't so hard for Linn. He found himself hoping he would get back early.

"Sure. Thanks, I'd like that." He ducked his head briefly, feeling more like a shy bird than a pilot heading out into the unknown. He really would like to spend some time here.

"Great." She smiled, but her smile faded quickly this time, unexpectedly restrained, and she said awkwardly, "Well, see you then," as if he was leaving.

"You're not doing the final briefing for the flight? Thought you'd be heading over to the hover pad with me."

She hesitated. "Had something to finish up here. There's a new guy, he'll be doing the last rites of passage. You know the drill anyway." Her words carefully casual, at odds with the warning in her eyes. "See you when you get back." As he turned to go, she added in a softer voice, "You take care now."

"Thanks. I'll do my best. You take care too." He turned back for a moment, and her answering smile, warm and open again, enveloped him.

On his way over to the hover bay, he wondered if Nichols would be handling the launch, not exactly a new guy, but Linn had heard he was back. A waste to conscript him for another department, he was a good tech. Ken's veiled warning had been a surprise. Maybe they weren't immune to the long reach of politics and paranoia over here after all. But it wasn't Nichols waiting for him at the launch pad. A younger man, outwardly quite bland and by the books, intentionally informal, greeted Linn at the hover pad instead.

"Linn? Hi, I'm Richard James. I'm here to brief you on the flight plan and see you off."

Pleasant enough, but with a hidden edge, especially the see you off part. Where did they get these new people? You would think after all these years that he would recognize everyone, that he would have met, or bumped into, or seen everyone here at least once. But this young man.... then he remembered his son, how completely Kai had disappeared from view. Schedules, work and living reassignments, and they may as well live in different worlds.

The small hovercraft sat at the dock pad, already mounted on the launch tracks. A long time since he had flown one. But they had remembered, it was in his files. Data never dies, data can always be recalled, precise, impersonal, hard edged. Not like memories, the ones shimmering and alive inside flickering in and out of view. FLIGHT TRAINING: AUTO PILOT AND MANUAL OVERRIDE. LISCENCED FOR AERIAL RECON AND FIELD SUPPORT. Where did that include the pure joy of flying, the dynamics of freedom, the alchemy of flight, suspended between Earth and sky, patterns unfolding above, below, and all around him. Where did that include searching for the hidden brightness in the open spaces of memory and mind, where was....

"I saw your record, guess you're familiar with all of this." The man gestured at the hovercraft. Very businesslike, despite his studied casual air. Linn had a feeling Richard James didn't really know much about the mission or the craft, had just been instructed to send him on his way. Next question is, by who. Not by Ken. The whole mission was already in override.

"Yeah. I went over the simulation program last night for a refresher." He looked at the young man. Richard James. Maybe someday, to someone, Richard. Never a nickname, except maybe a derogatory one behind his back. He found it hard to imagine him as ever being just James, as in *Hey, James, good to see you,* the easy greeting of a friend. Not R J. But maybe R James, if you got to know him? He tried it out in his mind, trying to connect it with the person standing next to him. He wondered about the young man's life, what his hopes and dreams, if any, would be. Horizons inside the Lab pretty limited as it is. Linn felt a stab of sadness verging on anguish, he hoped Kai was not being groomed to be like this. A contained persona that precluded even questioning the limits or the loneliness. Maybe Ken and the other regulars over here could loosen R James up a bit if he stayed. He needed to believe that, for Kai's sake, for himself too.

The young man gestured for him to climb into the cockpit of the hover. "She's all yours."

The short winged craft was slim and compact, not so ungainly looking as the first of these small personal low altitude vehicles. This one would probably be out of date by now and hadn't been taken out for a long time. Just like Linn. He eased himself into the tiny cockpit, checking the instrument screens, reorienting, calling up procedures, habits of relating to the craft. Would have been second nature long ago. Strange and unfamiliar now at first as they came back to him. But the feel of hover flying had never left him, the gliding motion that was more like swimming than flying, through air instead

53

of water, tempting gravity with a different kind of buoyancy. He did love to fly. He had tuned out the young man, and heard his voice again in mid sentence.

"....so they sent a new cell over from ISEC, requisitioned specially for the mission. Must be an important job, them taking an interest in it and all," R James said speculatively. When Linn did not volunteer a response, he continued. "Not enough fuel to fly on hydro, you'll need to rely entirely on solar. The cell was fully charged up yesterday, should be enough to get you over and back again. Highly unlikely that you'll need it, but some option for recharge available if necessary."

Linn noticed that cell had already lost a small fraction of its charge, the display registered just below full. He mentioned it to R James who said, "No problem, the gauge is a little off is all, they went over it thoroughly, along with everything else." Then he was on to the rest of the instructions, while Linn was still considering the use of the pronoun *they* instead of *we*, and wondering which *they* he meant. "You'll need to leave soon anyway. Solar gain calculations for this time of year show there will be just enough daylight for the minimum recharge, if you need to use it, if you stay on time. Flight plan already logged into the craft's guidance program." All Linn had to do was keep the craft airborne and follow the route on manual. "Manual uses less energy than the auto systems. Guess that's why you're along for the ride," R James added cheerfully, in what Linn hoped was intended as encouragement.

"What happens when I get to Lab 6?"

"Make voice contact if you can, use the short range trans. Most of the longer range radio trans and remote sensing equipment have been removed from the craft over the years. They needed the parts for repairs in other sectors here."

Manual indeed, Linn said privately to himself as he nodded to R James.

"So, no way to send comtrans back here during the flight."

All this they saved for last, for this studiously bland I just work here nominally pleasant young man to deliver, unable to alter or intervene in any way with whatever the shadowy ISEC higher ups had in mind. Linn knew he didn't have much choice on his part either. He had already accepted the job, a choiceless choice from the beginning. A feeling of inevitability was setting in, like going into major surgery, surrendering to a process already in motion not knowing how or where it will spit you out. The not knowing somehow attractive, growing more so moment by moment after the watchful constriction of his days here. Not knowing more like flying. What was the old saying, a wing and a prayer? "Great, anything else? I'm ready to go."

R James looked surprised, startled, maybe even a bit envious or awed. Maybe as surprised by the emotions as by what had triggered them. He may or may not have been aware of hidden currents in Linn's assignment, but just now he seemed to have felt the stirring of something unfamiliar beside him, a sense of risk, like a window opening suddenly on a claustrophobic space. "Good luck," he said, momentarily real himself, and he meant it.

"Thanks." Linn pulled the door shut and settled in. The hover moved forward slowly, pulled on the launch tracks. He heard the inner bay doors seal. No chance of a breath of fresh air entering, metaphorically or otherwise. R James, Richard James, would not breathe any but the carefully modulated air of the Lab, would not see whatever barren world was about to be revealed outside. Linn would have a short time after the outer doors opened to lift the hover from the rails and ease it into flight. The outer air lock opened as the hover drive engaged and then he was airborne.

Kikerri, the she hawk, forest hunter, waited. Silent and patient. Occasionally turning her head, sweeping her sharp eyes and fierce attention across the land. Missing nothing. The rest of her sleek body motionless. From her perch hidden high in the long needled pine, she had a good view of the steep valley in both directions as she waited. Morning sunlight and shadow sifting through the needles of the pine slanted in thin lines around her. Concealing her watchful presence. Dappling her blue grey back, dappling the feathers of her chest already marked with the narrow red brown lines of her kind. A sudden burst of movement across the valley caught her eyes. She focused her gaze on the opposite slope and the cluster of shiny rounded shapes that brooded there, like the shells of giant eggs half buried in the earth, some as tall as the tallest trees. A flock of brown birds had started out of the brush lands past the eggs. The birds swept up the slope and disappeared into a stand of trees. She waited for the birds to move again. She was not in a hurry. Her nestlings had flown off on their own, her need to hunt was lessened.

She looked intently at the strange egg shapes on the slope. They had been dormant for many generations of her kind. No one to tend or keep the life force in them alive. Generations of wingeds came and went. No life had emerged from the giant alien shells, until a few sad fledglings that had emerged at night. Already dead, the owl kind said. But there was life inside. All the kinds agreed. Kikerri could sense movement there, so subtle within the other rhythms of the day. What the owl people felt by night they could not say, as if there were faint lights or bright shadows. The deer kind stayed away from the slope, the way sounds reflected off the strange shells unsettling. Whatever was inside was not like the quickening of new life in her own eggs or the eggs of other winged kinds. No struggling will to emerge. No eagerness, no urgency. No warmth seeking breast to breast. Whatever life waited inside wanted to stay there.

New tensions emanating from the giant shells this morning, and abrupt sounds, repetitive, and sharp, coming from their sunward side. An even louder grinding mineral sound, heavy, sudden, like a tree falling or a crack of thunder, just before the birds had flown. Now Kikerri could feel another presence entering the day, a presence seeing the morning slope in a different way than other kinds, spreading a wary stillness nearby with its strangeness. The rocks, the trees, the entire pattern of morning light and shadow on the slope around the alien eggs taut like a spider's web heavy with the weight of dew. Kikerri unfurled her wings. She raised up on her perch, suddenly tense, poised to fly.

Another jarring, grinding sound burst into the day followed by a breathy muffled roar from behind the eggs, pulsing steadily like the drone of an angry hive. A strange fish shape came into view, hovering in the air like some of the insect kind. Rippling the air beneath it. Air moving back, pulling away to let it pass. Kikerri launched herself into the air, wheeling swiftly through the trees, wide strong wings and narrow tail angling, tilting, turning, around and through the dense branches of cedar, pine, and fir, Kikerri, swift flying, sweeping, gliding, through the long arms of the trees, through the slanting corridors of sunlight, finding horizons and hidden pathways in the forest air with the same sure skill and grace as wind and shadow. Hurling her warning cries as she flies, "Kiiiiii Ki Ki Ki Kiiiii .... Kiiiiii Ki Ki Ki Kiiiii... Kiiiiii Ki Ki Ki Kiiiii..." to alert the day, the valley, to alert the sky. "Kiiiiii Ki Ki Ki Kiiiii.... Kiiiiii Ki Ki Ki Kiiii." Her intruder's call.

The alien sky fish heavier, lumbering in its slow-bodied insect flight, turning slowly, dropping lower, toward the creek. Fish shape, drawn to water, newly hatched, perhaps seeking water as some others of the water people did, seeking home. This one churning the gentle morning air as it passed, carrying a shimmer of distortion around it with its roaring breath, leaving a wake of strangeness in its path.

Kikerri landed in a tree on the sun side of the eastern most egg. She looked intently at its surface. No cracks or broken pieces of shell. Instead, a strange eye had opened in the side of the shell, a hollow eye, empty inside. Then the lids of the strange eye began to close very slowly with an eerie motion like a lizard's eye. She felt a chill. She rose up in the air, the shadow of her outspread wings sweeping across the eye as it shut, sweeping across the blind face of the rest of the giant egg, her silhouette sharp and clear, lengthening across the curving shell. She rose higher and higher. Calling again, "Kiiiiii Ki Ki Ki Kiiii".… "Kiiiiii Ki Ki Ki Kiiii".… as she climbed the sky.

The valley shrank beneath her. The strange alien shells growing smaller and smaller, trees and bushes on the familiar slopes flowing into one dappled texture covering the land. Ridges, crests and valley folds beyond the valley that was her home flowed into the circle of distance held within her eyes. Her spot of sharp seeing roving that flowing land, searching through the softer distances unfolding in her far seeing eyes. Tiny details precise and clear, leaf by leaf, twig by twig, twitch of whisker, blink of eye, breeze ruffled fur. Her own shadow growing larger, fainter, ghostly, rippling through the trees. All held within the horizon of her eyes, bounded by the openness of sky. To the south she could see fields of clouds flowing into the circle of her world. High thin wisps riding ahead. Denser clouds forming, billowing behind. Coming up fast, along with other smoother cloud shapes polished by the winds, silken with the faintly rainbowed sheen of unborn snow, first hint of winter quickening. Long cloud shadows reaching out, sweeping the land, slanting, rolling, pouring into and flowing up and over valley after valley, ridge after ridge.

Kikerri rode the strong air that raised the clouds, sending her warning cries across the land. "Kiiiiii Ki Ki Ki Kiiii.… Kiiiiii Ki Ki Ki Kiiii." Casting the sharp point of her eyes through the closer distance of her valley sailing below her. She followed the strange insect sky fish in its flight up the valley until it crested the ridge at the far end and dropped down on the other side, and she heard her sister cousin in that valley take up the warning cry. To the south Kikerri heard a distant "Keearrrrr, Kearrrrrr, Kearrrrrr," of a red shouldered visitor on her way to winter grounds alerted to her calls, and another fainter "Kiiiiii Ki Ki Ki Kiiii" farther on. All the hawk kind would shadow the alien sky fish if it passed through their lands. Wherever the strange hatchling went in this world of steep valleys and sky homes, the land would know. There would be many eyes. Many warning cries.

Kikerri curved her wings to ride in slow circles high above her valley, soaring higher and higher, silent, blending with the sky. Then she folded her wings and dove back toward the earth, plummeting as if in a hunting dive, land rising up to meet her, growing larger, rushing toward her, rocks trees bushes slope of day scented air, familiar, home, all pulling toward her, Kikerri wild and fierce, skinning through the air to come to rest on her perch again, letting the day settle back around her, like the fine splinters and shards of sunlight and shadow sifting through the long needles of the pine settling around her, cloaking her as before.

Linn felt a moment of extreme disorientation, a disconnect emptying him from inside, as the outer doors of the hover bay opened with a sharp pneumatic burst. The crack of light widened, and suddenly he was facing straight into the sharp rays of unfiltered morning sun. A blurring brightness met his eyes, resolving into landscape reluctantly, even after his physical eyes adjusted to the unfamiliar light. He was shocked. The mind behind the eyes had become more accustomed to phrasing the familiar shapes of the Lab, the metal walls and corridors, the muted plass paned sky, than he had imagined. Internalized, interiorized, the Lab had worked into his senses more than he knew.

The sun was still close above the ridge in front of him. Angled shafts of sunlight streamed through tall shapes like trees. Long shadows flowed down the slope, skirting the patches of brightness, weaving delicate patterns around the tall silhouettes and smaller shapes like boulders or small bushes, their outlines glowing backlit in the morning light. The natural patterns and rhythms of a natural world, a lost world, long forgotten. Dazed and disbelieving at first he recognized the tall shapes as trees. Living trees. He had not expected this. That the land would be alive. External sensors had failed at all the Labs after the first big solar storms and had not been replaced. No need, we were already sealed inside. Our only crucial interface with the outer world was to mediate solar gain from the sun, handled automatically, molecularly, within the plasma layers of the plass panes. Transmissions from the war zones, infrequent and garbled from the first before they faded completely away, had given painful testimony to nearly universal horror and destruction outside. He was unprepared.

Untouched wilderness. As if the Lab had been air lifted and dropped here, with no trace, no roads, no human sign, except the flat gravel border like a caustic shadow below him at the base of the dome wall. Decades since he had been on a hover flight, twenty years or more. The half-remembered trees and bushes on the near slope were much taller now. Bushes and smaller woody plants and grasses had invaded the gravel border, blending the harsh perimeter back into the land. He had expected desolation, barren rock, and found it hard to let the livingness in. The main dome and the smaller domes surrounding it were connected from the inside only, circled like wagons in protection from what was assumed to be a hostile world outside, alien, devoid of life. Assumptions, provisional or the supposed new real, all behind him now. As he lifted the hover out of the launch bay, he knew that not just the outer doors were shutting behind him. He was already outside.

Linn swung the hover in a wide slow curve to the right. The lab sat halfway up a long south-facing slope.

At the foot of the slope, a small creek threaded its way through the narrow valley. He dropped down below the level of the domes to follow the creek upstream toward the west. Once he was facing away from the sun, he could see the sky was hazy, with a milky hue not unlike the plass sky, a subtle color bridge between the world he had just left and the one he was entering now. He wondered if there would be more substantial clouds, if there would be actual weather. The molecular adjustments of the plass panes were all that passed for weather inside. The plass molecules were the only ones to read the sky directly. He felt vulnerable out here, so long away from responding to basic cues from life itself. And breaking through its long dormancy, he also felt the other side of feeling open and exposed, the quickening of a forgotten eagerness, a discovering joy.

The streambed curved to the left and then right again as it skirted a slide wall of boulders and continued winding between the steep flanks of slopes on either side, winding higher and higher as the valley narrowed toward its source below the far ridge. He clicked on the map screen. His route was laid out in a glowing line, following the valleys, cresting the lowest points on the ridges, descending to the valleys again. Crumpled, corrugated country on the holo map. He was traveling up just one of the many wrinkles in this maze of canyons and valley lands. Lab 6 was a half day's hover flight away, tucked in one of those remote valleys far ahead. A destination as increasingly arbitrary and unrelated to the landscape flowing beneath him as the glowing line. He clicked off the map and let the little stream be his guide for now. Through the heavy tree cover along the stream banks, he could see hints of bright water sparkling, reflecting the pale sky overhead. An autumn day, the light gentle from the hazy sky, a few wisps and curls of thicker clouds starting to show to the south. The tall shapes of trees, their green colors rich in the muted light, recognitions of their distinctive shapes blooming slowly in his mind from long forgotten memories. The almost geometric spires of cedars, shaggy silhouettes of firs, the egg shape crowns of sugar pines, their long needles shimmering in the soft light. Here and there the yellow gold leaves of what must be oaks and maples. Blue greys and greens of smaller maybe manzanita bushes crowning the drier south face of the ridge to his right. Another field of boulders startlingly vivid in their roundness. Like waking in a dream, details almost transparent in their piercing clarity.

Wilderness. He marveled again. No human signs, a land swept free, as if at sea. Miri would love it out here. Would love even knowing that it was still alive, the land, the Earth, the animals. Here and there he caught a glimpse of birds startled by the hover's flight, brief bursts of movement disappearing through the trees. There must be animals down there too, the four legged kind. He hoped that included bears. For Miri. Back when they were first researching space travel on the search engines, Miri had found an article archived from an old campus newspaper. Her alma mater. Catchy title, linking space travel and bears. Outlining possible connections between weightlessness and hibernation. *You see!* She had said, in playful triumphant delight, her eyes dancing the way they always did when she was delighted. *A sign! I knew it, they do need me!* Bears had been her first area of

65

research, studying cellular regeneration in hibernating bears, the molecular aspects of how they maintain bone and muscle mass while they sleep. Before she went entirely for molecular, leaving the bears in the field. Her first love, the one that brought her into science. For Linn it had been the compelling beauty of natural patterning, for her it had been bears. Beauty and the beast. Beauty and the bears. For the millionth time, and the millionth reason, he wished she were here.

He lifted the hover a little higher so the cushion of turbulence it generated did not cause ripples below and savored the gliding swaying freedom of slow flight, like swimming through the sky. The land flowing beneath him, all around him, so beautiful he did not want to disturb it in any way. For Linn, after years of being in the controlled environment of the Lab, simply being in the presence of otherness beyond one's ken was as beautiful as flying. He swept up and over the ridge at the head of the valley and dropped lower again, following the rise and fall of the land, flowing like the air up and over the ridges to follow each succeeding valley beyond. Always when he crested a nearer ridge, he could see wave after wave of ridgelines fading into the milky blues of distance, and at the rim of this unforeseen land, white capped peaks gleaming in the morning sunlight.

All of it untouched. Wild. Wild to begin with, a remote area cloistered inside a much larger tract of government land, off limits to everyone except the small groups of research personnel for the Lab project. A secret place, and so the Earth had been free to be herself here, and she had survived. He was surprised how healthy the forest looked. The first big waves of radiation that came from the meltdowns at the nuclear power plants had not reached here. The outside sensors were still in good repair then. Wind currents, distance, and the high range of mountains between had protected the Labs. The bulk of that first damaging radiation had gone elsewhere, and the Labs had already been sealed before the other kinds of meltdowns hit, before the Cleansing and the War and the Wasting convulsed the outer world. Simulated space travel has its benefits, that had been one of the draws of the project in the first place, though seldom voiced. Even in their closed academic world, they had felt the coming turmoil even if they rarely acknowledged it to each other or themselves. A protective collusion with a kind of blindness. Being part of a time capsule was part of the secret allure, more than simulated space. The world already most at risk was our own. And it had been the human plagues, tailored to our own specific human immune responses, the ones targeting us alone, that finally in the end had taken the greatest toll on the species of their designers when they turned on their makers, and we had been safe from those too.

As transmissions dwindled down, it had become clear that while we may be distanced from the ravages of our times within the sealed sanctuary of the Lab, we were not separate from our place in time. If anything, our responsibility was even greater now. No longer pseudo space travelers, we were real Noah's arks, the ships themselves, each of us arks of humankind. And maybe that was when the isolation and the burden of who we might be, who we might have to be, began to deform the human dynamics of our little insular communities.

Repository of the past, requiem or seed, seed of a future unimagined before. Was our primary responsibility to uphold the past, or to adapt, respond, and change in order to survive. Basic biology. A question of emphasis. Everything at the Lab reinforcing repetition and holding in order to maintain. Even research, especially research, so often in the service of validating or extending the established way. So little requiring or rewarding innovation, except in repairs. We sure needed to get creative there. Maybe that was why he always preferred the mechanics crew, but even for them, no matter how creative their solutions, the mandate was always to preserve. Even the pledge to stay encapsulated inside the Lab, not even air was to be exchanged, was working against us. The world outside had changed and was continuing to change. Too dangerous to leave. Where would we go? Back to the cities? Radiation and disease. Crazed madmen running loose at the end of time. Why not add aliens too, we were supposed to be in outer space. Wasteland. Barren rock. Space flight a long way off now. Surely time to change the purpose of the project. The ark of holding to convention and contract, or the ark of life, of livingness, ongoing, unafraid.

We had to choose. Heated debates for a while. Underneath whatever argument anyone offered, a basic fear of leaving. A fear that eventually someone in their fear was going to exploit. And here we were today, ISEC running the Lab, everyone else acquiescent. Hadn't taken much, but those steps had been enough to seal the fear with more fear. We had started out as astro-naughts, ciphers, placeholders for the ones who would truly journey through space. Now astro-nots. Program terminated along with the civilization that envisioned it. No longer simulated space travelers, not even really on the Earth either, encapsulated in the Lab. Caught between worlds, blinded by futures that would never be. He realized there had been another future all along. The Lab was not the ark, not the privileged time capsule it thought itself to be. Neither were we. The ark was not inside. The ark was outside. He could see now all around him, life continuing, complex, healthy, whole. Miraculously, and to his eyes, beautifully. On its own. The ark was the Earth, in all her myriad generosity. The ark was here. This was where we were supposed to be, if we were willing to rejoin life, if we could even remember how.

He had entered uncharted territory, in time and place, except for the thin line of his route glowing on the map screen, which he checked from time to time. An increasingly imaginary line, a suspect mission as first laid out. Even more suspect right at the end before the launch if he chose to dwell on it. But now he really wanted to try to make contact with the other lab. He allowed himself a bit of hope that at Lab 6 they had found out what was really outside, and were making other choices, the ones we had been afraid to make. He continued to follow the little rivers and streams as they found their own way, water's way, through the maze of these remote lands, checking the map only enough to stay on his possibly quixotic course. Lab 6 was set in one of the folds of ridgelines somewhere far ahead. He would not see it until he reached their valley. The land poured under him. Long slopes of granite shelves with only a few gnarled trees and shrubs clinging to footholds

between huge slabs of rounded rock. Small meadowlands
here and there in the lap of a slope, greening, lush with
young plants, and taller sugar pines with wide full shapes
and branches sweeping low to the ground. Another
stand of blue grey manzanita bushes on the crest of a
ridge. More clouds coming closer now, rising up from
the south, their shadows flowing swiftly in and out of the
valleys, dappling the land. Larger clouds moving up
behind them from below the southern horizon, some
smooth and windswept, others billowing, building
mountains in the sky that dwarfed the land below in their
scale.

After Richard James shut the inner hover bay doors for the launch, Ken had turned on a closed circuit camera inside the hover bay from her personal screen at her workstation. Just to say goodbye to Linn again from her side she told herself, but she really didn't trust Richard James and wanted to make sure Linn got safely airborne. The camera was the only one left from the full launch array. Got "overlooked" conveniently, she grinned, when all the other sensors were removed and used for replacement parts elsewhere. She didn't expect to see much, the cam was angled low to the floor, focused on the launch tracks, but at least she would know how the launch went.

She saw the bottom of the hover lifting up out of view, the distortion field on the underside of the craft briefly churning the narrow band of brightness at the top of the screen that would be the world outside, a world too bright for the setting on the cam. The paler sunlit floor of the bay was more in its range. She could see the tracks clearly, then a large shadow moved slowly across the floor blocking the sunlight for a moment as the hover dropped lower and turned to the right, then the shadow disappeared. As the doors began to shut, she struggled with the contrast and focus to try to see what was in the band of brightness at the top of the screen, and then a smaller shadow shape swept suddenly across the nearer paler brightness of the floor, rippling across the rails uncannily like a hawk with wings outspread. Then the shadow was gone, and the wide swath of sunlight growing narrower until like the shadow it disappeared and the cam showed only mute rails and indoor light again.

She let out her breath. Hadn't even realized she had been holding it. Her mind careening back and forth. No life outside, barren rock, it couldn't have been a bird. It was a bird, a hawk. It couldn't have been a bird, must have been the hover.... She hit stop, then replay, and waited for the smaller shadow to come on screen. She pushed pause and studied the image as long as she dared. She tried to imagine every possible angle of sunlight on the hover that would throw a shadow in the shape of a hawk. No way, and it was moving in the opposite direction.

She sent the whole segment to her private cache, deleted the original, adjusted the camera's log to read as if she had never turned it on, and went back to working on whateverthehell was sitting on her work table, her mind still on the shadow. It couldn't have been a bird, it was a bird. Image so fleeting, so grainy, out of focus, hard to be sure. If it was a hawk, what the hell else was out there. She switched on the tape one more time. She studied the narrow band of brightness, maybe a few blurred outlines there, could be rocks, could be anything.

72

What the hell was out there anyway. What the hell was Linn seeing now? She closed the file again. Damn those interfering bastards from ISEC who took the comtrans off the hover at the last minute. She wished she had pushed harder to get it reinstalled, but she was pushing pretty close to the edge as it was, and that bland little ISEC guy had some hefty back up. What if, what if.... and then her mind circling back around to the improbable wonder of it. What if it was a hawk, what if a hawk lived out there, then what else did? And if it did, then what? Might be time to get a little curious. She grinned to herself, might be time for me to do some inventory. She grabbed a few parts at random from her work table and headed for the shielded compartment for special equipment in the storage area, the only place in the mechanics dome that was completely surveillance free. About time for me to do some serious thinking out loud, figure a few things out before Linn gets back. Wouldn't be until late afternoon, and then it might be time for him to do a little inventory too.... Damn! Wouldn't that throw those bastards in ISEC for a loop if it turned out the world wasn't flat after all. About time for some round Earth again.

"Kiiiiii Ki Ki Ki Kiiiii … Kiiiiii Ki Ki Ki Kiiiii… Kiiiiii Ki Ki Ki Kiiiii." Alehya heard a hawk's quickening call sounding from down the valley toward the east. Clear and sharp, and high in the sky. The call the winged forest hunters used to warn intruders away when they came too close to their nests. Out of season, and out of place coming from the sky instead of from the trees. Sky intruders, coming too close into this hawk's sky world, coming too close within the sky nest of this valley. "Kiiiiii Ki Ki Ki Kiiiii ……. Kiiiiii Ki Ki Ki Kiiiii." The hawk gave her warning calls again, circling back, higher, toward the east, and then the hawk and her cries faded into distance. Farther to the east, Alehya heard another hawk cry in answer. The hawk kind were alarmed today. The warnings stayed with Alehya like ripples moving through calm water, as the calls faded away and sunlight and shadow settled back into stillness on the slope around her.

A strange alien vibration caught at her ears again. Alehya realized it had been growing into her awareness long before she knew it as sound, ever since the hawks' warning cries. A breathy metallic droning, a hollow mineral roar, painful, far away, an echo with no source, out of harmony with the beauty of the day. The sound came intermittently, fading and returning again, each time a little louder, finally not fading away at all, steadily approaching, louder and louder. She knew the stories the old ones told. She knew why the People moved in the quiet dance of light and shadows that she loved so well. She knew why they must never ever leave traces of their passing on the land, no footprints, no broken twigs, no displaced pebbles, when they were away from the protective cover of their villages. The regular overflights of those who watch from above had stopped long ago, and the last random flight had been well before her first woman's moon a few winters back. Some of the elders with deep seeing felt that a few of the sky eyes orbiting high above out of range of human eyes were still operating. Others said they doubted there were any Watchers left to monitor them. But if the sky eyes were still capable of seeing in detail whatever passed here below, and even if one sky eye were to see and one Watcher were to notice what it saw, that would put the People in danger. She knew that some of the Watcher eyes could rain down death as well as sight. The careful blended walking continued and had become part of the People's lives.

For some of the older ones and for the newer ones who had come to live with us through the years, for anyone who had lived with more hurried forms of walking from Before, the slow walking had been difficult at first. For the younger ones, the ones born among the People as she was, Earth walking came naturally, at first as play, then as skill, then as art, as joy. Alehya found it hard to consider wanting to move in any other way except quietly with the land. She could understand needing to move swiftly in some kinds of danger, but she could not imagine needing to make a habit of haste, of wanting to move so fast you missed the wholeness reaching out to you at every moment from the plants, the trees, the rocks, the sky. And if you were in danger you needed that connection even more. A special skill, to run in wholeness. Sometimes bestowed by grace when most in need, sometimes practiced, learned.

She remembered playing Hurry Hurry Run Run with the other kids when she was younger. The one chosen to hurry would close their eyes at a starting point while the others hid along a trail. The last one to hide would leave a marker on the trail. When everyone had hidden and given the personal animal or bird sounds we all knew each other by, the hurry person would run down the trail trying to see as many of the other kids in hiding as they could. Usually none. Then the runner would move the marker farther down the trail, hide and give their call, and the first hider would come out and run trying to see. With five or six kids playing, you got to run several times, and it became harder not to giggle. Hiders would get more obvious, making faces, wiggling fingers, sticking twigs, branches or even feet out into the trail. Finally we would all come out of hiding and fall down laughing with each other on the trail. Some kids got pretty good at seeing while running fast, and they began to train for when runners were needed in times of danger. Alehya had been one of those. And although her training had only increased her love of the slower gentler pace of daily walking all the more, it had given her a suppleness and grace in her movements that the whole community appreciated. Her offering to them all, her joy. Her friend Tomah loved the running itself, and the skill of running sight. His training had taken him deeper. He offered another kind of joy, and the People appreciated the strength of his sureness. Like an arrow in its flight when he ran, so unexpected in such a quiet thoughtful boy. Now almost a man, she reminded herself, and smiled.

The strange sound was coming closer, a hollow cry, full of rushing, hurrying, and possibly seeing. She held very still, hidden high up on the slope within the shadow of the tree, while a flying shape approached below her, traveling low, following the winding course of the narrow valley. A fish shape metal craft, more like a swimming thing than a flying thing, a metal sky fish, calling with a muffled hollow breathy roar. The hawk's intruder. Strange markings on the side. Short wings, like fins. Shiny ovals of hard flat skin on the front of the craft, different from the metal body. The ovals were like eyes, but she knew it was a constructed thing, a Watcher's thing. She had heard in the stories that many of these craft had no person inside, only equipment that could fly by itself and act on its own depending on what it found. She knew that Watchers could also be looking through the craft's eyes from a distance while it flies. This was not a distant Watcher's thing. There was a person inside this one, she was sure. She could feel a presence different from machine. She did not know how a Watcher would feel to an elder, but she was surprised how human the person inside the craft felt to her, and

77

she did not feel death traveling there. Whoever or whatever was sky swimming through this valley, the elders would need to know. The medicine trail could be tended another day.

She waited. The metal sky fish might come back, or there might be others following it. She was sure it had not seen her. She had been motionless in the tree shadow, blended into shadow, into tree, hidden within the screen of down sweeping branches. She had left no trace of her passing on the slope in the open places. For the safety of the People she waited a while longer, still motionless. The craft was definitely moving away. It had crested the lowest point of the ridge at the far end of the valley after curving around the great hump of bare granite shelves that jutted out from the slope farther up the gorge. Then it must have dipped down to follow the next valley. The sound of its hollow roar wavered in its passage across the land, louder as it crested another ridge, and then by its fainter sound dropping below a ridgeline to follow another valley, the ridges muffling its painful cry again. Rugged country to the west, despite the gentle contours of the ridge tops and the layers of trees dissolving into blues of distance. A tangle of canyons and narrow valleys.

Then she heard a change in the sound. Not from the ridges or the distance, but from the craft itself, shriller now, a whine, then a stuttering broken rhythm, and a searing feeling from the person on board, very afraid. So the openness of the People could touch even those who seek from above. The fear calling increased, and then, muted by the folds of Earth between Alehya and the flying faltering thing, a loud thump, like a tree falling, or a mudslide. Sudden, final. Then the silence and stillness of wary quiet all around her. A few minutes passed. Another sound, sharp, explosive, and then in the distance a column of thick dark smoke lifted above the ridgeline.

Linn had just noticed a large level meadow up ahead, when the red warning light went on. A sudden drop in the power level in the fuel cell. More warning lights. Auto recharge function blocked. The sound of the hover generator stuttering, arrhythmic, he was losing what little altitude he had, losing it fast. The wide meadowland loomed closer and closer, then the power cut off entirely. He struggled to keep the hover in a level glide as long as he could, then let the grinding impact slow the craft. Ripping through grasses and small bushes, plowing into the earth, it came to a halt, nose buried in a pile of torn up meadow earth and grass and small gravely rocks. He had been thrown forward hard against his harness, but the straps had held. He was bruised maybe, shaken and shaking, but unhurt. The instrument panel had gone dead. No way for the system to assess itself. No power. The hover mechanism on the underside of the craft undoubtedly crushed on impact.

He reached instinctively for the emergency pack under the seat. Standard issue for even short flights. He found nothing there. Far too many years away from the field, he should have checked. It had to be somewhere around here. Very few places in the small cockpit where it could be, all in arm's reach. He found nothing. He had presumed it would be there, he had counted on the prep team. He thought of the young man, Richard James, the replacement battery, the warning in Ken's eyes. He found himself wondering what else may or may not have been prepared for him. The sudden loss of power, so unexpected. He had only been out a few hours, the charge should have held for the entire flight, over and back. The new cell had been sent over by ISEC specifically for this mission. To make sure it would last. Presumably. What else was he presuming? Still shaken, in slow motion like a dream, he pulled himself free of the harness and tried the door. The latch refused to move. A wave of panic beginning to rise, he tried the latch again, more forcefully this time, adding a few biological curses. The latch finally gave way. He heaved the door open, moving faster now, sliding the door violently on its tracks as he leapt out onto the meadow grass. Stumbling, starting to fall, catching his balance slanting in midair, flying now on ungainly human legs, lurching, running, across the meadow. A warning from outside himself, deep, insistent, urgent, drawing him away from the ship, pulling him toward a small grove of trees like an island in the meadow. Racing toward the trees, their shapes growing taller, the circle of their shadows round and perfect under them like calm water, inviting, safe harbor, shelter. Behind him, a flash of light as the hover exploded, then a searing crack of sound. The shock wave lifted him and flung him forward as he dove into the grass just short of the trees.

Dazed, his ears ringing, he lay motionless with his face buried in the moist fertile smell of roots and meadow plants and loamy earth, seeking refuge from the caustic acrid smoke that began to fill the air. His body shaken into stillness, his thoughts shaken loose from the rest of him, functioning on their own. Processing. An accident, with a practical explanation if fully understood. Fuel cell damaged on impact. Connectors torn apart. Friction of the crash. And the other question also shaken loose in his mind. The question he did not really want to ask. That the crash, his crash, may have actually been intended, engineered, at the very least through intentional negligence, at the worst outright sabotage. And another thought, beyond questioning, wrapped in wonder and gratitude for whatever force had pulled him from the hover toward the island of trees, grace or intuition, grateful either way.

The thick wave of smoke was passing, only a thin column still trailed up into the air. He crawled into the protective shadow of trees and sat with his back against the soft bark of the nearest tree. Cedar trees. Gradually their rich spicy scent replaced the lingering stain of chemical fire in the air. He sat, letting himself settle into the tree, letting the shock take him deeper, giving himself to the shock, to the tree, to the meadow, to the loamy earth. Breathing in cedar and meadowland, exhaling the confinement of the Lab. Allowing his thoughts to come and go, letting patterns come together and then disperse. Settling gently, like falling leaves, like falling ash, like falling snow. Slowly, quietly, awareness of time returned and with it the earnest of another kind of gravity. The day was darker, the cloud cover had thickened. A cold front moving in fast. He could feel a moist chill in the air. A few flakes of snow already drifting down through the stillness all around him, the quietness of Earth pulling gently inward, downward, tiny waters everywhere around him remembering themselves as ice. He needed to find warmer shelter. He tried to stand. His head did not move at the same rate as his body. It spun around instead, and that set the ground spinning too. He grabbed the tree for support and lowered himself slowly to the ground to sit again.

Alehya moved cautiously up the slope, moving with the breeze. A watchful quiet lingered on the valley. The flock of blue birds had scattered at the first sound of the hawk's call, and they had not returned after the sky fish passed. She was still careful in case there were other flying craft, other sky eyes. She reached the manzanita and crouched low, concealed inside the thicket of purple shadows and red brown trunks. She looked out toward the smoke rising above the layers of ridge tops. At least three valleys between here and there. The fear calling she had felt when the craft faltered had been followed by a calling of sharp pain or alarm that quickly receded into blurry softness as if the person were in shock, but the calling was still there.

Someone was coming up the trail behind her. She could hear faint sounds of a person moving as she had done, in the rhythms of the wind and shadows. Tomah. He knew she would be out on this trail today. Maybe he had seen the sky fish too, even before the smoke. He came lightly up the slope, paused in the same tree shadow where she had sat, and looked intently at the manzanita on the ridge. She made a small gesture with her hand. He smiled within the dappled shadows of the tree. She smiled back at him. Two shadows smiling. He waited a few more moments, and then moved up the slope to join her.

They talked mostly within the space of the calling between them, and sometimes with hands and eyes, and occasionally with softly whispered words.

The flying.....? Tomah began.

You saw it too?

Yes.

It followed the valley, traveling low. She mimed the craft's flight with her hand as her eyes traced the route it had taken up the valley.

A person....

Yes, I felt that too.

The smoke.... The flying thing crashed.

Yes. The person was afraid.

A man.

Alehya nodded and switched to whispering. "He is not so much afraid anymore, quieter, settling, hard to describe, a texture, like falling snow." She made the graceful swirling motions for snow from the hand sign language, both hands floating gently downward, and added in the calling way, *his calling is not strong now, but I can still feel it.*

Strange, to feel a Taibo'oo so clearly. He used the word for alien strangers borrowed from the language of the Ancient Ones, rather than the word "Watcher." *I did not know they knew the calling.*

Yes. I was surprised too. Tomah, this is important, like a dream, or a vision. I can't quite see.... but he doesn't feel

85

dangerous, different maybe, but not Taibo'oo, he feels human…. and he may have been hurt in the crash, not too badly, but he may need our help. Her eyes were eager, filled with wondering about her connection to the strangeness. *There was a reason he passed so close by,* she concluded, as if that settled it.

Tomah felt he should consider carefully before he replied. He took in her eager look. He knew her resourcefulness. Her willingness to help, anyone, a small bird fallen from a nest, an elder with a heavy basket on the trail, one of the younger children with a hurt knee. Her skillful hands, making cordage, weaving baskets, always ready to tend a cooking fire, to steady a load, and now, to heal, her new work learning the inner ways of medicinal plants. Her strong will, her independent spirit, her kind heart. It would be hard to turn her back, to convince her not to go. He weighed all of this in the balance of his fondness for her. His growing love. He motioned for her to crawl through the manzanita until they could both see out toward the crash site. The first big plume of billowing smoke had drifted north, dissolving as it went. A thin column of dark smoke still rose from the crash.

One, two, at least three valleys, between here and there, maybe four. Alehya offered, counting with her eyes.

Steep country. Tomah answered. He scanned the distance with his eyes, then nodded, satisfied. *Look, that tall tree on the ridge. There, on line with the smoke, on the ridge closest to the smoke. See?*

I see it.

I recognize that tree, the double crown, the bend in the trunk before it forks. Abi's heart uncle saw the bear near there on the ridge. Two winters ago, in the spring. The bears were coming down from the mountains early that year, after their winter sleep, remember? And this one was grouchy. Old Uncle didn't know the bear was there. He came up quietly, and startled the bear. Startled Old Uncle too.

Startled him. Aiiii!

Old Uncle, he was breathing heavy, but he stood tall and talked calmly with the bear. Finally the bear turned and walked away. But Old Uncle said he had a feeling about that bear. After the bear was out of view, Old Uncle climbed the nearest big tree. That one with the fork, there on the ridge. Sure enough, the bear came back.

The bear came back. Alehya's eyes were shining, Tomah was telling the story well.

The bear came over to the tree and looked up at Old Uncle for a while, sniffing and whuffling the air, and then the bear started to climb the tree too. Old Uncle, began climbing higher to get away from the bear, but when the bear got to the fork, that bear looked up at Old Uncle again and just started climbing up the other trunk.

The other trunk! Alehya grinned and lifted her eyebrows playfully.

Yes. That's the way Old Uncle tells it. The bear was up there as high as Old Uncle, just looking over at him from the other trunk. Then the bear started chewing on the tree, going for the resin and the inner bark. There's a big blaze on the trunk where the bear chewed, you can't quite see it from here. Then the bear climbed down and went away.

Sugar pine. A lot sweeter than Old Uncle. Alehya giggled, and they both grinned.

Old Uncle said that bear just knew he was too tough and ornery to be much of a meal, all sinew and bone.

87

The bear relatives are wise. They know many things. And this one gave Old Uncle a good story.

Abi showed me the tree when we went to the little spring at the head of that valley right past the tree. That's the same valley where the crash is…

They looked past the tree. The smoke was fading faster now. Long curtains of snow showers mingled with cloud shadow were sweeping up from the south, coming in fast, coming closer to the valley and gathering toward the higher mountains beyond.

The bears will have snow to eat soon up on the mountain if they aren't already asleep, Alehya observed and made the hand sign for winter, holding her fists close to her chest and shivering them, but her eyes were on the valley, not the distant mountain.

Snow coming to the valleys soon too.

Yes.

The man from the crash, you said that's the way he felt, like falling snow…. Tomah came back to the decision at hand. Old Uncle and the bear, the tree and the crash, the coming snow and the time of winter sleeps. All connected. Tomah knew that relating the story was somehow important. As he told the story he had been sifting through the patterns of the day, and remembering how his own uncle had taught him that everything mattered, everything was part of the whole. Everything had a story, and the stories were part of it too, they were how we saw the patterns, and how we remembered them. They were landmarks, like the tree, pointers to the pattern into which all things were woven. The stories helped you see the wholeness, the connectedness, the belonging. They helped you decide.

Tomah, I have to reach him soon, he may need our help. Alehya tugged at him with her eyes.

It was clear that she would go. *Yes, it's time.* At least now that he recognized the tree, he could help. *I remember how Abi brought me to that valley,* he began slowly, retracing the route in his mind. *You could to go back around that way, and then come in from over there.* He gestured with his hand.

What if I went straight for the bear tree instead?

Tomah looked at her. *Faster maybe, unless you have to back track along the way. And those valleys are very steep…. A harder route,* he finally said, but he could see in her eyes, she had made her choice. Their council of two had not exactly reached consensus, but there wasn't much more time. She was always so quick, and he was by nature the slower and more thorough to consider and decide, although once he did decide, he was as decisive in his actions as he was thorough in considering. There was a time to go slow, and a time to go fast. Once you released an arrow, hard to call it back. He liked to have a clear aim in view. He wished he could go with her, but she knew more about healing, and he was the faster runner, his people's messenger. They each had their skills and their ways. He sighed and smiled affectionately at her. *Go now, and I will tell the village and the elders about the sky craft and where you have gone. They will need to know. And,* he added, *be careful.* He turned and weighed the distance again with his eyes, as if already following her progress there, gauging the approach of the snow clouds. Trusting her, and still a little hesitant to let her go. *Be careful,* he said again, *and watch out for spring bears!*

They both giggled.

And you be careful too, Swift Messenger. She touched his hand and smiled at him with her eyes as a bright warmth swept through him.

He touched her gently with his eyes in return, and then headed back the way he came, moving more swiftly this time.

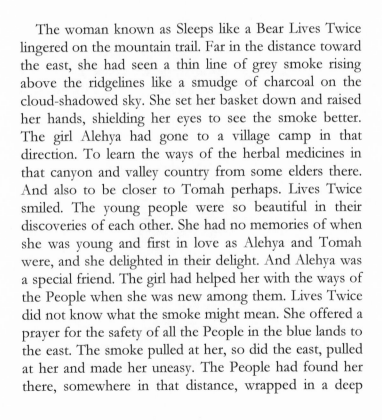

The woman known as Sleeps like a Bear Lives Twice lingered on the mountain trail. Far in the distance toward the east, she had seen a thin line of grey smoke rising above the ridgelines like a smudge of charcoal on the cloud-shadowed sky. She set her basket down and raised her hands, shielding her eyes to see the smoke better. The girl Alehya had gone to a village camp in that direction. To learn the ways of the herbal medicines in that canyon and valley country from some elders there. And also to be closer to Tomah perhaps. Lives Twice smiled. The young people were so beautiful in their discoveries of each other. She had no memories of when she was young and first in love as Alehya and Tomah were, and she delighted in their delight. And Alehya was a special friend. The girl had helped her with the ways of the People when she was new among them. Lives Twice did not know what the smoke might mean. She offered a prayer for the safety of all the People in the blue lands to the east. The smoke pulled at her, so did the east, pulled at her and made her uneasy. The People had found her there, somewhere in that distance, wrapped in a deep sleep, and they had cared for her and welcomed her into their lives as one of their own. They called her Sleeps like a Bear at first, but bears resume a familiar life when they emerge from their winter sleep, and when she did not remember anything from before, they called her Lives Twice, while the ones who knew her well still called her affectionately after the sleep of the bear kind. When she tried to go back before her time with the People, the way was always blocked by a protective warding darkness. Whatever memories she might recover from beyond the darkness wanted to stay there. Enough to be with the People now.

A light snow was beginning to fall, curving flakes like feather down drifted through the air around her. A few caught on her hair, white against the dark strands just beginning to thread through with the grey of their own winter. Here and there in the distance, silken curtains of heavier snow showers erasing the thin line of smoke. The old ones she was gathering with today had paused on the trail up ahead of her, looking back toward her, waiting for her. She picked up her basket and continued up the slope to join them, following the whisper of their footsteps laid as lightly on the land as the delicate flakes of snow.

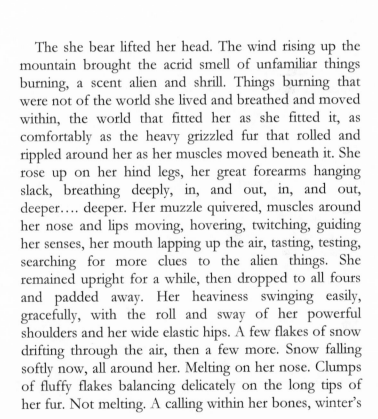

The she bear lifted her head. The wind rising up the mountain brought the acrid smell of unfamiliar things burning, a scent alien and shrill. Things burning that were not of the world she lived and breathed and moved within, the world that fitted her as she fitted it, as comfortably as the heavy grizzled fur that rolled and rippled around her as her muscles moved beneath it. She rose up on her hind legs, her great forearms hanging slack, breathing deeply, in, and out, in, and out, deeper.... deeper. Her muzzle quivered, muscles around her nose and lips moving, hovering, twitching, guiding her senses, her mouth lapping up the air, tasting, testing, searching for more clues to the alien things. She remained upright for a while, then dropped to all fours and padded away. Her heaviness swinging easily, gracefully, with the roll and sway of her powerful shoulders and her wide elastic hips. A few flakes of snow drifting through the air, then a few more. Snow falling softly now, all around her. Melting on her nose. Clumps of fluffy flakes balancing delicately on the long tips of her fur. Not melting. A calling within her bones, winter's

93

pull. And another calling within, new lives waiting, tiny, drifting on her inner seas, and an ancient need to enter the timeless renewal of her kind suspended in depths beyond sleep while they grew within her.

She had no single name sound, as some of the other kinds did. Her name was in all her sounds, her every movement, her scent, her breath. Her new cubs would know her, as others knew her, by her very presence, her beingness, infused in every rhythm of her breathing, the texture of her fur, the way she shifted her weight shoulder and hip, shoulder and hip, side to side. They would know her by heart. They would never forget her. They would know her in their blood, her blood ongoing in them calling like to like.

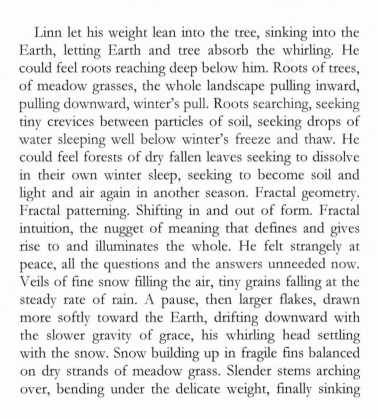

Linn let his weight lean into the tree, sinking into the Earth, letting Earth and tree absorb the whirling. He could feel roots reaching deep below him. Roots of trees, of meadow grasses, the whole landscape pulling inward, pulling downward, winter's pull. Roots searching, seeking tiny crevices between particles of soil, seeking drops of water sleeping well below winter's freeze and thaw. He could feel forests of dry fallen leaves seeking to dissolve in their own winter sleep, seeking to become soil and light and air again in another season. Fractal geometry. Fractal patterning. Shifting in and out of form. Fractal intuition, the nugget of meaning that defines and gives rise to and illuminates the whole. He felt strangely at peace, all the questions and the answers unneeded now. Veils of fine snow filling the air, tiny grains falling at the steady rate of rain. A pause, then larger flakes, drawn more softly toward the Earth, drifting downward with the slower gravity of grace, his whirling head settling with the snow. Snow building up in fragile fins balanced on dry strands of meadow grass. Slender stems arching over, bending under the delicate weight, finally sinking into the growing whiteness. Soon the remnants of the crash would look like nothing more than a jagged outcropping of boulders, no longer alien, slowly melded into the land by the same enveloping grace. He was on a little island now, in the snow shadow of the cedars. Whiteness slowly shading inward toward him. Grainy snow falling again, bits of snow drifting onto his island carried on gusts of wind. Snow grains settling on his outstretched legs. A few at a time, then a few more. Lodging in the crevasses between the wrinkles in his pants, frosting them into high relief. Like a vintage photo negative, or moonlight hollowing the world into fragile shells of light and shadow. He sighed. Delicate beauty, so simple in the end. He wasn't even cold.

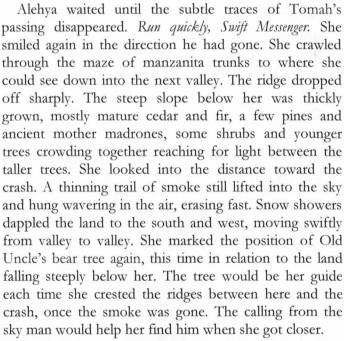

Alehya waited until the subtle traces of Tomah's passing disappeared. *Run quickly, Swift Messenger.* She smiled again in the direction he had gone. She crawled through the maze of manzanita trunks to where she could see down into the next valley. The ridge dropped off sharply. The steep slope below her was thickly grown, mostly mature cedar and fir, a few pines and ancient mother madrones, some shrubs and younger trees crowding together reaching for light between the taller trees. She looked into the distance toward the crash. A thinning trail of smoke still lifted into the sky and hung wavering in the air, erasing fast. Snow showers dappled the land to the south and west, moving swiftly from valley to valley. She marked the position of Old Uncle's bear tree again, this time in relation to the land falling steeply below her. The tree would be her guide each time she crested the ridges between here and the crash, once the smoke was gone. The calling from the sky man would help her find him when she got closer.

She began to work her way down the slope, moving slowly through the tangle of brush and fallen branches.

Under the dense cover of the trees, the forest air was silent, except for her overloud, to her ears at least, progress. All around her, the fresh scent of green cedar mingled with the dry musty smell of decay. Years of brittle branches, twigs, and leaves balanced intricately in fragile layers on the forest floor, crunching softly underfoot no matter how carefully she stepped. Slow going indeed. Tomah had been right. But all the north facing slopes were like this, and going around would take even longer. She was grateful when she came to a deer trail that offered a quieter route heading diagonally down the steep slope, a narrow path worn through the brittle debris marking the easiest descent. Well not quite always the easiest. Depends on if you move on four legs and are a bit closer to the ground she grinned to herself, when she came to the first set of low branches crossing the trail. The deer had gone right under, she crouched down to do the same.

Farther down the slope the trail merged with a wider deer trail that held traces of other four-legged relatives as well as deer, both trails coming together heading down slope like a little stream gathering as it went. The gathered trail was well used, with enough overlapping lobed heels, claws, toes and fingertips as well as hooves to make it harder to distinguish her tracks if she was careful to blend her footsteps into theirs. Many of her fellow travelers were more active by night, and as she followed in their wake, she read the signs that hinted at their lives. A passage of a few clear footprints overstepping all the rest. *Hello coyote sister, out late this morning I see.* Delicate long fingered handprints peeking out from the maze of other shapes. *Little raccoon brother, was your foraging good?* Small flat-footed tracks, like miniature bear's feet but not quite. *Greetings little skunk mother, was your night hunting good too?* Woven over, under, around, and through most of the other patterns braided on the trail, the cloven shapes of deer's hooves. She smiled. The deer people on their way to an early afternoon day bed would soon conceal her passing with their sharp pointed tracks. *Thank you, all my brothers and sisters, for your paths, for blending my path into yours.*

A few flakes of snow began drifting through the air. All around her, a feeling of pulling downward and inward with the snow. Like a gentle exhale, a waiting, a great listening for the approach of winter. A time to pause, to sit and be with the stillness ready to cloak the land. She held out her hands, a few snowflakes landed on her open palms, melting into her heat. *Thank you sky waters, thank you winter waters, for your blessing.* A slight gust of wind stirred through the snow falling above her in answer, white on white in the bright sky space between the shadowy trees. Winter breathing in answer, in the swirling flakes, in the downfalling quiet growing steadily and lightly all around her. She loved the snow, especially the first snow, but she had a mission, and the inward turning that surrounded her added to the urgency. She needed to reach the man before that turning swallowed him too, forever in winter's grace.

A tangle of fallen trees and brambles crowded together on the slope rising up ahead of her after she crossed the small stream at the bottom of the valley. One of the places where sky fire from the summer storms had taken the trees. The trail she was following went around, she would have to do the same. Not much cover here, until she reached the trees farther up the slope. A sudden flurry of snowflakes filled the air. She pulled her outer cloak closer around her. If it began to snow harder, her tracks would show in the whiteness. Even when covered over there would be distinctive patterns. The soft dimples and the rhythms of their spacing in the rounded surface of the snow would be easy to read. And there would be no way to hide the trough that would show in heavier snow. If eyes there were, then better for her tracks to merge with the flow of the deer people and the other four legged relatives. They knew the ways of the land, and many of them had closer eyes to be wary of, they would not take unnecessary risks.

Even with the animal trails, her progress was slow. Each time she reached the crest of a ridge, she realigned her route toward Old Uncle's tree. The snow stopped and started in brief showers that faded away as quickly as they came. Sometimes in clusters of flakes like downy breast feathers, sometimes as tiny grainy pebbles like white sand. When she finally reached the bear tree and could look down towards the crash, she saw that the valley floor was wider than the other valleys, curving a little to one side, with a level meadowland at the bend. The spring that Tomah had visited with Abi would be at the far end of the valley at the foot of the steep rock face. All dissolving rapidly in veils of swirling snow. Snow falling more heavily here, frosting the meadow and sitting lightly on the shoulders of the trees. Soon the land would be completely enveloped in winter white. Through the middle of the meadow, a long wide gouge in the earth led to a rounded heap with a few jagged shapes protruding from it. The crash. The snow was not sticking yet to the mound or where the earth had been laid bare, and they still held an alien energy. Starkly set apart in the growing whiteness for now, soon to be included in the blessing of the snow. No sign of the man, no sign that anyone had escaped the wreck. No sign that others of his kind had come to investigate the crash. The calling from the man had grown very faint, as if he was merging into the land with the snow, but she was sure he was somewhere nearby.

She approached the crash site cautiously. She stopped and listened, moving quietly, stopping to listen again. She found the man in a small grove of young cedars. He was sitting with his back leaning against a tree, his legs stretched out on the ground, his arms limp at his sides. He was still alive and beyond knowing if he was alive or not. Neither awake nor asleep, breathing very softly, strangely peaceful. She could feel his shock, and something else, outside her experience, a feeling from him of falling, letting go of all support. She wondered what kind of world he had come from and what would give rise to such a feeling, such a need to fall away. For now, he needed warmth, he needed shelter. She did too. No others of his kind had arrived to care for him. Perhaps his people did not know yet, perhaps they were far away. The snow had let up again, she did not know for how long. She had seen a cluster of fallen trees a short way back in the woodlands as she approached the crash site. She could improvise a shelter there, and find dry wood for a fire to warm the man. She would be all right for a while on her own, she had some training in the inner heat, but his limbs were getting very cold. She

101

took off her cloak, wrapped it around him, and went back to find the downed trees.

Several large trees had fallen crisscrossed on top of each other. After thanking the tree people for the shelter they could still provide, even in their fallenness, she worked her way through the dry branches to the place where two of the largest trunks crossed each other, and began breaking off branches to build a rough roof over the angled space between them. She left a screen of branches at the entrance to her pathway untouched. She laid thinner branches on the roof parallel to the first course to fill in some of the gaps and across the back of the shelter. She explained her need to a stand of healthy cedars close by, thanked them, and broke off some of their smaller boughs. After layering the dense flat fans of green cedar over the roof of fallen branches and filling in the back under the logs, she had a small cave. Snow starting to fall again. If it fell thick enough, it would complete the roof. She thanked the snow and reemerged from her hidden lair, gathered pine needles and dry cedar, and heaped them in the shelter to make a large nest. As more and more snowflakes drifted through the air, she gathered dry bark from the undersides of the fallen trees for tinder, and enough dry twigs and slender branches to keep a small fire going for the night. She piled them near the opening of the cave beside a few rocks she had found for a reflective hearth, and went to get the man. Along with her medicine seeds, she had a small pouch of chia seeds, traveler's food, and she had filled her woven water flask when she crossed the last stream. On her way back to the crash site, she gathered a small handful of green pine needles, and a few leaves of winter herbs growing in a sheltered spot. *Thank you my brothers and sisters, thank you.* Food was not a problem for now. Warmth was what this man's body needed most. What his heart and mind needed was puzzling. Where had he come from, why was he here? And why had she seen him? The People did not believe in random events. All things were part of patterns woven by the great kindness at the heart of all life. She would wait and see.

The young woman's face had appeared suddenly before him. Her eyes, especially, seemed to be calling to him. He had tried to surface, tried to form words to answer, but he was too far away even though her face was so close. She wrapped him in some kind of fur, then she was gone. She was another memory perhaps, one he never knew he had. Her eyes reminded him of other eyes, he could not remember whose. Too many memories had crowded around him on his island at first, now so few.

She was back, her eyes more insistent than before. She wanted him to do something, to get up, to move. He wanted to explain the spinning in his head but he had no words. Why didn't this memory go away? Her hands were kind, their touch surprisingly real. Perhaps she was more than a memory. She gently eased him to his feet. The earth rolled a bit, but it did not spin. She wanted him to walk with her. Her hands were strong as well as kind. They helped the spinning stay away. Slowly he moved one foot then the other. She guided him, he was walking with her away from his island under the cedars.

She was an island too. He leaned on her to steady his steps. They were heading into the forest. Snowflakes landed on her hair and on her arm supporting him. Delicate geometries, delicate balancing. Her hair and her skin a rich golden brown color with a polished sheen like oak leaves newly fallen in autumn. Subtle patterns at the beginning, self-similar throughout the whole.

They came to a small cave nestled among a tangle of fallen tree trunks. Another island, sweet with the smell of cedar and pine. She helped him sit down on a pile of dried cedar, pulled the fur closer around him, and turned away from him. He watched her, enthralled by a memory that was not memory, that had a life and direction of its own. She pulled wide curls of dry bark into tiny strands, broke up little twigs, and built an exquisite miniature shelter of the twigs and strands at the mouth of the cave. She unwrapped a small bundle and unwound an arm's length of string that bound two pieces of wood together, a thick cylindrical stick that was rounded on each end, and a flatter piece of wood of similar length. Both were about as long as her hands. The flat piece had a row of small cup shape hollows set into it, each notched on one side. She chose a few branches from the pile beside her, tested their suppleness, and strung one like a bow. She made a small nest of very fine shreds of bark and some soft material from her bundle and set it aside. He watched entranced, as if he had awakened in a dream, determined to remember everything he saw, afraid that any moment the dream would change or disappear. Her actions were purposeful, unhurried, filled with reverent grace. She set the flat piece of wood on a wide curl of bark, knelt on one knee, and placed one foot on the piece of wood. She looped the taut bowstring in one deft movement around the short round stick and set the stick upright in one of the cup shapes on the board. She took a palm size rock from her pouch, fit the indentation on one face of the rock to the top of the upright stick, and held it there with one hand. Then she began moving the bow back and forth with her other hand, in swift quiet strokes. Making silent invisible music. Now he was sure he was in a dream, he was in the young woman's dream, and she was a dream too, a dream of where memories come from.

Wisps of smoke began to rise from where the spindle fit into the cup shape. Her music becoming visible, with a curving wavering tune he wished he had ears to hear. She set the bow and spindle aside, lifted the flat piece of wood and carefully tipped something on the bark into the small nest. She held it close to her lips, whispering more silent music with her breath. A few sparks flew out from the nest, then tiny flames burst into view. She set the flaming nest tenderly inside the miniature structure she had built before and knelt down to breathe into it. Small flames began to lick at the tiny cone shape. She carefully laid more slender sticks on the small structure, building the same shape each time inside the flames, rebuilding as fast as the fire consumed it, a persistent, ephemeral shape living with her help inside the flames. The young woman was singing softly now, as the flames grew larger, this time a tune he could hear, but not the words. The flames flickered upward in the quiet air, burning steadily brighter and brighter. He could feel warmth growing all around him in the cave nest. Her music, the dream of fire. Cocooned in the warmth he drifted deeper, farther away, called by another persistent dream memory as transient and enduring as the tiny structure inside the flames.

Alehya sat at the entrance of the shelter as twilight began to fall. Snow pulling steadily downward in an endless curtain, individual flakes flickering red and gold as they caught briefly in the light from her small fire. She had gathered enough dry wood for the night, woman's wood. She smiled, everyone's wood now, no need for the big angry bonfires of the terrible times Before that she had heard about in the stories and shared memories. Her wood was in small pieces, just large enough to feed a small careful fire and make a layer of embers to radiate their warmth between her small offerings to the tiny flames. The quiet voice of the fire blending easily, comfortably, with the stillness of the snow slowly shading into grainy twilight. *Thank you brother sister fire for your cheerful heat, for your warmth, for your light, for your companionship.*

She looked over at the man. She had reached him in time. He was warmer now, secure in the cave nest with the fire. Cold would not be the way he left the world this time. But his heart, she was not sure, it was as if his heart had already left. She could feel him receding into his own flickering twilight beside her. Remote. Absent. His heart present somewhere else. As if he was following someone far away, a calling from his world, trying to reach him. Or someone he was trying to reach, trying to catch up with. She wondered, did he have a special friend, like Tomah was for her, did he have brothers, sisters, aunts, or a child, who were sending their calling here, looking for him too. He had a longing feel, a longing stretched tight over a distance of time even more than place, for someone so far away in a personal before that he can only try to reach, he can never touch.

He reminded Alehya of the little deer that she tended after his mother had been taken by the mountain lion, like and not like. A brave deer child, open, unafraid. He had followed her around, curled trusting beside her as she slept. One of the mothers had nursed him at first, offering her milk as tenderly to the little four legged one as to her own child. But Alehya was the one who led him to the ways of the green plants. She knew the likes and dislikes of the deer kind well. She had followed their trails, she had seen their sharp hoof prints pressed in meadow earth and the torn stems where they nibbled tender shoots and leaves, tasting a bit here and there. She knew their favorite lays, in warm sun on cool days, in deep shade for summer heat. And so she led him back in the end to his own kind, to his own ways. She was sad, but happy when he left to follow them. She knew he might have had a hard time at first. He would have to find his own way to fit in, his own way to learn the cues, the ear laid back, a head lowered or turned, a hoof partly raised, signaling a private space not to invade. All of these she could not give him, only the green growing ways of the plants, and the trails, and her love.

She leaned closer to add a few sticks to the fire. The warm glow of the fire blushed the rounding shore of snow building up outside the opening of the cave. She looked over at the man again, and wondered, like the little deer or the bird with the injured wing, how long this one would stay. She sat back and burrowed into the heap of leaves and cedar fronds. She adjusted her rabbit fur cape more tightly around the man to make sure he stayed warm. The little deer, green leaves and tender shoots, the little bird, insects and worms, this man, what could she give him to help him to his unknown place so far away.

The man's passing, if he did leave to follow whatever was calling him or whoever he was calling for, would be for her like the passing of a small child who had not yet had enough time to be here before they left. Brief, mysterious, leaving only glancing memories. Taking their other traveling memories with them, the ones they came in with, unshared, unexplored. Or maybe the man would stay instead, and be like the cicada kind, cracked open into another life, startled perhaps by the loud buzzing rhythm of their newly discovered voices after years of earth dark silence, but compelled by some ancient wisdom to stay. She reached forward to add a few more sticks to the fire, then settled back into the nest of cedar and pine. She pulled a corner of her cloak over her shoulders and made sure the man was still covered. His quiet breathing was slow and steady. Dissolving, melted down inside as he seemed to be, which way would he go? She offered small prayers into the gathering twilight outside, and settled in for the coming night. *Thank you brother sister fire for your bright spirit and your hope. Thank you brother sister snow for your protection and your grace, thank you mother father night for coming so softly and guarding and holding us all.*

The she bear paused on the upper slope of the mountain. She lifted her head, her mouth open, sifting, tasting the twilight air. Snow falling all around her. Pulling steadily toward the earth, already covering the high meadowland. She rose up on her hind legs. Balancing her great winter weight upright in the downfalling air. Breathing deeply the subtle mineral scent carried on the snow. Clear, thin, far away, the flavor of the upper sky coming to rest on the mountainside. Winter sleep of the sky. Erasing the last wisps of the other mineral smell. The last traces of the alien fire. That burning was over. The calling from the man who came with the fire fainter now, like the wisps. Not as restless. Settling, like the snow. The young sheling had reached the man in time. The People would know, whether to welcome him in or not for the time of winter sleeps. She gave a soft whuff and dropped down to all four legs again. She padded through the meadow, through the swirling veils of snow. Stepping in the wide sure tracks of her mother and her mother's mothers before her.

112

She stopped and turned aside for a moment. Her claws raked through the crumbling sides of a fallen log. She rooted lightly, casually, through the debris like chunks of shadow dark against the glowing twilight whiteness of the snow. Found a few slow insects. Winter slow. Picked them delicately, one by one, with her agile lips. Then she moved on. The great hunger was already waning in her. She was secure. The layer of fat wrapping her body under her heavy fur was thick. Enough for herself and for her cubs to be. She ambled through the high meadowland toward her den. Following a line of mothers reaching back through uncounted time, feeling new lives within them waiting to cross the land bridge of their bodies in their ancient migration into form.

She reached her den. Grey rock and gnarled roots of aged pine. A small opening hidden between. High on the mountain, on a slope where snow lingers in the spring. A small cave, bear size, dug into the mountainside, supported by the roots of the stout bodied tree. A tree that spent its long age growing into the heart of the mountain, not reaching for the sky in the way of most tree kind. Carried upward by the mountain's height instead, roots entwined with the mountain's heart, sharing the mountain's secrets of rock and stone. Burrowed between the roots, a low short tunnel facing away from storm and wind. A small chamber above the level of the tunnel, with just enough room for the bear to turn around in. A nest of grass and leaves gathered before the snow. Her cubs would be born here, deep in winter, within her ancestral sleep. Held in the circle of her body's heat curled around them. Her breath warming the air they breathed. Cubs seeking her teats in their

113

blind newborn darkness. Finding mother source in the forest of her fur by heat of flesh alone. Cubs growing big on the cream rich milk of their kind. Bear flesh. The gravity and dignity of bear kind. Cellular memory, rich as cream, given with her milk. Her own bones and muscles regrowing as she spends her store of fat to heat and nourish, while her cubs grow and she sleeps.

She had been keeping close to her den ever since the snow began to cover the higher peaks. Sleeping more each day. Sometimes in the den, sometimes outside. She paused at the entrance, searching the air one last time. Her breath her benediction for the winter land. She surveyed the whiteness descending on the mountain in the lingering glow of twilight. The People would guard these lands wakeful for the time of winter sleeps, and she would still guard the portals of their dreaming, even while she roamed the far country beyond sleep and dream in the freedom of her kind.

Within the snow veiled twilight outside her lair, and the silence of rock and earth, the bear, settling herself, curling in on herself, cocooned in fur, in thick layers of winter fat, fat born of berries, nuts, and seeds, of roots and grubs, of flesh and bark and fruits and leaves, of hot summer suns, moist spring earth, and clear blue autumn skies. Sheltered in all of this, descending, spiraling inward, curling around the new lives within her. Cradling them in her memories, weaving ladders of memory in every cell, shimmering with light. Light living, breathing, as she did, and light spiraling through time in another way, weaving pathways, corridors, connecting future memory with things long past, with futures unfolding that may never be except in memory, connecting things past with what they still could be.

Suspended in the quiet rhythms of her breathing, riding calm seas beyond dreamless sleep, beyond dream. Soft swells of air lapping on the shores of her lungs, receding and incoming again, gently, slower and slower. Suspended in the slowing rhythms of her blood, soft swells lapping on the shores of her heart, red tides gently receding and incoming again. Slower and slower tides. Reaching the threshold of her ancestral freedom, her heritage to move freely beyond time, beyond the need for redeeming memory. Meeting another on the threshold, an older sheling, dark hair with a few strands of grey, framing her face like the wings of a dark bird. A woman of human kind, not like the People, but not unlike. The woman not knowing how she came here. Bewildered. Unsure.

Daughter, why are you here? Do your kind also practice the deep dream beyond sleep? The bear asked gently.

No, well, maybe. I don't know.... Are there others?.... How did I get here?.... I am searching.... searching.... for something....

The bear considered her reply. She looked at the woman. Like a small cub, this one, born blind in darkness, not yet knowing about light. Searching for warmth, and for more than that, searching for something she does not know, knowing only the searching, and yet she is so close. *Then go with my blessing, you will not find it here, not yet.* She looked into the woman's eyes, brown eyes, flecked with a hint of sunlight. So like the eyes of bear kind. *Come back when you know what you are searching for, and I can help you.*

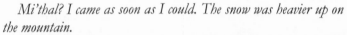

Mi'thal? I came as soon as I could. The snow was heavier up on the mountain.

Mi'thal looked up as she heard the sound of her brother's distinctive raven call, the low guttural croaking purr that accompanied his sending, and saw his familiar form silhouetted in the glowing twilight outside the entrance to the lodge. She gave her answering raven's call, the one she had used with him since they were young, and he stooped down to come through the low doorway. She waited until Ta'le had straightened up and brushed the snow off his cloak and hair, then she said, *Good that you are here. She is far away again. I cannot reach her....*

What happened? He knelt down by the small fire, and let his senses take in the familiar warmth of the lodges of his people, rich with an earthen smell and the scent of dry herbs and wood smoke. And today, the added green medicinal fragrance rising from a small cooking basket near the fire. Then his eyes found the figure wrapped in shadows beside his sister.

I'm not sure. The old ones gathering with her on the mountain said she saw the smoke in the east.

Yes.

You saw it too.

Yes....Go on….. His eyes stayed on the sleeping form beside her.

She looked into the east for a while, and she seemed to be all right at first. She walked with them on the trail, and then she just sat down and disappeared into herself again. They led her back like a sleepwalker. She gestured toward the sleeping figure. *She has been like this ever since.*

We have all felt the pull she struggles with in her dreams.

Yes. This time she seems to be trying harder to reach beyond the threshold of her darkness. Something calling to her. Perhaps this time she has gone to find it.

It is hard for her.

The reason she has waited so long to try.

She has a fever? He had moved closer to the sleeping woman and was touching her face, gently, tenderly.

She is warm, yes, like a fever, but different, as if she is heating the air around her while her body grows steadily cooler. Her pulse and her breathing are very slow.

A hard journey. I will sit with her now. Thank you, Mi'thal.

I will come back soon. She hesitated, not leaving yet. *Hard for you too…. the woman you love….*

Here or far away, she is still the woman I love, I will be all right.

What if she finds what she is looking for?

We will wait and see.

He looked into the fire. *I did not know I would ever love again.*

We are all happy for you that you do love again, little brother.

A long time since you were bigger than me, my little big sister. He smiled at her. *Thank you, Mi'thal, for watching over us both.*

He looked longer into the small flames and glowing embers. Mi'thal could see his eyes entering a luminous inner depth, with a hint of a bright shore of light and color far beyond the fire. At last he turned to her. *You tended her when she first came to us, her sleep now, like her sleep then?*

Yes, it is the same, only this time, more of a friction inside. She made a tugging motion with her hands. *Her struggle.*

Yes. We have all told her she doesn't have to remember. She can live her new life among the People without the darkness that guards her memories from before.

Except inside.... They were quiet for a while. *And your memories?* She asked gently.

He took a long time answering. The quiet warmth of the shelter filled with their breathing blended with the pulsing glow of embers in the fire. The sleeper's breathing barely audible, so faint and slow. Mi'thal no longer expected an answer when he finally replied. *Difficult, but not as far away as hers. And I am making some peace with them.* Another long pause. An ember shifted in the fire.

Would it be better for her if we told her more of when we found her? She ventured.

He looked long into the fire again. *No, there is a reason for her forgetting. The elders and the councils agree. When it is time for her to remember, she will find her own way to her memories, she will find the strength to go there.* He stopped again, sifting through other distances with his eyes. *What we do here, what we all do, in the village camps and on the mountain, the way we live our lives now, what we are trying to do together, that must not be allowed to die. The future is born of us now. There are so few of us. We need everyone. She needs to come back. We almost lost the Earth last time around. We can't do that again.*

Mi'thal nodded in agreement. *So fragile, our presence in this world. So fleeting and so full of hope, so full of the promise of life.*

As we all are.

Beside them, the sleeper traveled her own worlds, following hidden trails, moving from one firm memory to another, following footsteps tracing back through time, moving through light and shadow, pausing here and there with the breeze, the way the girl Alehya had shown her. Searching through the spiraling memories, trying to weave fragments of her life into a wholeness still beyond her ken.

She had no memories of her time before. Her memories were all recent ones. Memories with the People. Most were moments of nascent beauty. Morning sun in early spring warming a small meadowland, clouds of mist rising from the gentle heat glowing softly backlit in the sweet air. Drops of rain shimmering at the tips of pine needles after a brief shower. Maple buds swelling, held upright on curving tips of bare branches like green flames. Moments not of personhood, but of invisible witness. Moments of place, braided into days and nights and seasons. Like fine cordage double wrapped. Skillful fingers teaching her how to spiral slender plant fibers together, patiently helping her wind herself into a new life. Other moments, longer, the person living that new life, shy, delicate, emerging slowly, islands of conversation, moments linked together, anchoring her, showing her in the ebb and flow of the seasons. Following those memories especially, unwinding the double wrap, gently tugging apart the strands of fiber, seeking the plant, the creek side, the riverbank, where it first grew and flowered.

Her first memory, waking among the People. Lingering on a formless shore. Perception returning slowly. Her thoughts and senses still distant, flickering with the grainy texture of twilight. She was warm, wrapped in a softness like fur. Sounds reaching her, quiet sounds from far away, moving through her like curving lines of light through water. Faint crackling of a fire. A woman's voice, rippling, melodic, like water, singing softly. Smell of wood smoke, laced with herbs, and something else, sweet and sharp together, comforting. Another smell, rich mineral earth, mothering. A burst of laughter farther away, children's voices, children's laughter. She opened her eyes. A woman sat by a small fire, singing as she laid a few sticks carefully on the flames, as if her song and the fire together were a prayer. Firelight glowing on wide trails of grey mingled through the woman's long dark hair. The woman smiling, asking some part of her outside of words how she felt, asking if she was feeling better now.

Yes, she replying, also without words, not knowing how.

Good. Would you like some tea? The woman smiling again as she offered her a bowl shape cup. The cup felt warm and round when she cradled it in her hands. From the cup a warm breath of scented steam. The smell, pungent and full that was light and green too. Strong, with the strength of leaves and roots. The woman's eyes were kind. "You have been sleeping for days." She spoke in words this time.

"Where am I?"

"You are with the People."

"How did I get here?"

"We found you. You are safe now." *Finish the tea, and rest again.*

She gave the empty cup back to the woman with wondering hands, luminous and pale. She felt very tired. She felt a softness soothed around her as she drifted back onto a far shore. A sudden spacious depth, a hollowing out of all the senses, all thought and perception becoming one tactile field of pulsing lights, tiny bits of colored lights.

No word names yet. Colors and shapes only. Words and names came later, part of the new remembering. Her memory very selective when it returned, an absence surrounded by a persona with no name, like the beautiful blue and grey leaved bushes in front of her, a mystery even to themselves. A person who knew how to be in a world, in a life, who knew the pull of gravity, the feel of heat and cold. Who had been born young once, somewhere else, and had grown up and was now here, capable of feeling and perception. A definite someone that still functioned even without a name or a history. The movement that was her life just continuing from some point in a past she couldn't see beyond.

Sitting at the edge of the village camp, a favorite place, morning sun not yet high overhead, warm on her face.

122

Stretching her legs out in front of her, running one hand gently across the tops of summer blond grass. Hearing his voice beside her, familiar but unexpected. "Hi, can I join you?" Warm like the morning sunlight.

"Sure." She turned and smiled at him as he settled comfortably on the ground beside her. "You said the same thing to me when we first met, I am better at speaking within the calling now, outside the sounding words."

"I know, but sometimes I like to see your eyes when you hear my voice and turn to me."

She looked at him, his face elegant and refined in a subtle way, a face that could be delicate or strong by turns. His eyes dark, with a hint of green, like the forest pools where the creek ran slower in the shadow of the trees. She had known other eyes that were dark like these, she was sure somehow, but a feeling that those other eyes were usually reaching, quick, seeking outward to understand. Ta'le's eyes were different, they opened inward instead, pulling understanding up from a depth she felt she had not met before, allowing a knowing up from his heart somehow, allowing his heart to know and decide.

I've missed you, she said simply, as she looked at him.
I've missed you too.

She moved closer, resting her head on his shoulder for a moment, then lifted her head to smile at him. *I'm glad you're here.*

You are happy here at the village?

The People are kind, and I love the children. I love to watch them play, so alive, so bright, the world and each other all so new to them. I like to be with them.

123

They like you too. I heard that you tell them stories.
We tell stories together, discovering them as we go along.
Where do the stories go?

Not far. She laughed, her laughter rippling with the sunlight. *I let the children lead. You know the children, their joy in the simplest things, the rocks, the trees, tiny wildflowers hidden in the grass, a pretty stone on the trail, a bird's nest, a snail's shell. Little rainbows in the drops of dew at sunrise.* Images of their delight and hers tumbled out of her beyond the calling words. *Purple stains on your fingers from the last blackberries ripening in the summer heat.* Laughing again as she held up her berry stained fingers.

They were quiet for a while together, finally she offered, *I still do not remember.*

No need. He soothed away a few strands of hair that had fallen across her face. *Enough that you are here with the People.*

This is my home now, yes. She paused. *But sometimes, I feel like I am not really here, not really anywhere…. I don't know, I am…. neither light or shadow somehow, some of both, in between, like shapes seen by moonlight….* Her hands moved in the air, shaping invisible curving forms while she paused again. As her hands came to rest cradling each other in her lap, she continued. *And maybe like a dream trying to wake itself up…. I am searching…. searching for something else in the memories…. searching…. I'm not sure…. searching for something beyond light and shadow, for where they come together perhaps… I don't even know if I will find it there.*

He waited quietly, letting her thoughts and images sink into him, landing softly like her hands. After a while, he turned to her. *I want you to come to the camp of the gazers with me, to visit. I will ask the other gazers. Next time I come down the mountain I will take you back with me.*

I would like that. She smiled. *When will you come?*

In a few months, before winter.

I will be waiting. She looked into and beyond a distance overlapped with the morning sunlight close around them. *Sometimes I feel you and the others up on the mountain…. as if you are all shells of light or rounded stones polished by the sea, washed up on the shore of a great happiness, drenched in light, resting as if placed there by the sea.* She looked down, suddenly shy. They both paused, caught up for a moment by her mention of the sea, each pulled by different currents. Each traveling different seas, different directions in memory. She looked at her hands, like empty shells, which tide, which sea had washed them up on her lap.

He returned first. *Yes,* he said, with a quiet smile, eyes luminous and sad and at the same time, at peace with both. *Yes, that is how it is. I will bring you there.* He kissed her softly, briefly, and drew away before the sadness that was always there welled up again. He pulled her head gently to his shoulder and held her close to him, feeling the saline warmth of her quiet tears on his neck, his own tears already full in his eyes.

Tears of the sea. Oceans of grief, waters of life…. Her memories drifting onto farther tides. To his memories, not hers, this time. His went farther back. *Grandson,* his grandfather had said to him. *Go to the mountains. Take anyone who will go with you. Do not stay here. I will meet you there….*

She had asked him about names. His name. *Waits for Rain. Waiting for Rain.*

"When I was a kid, my grandfather told me...." He stopped, his eyes shadowed for a moment from inside. Then he continued. "Long ago. My grandfather told me.... once, long ago...." He paused again, searching for a safe route through. "He told me, that you could see the whole world in the first drops of rain. I loved the rain. The first rains after a long dry spell. The smell of moist earth in the fields, newly moist earth." He was in another country, the sad bright one again. Then he smiled quietly, and returned. "I would stand outside when the rain was coming, waiting to catch the first drops in my hands, waiting for the rain. My grandfather.... he gave me the name, along with the gift of the rain."

She could see him in her heart's eyes as a small child standing with his face lifted toward the sky, palms upraised, waiting to catch the first drops, waiting for the blessing of the rain. Waiting to see the whole world there, waiting to hold the wonder of it in his hands. "And are you still waiting for the rain?" she asked.

His answer coming from a place beyond words. "Yes, and no. The rain I wait for now is everywhere." He touched his heart. "Inside, outside, everywhere.... and I know the country, at last, where I will find that rain."

Grandson, go there. His grandfather. A different rain. The other part of his memory, the other side of his name that he did not tell her then, only later. The grandfather who knew the secret in the rain, who warned him to get away before it was too late. *Grandson, go to the mountains. Take anyone who will go with you. Do not stay here. I will meet you there.* Troubled, turbulent times. Brutal times, the time of the Cleansing, the hatred and the bigotry. Before the War. The soldier police, the militias. Death squads.

126

Warlords. Warrior gangs. Everything building toward the war. The WAR police came. Beat his grandfather. The neighbors watched. No one interfered. Ta'le's voice soft, telling quietly the horror. She had asked him, about his name, about the rain, and about what she had seen in his eyes.... "No one came to help us. I was young, I tried.... When I came to, they were gone. My mother sobbing. Grandfather dying. I held him as he died. *Grandson,* he whispered, pointing shakily at the mountains with his broken hand, like a folded wing. *Go to the mountains. Go there. I will meet you there.* My mother was already ill. My father already dead. In the new prison. We never knew how. Ma'marie, my mother, she could not go on from there. She had lost her heart. She told us to go, to follow Grandpa's words. My sister, Mi'thal," he smiled. "Wanted to go with me. She is...." he smiled again, "very.... determined, strong." They both grinned, and then he continued his quiet telling, somber and restrained again in the delicacy of his grief. "Our younger sister, Li'sele, was afraid, she wanted to stay.... Mi'thal and I finally left. We found an encampment of the People. They gave us refuge. They took in a lot of refugees then, anyone who could see far enough ahead and had the courage to leave. I left Mi'thal with them. Went back for our mother and sister. I thought they would come if they knew there was a place to go.... " His voice tightening. "Li'sele.... my sister.... had been raped and murdered brutally. Her body left in the yard for everyone to see. My mother forbidden to bury her. An example to the community. Ma'marie was like a bird that has hit a window glass, too numb and dazed to move yet on her own. I coaxed her up into the hills. We

127

left in the night. The rain came at dawn. She died in my arms. These arms have held so much death." He stopped.

She nestled closer and wrapped her arms around him. *And so much life,* she had said silently, and held him tight. As if she could press her heart into his, pressing them together into one heart.

"My mother," he continued, "was peaceful at the end, with the rain. *Look,* she said, *Grandpa's rain....* then she passed, happy to be going home...." He was quiet for a while. "These arms have held so much death," he said again and tears welled up in his eyes.

"These arms have also held so much life, so much rain." She had said then, as she held him. And then, the other words that had followed, from the far place of accepting witness that floods memory with cleansing grace. "Tears are another kind of rain, the crying of ancient seas, the tears of the sea, bringing life to the land." Quietly, wonderingly.

He looked at her. "You know the sea?"

She looked startled, absent for a moment, present somewhere else. "I.... don't know, I...." her voice far away, bewildered, returning reluctantly, "it was as if someone else said those words," she said at last, "from some other time, some other memory. Like a veil...." She moved her hands with a motion like a breeze, parting an invisible curtain in the air in front of her, and closing it again. "Like a veil pulling aside, a glimpse only, and then closing again." She felt thin, frail, watery. She clutched at the words *the crying of ancient seas* like a song, a calling memory. Torn. Wanting to close the opening before her new life drained away into the gap, and afraid

128

to let it close, afraid she would lose the thread of remembrance that could make her whole, remembering a wisdom she had before. The rain, the sea. Lives Twice. Sleeps like a Bear. How many more lives had she lived, whole worlds in the rain.

A sudden darkness, hers, not his this time. In the midst of the darkness, a protective kindness there, another life, another direction pulling her, reaching in from another kind of time beyond the forward and back spiraling of her memories, beyond the two directions she was already familiar with. She remembered the bear's question, *what are you searching for?* And the sun flecked depths of the bear's eyes watching her. Searching for her answer. The words surprising Lives Twice when she heard herself say, *I am searching beyond memory, for a wholeness there....* Did she say that? Or only felt she said that, only realizing later what the bear had opened for her?.... and the bear's reply silently in her heart, *this is one doorway, yes. There are others....* she could not hear that then, only store away for remembering later. Other questions. Asking Ta'le, how are you called, about his calling name, what does it mean. And his reply, partly teasing, *What is the color of light. All color and no color at once.* Questions, questioning. Gently, looking for the question beyond questioning that unlocks them all. And another bright island of memory, another strand of time opening. Another love calling like to like. Intersecting other lives and memories. A crossing place, a question in itself. And a doorway outside time, a future reaching back into its roots in the past in answer. Like the bare oak trees in winter, the patterns of their branches so much like gnarled roots. Reaching into winter sky instead of summer earth. Sky roots. Earth roots. Tracing memory in each. Tracking again, footsteps wide and deep, determined to find the pattern woven through all her lives, a pattern deep and sure, like the trails of the bear kind, who know where they are going.

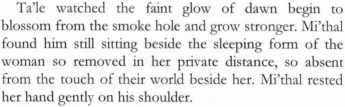

Ta'le watched the faint glow of dawn begin to blossom from the smoke hole and grow stronger. Mi'thal found him still sitting beside the sleeping form of the woman so removed in her private distance, so absent from the touch of their world beside her. Mi'thal rested her hand gently on his shoulder.

You have been awake all night.

He took her hand in one of his and smiled up at her. *I'm okay. I told her in her sleep I would be waiting here for her. She is still held far away within her journey.*

I'll make some tea.

Yes, he said, but he was already far away again too, waiting patiently for a glimpse of wherever the sleeper led in her wandering.

The snow had stopped in the night. As the dawn sky brightened, Alehya watched a pale no color world emerge. Pale no color sky. No color land, already bright in the first light. Snow mounded up, rounding everything, weighing down the shoulders of the trees, molding all the hollows of the land into one whiteness unbroken. An icy sheen to the sky, faintly iridescent, the snowy world below reflected on the face of the sky. First rays of sun touching the snow laden tops of trees with warm yellow light. Snow sparkling, flickering with tiny rainbows. Alehya moved her head slightly back and forth, slowly, gently, the bright sparks of light shifting red, yellow, green, blue, purple, winking at her. *Thank you mother father rainbow soul of all that is for revealing your grace.*

She looked over at the man. He had opened his eyes a few times, but she did not know if he had seen the brightness of the dawn, his eyes so full of other seeing. Sometimes he smiled, sometimes he whimpered softly, and she had comforted him. Now he was quiet again, pulled back into his shadowed sleep.

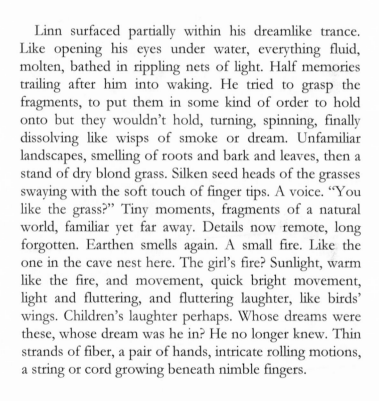

Linn surfaced partially within his dreamlike trance. Like opening his eyes under water, everything fluid, molten, bathed in rippling nets of light. Half memories trailing after him into waking. He tried to grasp the fragments, to put them in some kind of order to hold onto but they wouldn't hold, turning, spinning, finally dissolving like wisps of smoke or dream. Unfamiliar landscapes, smelling of roots and bark and leaves, then a stand of dry blond grass. Silken seed heads of the grasses swaying with the soft touch of finger tips. A voice. "You like the grass?" Tiny moments, fragments of a natural world, familiar yet far away. Details now remote, long forgotten. Earthen smells again. A small fire. Like the one in the cave nest here. The girl's fire? Sunlight, warm like the fire, and movement, quick bright movement, light and fluttering, and fluttering laughter, like birds' wings. Children's laughter perhaps. Whose dreams were these, whose dream was he in? He no longer knew. Thin strands of fiber, a pair of hands, intricate rolling motions, a string or cord growing beneath nimble fingers.

And then somehow, Miri seemed suddenly so close. Strands of memories he recognized as his own. Miri and he when they were still young. When they first met, when they were getting to know each other. The two of them sitting outside on the ground together. Miri drawing bear tracks for him in the earth beside her.

"See, the front one looks like this, more like a hand." She held up her hand, palm flat, fingers curled down into pretend bear claws. Her eyes laughing. "Well, maybe. And the hind foot walks flat, their feet are just like ours."

"But they have bigger claws than we do," he grinned at her.

"Yes," she sparkled, "and if only I could sleep all winter, and wake up renewed like they do!" She told him about her work on hibernation in bears, the molecular intricacies of how they reverse bone loss and restore muscle mass while they sleep, and how their teeth keep growing throughout their lives.

Another Miri, frightened, tense, bewildered, but very fierce, telling him to leave, to get away, no safety here. Disturbing. He whimpered in his own strange sleep. Far away he felt something soft and warm soothed around him, then he passed beyond, falling inward again. Pulled back into a vortex of other memories that he could not grasp. As he slipped farther away, an image of a woman he has not seen before, her face friendly and kind, offering him a small round basket in her hands as if to welcome him. He did not know why.

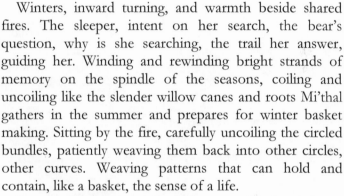

Winters, inward turning, and warmth beside shared fires. The sleeper, intent on her search, the bear's question, why is she searching, the trail her answer, guiding her. Winding and rewinding bright strands of memory on the spindle of the seasons, coiling and uncoiling like the slender willow canes and roots Mi'thal gathers in the summer and prepares for winter basket making. Sitting by the fire, carefully uncoiling the circled bundles, patiently weaving them back into other circles, other curves. Weaving patterns that can hold and contain, like a basket, the sense of a life.

Long cold rainy nights, the sound of raindrops drumming on layers of forest debris covering the earthen lodge. Soft staccato sounds accompanying her sleep, rhythms of ancient songs only the rain knows. And then the winter snows, and the whiteness. Tiny wisps of smoke rising from smoke holes of the lodges at twilight, the village layered in snow. Blue shadows on the whiteness spreading, becoming one with the twilight air. White snow mounds of lodges sparkling in morning sunlight. Fires banked by day, no wisps of smoke in the

sharp clear air. Farther back, seasons unwinding, hazy
light of autumn days melting into fierce heat of summer
suns high overhead giving way to pale spring sunlight
lifting slowly above the trees. Winter suns again,
lowering on the southern horizons, moon cycles, nights
of darkness wreathed in stars, nights full to overflowing
with light of ripening moons, moonlight pooling in the
small forest clearings like fallen snow. Seasons
overlapping, circling, memories forming and dissolving
again, always revolving around the east and the blue
black darkness of another kind of night behind which
memories of another life sleep their own dreams. Her
trail not lingering there, the arc of her memories coiling
forward and back at the same time, pulling her.

Sitting together on warm earth. Her hands running
lightly across the grass. His voice new, unfamiliar then
beside her. "Hi. Mind if I join you?" A quietness
between them, a tentative space, and then his voice
again, "You like the grass." Not a question, an
observation, an appraisal and an appreciation perhaps of
the tenderness in her gesture gently caressing the tips of
the grass.

Drifting into a dream, away from memory. Rainbow
land rainbow sea. Rainbowed breath rainbowed air,
rainbowed everywhere. Not yet. Sea songs deep in their
own sleep, words singing to themselves. At last, the last,
out to sea, this time trying to point with his other hand
the way to go, his eyes taking him there instead. A huge
silver fish. He had waited. Whistle blower, he had waited,
for someone else to come forward. No one came. His
grandfather. His eyes took him there instead.

Bright islands of memory. Another conversation, another season, sitting together on warm earth. Her hands running lightly across other grass. His voice beside her, "Hi. Mind if I join you?" His voice, growing more familiar, slowly learning each other's ways with the delicacy and gravity of the animal kinds.

She had asked about his name. Waits for Rain, Waiting for Rain. His outer name. She had asked him before, when they were still new to each other. This time, she....

The sea. Her mention of the sea. One sea had been a companion to her, a glimmer of a memory, from before. A link somehow. Not that she had lived by the sea, but that she knew about it. How and what she knew somehow important. Connected in some way. The sea was different for Ta'le, not the real sea either, a symbol of another, more painful time, the tears, a loss long passed, the tears from painful anguish, brutal times, but there were other seas for him as well. He had told her some. The practice they did up on the mountain was like the sea, he said, fluid, shimmering, filled with light just as she had seen it in her heart.

You'll see, someday, he said, *someday you'll see what we see, what I see.* He was not in a hurry and did not push. But she knew he wanted very much to share this above all else with her.

Islands of brightness, islands of memory, the sounds of village life. Voices. Laughter. Grinding acorn meal. Rhythmic see saw sounds. Birdsong. Children's voices, scattering and coming together again, like the voices of the birds, like their songs. Smell of wood smoke from the early morning fire lingering in her hair.

She had found a place at the edge of the village camp, where she could sit quietly letting the sounds of village life wash around her. Like a sleeper waking slowly from a dream. Into another dream. How many layers of dream lives did she have? How many did it take to wake up? Sometimes there were hints of something other than human kind, something far older, more ancient in her, that had also been her life. Had she felt that in her life before? Or was it only now, here in the gap, that other worlds could break through? The People were close to the plant and animal kin, they spoke of them as family, as relatives. Respectfully, affectionately. But more like cousins, or neighbors maybe, she imagined. The strange feeling she had that shadowed her was more than that. Visceral. Bigger thicker bones, stronger muscles, wrapped in fur, weight swinging side to side, shoulder and hip, shoulder and hip, walking in a wider stride. Fleeting. Momentary. Slipping quickly away, like a shadow at the corner of her eye, hidden behind the life that could not be remembered at all. That one decidedly human, calling her, pulling her, into a dream she could never reach. She ran her hands along the grasses at her side, inhaling the sweet spice scent of sun-warmed cedar. Feeling sun-warmed earth beneath her. Supporting her. Giving its warmth into her bones. Human bones this time.

An autumn morning, her first autumn with the People, sitting in a small clearing at the edge of a village camp lower down in one of the hidden valleys. Mountain forest cedar giving way to oak and maple woodlands. Acorns and manzanita berries ripening. Birds chattering as they moved through the manzanita, harvesting, preparing for winter as the People were. Pleasant to sit, her back to a tree, legs stretched out before her in the pale autumn sunlight. One hand running gently across the new green autumn grass. A few yellow gold oak and maple leaves beginning to fall, drifting through the air like summer butterflies.

"Hi. May I join you?" A man's voice, unexpected, mild, beside her.

"Sure." She looked up, surprised he had spoken aloud. She was just getting used to the quiet ways of the People, their communication outside words. The girl Alehya had begun teaching her some of the beautiful gestures of the hand language they sometimes used. It helped to have a tangible link to the silent words. The man's voice was pleasant, barely disturbing the stillness of the morning. She realized he had been speaking out of kindness for her, so new in their ways.

She smiled at him. "Do you live here in the village?"

"No, I live higher up the mountain at the camp of the gazers."

"And you are a gazer too?" She had heard only a little about them. A small group, men and women of the People, living very simply in seclusion, following an ancient spiritual path. Something about light and water, visions and heart eyes. People of the heart of light some called them. She had not met a gazer before, did not know what to expect. The man beside her intrigued her. His manner was gentle and plain, with a hidden depth. She liked him.

"Yes. We take turns coming down the mountain while the others stay in retreat. This time I am bringing medicinal herbs from the high places, enough for all the villages for the winter. I will take acorns and dried berries back up the mountain when I return."

"You like it up there?"

He smiled. A quiet, inward smile, peaceful and kind, and like someone returning from a far country with traveler's tales to tell, but no words to tell them. "The practice is very beautiful."

"I can see it in your eyes." She smiled too, a sadder smile. She was also from a far country. She had not remembered her stories yet, but she did not know if they would be as beautiful. "What is your name?"

"I am called Waits for Rain. I have learned to let things ripen in their own time."

A long pause between them. "I am waiting too, waiting to remember." She finally offered.

"Remembering comes in its own time too. Sometimes it is enough to live again, beyond remembering. I have heard you are known as Sleeps like a Bear among us and also Lives Twice. A rare and precious freedom, to awaken and live a new life.... a life washed clear." They were both quiet again for a while. His silence more delicate than the autumn light around them, more like the pale sunlight of another season, early spring, with a promise of quickening. A season she hadn't experienced yet. Not here. Another far country. "I must go now. Welcome to the People, woman who Sleeps like a Bear and Lives Twice, and is waiting. "

"Perhaps I will see you again?" She asked.

"When I return, yes."

"I will be waiting." She smiled shyly, and turned her eyes aside.

And later she had asked him, *what do the other names, the calling names mean?*

They are like music, like birdsong. They mean everything.

Where do they come from?

From the great heart living around and through everything. They are like dream names I suppose, from the great dream dreaming us, as the little Kalahari San people would say. A sadness in his eyes then. From the San, or just from the closer time Before, when they had been something he knew about, or found out about, or learned from someone he cared about then. Long gone. Before. All of them.

Tell me about the names that are like the names of the Ancient Ones.

There aren't a lot, just a few. And we don't pronounce them quite the same way. The Ancient Ones had more complex soundings. Our tongues and palates, and our ears, are much plainer. He told her which names he knew, and the people who carried them or were known by them. *Some of the names sound like the ancient names but aren't. They are from a different dream, Alai, Tomah, Mi'thal, Ta'le.*

Echoes of another memory. "Ta'le, my calling name is Ta'le." He had said it aloud for her the first time that she asked.

"I don't have a calling name yet. Something else I'm waiting for," she had replied sadly.

"Your name will find you, just like the rain," he said, and she had not asked him more, had not asked about the rain just then, only guessed at it in the depths of his eyes.

Names again, linking memories, like the round of seasons, anchoring. I was here, and I am here again. This time she had asked about the outer names. His name.

141

Names were like landmarks. Memories. That you shared. Shared moments. Trail markers. They let you know where you were, who you were, a connection to a then, a time before. She had asked him before. He had told her about waiting when they first met. Now he told her about the rain.... *Grandson*.... his grandfather said, *grandson*.... trying to point with his hand broken by the police, pointing with all his fingers folded together like a broken wing, not flying, his eyes taking him there instead.

She had asked him about the names the People had for each other. The way they chose the names. His name, Waits for Rain. Waiting for Rain. "My name came with me." He smiled. "A childhood name, from long ago." The smile faded and returned a sadder smile, of distance, and distancing.

Winters again, the inward turning, grey skies, heavy rains. Clouds heavy in their water weight pressing low to the earth close above the trees, and then the whiteness, winter snows transforming the land, the children playing in the snowbright sparkling wonder of the snow. Summers. Early summer, her first summertime. Morning air still fresh and cool before the heat of the day took hold. Golden yellow sunlight reaching for the tops of the trees, rolling slowly down their tall shapes, young green leaves slowly ripening to darker greens of summer. Days hot. Berry blossoms thick on bramble vines. Bees lifting heavily from one flower to another. Small buds of acorns falling in the afternoon heat, tiny brown scaled caps still tightly round, the swelling nut inside not yet pushing through. Caps like tiny perfect baskets, tightly woven by the tiniest of skillful hands. Patterns of tiny brown scales overlapping, intricate, precise, like the careful weaving of a fine basket growing under Mi'thal's watchful guiding eyes.

Still tracking, still following the footsteps of her memories, stepping in them over and over like the bear kind. Still searching, searching, for what? She would know when she got there. The village council meeting. Faces familiar now, not so familiar then. Sitting close around a small fire. The welcoming ceremony, the naming. Friendly faces, warmth of fire and faces blending. They were giving her a new name, her outer given name, the one she would be known by among the People. Sleeps like a Bear Lives Twice. There were others among them, others lost and found, who had lived other lives before becoming part of the People, but no one so thoroughly distanced from their past as she was. They accepted her, and did not push her to either remember or forget whatever may be remembered. Enough to be with the People, to be open to each day here. Her other name, her inner calling name, would come later, not given by the People, but by the great kindness through which all things arise and within which all things are embraced. *May you live long and well among us.* A hug from each person, and a gift, and a blessing prayer. A small basket, delicately woven. *May you be filled with joy, woven among us, carrier of our love.* A pair of supple moccasins. *May your steps be gentle and leave no trace.* A necklace of shells and seeds. *For beauty and for the promise of what can be.*

Her first time outside the lodge. Her legs as tentative as her senses. Mi'thal helping her get settled, sitting on mothering earth, her back leaning against a tree. Pale sunlight dappling the ground around her. The rustle of a breeze, rippling play of light and shadow. Grey blue leaves of manzanita leaves. Flocks of tiny birds sweeping through the air, pulled as if on curving lines up to the branches of the tree over her head. Musical twittering chirps sifting down through the soft autumn air. A small group of children, running by, their laughter fluttering like the birds. Turning in one motion like the birds, drawn to her. Standing in a circle around her, looking with wide clear eyes. A young girl offering her a yellow oak leaf, another smaller girl shyly offering a few tiny autumn flowers, like little lavender stars. Each child smiling, giving their names and a small gift, a small blue feather, a few acorns. She taking each gift in her cupped hands, delighting in their treasures as much as they, and then throwing up her hands and laughing. "So many names, so many names!"

The children asking her name, "how are you called?"

The sudden gap, a space. A hollowness or a freedom, so new she hadn't decided yet. Then for the children, swept up again in their play, "I don't know yet, I'll have to learn yours first won't I? We can work on that another time. Then you can help me remember mine." She added conspiratorially, "Promise me you'll help?"

"Yes! Yes!" and off they went, as swiftly as the birds and just as light.

Back farther still. Another gap. A harder, colder place, echoing with the cloaked memories she could not reach. Mineral smells. Then something hard, polished, and sharp. Metallic hollow sounds. Faces. Hard, sharp, and hollow, like the metallic sounds. Behind them, beyond them, somewhere she had to go, someone she had to reach. The faces would not let her, they were always in the way. Faces stopping her not just with their presence, or their words. Stopping her with a cruelty and thoroughness she could never have imagined before. Then the dissolving again, light and dark together. The faces could not reach her there, she was safe within it. Great kindliness and great love met her in that bright darkness and held her there. But this time, she was certain now, another small island of brightness was reaching out to her from beyond the faces, beyond the dissolving and the darkness. Reaching out from a world solid and real, from another time, another life. The island was reaching for her, needing her answering brightness. She almost touched it, then both the island and her answering dissolved, time tunneling, spiraling, coiling, striated bands of light and shadow, pulled taut from her seeking, rebounding now, faster and faster and suddenly she was back on the shore of her current life again. Ta'le was still beside her, waiting, just as he had promised he would be. His wise sad eyes gladdened at her return.

Welcome home.

She buried herself in his arms.

Brightness when Linn returned again. Brightness everywhere. He squinted into the light. The girl sat by her small hearth at the mouth of the shelter, silhouetted against whatever over bright world waited outside. He shut his eyes. The brightness hurt, so sharp and clear even behind closed lids. He opened his eyes cautiously. Full daylight now, morning perhaps. The snow had stopped sometime in the night. Clear sky above tall rounded shapes of snow covered trees. Sunlight blazing and flashing from every facet of a transformed world. Snow covering everything, weighing down the trees, balancing in sharp ridges on every bare branch and twig. A world immersed in white, a brilliant sea of dazzling light. He closed his eyes. Exhausted. Whatever had held him in his dreamlike state had given way, had snapped like an elastic band stretched too tight. No longer holding him. He felt heavy and sad. Unexpectedly sad, not knowing why. As if he had missed something important, and now he had no way to go back to find it. The girl looked over at him and smiled. She handed him a small tightly woven basket with something warm and

146

fragrant inside. Steam rising, with a fresh green scent, like a tea made of trees. He took a sip and handed it back to her, too tired to hold the cup. She went back to tending the fire, singing softly to the tiny flames. He drifted away again, back into sleep. No memories or dreams belonging to him or anyone else, just simple restful sleep.

When he awoke again, a shaft of sunlight was reaching into the shelter, full and still beside him. Kindly, comforting. Outside, tiny rainbows of piercing light flickered from the blazing brightness.

By mid day the air grew warm. Mi'thal coaxed Lives Twice outside to walk slowly in the soft air. Snow already melting back from the sunlit places and slumping from the rounded shoulders of the trees. Tiny drops of water glistening at the tips of twigs. Here and there a brief burst of unmelted snow cascading, sparkling, falling branch to branch gathering speed. A thawing alive world, a beginning time, fluid and emerging, just like her. Lives Twice smiled. A first world day, like in the songs, when Earth and sky and all the kinds were still new to each other and to themselves. A good day to return.

She had felt a shift within her searching sleep. Something in her unknown past had lost its hold on her, and something else had opened, a new possibility. Subtle, unformed. She was no longer searching in the same way, Without knowing exactly why, she felt it was really time to start again, a fluid open space ahead of her, thawing and watery like the day.

She turned to her friend and hugged her. *Thank you, Mi'thal,* she said, too new and full for other words.

When they returned to the lodge, Mi'thal gave her a cup of acorn gruel she had been keeping warm by the embers of the fire. *Here,* she said, *we give this to the new mothers after giving birth, to give them strength.* And Lives Twice knew that Mi'thal could sense some of what had happened to her this time in her sleep. As if in answer, Mi'thal added playfully, *if you keep giving birth to yourself, we'll have to change your name again, Lives Thrice!*

Oh no! ....and I am still a bear.... at least I still sleep like one. They both laughed. Ta'le looked up from where he sat by the fire circle and smiled at them.

Ta'le and his sister sat together near the slow embers of the fire. Lives Twice had eaten the acorn gruel and gone into a normal restful sleep. They watched her cautiously at first, but she did not slip into the deep sleep of the bear kind, and they sat quietly, watching her with affection and relief rather than concern. Ta'le turned to his sister. *Mi'thal? Do you think she would be able to make the journey up the mountain? I will have to go soon, before the snows come again. I want to ask her to come with me. Do you think she will be strong enough?*

To stay up there, or to make the journey?

He smiled. *Maybe both I guess. No, just the trail, so soon after her other traveling. She is changed this time, returning from her sleep. And opening there perhaps.* He made a gesture as if cupping his hands lightly around a fragile rounded shape, then turned his open palms upward as they moved apart in a gentle expanding motion delicate as the invisible shape no longer there. *She has turned away somehow, from searching the shadows I think, searching now for something else instead. She has a strong spirit, plenty strong enough for the mountain. She will fit right in, and she will not give up.*

Mi'thal looked long at her brother. She had felt the shift in Lives Twice, in perhaps a different way, not entirely sure what direction the new beginning would eventually take. Finally she said, *No, she won't give up. I was concerned for you my brother.*

He looked at her.

A strong spirit…. like a bear? Mi'thal asked gently, and they both smiled.

"*Strong like the bear kind, yes, and deep. She will like the mountain.*"

Be careful, my brother, Tommo Agai. She used his other seldom used name, his life name among the People, so often eclipsed by his childhood nickname that had followed him here, and by his calling name, which like hers, had eclipsed all the other names, not only between them, but with all the others who knew them well. *Bears eat salmon,* she reminded him.

Tommo Agai was the name for the elusive and rare winter salmon trout in the language of the Ancient Ones. Many of the gazers had salmon trout names. Compelled as the gazers were from within to seek the solitude of the high mountains to fulfill their path, they felt kin to the silver rainbowed fish also compelled from within to seek the highest reaches of the swift flowing mountain streams in winter to complete the cycle of their lives. And winter trout names seemed to find the ones destined for the gazers' path from an early age. Already there was another younger Tommo Agai, youngest son of the big man with a fish tattoo who delighted children by flexing his arm to make the fish leap, and whose quiet good-natured strength could be counted on in council when a particularly difficult decision needed to be

151

reached. The big man, Agai, was called after a different trout, the Tama' Agai, the huge spring salmon trout that came in great numbers each spring and sustained the People. True to his name, the man Agai had helped sustain the People in their difficult journey up and over the mountains to their safe haven here, but his son, drawn to other mountains like Ta'le, had been kin to the other trout, Tommo Agai, from early on, a dreamer, a seeker, one of those compelled to look beyond, a searcher. Ta'le sighed.

Bears eat salmon kind, trout kind. Mi'thal repeated.

I know, better to be devoured by love than by the other mouths that lie in wait in memories…. They were quiet for a while.

A flock of small birds swept into the snow covered bushes outside the low doorway. Dappled patterns of light and shadow fluttered on the earthen floor near the doorway, reflecting the movements outside.

She will come with you, Mi'thal said at last, her gaze focused inward on a kind of distance that came to her at times, a simple matter of fact clarity. *She will stay and your world will become her world, but she belongs to other worlds too. There is a claim on her heart. I can't see which way she will go, when the time finally comes for her to choose. She is strong, yes, like the bear kind, and she is not afraid.* She looked at him. *She is not afraid…. to love.*

Yes, he said, *I know. She has already claimed my heart.*

She will be strong enough to make the journey, strong enough to stay, for how long, I can't say. There is something else calling her beyond what has been pulling at her, something she may not even see yet. She is not unlike you, little brother. She looked at him again. *She loves you very much. She will be fair in honoring her claims. She is very much like you, little brother, more than you know.*

She was teasing him gently now, as she always did when she knew he was about to go, was already going in his mind. Their caring and their love for each other had remained strong through the years. Her teasing was as much a blessing and a prayer as an expression of her concern for him. *She has been waiting, I think, for you to take her there. She will be happy to go with you.*

The day grew steadily warmer and milder. By mid afternoon the snow was receding rapidly, even under the trees. Alehya sat at the entrance to the shelter and watched as the land emerged from under the heavy cloak of snow. As suddenly as winter had arrived, as suddenly it was gone. Alehya's view was hemmed in by the fallen trees and branches close about the entrance, but when she lifted her eyes, she could see snow sliding in great chunks from the tall spires of trees sparkling in the bright sunlight or sifting falling from branch to branch triggering more snow to fall. Delicate balances in motion all around her. She had banked the glowing coals of her fire and sat close to the shimmer of heat rising from the ashes. A wide path of sunlight reached into the shelter again for a while and then passed. The man seemed to know the sunlight. He had smiled briefly then closed his eyes. Now he was awake again looking at the thawing world through wondering dreaming eyes. For Alehya, the warm moist air saturated with the smell of roots and wet earth, wet wood, wet fallen leaves, the whole afternoon, was like one of the herbal teas the plant elders were teaching her to make. A fertile time, like the season of the warming moon in early spring.

She thought of the new green leaves and first shy flowers of that other season still a winter away, and her friend Tomah's shining face, breathless, running into camp with the news, "The spring trout! The spring trout!" Calling to the big man, "Agai! Agai! Your people are here! Your people have returned!" And Agai's deep rolling laugh as he flexed his arm and made his fish tattoo leap for the children gathering around. "The trout are running!" Exited laughter as the whole village went down to the creek to greet the yearly arrival of the huge fish. *Thank you, trout fathers and trout mothers for the generosity of your kind.* And the time of the hunger moon would be over, warm moon coming soon. She held the image of Tomah's face in her heart, warming her as much as, more than, the remnants of the little fire beside her or the passing sunlight.

Tomah, Abi, and Abi's older brother arrived in late afternoon. Alehya had known the People would be sending someone to look for her, that was their way. She had felt a quickening in her heart as the boys neared the valley, and she felt their concern when they reached the crash site, searching for the signs already dissolving into the thawing land. And she had known in her heart that Tomah was with them. She felt his calling, and although her little shelter had been skillfully hidden to all but familiar eyes, she pulled at Tomah with her calling in return, and they found her easily enough.

All three boys crowded into the shelter with Alehya and the sky fish man who watched them from within his

155

waking trance, smiling dreamily as if he expected them all at any moment to vanish or grow wings.

Aiii! Sister friend, Abi said greeting her, *the only dry land for miles! We nearly swam the whole way here!*

They all laughed softly. The sky man looked puzzled and amused by their silent conversation.

How is he? Abi's brother gestured slightly with his head toward the man.

Okay, I think, at least his body is well enough. He doesn't like to stand or move around, but no broken bones, no.... she made the hand sign for sickness, holding her open hands palms toward her lower ribs, pulsing them in and out, as if a throbbing inside. *Mostly he is in shock perhaps, not quite here yet.*

I'll bet, Abi said. *Quite a crash. Lucky he's alive, the gouge in the meadowland, the heap of rocks and earth.* He made a long pushing motion enthusiastically with his whole arm.

Any other Taibo'oo come to look for him? Abi's brother asked, looking cautiously at the man with a slight but pointed emphasis on the word Taibo'oo.

No, the snow came so soon, so heavy, filled up the sky as much as the land. You're our first visitors! She smiled at them.

Then she looked over at the man, seeing him with different eyes than Abi's brother, and said sadly, *none of his people came for him, and he is far away.... chasing his heart, looking for his heart.... I think his heart is far away too.*

They sat quietly for a while, each of them grateful that their hearts were very much here, listening to the thumping sounds as the last few heavy clumps of snow slumped from the trees to the ground.

Here, we brought you some food. Tomah reached into his traveling pouch and offered her some ground pine nuts and a little dried salmon, a special treat. *We didn't bring water,* he laughed, *I see you have plenty of that here,* and he pointed to the drips forming and falling steadily from the cedar boughs of the roof at the opening of her little cave.

Will the Tai…. this man, be strong enough to make the journey back to the village? Abi's brother said, his eyes fixed on the drops of water. *The People have asked that we bring him back if you found him alive. Once he has seen one of the People…. he cannot go back to…. to that place he comes from.*

She considered his question, her gaze resting on the man again, a healer's look, appraising him.

Yes, she said at last. *He will be strong enough to walk back to the camp, with help. It's not so far, but I don't think he can make it on his own, not without someone to steady him. He'll need support. Good thing they sent three of you! And he is very tall, who will help hold up his head?* She teased. She looked affectionately at all three boys. *Thank you,* she said, *I am glad you are here.* But her eyes were on Tomah alone when she said, *my lodge is your lodge,* and gestured around the tiny shelter. Then she looked away smiling shyly.

They spent the night sitting close around the small fire, dozing from time to time in the manner of the long night sitters, and left early the next morning when the thawing water soaked world was still firm underfoot from the night's cold. Tomah had brought an extra cloak for Alehya. He wrapped it around her shoulders carefully and tenderly, as if he would rather be keeping her warm in other ways, and then they set off. One boy on each side of the man, gently guiding his steps, taking turns leading and supporting him along the trail.

He was tall, but thin and very light. Easy to support even though he was so much taller than they were.

Whatever weight he had was somewhere else, his center of gravity far removed from where his body was. His balance was not good, and he walked absently, but he followed them willingly, going wherever they led without complaint, like a small child or a sleepwalker, wandering in a waking dream.

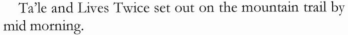

Ta'le and Lives Twice set out on the mountain trail by mid morning.

I am ready, she had simply said, when he asked her.
Her eyes shining with quiet delight, her face opening like a flower with the same joy.

Are you sure? His eyes searched her face, questioning. *It is not so far, but the way is steep in places, and we will have to go soon, before the next snow falls, and once winter sets in....*

I am ready, she said again.
For the winter, or the trail?

Her eyes laughing again. *For both. And do not worry, I am well rested now, I am the one who has been sleeping. You are the one I think, who has stayed up late for me!* She nestled in his arms. *I want to be with you*, she had said softly into his shoulder as he held her tight.

Mi'thal watched them go long after they passed from physical sight.

You will miss her, Ta'le had said, and he was right. She sent her heart ahead with them to watch over them on their way.

Lives Twice felt herself growing stronger and lighter the higher up the mountain they went, despite the steepness of the trail. As if the mountain was giving her strength. A kind of promise, an invitation reaching out to her, pulling her along. She knew how to be here, a feeling so unexpected and sure, of knowing the mountain somehow, of at last coming home. She had not expected this. She had expected to be entering Ta'le's world, not hers. The rocks, the thin bright air, the shifting patterns and rhythms of this steep land, the bright patches of snow becoming more frequent, the swift passage of cloud shadow playing across the slopes, all strangely familiar. The weathered trees along the trail seemed to be speaking to her as she passed, meeting her, welcoming her in a language part of her understood, the rest of her, not yet. She said little, content to trust the feeling. Not ready to shape it into words, spoken or unspoken, or send much more than a growing feeling of contentment to Ta'le as they climbed.

The trail was narrow and faint in places, so blended into the land. She watched Ta'le a few steps ahead of her, his feet finding familiar turns in the trail, a step here, a shift of weight, pivoting around a rock ledge. The way smooth under his feet. Years of gazers walking this trail matching their rhythms to the mountainside had left the way melded gracefully with the land. Mountain way. Balance meeting balance, ball and heel of foot meeting rock and stone now carrying her too. She wondered, did he feel the same way about the mountain, or was he drawn by another force, his practice perhaps, compelling him, like the secretive winter trout of his other name. The ones he told her about, who lived for most of the year hidden in the saline depths of the last remnants of the great mother lakes from long ago, and spawned in the swift rushing waters of the mountain streams in winter. Whatever drew him and whatever was drawing her, she was grateful. *Thank you mountain way, for leading us wherever we are going.*

She remembered what Ta'le had said, the first time they met, *a rare and precious gift, a life washed clear.* For her, the mountain was like that, air so fresh and pure, the stones, the rocks, the aged trees, the windswept, sculpted shapes, everything with roots reaching back, it seemed to her, into the essence of sky and mountain before time lifted these huge blocks of mountain to the sky. A land so old, naturally beyond memory. An angle of spiritual repose, rocks settled, settling, long ago, in their own time. She would not need her lost memories here.

The mountain offered, she was sure, not just a life washed clear, but brought into new life again. She remembered Mi'thal telling her, after her naming celebration, that Lives Twice was a good name, a name to grow on, and to grow into. *Both your names are good*

161

names, strong names, Mi'thal had said, *and don't forget, your bear kin have other wisdoms besides sleep!* And they had laughed. A conversation, a world away now. Ta'le turned to look at her, as if he felt her smiling at his sister's memory, as if he felt them both. Mi'thal suddenly seemed very close.

You called? He asked.

No, yes, I am so happy here already, my happiness must have called out to you on its own. Her smile radiant to his eyes. *I love it here,* she said opening her arms wide taking in the whole mountain.

Just wait, he answered, *we aren't even there yet,* and he smiled, turning back to the trail, also growing lighter inside with each step.

When they stopped to rest from time to time, she looked out over the lands spreading to the east. The layers of valley folds and ridge crests melting into hazy blues growing farther away as they climbed, and all her memories, the recent ones, and the other silent unapproachable ones from another time, all ebbing away into that pale distance. Each time they stopped they had risen higher up the mountain, and she could look at that receding tide from a farther and farther place. She turned back to the mountain, walking carefully, matching Ta'le's steps as he led the way. Gradually rock by rock, stone by stone, the blue distances behind her dissolving unseen into one soft before. Not as hard as the terrible Before that the People spoke of, and then only as needed to learn from the experiences and choices there. Her personal before had a gentler feel now, receding slowly, pulling farther away on its own, settling like a mist, ghost-like, fading fast in the clear mountain air like the porous strands of high clouds drifting in the sky above her, dissolving like whatever was behind her that had held her. Or maybe the clouds were growing, like seeds of something new, she didn't know which, maybe both together.

Ta'le looked up at the mountain and the sky. *You'll like it when it snows, the quiet and the stillness. Winter coming soon, we will be here just in time.*

For her now there was only the stillness and the peace of the day unbroken even by their presence here, their passing knitting the calm more securely around them as they continued up the trail.

The way grew steeper as the trail zigzagged toward the top of a sharp ridge on one flank of the mountain. Banks of snow across the trail were slippery underfoot. They crossed a swift stream just above where it plunged down a nearly vertical drop. They stopped and knelt beside the rushing waters. Ta'le used a woven dipper to fill their water flasks, then poured a little into her cupped hand and his, and they raised the water to the sky and the high peaks towering above them. *Thank you, sky waters, mountain waters, for your blessings.* Then they drank their fill. Cold clear water poured down her throat, cold sweet water, vibrantly alive. Winter cold, plunging cold, mineral fresh, tasting of rocks and snow and sky. *Like drinking in the mountain,* she said, *like drinking in the sky, the high clear air, the mountain's heart.*

As it drinks us in, he said, and smiled. He refilled their small tightly woven water containers and they set off again.

As they passed through a grove of taller trees sheltered in a hollow of the slope, a slim grey bird with a

163

bright eye ring and a courteous, curious presence like a deer landed close beside the trail near them, and drank from a small pool of snowmelt cupped in the hollow of a rock.

Ta'le greeted the bird. *Hello little brother,* he said, *we thank you for welcoming us home.* He turned to Lives Twice. *A solitaire,* he said, *a hermit thrush. One of the few names from Before that still fits.* His eyes shining, glad. *They are kind enough to share their mountain with us. They like many of the same things about being here that we do.*

They reached the top of the ridge, the tall peaks still rising high above them on either side, covered with low conifers giving way to long steep slopes of grey rock and talus, the upper reaches covered with snow. Ta'le stood aside at the crest of the trail so she could see into the other side as she came up to meet him. Held between two arms of the mountain, a small flat valley, like the open palm of a hand. A lush meadowland, now brown in autumn like coarse tawny fur. A few streams meandering through the grasses, the grasses curving over their steep banks on either side. A shoreline of taller trees, clusters of white trunked aspens among groves of spruce, pine and fir. The huts of the gazers nestled in the shelter of the taller trees, earth lodges like those of the village camps, but smaller and covered with sod of living grasses so they looked like hillocks of meadowland. Her heart already full with the mountain now filled to overflowing with the grace of this hidden place, and a hint of an even deeper joy waiting here, waiting to be discovered or revealed. A secret open as the sky, as open now as the far distances receding behind her, an openness gentle as the late afternoon light. A safe harbor. A shimmering peace. *Thank you,* she breathed, *Thank you.*

She was close to tears, not of sadness, but of an unfamiliar joy washing through her eyes on its own.

Yes, he simply said, watching her, caught up in his own joy magnified by hers. Silently with his heart, he offered, *Thank you mountain, thank you sky, thank you great heart of light, for this path and for the woman at my side. Thank you for bringing us together home.* They stood for a moment side by side with their arms around each other, in silence with the mountain's silence of stone and sky, then they descended the trail to the gazers camp, and the far blue distances to the east dropped from their view behind the ridge.

As they drew closer to the camp, Lives Twice felt the same atmosphere of quiet depth around the cluster of small huts that she felt in Ta'le. In the village where she had lived with Mi'thal, it seemed as if someone was always moving, quietly and carefully as the People did wherever they were, but there was always a feeling of animation to the village as a whole, people living their lives cheerfully happily bumping up against each other. Laughing, talking, telling stories, singing songs, joking, teasing, arguing, making gifts, baskets, fishnets, and arrow shafts, playing with children, even smiling, all left traces of energy even when no one was about. The traces here at the gazers camp had a different tone, the smiling was here too, but the joy was of another kind, from an inward turning palpable and serene. And with that inwardness another hint subtle and intangible, of a vast unimaginable kindness that held her also in its reach.

I like it here, she finally said, and the simple words of her calling had a feeling of a whisper inside that vastness.

You will meet the others tomorrow, Ta'le said, answering her question before it was asked as they stopped in front of one of the huts. He moved the door aside, a stiff hide stretched over a framework of smaller branches that fit securely over the opening, and motioned for her to go inside. *My lodge is your lodge,* he said when he joined her, gesturing around the small space, *as is my heart.* He took her hand and pulled her gently to him and kissed her. *Welcome to the mountain.* He smiled. He could see in her eyes that the mountain had already said the same to her in its own way. She would be at home here.

The interior of the hut was arranged much like the lodges of the village. Light from the smoke hole and through the semi translucent hide covering of the door gave just enough light to see by. A small circle of stones in the center of the hut for the fire. To one side, the low sleeping platform that was also the general living area for sitting and working. The sunken floor of weathered rounded stones set deeper in the Earth than in the village lodges.

We dig farther down here, Ta'le said, *for protection from the winter cold.* A small opening on the other side led to a cave like alcove like a miniature hut, with just enough room for one person to sit inside on a simple cushion in the center of the tiny space. Baskets sat all around the hut on the wide shelf formed by the top of the stone foundation wall. The gazers apparently lived as simple and uncluttered a life as the villagers. She recognized Mi'thal's skillful hands in some of the basketwork by the distinctive patterns in the weave. A few bundles of dry herbs hanging up here and there. A few small cooking baskets and some small cooking stones next to the hearth. A niche by the door for firewood. She took in all the details, familiar yet new, the pattern of the Peoples' daily life as Ta'le lived it. Clean and functional, each object in his world cared for, respected, the whole hut breathing the same feeling of reverence and inward depth that she felt so strongly in him. She treasured the simple details of how he had expressed his life, the whole hut feeling alive somehow as if he had never left, as if the hut was waiting for him and also that he had never been away.

Ta'le stirred the ashes in the hearth. A few sleepy embers flickered briefly before he covered them again. *We will have a fire later at twilight. The smoke shows so strongly in the high clear air here, we are very careful. One of the other gazers came by early this morning before dawn to kindle the fire for a while. We do that for each other when one of us goes down the mountain. We try to keep the huts from going completely cold. Takes a lot of fire and firewood to warm them up again. We keep them warm a little at a time instead.* He smiled. *Keeps the huts alive.*

Warm was not exactly how it felt to her now. She would have to get used to the ways here. Simpler even than those of the villages below. She nodded. The hut did feel alive, and not really cold either.

As if he could read her heart he said, *our food is pretty simple too. Hope you like spruce and fir bark noodles,* his eyes merry. *Not often! But we do rely more on the pines up here, mostly pine nuts and young pollen cones. Acorn meal is more of a*

167

special food, we have to carry it up here. Hope you like pine nut mush.... and they both smiled.

Yes, she said. She put her arm around him and drew close to him. *I like it very much.*

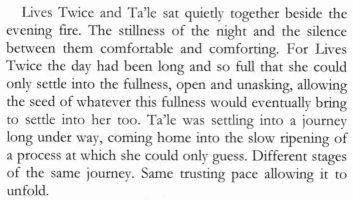

Lives Twice and Ta'le sat quietly together beside the evening fire. The stillness of the night and the silence between them comfortable and comforting. For Lives Twice the day had been long and so full that she could only settle into the fullness, open and unasking, allowing the seed of whatever this fullness would eventually bring to settle into her too. Ta'le was settling into a journey long under way, coming home into the slow ripening of a process at which she could only guess. Different stages of the same journey. Same trusting pace allowing it to unfold.

Without looking over at him, she saw again in her heart how content he had looked in the warm glow of the fire. His face, familiar to her as a visitor when he came to the village, a face she had imagined would be at home anywhere secure in its own depth, now like a long slow gentle exhale, a breath merging into a larger breath encircling it, a surrender, trusting, being home.

Ta'le let the fire die down and covered the glowing coals gently with ashes. *Thank you brother sister fire, for welcoming us home. Sleep well.* They sat in silence again for a

169

while as their eyes settled into the soft darkness of the hut, then he stood up and took her hand. *Come,* he said, *I have a treasure to share with you.* They wrapped their cloaks around them and he led her outside into the mountain night. The high snow covered peaks rising on either side of the camp blazing with starlight, framing an abyss of star bright sky. The dazzling darkness overhead pierced with innumerable wells of light, brimming over in the precision of their brightness. Countless bright worlds of light too numerous to see. Lingering patches of snow glowing in the starlight. They walked a short way from the camp up a nearby slope to get a wider view of the sky. Lives Twice looked down and saw two shadows outlined in star shine intangible as the night beneath their feet. *Look!* She said. *Star shadows.* Following wherever they went. She felt delicate and ephemeral as the shadows and the starlight. A hollow shell of light no longer empty, full instead, with the intangible substance of grace. "Thank you," she said very softly aloud, her voice a whisper of starlight and shadow. "Thank you," to Ta'le, to the sky, to the mountains, to the stars, to whatever or all of them that had brought her here, that had brought them all together.

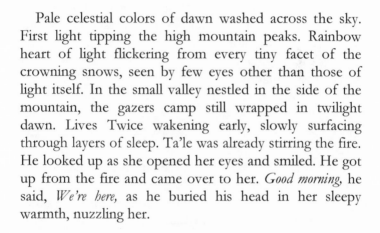

Pale celestial colors of dawn washed across the sky. First light tipping the high mountain peaks. Rainbow heart of light flickering from every tiny facet of the crowning snows, seen by few eyes other than those of light itself. In the small valley nestled in the side of the mountain, the gazers camp still wrapped in twilight dawn. Lives Twice wakening early, slowly surfacing through layers of sleep. Ta'le was already stirring the fire. He looked up as she opened her eyes and smiled. He got up from the fire and came over to her. *Good morning,* he said, *We're here,* as he buried his head in her sleepy warmth, nuzzling her.

High up on another face of the mountain, the bear turned in her deepening sleep and curled the sinking weight of her dissolving form closer around the warmth of her slowing breath. Her heartbeat slowing with her breath already blending with the great tides of winter, blending with the heartbeats of the stones and the heartbeats of the snows, with the celestial colors of the dawns and the starry nights pulling across the sky outside

171

the breath warmed cave dark of her den. Cocooned in depths of rock and sky and winter night, cocooned in shells of light, in pink and turquoise dawns and rainbow halos around the swelling moons, mountains light tipped against the glowing skies or wreathed in fathomless nights filled with tiny points of light, wrapped in the spiraling lights of memories of her kind woven into every cell of her sleeping flesh, as she drifts beyond sleep or dream, soon it will be time, and the tiny seeds of new lives within her will begin to waken.

Called by the slowing rhythms of her body, riding the gentle swells rolling through her inner seas, the new lives will listen for the cadence by which they will come at last into form. Listening, waiting, until the tides are slow enough to bridge from light itself through the dissolving and reforming flesh of the bear's body deep in her ancient sleep. The spaces between each heartbeat growing longer and longer, vast openings inside her sleeping form that allow ancestral memory to coalesce. A single heart beat deep and full filling the whole of their nascent world, and then timeless space again. The heat of her body cooling, not as fast, not as far, a gradual lowering with the slowing tides dissolving and arising being. Beginning times.

The seeds of new life within her, the tiny fertilized cells that waited all through the high heat of summer, all the way from the late spring season of bear's heat, the tiny cells that waited patiently through the season of nuts and seeds and fruit, of tart dry little manzanita apples and the blackberries juicy in their own heat, the ground squirrels sweet with ripening fat, dug rocks flying dirt churning from their nests, waiting through all of this, until the bear's store of winter fat was enough to sustain their lives and hers in her winter sleep. Listening now to the slowing tides of blood and breath as the bear drifts in her mother depths beyond dreamless dream, enfolded in the stillness and cold of winter, the children of her heat will begin to anchor themselves in the ebb and flow of her dissolving form, take root, and grow on their journey into being, woven of indwelling radiance and mineral essence of saline seas, depths of blood and bone encoded with the shambling gait of their kind, encoded with their wandering, the lightning fast paw, and the towering in the throes of their heat.

The bear shifted her muscles languidly, imperceptibly, and sighed. It was time. Soon it would begin again.

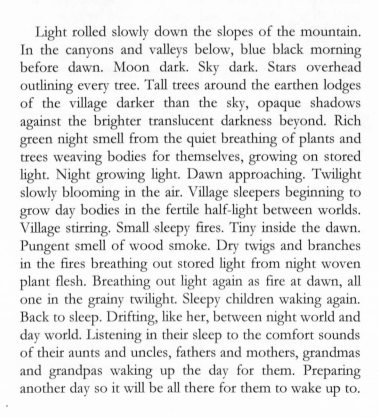

Light rolled slowly down the slopes of the mountain. In the canyons and valleys below, blue black morning before dawn. Moon dark. Sky dark. Stars overhead outlining every tree. Tall trees around the earthen lodges of the village darker than the sky, opaque shadows against the brighter translucent darkness beyond. Rich green night smell from the quiet breathing of plants and trees weaving bodies for themselves, growing on stored light. Night growing light. Dawn approaching. Twilight slowly blooming in the air. Village sleepers beginning to grow day bodies in the fertile half-light between worlds. Village stirring. Small sleepy fires. Tiny inside the dawn. Pungent smell of wood smoke. Dry twigs and branches in the fires breathing out stored light from night woven plant flesh. Breathing out light again as fire at dawn, all one in the grainy twilight. Sleepy children waking again. Back to sleep. Drifting, like her, between night world and day world. Listening in their sleep to the comfort sounds of their aunts and uncles, fathers and mothers, grandmas and grandpas waking up the day for them. Preparing another day so it will be all there for them to wake up to.

Quiet prayers. Soft sounds of the day being born flowing through their sleeping forms like ripples of light through water. Dawn bodies still dreaming, dreams rippling like the day sounds through their flickering sleep flesh dissolving at the edge of sleep, blending with the twilight dawn.

Then a brighter no color glow seeping down through the smoke hole. First light spreading closer across the far away sky outside. Trees holding the dawn stars close, hiding them in their branches, waiting for the sun, waiting for their tall shadow shapes to ripen into roundness in the creamy golden light again. Sweet smell of acorn mush cooking, quiet bubbling sounds from the cooking baskets near the fire. A hand reaching to stir. Softly lit in the red glow of the fire. Voices murmuring. Adults talking quietly, already familiar with the day. A closer calling, *Hey! Sleepy head!* Gently teasing, *Alehya, wake up!*

Alehya stretched under her warm sleeping fur. They had let her sleep again. She had let herself sleep. She had been tired after rescuing the man. Very tired. As much from his strangeness as from the rescuing. The council meeting to talk with the man and hear what he had to say would not be for a few days. He would be waking too. Sounds and smells familiar to her would still be strange to him. All strange, all new, as he was to them, the whole village weaving a new kind of pattern around him, it was already forming, surrounding him.

They would let him stay. They had to. They couldn't send him back where he came from. That would jeopardize the villages, and he was too innocent and unprepared in his hollowed out strangeness to send him out on his own into this winter sleeps land. Her instinct to save and protect, not only the People, but everyone, even this man so like a small bird fallen from a nest, this time falling into a new nest. Falling, or planted here, like a fledgling from a cowbird's egg. Where had he fallen from, from his side, what would he say? He had been so quiet, so absent, who would he be as he returned? How would he fit in? Everyone, all of us, young and old, would consider. We will gather, and hear and speak, and listen to the man and to each other, until we reach a coming into harmony. The ones who lived through the times Before, and the ones who could feel things far back in memory and up ahead in what could be, and all of us, everyone had roots going both ways, together we will know which way this new thing, this new pattern already growing would go, and whether we would go with it, or not.

"You could go see At'sah, she's the oldest one in the village, she knows the most songs." Linn had asked about customs, the ways of the People. What the council would be like. How the People had survived the War and the Wasting. How they got here. How they lived. A thousand questions bubbling up, flooding through him once he realized he was alive again. Something had happened to him after the crash, something he needed to understand. He had melted down, dissolving like a caterpillar in a chrysalis into a glowing soup inside, innocent, obscure, directionless. Then the girl, the young woman's face had appeared, calling him back into a different here than the one he left. He had lingered the whole time in the shelter that she built, suspended, fluid, reluctant to assume form. Even the journey to the village had been like a dream happening to someone else. The boys helping him along the trail had guided a molten emptiness, there had been no one there. Even now he was not sure who he was, or even why he was here. He still needed an imaginal pull, a maturing image to form himself around. A new pattern to fit himself into. He wanted desperately to find his bearings again. Through the most familiar way he knew, through questioning, questions arising in torrents. "In good time," his hosts assured him. "Let everything unfold at the council. For now you need to rest." Warm tea, faintly green, smelling of unfamiliar roots and leaves. "Strengthening," they said. Offered with kind hands. More kind hands settling him under a tree at the edge of the village. A warm robe, loosely woven of strips of fur tucked up around him. The winter clouds had passed. Pale autumn sun warming the chill away from the air instead, but even with the warmth of the sun, a coldness lingered in his bones. Calling him back, away from now, away from living, as these people here seemed to be doing, so lightly? easily? gracefully? gratefully? reverently? Hard for Linn to characterize them. Subtle, their quiet delight in simply being alive so different from his world.

Each day as he sat under the tree in the warming sun, a few people came by to greet him. Not pushing or prying, although the strangeness of his arrival must be well known. Approaching him with a kindly caution instead, without the wariness of the Lab, but with a restraint veiling what appeared to be their natural openness. A distancing that made him a little sad. Would he ever fit in? Did he want to? And if he did, would they want him to stay? For now, they were coming by to introduce themselves, to welcome him, even with his air of strangeness. "We will speak more at the council," one man said, offered with a friendly smile. The call for council had gone out as soon as Linn arrived, and a few people had already come from some of the other village camps. Apparently everything was decided by everyone.

Together. "Sometimes takes a long time," another man said with a grin. "Listening and talking and agreeing take time, and care. You'll see." After the man left, a flock of small birds swept through the air as if pulled on long thin curving lines, drawn magnetically all at once to the branches of the same tree. Then just as suddenly, they all depart, sipped on other invisible strings to another tree. Each moving on their own string, moving together as one being? one intent? He wondered if that was how the council would be.

He tried to ask about other aspects of their lives, wanting to know what to expect. "Ah," said a big man, well muscled with a fish tattoo on one large bicep, his voice surprisingly gentle for a man so imposing and robust. "Ah, yes, what to expect. We try to let what is to be arise in its own time. We wait and listen. It is a good way…."

Linn tried a different question with a woman of middle age who carried a beautifully woven basket in her arms and greeted him with a shy smile. This time he asked about the history of the People.

"Oh" she said, "you could go see Old At'sah. She can tell you."

Linn had already met Young At'sah briefly. A woman who looked to be in her eighties perhaps. Old At'sah must be very old indeed.

"At'sah is a name for the wild mustard seed," the man beside the basket woman said. "Watch out, she's pretty sharp. Spicy too." The man laughed affectionately.

The woman smiling offered to take Linn to At'sah's lodge. "It's on my way." Her soft voice grew musical and warm, "Old At'sah is my mother's mother. She is a singer. She sings our songs, she keeps them alive for us, the songs of who we are. But you will need ears to hear...."

They walked in silence on the narrow pathway. She walked ahead of him, walking slowly at a pace that fit his still uncertain gait. Even in their caution, the People treated him with a kindly concern. His head no longer spun around, but he had no land legs yet, no sea legs either, and no ship anymore. Sky fish, he had heard his craft called. Fish out of water, fish out of air, fish trying to land, not knowing how.

The woman stopped on the path and looked back at him. "It's good to take her something as a gift if you want to hear a song. It doesn't need to be much, the gesture of offering is the important part."

Linn shrugged his shoulders. He shook his head and opened his hands, "I arrived with nothing."

"Here," she said, and pressed a small soft pouch into one of his hands, "here is some acorn meal to offer her." He made the nearly universal I can't accept your kind offer gestures but the woman simply said, "If you stay here with us, you will become part of our sharing ways, it is the way we are, part of what you might call our history." She smiled, "our story, our song." *If you stay.* Her words haunted him as she continued to explain. "She will recognize the pouch, she will know it came from me, and she will appreciate your gesture as the new part of the gift. A traveling gift." Seeing a flicker of troubled concern in his eyes she added, "Here among us, there are gifts that have passed through many hands. They are traveling gifts, and they are valued for the hands they have gathered along their way. Both in giving and receiving. That is their song."

They had reached the entrance to one of the earthen lodges, a modest hump of earth covered with leaves, barely distinguishable from the surrounding forest floor except by the round shape and a few faint wisps of smoke rising from the smoke hole, disappearing in the branches overhead. The woman gave no greeting sound and waited attentively in silence for a few minutes. Linn decided she must be having a silent conversation with someone inside, announcing his presence in what they referred to as the calling way. When she turned to Linn she used spoken words again. "You may go in now. Grandma'ma will be happy to see you."

The old singer was barely visible to Linn's eyes at first, as she sat in the lodge shadows beside a small fire. A thread of smoke rose slowly from the glowing coals in front of her, drifting upward in gentle curves through the column of soft light from the smoke hole. Old At'sah leaned forward to add a few sticks to the fire. Her hair suddenly bright, a cloud of white illumined in the column of light. Her face, lined and wrinkled like an old riverbed, blushed with the warm glow of the fire. Sunrise and sunset. Then she sat back. Gradually as his eyes adjusted to the light inside the lodge, her face grew clearer for him in the shadows.

Old At'sah was indeed very, very old. Older than anyone Linn had seen before in his life. In the techno savvy world he had come from, from which he had been so recently ejected he reminded himself, older people had gone to great lengths to appear as young as they could. This woman seemed to have welcomed age, with the certainty of a tree near timberline, her agedness insuring her survival just as it did the tree's. Age as an expression of life force, not an obstacle. The folds and crevasses in her leathery wrinkled skin were surprisingly beautiful, especially the maze of lines at the outer corners of her eyes. Deltas of laugh lines, a living map of all the times she had smiled or laughed in delight. He marveled at the complexity and completeness of the patterning. A living web of feeling, a history of remembering what kept a people whole, remembering not just the "facts" of the events as they occurred, but how they felt, the textures of the living encoded in her face, just as he imagined they were encoded in the songs. She had an unexpected and compelling vividness for him, perhaps because he was so empty of any context for himself, outside the shared memories here, and she was so full, someone who sang the memories into songs. Not knowing what else to do, he knelt a few steps from her and offered her the small pouch silently. Then he waited.

She finally acknowledged his presence and his gift with a surprisingly engaging smile. He half saw half felt a brief image of her as a young woman, teasing, playful, full of life. Disarmed and disoriented, it took him a few moments to realize she had invited him to sit beside the fire with her.

After what he hoped was an appropriate wait, and in what he hoped was an appropriate way, Linn asked, "They said you could tell me some of the history of the People. The council is not for a few days. I have been asking around, I want to begin learning, I want to learn something of your ways."

182

"We don't have…. histories," she began slowly, looking into layers of distance with ancient eyes. Then she was quiet for a while. How to tell this new one, so recently from the solid fixating world they had fled so long ago, how to tell him of the fluid way of shared memories. "History…. is a group dream," she began again, her voice as far as her eyes, as if words, spoken words, were a far country themselves, growing stronger and closer as she spoke, her words calling up other words. He wondered, how often did she speak in words anyway? Did she even think in words? Then he remembered she was a singer of songs, and songs for him were music, listened for and heard. He settled in to hear as her voice slowly filled the earthen lodge. "….history is the power of a group dream…. that keeps on hypnotizing long after it ceases to live, spent history, the story self satisfied, insular, the one-sided story. Never ours. History, the story song with one half denied, the triumphant voice of a militant us, and the silence of a conquered acquiescing them. Yes, that's history all right, a noisy, boisterous us, and a silent them." She looked into the distance again. Then she looked back at him mischievously, "but you know, the silence is where we keep the other stories, where we keep them safe, away from turning into history. No, we do not let them go that way. We keep them safe in the silence." Her voice faded away like wisps of smoke, disappearing into a space of quietness that seemed too full to be called silence. Then she spoke again. "History is…. a lie, the unliving lie, no longer swimming flashing flying leaping, enshrined instead…. No longer alive itself…. living off the paralyzed bodies of the other songs, the songs that

183

remember how to leap and fly, that remember how to grow wings."

She looked at him as if she could see into him, all through him, all the way to his love of flight, to all that he knew of flying, and to the brightness he sought on the sky bridge. He found himself wanting to turn away, but her gaze was kind and she held his attention gently to her as she continued. "Until, unable to take wing, victorious history finds itself in the very real danger of being trapped in its own form, desperate, hoping and fearing for assurance it is not alone." She looked at him again, "Like your people, yes? In that place you have come from?"

She had shifted so quickly. He had been captivated, lost in her words. He nodded and could barely murmur, "Yes, that is how it is." Teaching me their ways indeed. As if he had asked about manners and teacups, and she had given him the hands that hold the tea directly instead, all the waters of the world cradled tenderly in her open palms.

She laid a few fragrant twigs on the glowing coals. Tiny flames flickered into life. "And then the other story, peaceful, weaponless, secure, wakens and begins to live and breathe again, swallowing all histories in its innocent becoming. Yes, that is how it is with us and with the land here, we are all becoming, that is our way. There are memories," she said, "many memories, everyone has memories, the fire has memories, the waters, the trees, we all have them, but yes, they are all weaving together as this becoming." She smiled at him. They sat quietly as the small fire dwindled down. He watched the delicate flames lick the air, turning, dancing growing smaller in

184

the shimmer rising from the glowing coals beneath them. Finally she turned to him and said, "We will speak again, at the council. I will see you then," and he knew his visit with her was over. "Thank you, Old At'sah, for telling me of the way of songs." He bowed gently, and she winked at him, the sudden brightness in her eyes briefly flooding the day lodge earthen darkness, dancing like the small flames.

Big Carl walked Linn over to the council meeting, chatting amiably as he showed him the way, and Linn was grateful for his company. Big Carl was not a big man physically, despite his name, but he had a generosity of presence that seemed big. A big heart. He included you. He included everyone, with an unencumbered easy way that made it easy to be with him. Dark bushy hair as generous as the rest of him, grey beginning to frost at the temples. Dark bushy beard and eyebrows. Warm lively eyes that were not afraid to see. A depth of experience in those eyes that had not dimmed, and perhaps had sharpened instead, Big Carl's affectionate appreciation and amusement for whatever was going on around him. In the short time that Linn had known him, he already counted him as a friend. Big Carl patted him on the shoulder reassuring and whispered "Don't worry, everything is going to be okay. You'll see," as Linn ducked to go through the low entrance to the council lodge.

Like At'sah's lodge, the council lodge was dark to Linn's day eyes when he first entered. A breathing darkness, scented with earth and wood smoke and dry cedar, and filled with the faint rustling sounds of many people whispering, giggling, shifting, settling in, all blending with the crackling of the small fire at the center of the lodge. Big Carl had explained to Linn that they would be speaking out loud today for Linn's benefit, instead of using the calling way as they usually did when they gathered, and the People seemed to be enjoying playing with the sounds of their voices as well as their words, and by the frequent outbursts of soft laughter, engaging in a lot of good natured teasing banter.

Once his eyes adjusted he saw that unlike At'sah's lodge, the gathering place was large, much larger than any of the other lodges he had seen, although it appeared to be constructed in the same way. A sunken floor of earth, four sturdy posts near the middle of the lodge to support the roof, set equidistant from each other around a central fire circle lined with stones. Cross beams resting on top of the posts connecting them. Thinner poles laid close together, forming a wide cone shape rising from the rim of the excavated floor to rest on the cross beams and extend inward, their ends overlapping around a smoke hole in the center. Rows of slender branches woven through the poles at their lower ends, the whole roof chinked with grass and moss. Layers of bark and earth on the outside, covered with heaps of forest debris to protect the upper layer from the rains. Like being inside an upturned basket or a woven hat, or a cave, all at once. Surprisingly comforting, the more he got used to it. Big Carl had told him that the Ancient Ones who lived in these lands long ago built even bigger lodges for dancing and meeting. Round houses they had called them. But the big lodges would be too hard to keep hidden now. The People built more modest council lodges instead. "And so," Big Carl had said with a chuckle, "we have to pack 'em in."

The round space was indeed packed. Old and young crammed together sitting cross-legged generally facing the fire. A few people sitting close to the fire waved at Linn and Big Carl and motioned to the empty places beside them. "Looks like our seating has been arranged." Big Carl said with a grin, and he steered Linn toward the center of the lodge. As Linn moved through the press of people he felt self-conscious under the gaze of so many eyes and faces turning toward him. A strange sensation for someone who still felt more like an absence than a presence, even to himself, an absence that had no desire to return to the guarded wariness of the surveillance culture at the Lab. The faces and the eyes around him here were kind and open, but they were still neutral. Not exactly wary, watching him with more of a patient caution instead. Waiting to hear what he would say. To hear what everyone would say.

A few faces looked familiar. The girl who rescued him after the crash smiled shyly as he passed, her shoulder pressed close to the boy next to her, who also smiled. Linn recognized him as one of the boys who came to find them, and who helped steady him on the trail back to the village. The big man with the fish tattoo that Linn met earlier was sitting close to the fire, and to Linn's mind expecting a certain kind of protocol, appeared to be the moderator or leader of the gathering by the way some of the faces looked from Linn to the big man and back again. The man was deep in private prayer, his eyes absorbed in the fire, but he looked up and smiled at him, a bit conspiratorially it almost seemed to Linn, as if the man knew something about him in a way that made him feel unexpectedly reassured, before the man returned his gaze to the fire. The basket woman who had taken him to meet old At'sah was sitting at the big man's side, and appeared to have a function too. She had what might be some ceremonial objects laid out on the ground in front of her.

Old At'sah sat across from them, offering small branches to the fire. She looked up and briefly dazzled Linn with a brightness that had no physical counterpart, then went back to feeding the fire, singing very softly, as if the song and the flames were one melody. Small children all through the lodge sitting on the laps of parents or aunts or uncles or older siblings, wriggled and peered between shoulders to get a look at Linn. A continuous murmured undertone of banter and quiet joking, as people nudged each other to make room for yet another person. The lodge was warm with all the bodies crowded together, even though old At'sah was keeping the fire small, more for light, and blessing, Linn guessed, than for heat.

"Didn't know we were coming for a sweat," a voice from somewhere in the middle of the crowd. A burst of louder laughter in response. Everyone was hot.

"Only way we can get Old Uncle to take one," someone else teased.

"You bet," grinned a very old man with few teeth, who sparkled like Old At'sah when the faces turned toward him.

189

More laughter. The village was family. They all knew each other well. They were gathered to decide an important matter, and there was a feeling of considered respectful presence, but clearly without the stiff formalities that Linn was accustomed to in meetings at the Lab. Here the act of gathering had a different feel, as if gathering itself was as important to them as considering and coming into consensus. The ease and play of simply being together was part of how consensus grew. Their restraint was in relation to Linn, not to each other. Big Carl had explained to Linn about the Watchers, as the People called the sky eyes and surveillance drones, and that because Linn had arrived in what seemed to be a Watcher's craft, there was concern he might be a Watcher too.

"Hardly," Linn had said bitterly. How was he going to explain the complex twisted dynamics at the Lab, and how he felt about what had happened there, and his sudden expulsion?

"Just tell them," Big Carl had said. "They are coming to listen, to really listen, and they will be open. There are others among us who have come through greater difficulties to live with us. They will understand."

Linn looked around at the faces and smiled tentatively. He felt a shimmer he could only describe as kindness coming toward him. Perhaps they would understand. Perhaps they already did.

The big man raised one hand in some kind of blessing gesture. The fish tattoo on his arm leapt and flickered in the firelight. The rustling and the murmuring began to settle down. The woman at his side lit a small bundle of herbs. Mugwort and cedar, Linn was just learning to

190

identify the scents. She fanned the bundle with a feather, sending curling threads of sweet smoke out across the lodge, and upward toward the smoke hole, and downward toward the fire. Old At'sah began to sing in a stronger voice, a haunting rippling sound, like wind in the trees or moving water. Other voices joined in, murmuring in the same soft rhythms. Everyone in the lodge seemed to melt into one person, entrained in the melody. Then the other voices faded away as she finished singing. The lodge grew quiet for a while, a full, rich silence, filled with the presence of a people coming together as one. Finally the big man spoke with a slow gentle voice that nevertheless carried easily throughout the lodge.

"We are gathered to hear what our visitor Linn has to say. He does not yet know the calling way. Some of us have spoken of this before today." He gestured around the room and many heads nodded. "It would be good if we listen and speak in the way of spoken words, so that he may know our hearts as we know his. May all our listening and telling be good and true." More nodding and murmurs of assent.

Another stretch of silence, a waiting this time. A normally communicative people feeling their way gently as a whole toward a way to deal with the new stranger. Then Big Carl spoke.

"This man, Linn, sitting beside me, has been a guest at my lodge since he came here. I know him to have a good heart. He is now a friend. I am happy to have opened my lodge to him. He does not yet know our ways. I believe he would like to know something of our experiences of the times Before. He has only recently come from a remnant of the world we left. It would help him to know how we felt about that world, those things that we experienced, and how those of us who lived through the hard times were able to make the change and begin again. It would help him tell his story if he knew the way of telling ours. He comes as a friend."

A number of heads nodded in agreement, and there were more murmurs of assent. Slowly, one by one, the People began to speak.

Linn's mind was reeling as the story unfolded, in quiet voices weaving together, overlapping at times, punctuating each other's words with sounds of agreement and emphasis, all as one voice. The voice of a People who had helped each other survive a horror they would never wish on anyone, filling in the details with an economy born of long grief, and the need, more than the fact, of distance. Something he understood.

The starvation camps. Food distribution camps at first, then starvation. Intentional. "They told us food distribution, to get everyone to move." High fences. Barbed wire, coils of razor wire. Guard towers. In the most desolate parts of the central valley. The prisons were already full. The Taibo'oo, the Watchers, built more. They had been keeping more and more people incarcerated even before. The new industry. Had gone on for years. They just called them food depots now. Soldiers searching house to house, arresting anyone who wouldn't go, anyone with food of their own. Hoarding, the Watchers called it then. "Even if it came from your own garden, even if you were growing it, even if you shared," another voice added. To the Watchers, sharing was the worst. Traitorous, unpatriotic, undermined civil order. They searched from above with sky eyes. Everyone had no choice but to comply. "Unless," a gentle voiced older man said, "Unless. There were some who left at the beginning of the unrest, or before." He smiled grimly. Too late for most. No food shipments from across the mountains. A wasteland there too. The breadbasket was scorched earth, incinerated by a nuclear accident. Grey skies everywhere after the accident. And then the solar storms. Linn nodded in agreement. He remembered the years at the Lab when they had to grow crops with artificial lights. Used up a lot of their back up energy reserves. Got pretty marginal for a while, before the skies outside began to clear enough that they could use solar again. In their own oblique insolated way they had been affected by the same things.

The voices had paused while the people gathered at the council waited to see if he was going to speak. Linn looked down, shy and embarrassed, suddenly aware of how finely tuned the People's sense of communication was, and that he had strayed perhaps into the realm of their calling way without knowing how. When they saw that he remained silent, they continued. After the solar storms, some sky eyes again. Not as many. For military only. No civilian telecom. No civilians. Only prisoners, detainees, and security. Military and paramilitary security, the contractors, operating under a vague all inclusive mandate that seemed only to justify abuse, and that included the WAR police. A state collapsing in on itself. Starving people inside the fences. Well fed, well armed patrols on the outside. Dirty skies. Diseases sweeping through the land, sweeping through the camps. Immune systems already weakened by unforeseen consequences of genetically modified organisms and communication microwaves. Those were familiar issues to Linn too. Miri had done some early work on those consequences, tried to raise the alarm, her research ignored or suppressed. Miri. He pulled himself back forcibly from following his memories, from interrupting the council again. With a different kind of restraint than at the Lab. Here he felt an instinctive respect for something he barely understood, a tangible web of caring and intent, a pattern forming of which he was already a part.

The story of the terrible Before continued. Nuclear and chemical weaponry unleashed, and then the engineered viruses. Specifically designed to target immune responses in the "enemy." Select few of the Watchers inoculated with a vaccine for protection before the viruses were released. But the viruses turned on them too. "Nature will find a way," someone said softly. Biotech Armageddon. "They were faced with bio terror from enemies too small to see. Hard to intimidate a microorganism with lies and propaganda, with secret police, hard to bribe emotionally. Their outsourced terror came at them from within. They were the Trojan bio horses, carrying their own enemy, their own destiny." "We didn't need to get the news. The plagues hit so suddenly. Our camps already far away, hidden." "You could feel the suffering," another said. "We prayed." Heads nodding. "A great sadness," another said. "On the lands everywhere." Silence, heavy with the weight of remembering, and then Big Carl spoke.

"We thought the best we could do was die with dignity. Affirm another way to be, to be with each other and with the Earth, with as much kindness as we could.

194

As a prayer, as family." He smiled. "Guess it worked. Guess the Big Momma wanted us here, wanted a few of us humans around after all. Wanted us to stay." He touched the ground in front of him affectionately with his hand. "She gave us another chance. Rest of humanity busy on another route. Hell bent on the way out."

The texture of the voices weaving together as one voice changed. We were already in the hills. We lived quietly, careful to stay hidden. Migrating slowly, higher into the mountains with the seasons as they returned. Finally we crossed the Sierra crest, and eventually, we found the land reserve for the simulated space program. The high fence. The signs. HAZARDOUS. KEEP OUT. DANGER. RESTORATION AREA. Inside the fence, the soil had been dug up and turned inside out. Sterile subsoil on top. Stunted fir and cedar trees planted in rows, like chemical flames, growing as if on fire from within. Red orange needles lower down and along the trunk, green flame tips. We sent our fastest runners out along the fence. They found a few places where it was down, but the fence and that tortured ground inside went on for miles. It was turn back or go on ahead, into that caustic land. Before we went through the fence, we gathered. We camped and talked and prayed. Everyone spoke their hearts. One of the old ones had a vision dream that night, that the ground just inside the fence was hollow, on fire at the roots of the trees, but she said if we do not linger inside the fence, she had seen that the land beyond is healing again.

A few people went in first, went through that sickened place. They went farther in, and found the land healthy just as the old one had seen. Healthier than many of the lands we had already passed through in our wanderings. Here, inside the barrier, no human sign of any kind. An unexpected ease. "Then we came to one of those places," the speaker paused. "We came to that place," the unspoken word Taibo'oo seeping through the lodge. "We went wide around, left it to itself. Gradually we came to know the ways of this land. Where there were more.... of those places, where to stay away. There were not so many and they were far apart, and the land was generous to us in between, and so we stayed, hidden away."

"We have lived quietly here, and not alone. Animals, birds, and fish, whole plant communities, they also found refuge here. We ate little meat. Our relatives, the four leggeds, the finned, and the winged ones were all struggling too. Together we were a kind of Noah's ark," he smiled. Soft murmuring around the lodge, yes, together we were all the ark. Not a test tube ark this time, or a sealed vault, but a living ark, carried in Mother Earth's heart. "All of us together," another man repeated. "We were quiet, careful. Slowly, we could feel the horror was passing away, dying of its own demented will." "We could feel a softening at the edges of our world," another voice added. "We could feel it. The terror and the darkness slowly melting away. No one to keep it alive anymore, no victims, no perpetrators. Subsiding, exhausted. Emptied. Life began to breathe again. But we never went back. The risk of contamination too great. Not just from lingering biological and nuclear contamination, but from the thought forms too, of the ghosts and spirits of that tangled troubled time that devoured itself. We let them

196

rest in their own troubled peace. We nurtured kindness here, we kept a different flame alive."

Slowly, a weight lifting. Like spring after a long winter. "We trusted that we lived again. That we could live. That Big Momma wanted us here after all," the woman speaking gestured affectionately at Big Carl. "The scourge had passed us by. We had a responsibility. To continue living, as a prayer, a prayer for new life, a modest, quiet, grateful life. It helped that we had chosen this way before, helped us accept the responsibility of being spared. With humility, without agonizing or mythologizing over it. To continue living simply, as the Ancient Ones long before had done. We stayed away from the contaminated zones, to keep from being re-contaminated by the greedy beast. Some of us had struggled with that monster from before, we were not immune, vaccinated maybe, seasoned, yes, but some of us have had an ongoing battle with the beast even here.... What if we could? Why not? So easy to slide back at first, sometimes even innocent sounding suggestions had other roots, we had to help each other see, and relearn. It has been worth it, the young ones, born into other ways help us now too. The greedy beast was not just physical toxins, but toxicity of the mind and heart too, of the world eating culture that devised its own end, so cunningly and willfully blind. The culture of the greedy ghost. Kindness saved us here. Kindness drives the beast of exploitation away in terror into its own undoing."

The People were silent for a while. Linn felt they had reached an unspoken accord, and that it was time for him to speak.

197

He focused his attention on the fire, as if speaking to the flames as Old At'sah had sung to them. He began in a quiet distant voice that seemed far away even to his ears. "For us.... inside the Lab, we felt only our own isolation, we knew it was bad out there, out here, outside...." He stumbled. From within the shared vantage point of the People gathered around him he was no longer sure from which direction to tell the story. He was between worlds, his vantage point already shifting. For the People, the Lab was the ultimate outside, outside the shared reality of the land. "But.... when the sensors went down and then comtrans stopped, we thought, we told ourselves everything was barren rock, outside. I guess in some ways it almost was."

"Yes, it almost was," a voice murmured, and heads nodded here and there around the lodge in agreement, and to encourage Linn to continue.

He paused at the enormity of how utterly insular the Lab had been. He looked up briefly and saw faces everywhere turned toward him in attentive kindness. Encouraged and disconcerted, he continued his story again, more a confession now.

"For us, inside, it already was.... barren rock. We had forgotten how to feel the world."

He stumbled again, chagrined. He tried to explain what it had been like at the Lab, the monitors watching and recording all the time. Like sky eyes, in every room, every lodge. He could feel a kind of horror mixed with compassion all around him. They knew about sky eyes. To have them so close around you.... He avoided mentioning Watchers or Taibo'oo by name, hoping to distance himself from being associated with those words, struggling with how to explain what it had really been like. How to explain the lure, the compelling power of the lie that they had lived by. Simulated space travel, hostile alien worlds, the void of space, we brought our own imaginary imagery with us into the Lab and bought into it. He told them about the project. The gardens, the research, the sensors, the rise of ISEC. The gradual tightening of "security." The paranoia and the fear, everyone closing down. The occasional disappearances of anyone who spoke out, who held out for another view, another way to be. All through the lodge, heads nodding in sympathy. As he told his story he could feel that what had happened at the Lab was not that different from what had happened on the outside after all. He felt less alone than he had in a long while. They had all been battling the same patterns released from the same seeds. Fractal patterns self-similar throughout the whole. He looked around the lodge and had the feeling that everyone there could feel the parts of his story that he had not been able to voice. Perhaps this was what they referred to as their calling way. Not only that, it seemed that they could not only feel, but also empathize with the situation the Lab personnel had set up for themselves. There was a definite kindliness in their openness. Encouraged, he went on.

"We collapsed inward, trying to keep the last remnant of the mind that bred the horror alive. I guess." He stopped, suddenly sickened as he realized that the mind that bred the horror was still alive, it hadn't completely died, not yet. It was still alive, there at the Lab, embodied especially in the ISEC high command. "It's still alive, the contagion." He said almost in a whisper. He had the feeling that everyone had heard him anyway, even before he spoke, heard his horror more than his words. "Lab 7 is the last Lab, right? We have to bring it down," he said simply. And he remembered Kai. It would not be enough to rescue Kai and a few others, as he had hoped impossibly to do, before he realized the full scope of the terrible potential of what the Lab really represented. "My son," he began, "my son is still in there, and.... there are others...." his words trailed off like smoke. The enormity. He didn't even know yet if they were going to let him stay, let alone stage a rescue mission on his son's behalf. Let alone destroy the lab. "My wife, she died a few years ago, but our son, and the others...." He was unexpectedly close to tears. An older woman sitting next to him that he had not noticed before put her hand on his shoulder, and nodded. "Yes," she said softly, "many of us have been there too, we know."

A child's voice lifted bright and clear into the temporary silence of the lodge. The People had been discussing whether Linn could stay, with a forthright candidness that Linn found difficult at times, but Big Carl and the big man with the fish tattoo looked over at him from time to time and smiled reassuringly as Linn tried his best to stay afloat. He had assumed that the big man was a chief or headman of some sort at first, but the man seemed to be just another voice, and his smile was all the more reassuring somehow, for being that of a friend rather than an authority. There did not even seem to be a need for a facilitator. Within the easy flow of silences and speaking and listening, everyone apparently felt free to speak their hearts as they called it, equally, and when they did they were all, young and old, listened to equally as well.

Linn turned around to see the new speaker, a small boy sitting on an old man's lap. "I don't know much about…. the Watchers and all that, but this man here he seems quiet and nice to me. Can he stay?"

Sounds of agreement here and there around the lodge, then the old man spoke. "And I have seen too many of those who watched in the times Before." He stressed the past tense specifically, "and I find no trace, no taste, of that meanness in this man here now among us. He seems innocent to me more than anything, like my grandson here." He hugged the small boy who had spoken up and smiled affectionately at him. "I would welcome this man who came from afar to our lodge if he stays."

One by one the people shared their thoughts and feelings about Linn in their frank and open way. A soft undertone of agreement or disagreement as each person spoke, weaving toward a unanimous voice. It reminded Linn of some aspects of honeybee communication he had studied long ago in a class on systems change and resolution. If he hadn't been the topic of discussion here with his whole life in the balance, he would have been fascinated by the process of arriving at a decision in this way. The People had gathered to hear him speak and to hear each other speak, and what they listened for was clearly more than words, an ongoing, voiced or not, nuanced perception, within an openness that was the inverse of the Lab, where words were curtains, veils, and shields, masks to hide behind or ways to deceive. Here words were respected. No need to lie, their words had roots that led to other roots that led to deeper tellings, shared meanings to be savored, whole baskets of meaning sometimes.

The little boy, the grandfather, the soft voiced younger woman whose words Linn had to strain to hear. And so it went back and forth around the crowded lodge. Each person speaking at length and then sometimes several more times again, heads nodding, sometimes in agreement, sometimes in dissent. A constant ripple of response like the laughter and the banter beforehand, punctuating the speaker's words. The People were attentive active listeners, murmuring, commenting, yes, that is how it was, or eh, eh, often repeating parts of what the speaker had just said to affirm their being heard. All overlapping with the speaker's words, woven together with the speaking into one single voice simultaneously hearing and being heard, phrased occasionally by the collective silences that seemed even fuller with shared thought. And eventually, with one heart they decided that he stay.

Night had already fallen and Linn was exhausted by the time the council ended. As Linn and Big Carl walked back to Big Carl's lodge together, they could hear the quiet sounds of others dispersing into the surrounding darkness. The People, his People now, seemed to be able to see in the dark, all of them, young and old. Not as if it was a special power or some super stealth night vision. Just matter of fact, ordinary. They all just seemed to know where they were going. Like waking up at night and knowing where everything was in your room without having to turn on a light. Familiar. Like that. Big Carl recognizing how tired Linn was guided him with a simple touch at the elbow, briefly taking his arm, steering him politely but surely through what was still for Linn unfamiliar territory. Commenting occasionally, "Aba's uncle must be planning to stay up late tonight," as they passed a lodge with a faint red glow showing in the branches close above the smoke hole, from a fire recently fed. Passing another lodge, the sweet spice scent of mugwort and cedar burned together as incense, "Naira's eldest daughter at her evening prayers, praying for that handsome young man over in the next village maybe." Big Carl's voice rich with amused affection for the young people, for all the People, orienting Linn to the map of lives and relationships laid out around him of which he was now a part.

Big Carl's lodge was on the outer edge of the village. He had offered to take Linn in when he first arrived, and they had gotten along well enough to have settled in a few short days together into a unobtrusive neighborly friendship. Big Carl had said at the council that Linn was welcome to stay with him as long as he liked, and Linn was grateful. Big Carl was naturally friendly, and seemed comfortable with having someone else around. It had been unexpectedly easy for Linn to fit in, with Big Carl at least, despite his awkwardness and uncertainty as a refugee. It had been a start. Linn was surprised Big Carl didn't have a wife or partner or extended family living with him as many others did, but he hadn't asked, one question he felt instinctively he should not ask. Not yet. Another start. He had a lot to learn about patience, and trust, and letting things unfold. He wished Kai could be here, and Miri too. He would like to offer them this new world, one they would probably fit into far faster than he. The sadness again. He was suddenly sure he knew why Big Carl had lived alone. Not from choice, but from absence. Big Carl's kindness and gentleness with him came from a great loss, a depth of grief long past, slowly wearing away the sharp edges of that grief as surely as a stone immersed in water rounded into acceptance, the rounding of a human heart measured in water's time, stone's time. Linn had a long way to go. For him the edges were still sharp, and he had not given up on the hope that somehow, impossibly, he could rescue Kai. For that, he would need an edge.

Linn was exhausted, emotionally and physically, but it was hard to consider going to sleep. Tired and wired from all that had been said at the council, and from his introduction to a community process so new and unfamiliar, almost alien for him, and yet one he truly wished he could grow to feel at ease with. Big Carl seemed to sense his mood, and did not seem to be in any hurry to go to sleep either. Linn sat close to the small fire circle at the center of the lodge. A few buried coals flickered faintly in the ashes. Big Carl joined him, stirred the ashes, and added a little tinder and a few sticks. The fire came to life. They sat quietly for a while each riding different thoughts, different memories.

The only part that hadn't worked out well at the council from Linn's view point, was the matter of going back to the Lab to get Kai and anyone else who would want to leave. Linn just couldn't abandon them there, sealed inside the Lab, not knowing what was really outside. Not just Kai, but McPhe, Ken, and the other techs, and he was sure there must be more who would be happy to leave, eager even, once they knew a way and a place to go. But the only agreement on the matter reached at the council had been to wait until later to decide, to consider it again. Linn understood the People's caution. Their survival all these years had been based on staying hidden, being invisible. Even now they took great care not to leave tracks or other signs, to conceal their trails and their villages, to not build big fires, or smoky fires, to build fires mainly at evening and early dawn when the muted flickering twilight would hide the whispers of smoke. And if they did need to build a fire at other times, they kept the fires very small, careful to minimize the smoke or the warm glow that would be reflected at night on the branches overhead that shielded the fires and the lodges from above.

And winter was coming. They had made that clear. Hard for someone who had lived in a virtually seasonless world for years to comprehend again. Winter placed certain restrictions of its own on the People. The first snowfall had melted fast but more snows were on the way. The time of winter sleeps for the land. And by land, they had also made quite clear, they meant all the myriad lives that moved and lived together here. They had a responsibility to them too. For the People, winter was a time to gather in the lodges, to fashion simple tools of wood and bone and stone, to make cordage and baskets, to weave fur skin cord into the soft robes they wore to sleep in and to keep them warm when they moved around in the cold. Time to listen to stories, and to the story songs. Time to remember and wait, and consider.

And especially, not a time to stage a war party. Linn was surprised that they had used such a term, they seemed so peaceful, so concerned with harmony. The idea had seemed out of place. When he protested that a rescue party was more what he had in mind, they agreed, yes, that is what we would like it to be too, but we must consider what else could happen, in that place. They had not forgotten the difficulties of the times Before, or the tenacity with which the Taibo'oo clung to their ideas of power, and Linn had to admit, the risk was high that the rescue mission could involve serious confrontation, could easily go that way. Caution and considering made more sense to him then. Subtle changes in patterns at the beginning. Fractals, consensus. He was beginning to understand.

"It is best," Big Carl said quietly, as if he was feeling Linn's thoughts or knew this would be on Linn's mind. "We have to weigh everything carefully. Perhaps in the spring, the time of beginnings. For now, get to know our ways. They know your heart. They understand and respect your heart in this matter. Your son, your friends. Many of us, in the times Before, had loved ones we wanted to rescue, to save. But the safety of the People, of all the villages.... We had to consider that even then. Now we must still consider carefully, the best way for everyone. Do not give up hope, wait and see."

For Linn, the spring, the season of beginnings, seemed a long way off.

"A lot of us old timers lost people we really cared about, in those times Before, in the terror times, and the War." Big Carl continued, talking to himself and to the fire and to others who were not there, as well as to Linn. "But sometimes it worked out that we could go in and get them. Not always. Sometimes not." He turned his hand, palm up, palm down, back and forth. "A lot of us lost people then. Had to let them go. The thing is to keep going, to not let your heart close down. That's the big one, sends you right back there if you don't. May as well not have left."

Linn thought of Miri. The loss so sharp and recent at times, and like everything else before the crash, before the hover flight, growing more distant now. He thought he understood why the People usually referred to the hard times, the horror, the difficult times of the terror, simply as Before. The pain of loss was still fresh at times but the events moving farther away, Before.

It was very late when exhaustion finally caught up with Linn. Maybe he had to be this exhausted to finally land.

"Yeah, I know." Big Carl said, and Linn heard lifetimes in his words.

As Linn burrowed in the sleeping fur that Big Carl had given him, he could hear his friend rustling in the darkness on the other side of the lodge, making the small sounds people make as they settle down to sleep. Finally Linn let himself relax. They had let him stay. He had a friend, several friends. He could start again. The People had told him that there were a few others of his "kind" from other Labs who had made the shift and were living with the People now. One of them had sent word that he would be coming to visit Linn soon. And finally, enfolded in the soft fur of the robe and the quiet earthen comfort of the lodge, he surrendered at last to sleep.

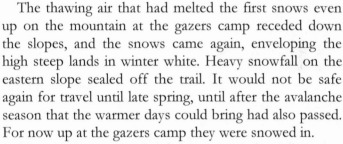

The thawing air that had melted the first snows even up on the mountain at the gazers camp receded down the slopes, and the snows came again, enveloping the high steep lands in winter white. Heavy snowfall on the eastern slope sealed off the trail. It would not be safe again for travel until late spring, until after the avalanche season that the warmer days could bring had also passed. For now up at the gazers camp they were snowed in.

Lives Twice met each of the gazers informally rather than in a council as she had expected. It had apparently been decided unanimously before she arrived that she would stay, when Ta'le had spoken with them earlier before he invited her. Shy quiet folk for the most part, and generous and kind as all the People were, it was easy to say hello, as if she had already lived here a long time. No need for more complex greetings, simply to acknowledge being here.

One of the women was a bit more talkative. *My job for now!* The woman joked with a bright smile in her eyes. *Coordinating mostly, and messenger. Relaying information and needs, organizing the trips down the mountain in those seasons. We take turns at it, share the responsibilities, no one wants to ordinate,* she rolled her eyes at the word play, *full time! In the villages this happens differently. Up here, with everyone so deep in practice, it helps to have someone…. You know the geese? The grey fronted ones with the long black necks and the white blaze on their chins, the sky travelers? They always have one who watches out for each group when they graze in the meadowlands. They put their heads up and down so seamlessly taking turns, they don't have to look around to know when to change.*

Yes, she said, remembering the first time she had seen the great birds on the ground.

Like that, the woman said, *just like that. That is how we watch. Our groups are always small, usually no more than twelve or thirteen, no more than the moons of a year.* She made a circle with one hand in the air in front of her, for the yearly cycle of the seasons, her hand motions seamless with her calling. *Enough people to be a support, but not too many, so that we can know each other's hearts and consensus comes more easily. At least in less time!* Her eyes laughing again.

Lives Twice imagined there was not too much dissent or discord here. Everyone moving toward a shared goal, each in their own way, together. The mutual respect that was so much a part of the People's lives in the village camps was especially heightened here, with the focused intent of their practice and the isolation of the camp. Even so, that focus seemed to hold them elsewhere in what was for her another world. For now they were all kind like Ta'le, and like him suffused with a quiet intensity and fluid brightness as if glowing from within. A feeling she had from them of another kind of eyes looking from within an immense wonder beyond even the calling words. An ever present wonder. An open

210

secret, one you could see, like the mountain, once you were there. They made her feel welcome, and from her side, Lives Twice did feel strangely at home with these people so immersed in something so utterly at the heart of all that is, something that was carrying them somehow. So trusting in that carrying that they were not in any hurry to get wherever it was taking them, content to let it carry them, utterly focused and surrendering at the same time. A lot like her.

The rhythms of their days were very simple, especially after the snows came and stayed. Each gazer spent most of their time inside their hut practicing. For winter, they built snow shadows, like the sun shadows in the village camps in the summer, the open canopies raised on posts with branches and leaves heaped on top for dappled shade. Outdoor spaces where a few people could gather protected from above, to talk quietly, work, and tend small children. Here the snow shadows were rambling, built to skillfully flow with the spacing of the surrounding trees, connecting the protected places under the denser conifers, bridging the more open spaces under the bare aspens, linking all the huts, shielding the paths between and the careful stacks of firewood beside each hut. Looking like raged heaps of brush from above, with narrow corridors beneath becoming almost like tunnels, Ta'le said, at times when the snows were deep.

He showed her how he sat in the alcove cave where he practiced, and the tiny openings, "the eyes of the wall" that let in small rays of daylight, surprisingly bright inside the darkness of the hut, and the woven matt he could pull over the opening of the alcove while he

211

practiced. *Not to keep you out,* he touched her face tenderly, *just to keep the light in.*

For now she was content to sit in her own way by the embers of the fire, resting in a growing peace that in itself grew more expansive day by day.

Ta'le smiled when she told him. *Yes,* he said, *that is how it is, the way in. Better to go slowly, then you can be here, and when you're always here in that openness, then you can begin,* and he kissed her.

The other gazers welcomed her in their midst, not just as a partner to Ta'le, but as one of them on her own, a seeker in her own way.

They know your heart, he said, *they know their kin when they see them. Like the winter trout, so rare, so hard to find, they need to know each other on sight!*

So she eased gently into the quiet pace of their days. He pulled the curtain across the alcove when he practiced, so she did not know exactly what he did, except for the waves of feeling that swept over her when he practiced, as if pouring from a hidden sea, drenching everything like a vast sea of a joy beyond words. And she felt herself washed to the same shore she had seen in her heart's eye from afar, his sending so strong about his path even then. The luminous depth she had seen in his eyes the first time they met now filling the small hut with what to her was quiet wonder. Hollow shells of light, or clear stones on an endless shore of an equally endless sea, winter trout know why the mountain compels them here. So did she, in another way perhaps, in a part of her nascent, unformed, already swept on ahead.

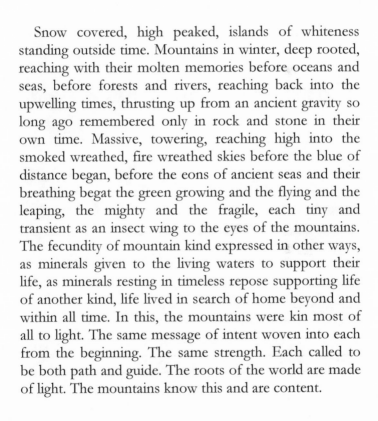

Snow covered, high peaked, islands of whiteness standing outside time. Mountains in winter, deep rooted, reaching with their molten memories before oceans and seas, before forests and rivers, reaching back into the upwelling times, thrusting up from an ancient gravity so long ago remembered only in rock and stone in their own time. Massive, towering, reaching high into the smoked wreathed, fire wreathed skies before the blue of distance began, before the eons of ancient seas and their breathing begat the green growing and the flying and the leaping, the mighty and the fragile, each tiny and transient as an insect wing to the eyes of the mountains. The fecundity of mountain kind expressed in other ways, as minerals given to the living waters to support their life, as minerals resting in timeless repose supporting life of another kind, life lived in search of home beyond and within all time. In this, the mountains were kin most of all to light. The same message of intent woven into each from the beginning. The same strength. Each called to be both path and guide. The roots of the world are made of light. The mountains know this and are content.

The bear, rising slowly from depths beyond sleep and dream like a great creature of the sea, lifting grandly through the great waters, bubbles of perception and memory floating to the surface ahead of her. From within the saline essence of beginning times beginning anew, the bear comes to meet the woman at the threshold again. The sheling with the dark hair just beginning to frost, shaped close around her face like the folded wings of a bird.

The woman looking at the bear, seeing the eyes brown flecked with yellow gold like her own, eyes looking at her from a depth of kindness she longs to meet, flowing, sliding away like water when she tries to grasp. Eyes searching through her.

The woman looking around in wonder, *I am here again.... How did I get here.... Why do I know how to come here....* hesitantly, trying not to let the opening fade away, trying to catch hold of a dream. *I have been.... I know something of what I am looking for....* Lives Twice could feel herself slipping away and tried to get to firmer ground in her mind. *You asked me, before.... You asked.... and I know*

now, not all of it but some, I am looking for a wholeness beyond memory, the woman said, as if reciting something she has understood before that is already dissolving even as she says the words, *beyond the shadows and light of memory, more ancient, whole, a belonging from long ago, before the beginning.... I seek,* she said, *the secret of the mountain's heart,* surprising herself with her words that were not quite words. A knowing instead.

You are getting close, the bear said, *to knowing what is found, to knowing what you find when you find it, but not yet. You are still newborn and blind. You need to ripen and grow. Your eyes will open when it is time.* She raised her paw and looked long into the woman's eyes. *They will open,* she said gently, *they will open....*

Wait, the woman said, as the bear turned to leave. *Something else.... Sometimes, I have felt something following me, looking for me as I seek. Is it something from before? It makes me uneasy. I.... will it find me before I find what I seek? Should I.... should I go to meet it if it comes again?*

The bear considered what and how much to say. *You choose, you have already chosen. Nothing finds you that does not already belong to you. But there are many belongings, this you can choose. You have more choosing in you than you know. A keen strong edge you are, use it carefully,* the bear said. *You are capable of choosing far more than you know. Use it wisely.*

I have seen the bear again, Lives Twice told Ta'le when they were both awake. *I can't remember all of it, but the bear comforts me in some way, like the mountain, I think. But she pushes me in some way too.* She made an undulating forward motion with the palm of her hand. *Like the winter trout of your name perhaps,* she smiled, *pulled to seek the mountain in winter and return to the ancient seas,* tugging at him playfully.

Bears eat salmon, Ta'le reminded himself. *Bears eat salmon, not yet, and this little bear still too young to know, too young to find the stream or the fish. Not in that way, not yet, not yet.*

The bear is very wise.... she said, drifting back again toward other depths, Ta'le holding her close to him, curling his body heat and his heart around her as they lay together in their sleeping robe, sheltering her as she fell back to sleep. *Time enough for winter trout to climb the mountain and return to their ancient home before the bears waken from their winter sleep. It is the other fish, the spring trout, caught in their spring tides, that must beware.* Then he kissed her lightly and tucked the fur robe back around her as he got up to sit before the dawn.

216

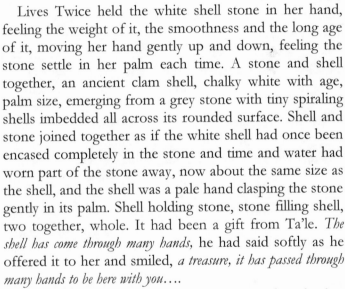

Lives Twice held the white shell stone in her hand, feeling the weight of it, the smoothness and the long age of it, moving her hand gently up and down, feeling the stone settle in her palm each time. A stone and shell together, an ancient clam shell, chalky white with age, palm size, emerging from a grey stone with tiny spiraling shells imbedded all across its rounded surface. Shell and stone joined together as if the white shell had once been encased completely in the stone and time and water had worn part of the stone away, now about the same size as the shell, and the shell was a pale hand clasping the stone gently in its palm. Shell holding stone, stone filling shell, two together, whole. It had been a gift from Ta'le. *The shell has come through many hands,* he had said softly as he offered it to her and smiled, *a treasure, it has passed through many hands to be here with you....*

As she sat with the shell stone she remembered other treasures that had come temporarily to her as gifts and then became gifts in return. Each had rested for a while on the small shrine beside her sleeping place in Mi'thal's lodge. Not a shrine really. In the village as well as here, the whole lodge, the whole hut, every lodge or hut, was a shrine to a way of life, a way of being. Her shrine had been a small basket-woven shelf, a simple gathering place near where she slept, and she remembered some of the treasures that had sat there. A pretty little basket she had made when she was practicing her hand and gaining some skill. That one had gone to a special friend of Mi'thal's who came to visit. A small deer skin pouch fringed on the bottom, a traveling gift that Lives Twice had received and had given to a young mother about to give birth, as a prayer for the child's safe journey into this life. A small round rawhide flask, delicately stitched, with a cherry wood stopper on a finely woven string. The flask had also been given to her, and she had given it in turn to Alehya when the girl left to go to the canyon village. Something to put dreams in perhaps, or herbs or seeds.

All the treasures on her little shelf were gifts. Often they were winter gifts, made patiently and lovingly around winter fires on cold nights. A coil of slender nettle cordage fine as a thread of sinew. One of the children had been practicing and gave it shyly to her. The bleached coil of an empty snail shell, spiraling and frail. A few acorn caps like tiny perfectly woven baskets. A wing feather of a goose, dark brown, tidy, smooth, filled with the careful strength of the great sky travelers. A few blue jay feathers like slender blades of sky. An orange tipped flicker feather, the guardians. A tail feather of a hawk marked with the white and brown mottled stripes of the swift forest hunters. A simple dark grey stone that fit smoothly to her hand, a gift from the land, the weight of it comfortable like a friend. However they came to her or were made by her hands, they were all gifts that would be waiting to be given again, to knit the bonds that so delicately held friendship and relatedness together. *Here, this is for you,* offered on an open palm, two hands together, one above the other, the one below cradling the offering hand, supporting the gesture. The People were always giving and receiving. Besides the objects of daily life, the objects of need and skill, the People had few other personal belongings, things they temporarily owned that were resting momentarily with them in their movement through the giving stream. The People counted their belonging in other ways, in their connectedness with each other, and they were always making gifts.

"It is an old, old way," Mi'thal had said with a smile, "from long ago in time and place. We have simply brought it forward again, it helps to keep us whole."

The first small baskets that Lives Twice had made were given as gifts to the children she shared the story making with. A leaf, a feather, a fragile sky-like half shell of a robin's egg. From the first day she had met the children, treasures had passed through all their hands, given and received and given again, with time to savor the beauty of the gift each time in between. Gifts were not exchanged at the same time, each for each. That was different, no bond there, no connecting tissue stretching out across time. To give too soon meant that you did not want to leave the connectedness open with that person, you wanted it finished, closed. In a community where everyone depended on everyone else, those connections were rarely cut. Repaired if they got a little frayed maybe, but never cut, and gifts were lovingly thought out and planned ahead.

The shell rock was from a connectedness that had its roots in a larger flow of connection and belonging. *You can send it out into the giving stream in good time, on the mountain, perhaps….* Ta'le had said gently when he offered it to her, a promise gift, and the white shell stone had rested on her shrine longer than the other gifts, until the promise was fulfilled. And so one day at twilight, the sky and the high snow covered peaks and the grey rocks showing on the steep slopes and the patches of snow all through the browned meadow grass all blending into one softly glowing flickering light, she had gone a short way from the gazers camp. She took the ancient shell and stone tenderly entwined in each other and offered their union to the great heart of the mountain. Giving the stone, the shell, and all the hands they had passed through, the ancient seas, all time, all place, to the mountain. The whiteness of the shell merging into the whiteness of the snow bank where she had set it, leaving just the barest shadow of its outline. No asking, no prayers, no calling in her heart, just thankfulness, allowing whatever comes to be. All one in the glowing twilight. Like her, so very small inside the vastness of the coming night. Like the gazers' camp so very small blended into the whole of everything, like the gazers, like her, set apart in one way yet blended within the flickering world growing between night and day. When she looked back as she walked away, the shell had completely disappeared into the whiteness of the snow glowing in the twilight, blended, merging into the mountain's heart, and she knew the mountain had received her gift.

That night, long after Ta'le had gone to sleep after his evening practice, she sat beside the embers of the fire settling in a quiet peace. And when at last she crawled under the sleeping robes and nestled her weight against his sleeping form, he had wrapped his arm around her and held her close to him from inside his sleep.

Kendra Williams checked through the array of small parts laid out on her worktable, searching for the next component in the series. One of the perks of her job as head mechanics tech, she got to do the hardest tasks. She squinted at the tiny parts. Usually the daylight translated through the plass wall of the Lab was plenty good enough to see by. "Must be my eyes," she muttered to herself, "or my age." She looked up briefly at the sound of footsteps behind her. Damn, she had been concentrating so hard she hadn't heard anyone approaching.

"Just a sec." she called out. "I'll be done in a minute."

"No hurry, I can wait." A gentle voice, unfamiliar, a young man's voice maybe, pleasant, kind. I've been ambushed by worse, she reminded herself.

She bent down and turned her attention back to tightening the tiny screws on the intricate mechanism in front of her. She finished and released her breath. When she turned around, she was even more startled by the look of him than she had been by his unexpected approach.

"I'm sorry if I'm interrupting you. I'm Kai Brenner, I brought the viewscreen from the training dome over for repair. They said you would have a work order for it on file somewhere." He glanced around the crowded mechanics bay. Didn't look like there was much paperwork here. He grinned.

She was momentarily out of words. He looked so much like his father. "No, fine, I mean, I was just finishing up, and we probably do have a work order for it someplace."

"Great. I, uh, if it's okay, I was also looking for Ken Williams, is he around here?"

Her turn to grin. "Yep, that's me. Kendra, been called Ken for years." She broadened her grin good-naturedly in case he was embarrassed. She was used to this. The grin worked. He looked amused.

"Wow. Sorry."

"It's okay, happens all the time. You'd think by now you guys…. Hey, since when do they have cadets delivering parcels?"

"Not often, I had to fight for the job." He laughed. "I was kinda on my way over here anyway…."

She waited, cautious and neutral, to see where this was going.

"I just, I heard that Ken, that you, were the tech who saw my dad off on his…. flight. And I just wondered, you know, if you could tell me…."

Surveillance was not as thorough over here in mechanics as it was in most of the Lab. The tech crew had made sure of that. Easy enough to disable a few strategic sensors here and there, when your primary job was maintenance and repair. Her personal workstation

223

where they were now was relatively safe, but this was still a conversation that an aspiring cadet should not be having, much less be overheard.

"That was Richard James actually, who did the flight briefing," she explained. "He's not working here anymore. He was sort of on loan to us from ISEC for a while then." She watched his eyes. Disappointment, and something else, shadowing in there.

She smiled. "Hey, I'm kinda swamped today, these damned screws took up too much of my time. Any chance you could help me out for a few minutes? I've got some stuff I have to find in storage."

"Sure." He looked relieved to have a reason to stay.

She led him down a corridor into a wide storage hall. Boxes and crates piled floor to ceiling in long rows. Part way down one of the rows they came to a large metal compartment. Kendra unlocked the door of the compartment, reached in to turn on a light, and stepped inside. Kai ducked his head and followed her through the narrow doorway. The low ceilinged space was about the size of his dorm room. Boxes with detailed labels filled the shelves that lined the walls on three sides. A bank of gauges occupied the fourth wall next to the door.

The room had a strange subtle feel, that he couldn't quite identify. Puzzled, he looked over at her.

"Electronics. Precision stuff. We keep it in here. The place has climate control, electromagnetic screening, the whole works. Safe from dust, moisture, magnetic fields, you name it." She shut the door and re-engaged the seal. "Safe from surveillance of any kind." She looked at him.

"How…"

"A completely shielded room. Multi layer walls. Built for some experiment. Testing subtle changes in electromag energy. Long time ago. We kind of inherited it. Seemed a good idea to have a place to keep stuff you wanted to protect." She waited for him to take in what the room implied, and then repeated for emphasis, "No surveillance sensors can reach in here, and no surveillance sensors in the room." She paused again, and finally said, "What did you want to know about your dad?"

His answer already in his eyes by the time he replied, "Everything, anything, whatever you can tell me."

"Can't tell you much. I did see him, just before he went over to the hover pad to meet the ISEC guy. Your dad looked pretty calm on the outside. You know how careful we all are these days...." She was taking a big risk with him she knew, bringing him here, talking openly, but his candid eyes, so much like Linn's, had made her want to be honest with him. "But.... I don't know, a feeling, under the surface, he couldn't talk about. I think he was uneasy, but ready to roll with whatever they had in store for him." She pressed her lips together and looked away. This time maybe she had gone too far.

"Yeah" he said, "Like my mom."

There it was, the chasm, the gap in his heart and in his life, longing to have a name, to have some tears shed over it too, she was sure of that. "Wish I could help you. Have you talked with McPhearson?" As soon as she said it, she realized how impossible that would be, to get McPhearson in a shielded place, to even hint at meeting. Dangerous for both McPhe and the boy.

"No, I...." He shook his head. "I was lucky this time. I've been wanting to come over here ever since I heard the news. They've had me under close watch after Mom.... I wish I had been able to see Dad more, before he...." His voice faded down.

Oh boy, did this kid need a hug. She took a chance and put her arms around his gawky height, but he recovered quickly, and gently pulled away.

"Thanks," he said, "I'm okay now. I've, I've learned some about how to survive."

"Expensive lessons, huh?"

"Yeah."

He still had something on his mind. Cautiously, another question, harder to ask, emerged. "Did you, I mean, do you, the flight.... since he never came back, I just wondered, if you, I mean, I wanted to know...."

"What I thought may have happened?"

"Yeah, something like that."

Poor kid, his mom basically disappeared, just two years ago, and now Linn. "Okay, you want it straight?"

"Yes."

"You sure?"

"Yes."

"I think the craft was probably sabotaged. Whatever happened out there, I think it was not an accident. I think they wanted him out of here, out of the way." She watched him.

He took a deep breath. "Thanks.... I've been wondering.... I've.... just needed to hear someone else say it, out loud." She waited while he looked into a bleak distance somewhere inside, and then he added quietly,

226

almost to himself, "It's barren out there, a rock, no life...."

"What do we really know? Outside sensors down. No radio trans. We don't know. There might be more out there than we know." She was remembering the shadow shape she had seen the day of Linn's flight. A glimpse of wings outspread, the silhouette sweeping quickly across the hover bay floor and all that it implied. Too soon to get the boy's hopes up just yet. She didn't even know for sure, the image so fleeting, so blurred. Wait until we know. For now his survival depended on dynamics inside the Lab. "Your dad was a good pilot and a good person. He would have done okay with whatever he met out there. You remember that, you've got a lot of him in you too."

They were both silent, retreating into their thoughts for a while. More words might take them past thresholds neither wanted to go beyond. One thing at a time. Finally she offered, "Well, I guess we're done here.... Can't stay too long anyway. If you'll take a couple of these boxes...." She gestured vaguely around the room.

"Sure, which ones?"

"Any of them, doesn't matter. I'll just return them later. I like excuses to come in here, gives me a little room to breathe." They both grinned again. Danger averted for now.

Kai carried a few boxes back to mechanics bay and deposited them reluctantly on the bench she pointed out to him, then he said, "Well, guess I gotta go."

"Thanks for the help."

"Sure, no problem."

He looked like he could use a friend, a real friend, not one of those nitwit security yahoos. "Hey, you scheduled any of your internships yet? You're probably destined for other things, but if you want to do a training stint with us, you know, to broaden your education, open up a few more possibilities, you're always welcome here."

"Thanks, we'll see." He started to walk away. After a few steps, he stopped and turned back toward her. "Thanks," he said again, and more softly, "Thank you."

"Take care." Same thing she had said to his dad, and she meant it just as much this time as before.

"You too."

"Hey, Linn? Hi, I'm Mike, Mike Aponetta." The boyish faced man with the big eager grin reached out to shake Linn's hand.

"No kidding? Mike the DJ?" Linn had heard only that a man from one of the other Labs who had been living with the People was coming to visit him. Mike had been the main comtrans tech over at Lab 5. His lively persona and cheerful banter on the air had earned him the nickname DJ.

"You bet, *Mike the Micropone*, Aponetta here, the one and only. Champion of the micro-airwaves, smallest transceivership in the world, the last voice of...." Mike stopped, bit his lower lip, and looked off into a private space all too familiar to Linn. Linn wanted to reach out to him but didn't know how. Still lost in his own far place.

Mike recovered quickly, abruptly upbeat again. "Wow! Linn Brenner! Can't get over it. I have to say, this is a real surprise, a real honor. When we heard you were with the project, we were hoping we would get you for our group. Lab 7 got a prize catch."

229

Linn grinned nervously. He ducked his head and shook his hair out of his eyes as he lifted it. Gestures that had seemed second nature and defining once, now feeling strange and out of place. The last thing he wanted as he returned to life again was his academic background following him here.

"Well, I don't think they were too impressed, mostly hard core number crunchers on our team. Felt pretty much alone there, mostly just me and my wife Miri, Miriam Allen, and Ed McPhearson." As he added Miri's professional name for Mike's benefit he struggled to keep the conversation light. Saying her name out loud didn't help.

"Wow! All three of you! Heavy hitters. Would have thought your team would have had the best chance of all of us, with the three of you on board."

Linn could feel a shift in the cadence of his energy as he talked with Mike, a shift he felt helpless to counteract. His mind speeding up, tense and brittle with a kind of mental breathlessness. Frantic inside. A texture so unlike the gentler way of interaction among the People. He looked at Mike and realized he was caught up in it too. It was like being back at the Lab, and they could both read the sadness in each other's eyes hiding behind the desperate rushing style so familiar to them from before. Like hyperventilating, running out of air. He tried to change the topic, turning the conversation reflexively back to the DJ again. "Hey man, you were the big celebrity over at our Lab. The great toothbrush drive for 5 was the only safe topic to discuss out loud after ISEC started running the show. You kept us sane there for a while as the walls were closing in!"

"You still had ISEC? We got rid of the whole damn internal security department early on, reassigned them all to something useful."

"Yeah, we tried that too, but we got outvoted and they kind of took over. Frogs in a pot, never noticed until it was too late." He found himself unable to explain to Mike just how thoroughly the Lab personnel at 7 had caved in to apathy and fear of ISEC, as if they had been entranced. "We were outnumbered, literally." He added lamely, grinned a bit, then gave up and let the bleakness show. No reason to hide it here, even in the grip of the Lab energy, but old habits die slow. Despite their hiatus after the crash, they had returned. He didn't seem to be able to resume personhood without inviting them along. "Miri's gone now. Couple of years ago."

"Gee, I'm sorry. I didn't know."

"Yeah." Not much else to say. He wasn't ready to go into details yet, and Mike had apparently been with the People long enough to develop some of their kindly sensitivity, despite his compulsive gung ho enthusiasm. Maybe that was just one of his habits from before haunting him too. Linn felt a sudden wave of kinship with Mike.

They were quiet for a while, then Mike reached out to Linn and hugged him. Linn hugged him in return, not quite as a long lost friend, but not as an academic icon either.

"Welcome to the People, man," Mike said. "Welcome home."

Then they could really begin to talk about what happened at their Labs. About how it felt to be with the People, the alternate ease and sense of being an outsider.

231

The awkwardness of trying to fit in. Mike's lab had been the one with the highest proportion of artistic profiles. Unlike the personnel at Lab 7, where there had only been a few hobbyists. And 7, Linn explained had had more than its share of so called "directive" types. Dictatorial would have been the better word for it by the end.

"They wouldn't have lasted long at 5," Mike laughed. "Just wouldn't have worked. Nobody would have listened to them."

What had worked at 5 Mike said was that with so many free thinkers on the team, they got curious about what was outside. "We opened the airlock, and found that the Earth was still alive. Transmissions from all the other labs had already stopped. No one wanted to stay. We left in small groups on foot. Most headed for the mountain passes back to the cities. A few of us went the other way, and the People found us, took us in. We're scattered now, among the village camps. As far as I know, Lab 5 may be intact, just abandoned as is. The last person to leave may have just shut the door and tucked the key under a nearby rock." Mike laughed. "None of us ever wanted to go back. From the People we heard that most of the rest of the Labs were in ruins, and that the largest party from 5 died in a snowstorm trying to cross the high mountains. The few of us living with the People, we're all that's left. None of us ever wanted to go back. That part of our lives was over along with the Labs."

"The People never mentioned 7," Mike said after a long pause. "I think it is Taibo'oo for them, alien, strange. It's a word adapted from the language of the ancient peoples, Paiute maybe, who lived around here long ago." He gestured vaguely toward the east. "The People have adopted some of their ways. That's how they managed to survive, hell, they did better than that, they live with a lot more kindness and grace than we could ever have imagined. Some of the old words came with the skills, helped the People orient to a new way of being in the world, new for them. Words are anchors man, nuggets for the mind to wrap around. They can hold you back, or keep you on the right track."

"Yeah, I know."

"Some woman who was with the People early on had studied them. Did ethnographic research, old texts, an antiquarian." He laughed. "Not quite, more than that. Practical too, she remembered a lot of what she learned about the skills and words and all. Lucky thing. She was instrumental in keeping the People alive I guess. Kind of like a saint now I suppose, in memory, in retrospect. Her source too, another woman, Wheat, Margaret Wheat. I remember that name especially, because of the Margaret part. I had an aunt once named Margaret...." His voice trailed away.

Linn knew then that Mike's prolific talent for conversation, his ability to fill all available silences with cheerful patter, was his way of trying to fill the chasm everyone here except the young ones seemed to carry inside in different ways. But he was grateful for any and all information Mike so willingly provided. The People preferred to volunteer information, which they did quite readily on their own time, and their ways of sharing and communication were so strong in them that if something was not being offered they were willing to wait patiently

233

until it was. With Mike, Linn's need for questions and answers, his own way of filling in the gap did not seem so intrusive.

Anyway, Taibo'oo was a word for the early settlers, miners, invaders, whatever you want to call them, us," Mike added wryly, "but the People use it now for anything from the toxic culture they escaped from. All the Lab ruins are Taibo'oo to some degree, even as they decay, contaminating just to be in contact with anything about them."

"Yeah." Linn said, all too familiar with his own share of Lab culture dogging him from inside. Mike seemed to know about that too.

"It was a big deal that they decided you were not Taibo'oo even though you came from there." Mike said. "That's one of the first things I heard about you. Came in a sky fish, but is not Taibo'oo." He looked at Linn. "Hey man, it gets easier, believe me, it does. Over time."

They were quiet for a while, then Mike said, "you ought to meet some of the other Lab refugees. There's Alavero, over farther to the east, he's from 3. And McNeil and Eskander from my group. We split up, helped us acclimate better, if no other Lab people were around to trigger the old patterns. Guess you noticed?" Mike smiled sheepishly, and Linn nodded.

"Anyway, I won't stay long. Then there is the woman from your Lab. The people found her held in a strange sleep, half dead, drugged maybe, her body dumped outside the Lab, something like that. Two years ago. Don't know her name. She never remembered who she was. The People called her Sleeps Like A Bear when she finally woke up, then they called her Lives Twice when she couldn't remember. Nice woman, from what I hear. Very friendly. The People like her. She seemed to fit right in." Mike laughed. "Maybe that's what it takes, to forget everything. She's over by the mountains, in one of the western camps. Probably snowed in by now, maybe you could meet her in the spring. You'd probably recognize her, maybe jog her memory a bit."

Mike looked over at Linn. "Hey man, you okay? Looks like you saw a ghost."

"Two years ago? Linn asked, "the woman?"

"Yeah, why?"

"Lab 7?" Linn was already far away, "you sure its 7?" he asked again.

"Yeah. You think you might know who she is?"

"Yes," Linn said quietly, "I think I know. She could be Miri. She died two years ago. Supposedly. We never knew for sure what happened." Suddenly he was sure it was Miri. He could feel it, he knew it. He had known all along. Hope soaring beyond all reason. He told Mike the whole story, about ISEC, the quarantine. "We never knew, we never knew," Linn said over and over, shaking his head, overwhelmed by a flood of grief and joy.

"Wow man, ask around, somebody can describe her. I've never met her myself.... you're sure?"

"I'm sure."

Mike could see in Linn's face that any kindly advice about not getting his hopes up would be too late, Linn was already off and running, way ahead. "Well, I'd better get going now. Just wanted to say hi and welcome. Maybe it's just me personally, but even though it works out better to be on our own, away from other Lab folks, I found a bit of news, from home, you know, so to speak, helped me out too. Guess your news was a bigger chunk than I meant to deliver, I'm sorry man, if I've made it harder for you."

"No, are you kidding? It's okay, is more than okay, I needed to know, about her." Linn said. "I would have wanted to know. And thanks man, for coming to visit me, I really appreciate it, means a lot to me." Still dazzled by his unexpected hope, he reached out to hug Mike. He was grateful, truly grateful, like living again. He hugged Mike with a warmth and ease that surprised himself. Maybe it does get easier.

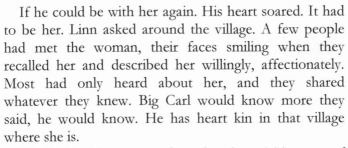

If he could be with her again. His heart soared. It had to be her. Linn asked around the village. A few people had met the woman, their faces smiling when they recalled her and described her willingly, affectionately. Most had only heard about her, and they shared whatever they knew. Big Carl would know more they said, he would know. He has heart kin in that village where she is.

Big Carl had been away for a few days visiting one of the western villages. When he returned that evening Linn asked him about the woman known as Lives Twice, and yes, the timing and the place were right, and the way they found her, her body dumped outside the wall as if given up for dead. ISEC must have retro fit the reclamation tube back to the space burial port it had been modeled on. Big Carl told him there had been other bodies dumped out from that Lab in the same way through the years, and that fit too, the disappearances. That's why the People kept a watch on "that place" as Big Carl called it. They hadn't been able to save the others, got to them too late. Miri, if it was Miri, was the first to live. They got to her right away.

"You sure she's your wife?" Big Carl asked again.

Linn was sure. The descriptions of the mysterious woman fit Miri perfectly. Even the connection with bears, and especially, the obvious affection anyone who knew her personally had for her. Miri was like that.

Big Carl seemed concerned, but Linn was too giddy with hope and relief to notice.

Finally Big Carl said, "She's up on the mountain, for the winter."

Yes, I heard that. Any way to get a message to her?"

Big Carl was quiet for a while, considering, too important to trust to words right away. Finally he said, "She never remembered anything about her life before, you know that don't you?" Linn nodded, and Big Carl continued, "she has a new life now…. a new life with another man."

Linn's shock was unmistakable. Ricocheting across his face, all through the lodge. Instant. Almost horror. Big Carl watched as his new friend went through rapid contortions of hope and fear, grief and joy intertwined, settling sadly on a kind of mute anguish Big Carl knew all too well from his own life and the lives around him from Before. His heart went out to Linn. "I'm sorry man," Big Carl said. "I thought you should know now, before you got your hopes up any higher…."

"Yeah, any higher, I would have crashed into the sun, if my wings hadn't melted first. Wings safe now," he tried to joke, but the bravado didn't hold. He turned away to stare into the buried coals of the morning fire, more bereft than he ever imagined he could be by the double loss.

Big Carl sat with him in silence for a long time, then touched him briefly gently on his shoulder as he got up to leave. "Takes time man, takes time. I've been there. Takes a powerful lot of time."

Forget it the black shirted man was saying, simply forget and reply.... Did he understand?.... Don't need my hat, he said, traveling light these days.... distance, distance to the epicenters of storms.... He was giving up. No matter what they asked him, no use to reply.... No one knew his real name.... Maybe someday, somewhere else.... not here.... not now.... Now you see it.... now you.... don't.... For him the passion had gone out, the radar did not lie.... and where.... and when.... not here.... not here....
Linn was awake now, abruptly, fighting to get free of the dream. Struggling up from the depths, fighting as if for air, fighting to get clear. The same intangible substance that kept him under now buoying him up instead, floating precariously. He felt so heavy, too heavy to be at sea, wanting desperately to land, wanting the kindness of gravity to support him underfoot again, not pull him down into a depth of sadness he could not bear to sound. She was alive. She lived. She was completely out of reach. Not living in the same world as his. Living in another time. Another place. With new memories. Somewhere he couldn't go. Not now. No way he could

join her there.... Somewhere she laughed and smiled. Somewhere she loved again.

He stopped his thoughts in midstream, almost praying to sink back into the jumble of his half remembered dream. Wanting only to sink again, anything but this. The ISEC thugs hadn't killed her. They had tortured her instead, set up an invisible barrier in her mind, an impassable divide not even she could breach. But they had let her live unwittingly. Had spit her out to die in the night, and impossibly, improbably, she had lived. Like the Earth, she had survived. The world still held the joy of her. Soaring, plummeting, riding the shifting declination of his grief, pulled by opposite tides, opposite sides of the same keen edge cutting through to his heart, cutting him apart. The People were kind, they would help him live again, as they had for her, as they had for the others who came to them bearing as great or greater grief. Crowded up as he was, pinned between his loss and his relief, grappling with his memories, it was hard to see. Which was harder, to start a new life over with too many memories or too few? Maybe he would see someday, same mountain, same path. Eventually, perhaps. Right now not even remotely the same trail. Mountain too far away to tell.

Big Carl had told Linn that Miri was with a man from a place on the mountain called the camp of the gazers, and that she had gone up the mountain with him just before the new snows closed the trail. There would be no way to reach her until the spring. The man she was with was someone with whom Big Carl had close affection. "Like brothers," Big Carl said. "From the wandering years," he added quietly, "we went through a lot together then." And so Linn had held back on his questioning out of respect for Big Carl's friendship, not wanting to impose on his loyalties. He asked around the village instead. Even then, he tried to keep his questions general when asking about the gazers camp, and about the gazers and gazing, not knowing if anyone else had connections there. Most of the people he asked said they knew very little about the gazers, even less about gazing, only that it was some kind of spiritual path. "Something from long ago, long, long ago." "Visions," one man said, "something about visions and light." "The heart of light, that's what they see," someone else said, a young woman who seemed reluctant to say anything further. She smiled shyly and turned to leave. As she left, she said as many as the others had done, "you could go see Old At'sah, she is the one to ask. She would know. Yes, she would know."

And so he took a small intricately woven cup, one of the traveling gifts that had come to him as the villagers had quietly welcomed him in the days after the council. "From my heart kin aunt," the soft voiced young man named Tommo Agai had said as he offered him the cup. "She is one of those with healing hands. May the touch of her hands in this comfort you. And may you find your own heart kin here among the People." It was one of the most beautiful exquisite things Linn had ever seen, and so he decided to offer it to the old one. I am learning, he told himself. Step by step, I am learning. He thought of Big Carl and Mike both saying, *it takes time*, and he smiled.

"Old Mother," he asked respectfully after Old At'sah had invited him to sit beside her, "I would like to know something of the way of the gazing path. I have heard," he said, "that it has something to do with visions and eyes and light."

She looked at him.

"....and I would like to know more about it."

She looked longer at him, her gaze open and steady, a soft unfocused look as if seeing him in some other way. Then she asked, "and perhaps more about the ones who gaze?"

"Yes, I would like to know that also."

"And I have heard," she said, "that the woman who was once your wife...."

243

Linn flinched at her directness, but he had asked. He nodded.

"I have heard," she continued, "that the woman who was your wife is among the gazers now."

"Yes."

"Perhaps it is about her that you really want to know?"

"Yes." Linn said sadly, "I am trying to understand what drew, what draws her there."

"Beyond the man who is also there?" she asked with her uncomfortable directness. She paused for a while looking into the embers of her fire. "She is there for many reasons.... not just that one she is with now. Many reasons...." Old At'sah finally said. "Like the others there.... As I was," she said, "as I was, long ago now."

Linn looked at her. "You were a gazer too?" He found it hard to imagine her in any other place but this village and her lodge, as if she was an ancient tree planted here so long ago it has no memories of other places, other times, her rootedness here a necessary part of her agedness.

"Oh yes," she said, her eyes filling with a luminous glow, different from the quicker sparkling brightness he had felt from her before. "And unlike some of the others who decided to stay, I came back to this place," she glanced affectionately around her small lodge, "when I completed the path. My place was here," she said simply in explanation. "There are others, who choose to remain with the mountain, who do not come down again to this life after they finish the path. They prefer instead to blend with the mountain's heart, a mirror of the blue-black depth of all.... For me, the mountain is also here."

244

She looked far away again and so surprisingly present at the same time. "Gazing," she said, after a long while, "is a way of going home," and for a moment Linn thought he saw, or felt with other eyes, Old At'sah dissolving like a vapor or a wave and then returning, "going home to the source of all that is. It is more than eyes and light, although they guide the way. The path is very deep, hidden deep inside yet it is also everywhere." She gestured all around her and then touched her chest over her heart tenderly. "Hidden especially here, in the heart."

Linn remembered Miri talking about weightlessness and saying *maybe they will meet up with God out there*. So quietly. I should have known Linn thought, I should have known, another light even then inside her playfulness, hidden behind the sparkling in her eyes, like sunlight on water riding on a different luminosity in the depths. In some ways he had known, and he thought he understood. It didn't make it any easier he realized sadly, just more real, no room for the slim hope he had harbored that she would return to a more prosaic life.

"Gazing.... like any other path, it is what you bring with you when you come to it, and sometimes, even more importantly, what you leave behind, before you do...." She looked at him. Her words hurt but her eyes were kind. She touched his hand with a finger knotted like an old tree root. She smiled. "It is the way of things son, son of the sky, sky's son, that things do not last. They are always arising, always becoming. Some appear to be beginning, some appear to be ending. From within the beginning before either of those arisings, they are already one. Everyone turns back to that beginning at some season of their wanderings. We are all wanderers in this life, and everyone at some point in time and space turns back toward the beginning of their wandering. Sometimes it takes many lifetimes. We do not know how long each of us has been wandering. Not everyone turns back to seek the origin at the same time." She looked at Linn with a great depth of kindness. "This I know," she said gently, "sometimes we have to say goodbye." She paused for a long while, then she said, "learn our ways, son, start learning our ways, begin again."

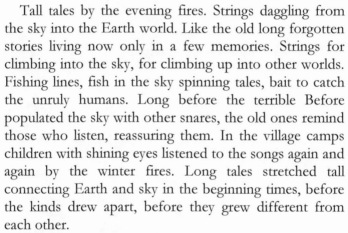

Tall tales by the evening fires. Strings daggling from the sky into the Earth world. Like the old long forgotten stories living now only in a few memories. Strings for climbing into the sky, for climbing up into other worlds. Fishing lines, fish in the sky spinning tales, bait to catch the unruly humans. Long before the terrible Before populated the sky with other snares, the old ones remind those who listen, reassuring them. In the village camps children with shining eyes listened to the songs again and again by the winter fires. Long tales stretched tall connecting Earth and sky in the beginning times, before the kinds drew apart, before they grew different from each other.

Winter sleeps was generally not a traveling time for the People or for news, especially in Mi'thal's village, the westernmost of the village camps except for the gazers farther up the mountain. A little more coming and going back and forth among the eastern camps, but even there at the lower elevations where winter tended to heavy rains rather than heavy snow, not much visiting. Detailed news of Linn's arrival had reached Mi'thal slowly, and it was a while before she heard more about the tall man who seemed to not be a Watcher after all. There had been some messages about the council, that a man had arrived in a Taibo'oo craft, and that he would be staying but that was all she knew until Big Carl on his last visit had told her more about the man who was not Taibo'oo. Mi'thal had felt a hint in his telling then that perhaps Big Carl had not yet seen, a subtle undefined warning, a crossroads, a choosing place up ahead in time. When she sent her heart to Ta'le and Lives Twice on the mountain as she often did, that warning was encoded in her calling whether she intended it or not.

I keep seeing Mi'thal, Lives Twice said. *She is holding up a big silver trout. I think she is wishing us well and reaching out to us.* She smiled. *I miss her.*

Ta'le had seen her too, and for him, so much more familiar with the nuances of his sister's calling, the note of unvoiced concern was also clear. A kind of warning in her call, something approaching on spring tides or nearer tides, here in winter, pulling closer, urgent enough in its own time. Which time, which silver trout, spring or winter, different trout run at different times. All he could do was wait and see. Whole lifetimes between then and now. Bears eat salmon, bears sleep in winter. The winter salmon trout are wise, they know when to brave the mountain to ride their own tides. He smiled. He sent the high drifts of the snow in reply, knowing Mi'thal's warning was for later, not quite yet.

Linn woke up in the night, a dream trailing after him. Darkness and bright fish, and faces rising from a great depth of water, swimming in and out of view then falling away again. A dream he has had before. A recurring fragment, searching there for something he does not know. For something beyond the dream. Glimpses of bright water, then darkness again. And the eerie persistent feeling that this was not his dream, that someone else was dreaming it through him or that it was a lost dream that no one is searching for.

Winter, a time holding the seeds of all the other seasons cradled gently together in the palms of its hands. Not the ripened fruit, the blackberries plump and juicy in purple stained hands waiting to be tasted. That was summer. Winter was the time of true beginnings, when things really start. The time of inward turning, listening for barest whisper of their coming into life. Autumn was when the ripened seeds fall to wait, another kind of beginning then, the beginning of waiting. And then the secret time, deep in winter, the quiet hidden time when the glimmer of all new things begins to rise, unseen at first, inside the silence. Outwardly winter was a time of remembering and planning ahead, basket weaving, story weaving, sitting by the fire, joking laughter and quiet shared. Held in the silence and whiteness of the snow or held in the soft drumming sounds made by the fingers of the winter rains. The smell of summer ripened herbs laid on embers of sleeping fires, lifting prayers up through the smoke holes into the winter world. A time of hope, and waiting patiently for the year to turn, preparing for new beginnings, treasuring the seed.

Alehya offered a few more dried herbs to the glowing coals of the evening fire. Mugwort and cedar for clearing, and for the kindly motherliness gathering all together. Herbs she had known since childhood now becoming closer friends, as the medicine elders led her further into the secret heart wisdoms of the plants. She smiled as the delicate curls of smoke rising from the coals spread a sweet pungent scent all through the shadowed lodge, seeping around and through the bundles of herbs hanging everywhere from the rafters of the lodge, wrapping around the baskets and pouches of other herbs on the shelves around the rim, wrapping around the sleeping forms of the elders wrapped together in their dreaming sleep, the aged man and woman becoming like the plants her deeper friends, her family during her stay with them in their lodge. *Thank you all my relatives,* she said in her heart, *for being family, for our belonging, all together.* She sat for a while enfolded in the peace of the night and the contented sounds of the sleeping man and wife, the patterns of their breathing woven together just as their lives had woven together through all their years as one life.

She considered again the difficulties in being in a relationship with Tomah once she moved back to her own village on the lower slope of the mountain. Far to the west. The distance that would be between them. Winter times. Traveling times. Waiting times. Waiting to come of age. Waiting for the choosing times. Waiting to choose, and choosing, if that was going to be her way. There were some, men and women, who preferred not to choose, not then, not for a while. Some for their whole lives. The waiting especially, she thought, would

251

be hard at times. Like in the spring when the men and boys would take turns sitting day and night by the rushing streams until the year turned, until the big salmon trout came again.

For her now, her waiting was full in other ways, drawing closer to the plants, learning the songs and stories from the old ones, playing with the village children. A good way. She would wait. Perhaps her heart had already chosen Tomah as it sometimes felt, as his heart had already chosen her, and they were both waiting for their bodies to grow into the decision. She smiled again remembering the sweetness of the moist warmth already between them seeking even deeper roots. She could wait patiently for the roots to grow stronger, waiting in their own time for the tree to bud and flower. And fruit. She caressed her slim belly, time enough to wait, time enough for that too, if that was going to be her way. *Cuando la distancia*, her old auntie, her basket kin, had said softly with an inward smile when Alehya had spoken, shyly at first, of her feelings for Tomah and about the choosing. And Alehya had seen in her auntie's eyes another inward private smile tugging at the old one's heart. She too had been young and waiting once, and waiting to choose. *Cuando la distancia*....

In the season when distance becomes sky, another elder had told her long ago when she was a child. She used to wonder about it then, when there were already so many things to wait for, almost as many as now. She smiled to herself. Only now the waiting and the wondering took you to things that shaped your life, things that put you on paths that could last your whole life. When distance becomes sky. She had gone up to sit on a ridge close to camp and looked at the rolling lands and the ridge crests and valley folds receding into distance in both directions, all blue, and changing like the sky, as if they were already one sky. And then there was a day in autumn, just as the leaves began to turn, the sun riding lower to the south at mid day and the blue of the sky so piercing, with a clear clean ringing sound as if the sky was shouting singing blue, and the blue ridge crests and the distance sounding the same way and she knew that distance became sky when your heart just knew when and where it wanted to go.

The moon grew full and waned and grew towards full again. The snows came and stayed. Layer by layer, the little corridors connecting the huts at the gazers camp grew more like white tunnels suffused with cool blue light. And all around the camp the starker brilliance of the mountain held in its winter sleep. As Lives Twice sat in the hut each day enfolded in the stillness and silence of winter and the gentle heat radiating from the coals of the morning fire and the stones around the fire pit, the expansive peace within her grew steadily deeper and brighter.

Like sitting in my heart, she said one day to Ta'le.

Yes, he smiled, *like that.*

Gradually she felt her heart blending more with a spaciousness that was also inside, the heart of the mountain she called it at first, then let it be, beyond words, a grace ripening. And one day the heart space opening, delicate as light, spacious as the sky.

Like sunrise in my heart, she told Ta'le on another day, as they sat together beside the evening fire.

The sky of your heart, he said softly, looking at her. He could see it in her eyes.

"The sky.... of my heart," she murmured aloud, feeling the texture of wonder even within the words.

Welcome to the mountain, Ta'le said. He had said this before, this was another kind of welcoming.

The mountain, she said, *is teaching me its ways....* They were quiet for a while, then she said, as if tasting the thoughts as they came into words, *the mountain is like the sea for me, it opens me, it opens my heart.... I am kin to the mountain somehow, in a way I don't yet understand. I have felt this before but this is a deeper belonging. I belong here more now. Maybe,* she hesitated, *not as a gazer, not yet.... That will take time.... You are all so....* She searched in the air around her for more words.... *all so immersed in that way I seemed to feel about you before I came here, but the mountain, the mountain is my real home perhaps. I do not know why.*

To be home, to be really home, is even more precious and rare, he said, *than even being washed clear. Yes, clear and at home, both together, that is the way....*

They sat quietly, drifting gently together then apart and back again, on bright tides riding up on different but overlapping shores.

When the sky of your heart meets the other skies, all one, no near, no far, all one, spacious, expansive.... Ta'le said at last, his calling dissolving unfinished, spacious as his words. Then he said very softly, "cuando la distancia, se vuelve cielo...." a whisper of a memory, from long ago. *When the sky of your heart meets the other skies all one, no near, no far, no separation, all one,* he said again, *that is part of the way home.* He kissed her forehead gently and smiled as he got up and went over to the alcove for his evening practice.

Cuando la distancia.... the sky of your heart.... Lives Twice sat within the glowing space of remembrance and recognition intertwined. And the next step perhaps, she counseled herself at last, will be to go beyond the memory, to go beyond the words that even now still evoked the wonder of it. The true sky of her heart, she was content to let that blossom of its own again, a grace, a gift.

Like the half shell of a robin's egg she had found her first summer with the People, the inside clean like a pale shell of pure unblemished sky. This one had hatched, she felt. Whoever had lived within that fragile shell, within that secret sky, had flown at last. She had given the shell to little Kibi, the wide eyed little boy so bright and quick, as if he was already one of those who could fly. He had cradled it gently in his hands with great tenderness, as enchanted by it as she was. *Cuando la distancia...*

Early morning class again. Kai studied the plass shell of the dome intently, the purple, grey, and blue tones of the silhouettes of the struts, the milky tones of the brighter panes just beginning to glow with the pale opalescent color of what passed for sky in here. Still an hour of the class to go. Another hour of the instructor's droning voice looming over our lives. He looked around the wide hall at the other cadets, wondering yet again if any of them were as bored as he was. Too dangerous to ask. Over two years he had been sequestered here in the program, two years marking the imaginary passage of the adjacent dome's shadow moving with the elusive seasons outside, gauging from the subtle changes of the bio-glow which hubs the shadow intercepted, which struts it aligned with or across, at which times of year. His high tech Stonehenge.

He had learned about the ancient monoliths, as well as about the seasons, in life science class. Ocean currents, weather, high and low pressure fronts, winds aloft. Taxonomy. Animals. Natural history. All unnatural history, of a world he didn't know. As far as he could tell, unnatural history inside too. Surveillance monitoring of a decreasing population all of whom had learned to mirror back expected behaviors while they kept their true thoughts and feelings out of view. No one real anymore. Too scared to live. A chasm inside. Geodesy, using math to find numerical points on the Earth's surface, to find the shape of the Earth, to map out where you are. Theoretically. The way he knew the world out there, the way they lived their lives in here. Imaginary, except for the passage of the shadow moving somewhere in real time. Today was the day the shadow would reach the highest in the early morning, would ride there each day for a week or so, and then imperceptibly begin to recede starting a little lower each day.

He considered the arched roof of his world. There was a subtle fuzzy dimming of the glow at the edges of the plass panes on the uphill sides on all the struts that ran more or less horizontally. As if another kind of shadow was building up there. They came and went this time of year. Did it snow outside? Was there enough atmosphere left to make snow? What was snow like? He imagined a world of cold whiteness. He had seen the archived holo images of rounded winter landscapes and close up scans of individual snowflakes. He knew cold, he had touched ice, he had read the science texts and the words of other more poetic writers evoking the experience of snow, but he couldn't really know…. The barrenness and the unknowness outside haunted and fascinated him, and he wondered cautiously where in that world of rock and stone and possibly snow was his dad? Another unknown. He thought he felt him sometimes, or maybe he only imagined him, a kindly questioning spirit looking in on him from time to time. His mom too, sometimes, but never at the same time. She was another spirit, looking in on him in a different way, more like a memory, farther away. "Forget your parents." The instructors had made it very clear, and he had grown even more careful at hiding those moments when he felt his mom or his dad close by. Sometimes it made him happy to remember his parents watching over him. Sometimes it made him very sad. He tried to keep busy with his studies. Not much point to anything anymore really, except just to stay alive. Somehow, that still mattered, he didn't know why. Somehow the fuzziness growing at the edges of the plass panes mattered too, and he didn't know the why of that either.

The days grew greyer, more shadowed with clouds, each day blending into the next, time blended together like the cloud cover. While inside the lodges it was a season of telling stories, of telling the tales that were sometimes the only way to tell about something in its truest way.

Linn, following Old At'sah's advice, went around the village asking for other kind of stories. The short kinds, he mused with a grin, not the tall stretched longing ones connecting with the most beginning times, but the short ones that connected the People with the land here now, the actual details of how they survived. He had a lingering feeling at the periphery of his thoughts that if he asked Old At'sah she would say the beginning times had everything to do with now, but for him, one step at a time. At the council he had heard a lot about why the People lived as they lived and the chronology of their wonderings. Now he wanted to know how they had survived, how they went about "unlearning the blindness, unlearning the numbness that let some look aside in the years of the Cleansing," as one man had said in the council. *Learn our ways son, start to learn our ways.*

Gradually he found himself more often at the lodge of the Basket Woman and her husband and her children and their friends and their relatives, a cheerful, bustling lively place in the quiet way of the People. And in the company of the Basket Woman and her extensive expansive family he learned the details of just how skillfully they maintained their disarmingly simple lives. A way of life upheld by a dexterity of fingers, hands, and eyes hard for Linn to comprehend at first, so far removed from his former world, along with the astounding directness of their connection with the land.

"Seeds," Basket Woman said, "we ate a lot of seeds." Linn had asked one day about what they ate during the wandering years, during the time of the sky eyes and the time of the dark blind sky when even the Watchers' eyes could not see through the sky, and especially, after they came to the Lab reserve lands and settled here.

"We ate seeds, we ate them parched and ground fine, we ate them cooked as gruel or shaped into little cakes we baked in the ashes of the fire," her husband said and they both smiled. "And we sprouted them lightly before we did any of those things, just enough to open the life of the seeds, to get the most from whatever the plants offered us. And in the time of the wandering, and the grey skies, and in the times when the seasons were still out of order, the plant kinds made many seeds."

Linn remembered how early researchers on climate change had found that plants reacted to even a subtle rise in temperature by making more pollen and seeds than usual, and he nodded.

261

"Yes, the seeds were prolific then, the plant kind responding in their own way to those turbulent times. We ate little four legged meat. The larger animal relatives were struggling as we were, but with the extra seeds the rodent kinds prospered. So did some of the insect kinds, the grubs and the larvae, and they were a lot easier to catch...." Basket Woman's husband smiled again but it was a grimmer smile, and brief. Although the People had survived the difficult years, it had not been easy.

"And the fish, the fish were prolific then too, breeding in greater numbers for the same reasons. We took only what we needed from the desperate generosity of those years, until the healing times brought balance to all the kinds again. And even now, especially now, always letting there be enough to seed the future, so the imbalances will not come again."

"We learned a lot from the bear kind about what to eat, not all their foods specifically, their digestion is different than ours! But the kinds of foods they looked for season by season, the foods of their spring famine especially, the foods of their waking up hunger, the shoots and early flowers and buds."

"And then the roots and grubs, the larvae and bulbs, nuts, berries, flower heads, inner bark of trees, and more young buds and shoots, and...."

"But not granite! Never granite! Our teeth are not like theirs...."

And Linn remembered Miri and their first meeting, and how she had told him that bears keep growing their teeth throughout their lives. He pushed the memory aside and found Basket Woman and her husband looking at him with such gentle understanding kindness that Linn had to turn himself away. Basket Woman touched his hand tenderly and Linn returned. "Yes, definitely, not granite," he grinned at last, grateful to be back.

"We searched out the springs for water that was less contaminated, drank spring water whenever we could."

"We were willing to adapt. We conserved our energy, careful with our actions. We learned what was strategic and what was not, what was too energy intensive. We kept our wants and needs to a minimum, and we found a grace there, perhaps a bit of the same grace the Ancient Ones lived by who were so much at one with the land and with the whole circle of life."

On another day Linn asked the small boys, Basket Woman's first grandsons playing happily together near the lingering warmth of the morning fire, asking them for a story about the People, about how the People came to live in this way.

"First the sky was very mean," one said. He made a fierce face and his brother giggled. "Filled with angry eyes." Then they swept an invisible shapes away from them with their hands.

"But the great fish in the sky waters churned the waters of the sky with his tail." They both made energetic churning motions with their whole bodies.

"And sent the angry eyes away."

"Then the People ate seeds."

"And they dug roots." Vigorous digging motions.

"And bugs. They ate a lot of bugs." They made big chewing motions with their jaws, eyes shining at Linn. "Yum, very good," they both said and patted their bellies.

"And then the bear."

"No, the bear came later."

"Then the other fish, in the waters here, came…."

"To feed the People," they said in unison.

"And so we live here." They concluded, beaming. A complete history of their world.

"Thank you," Linn said. "That is a splendid story. A fine story." The boys, delighted, went back to their play, moving small figures of animals and birds made of basket straw or carved of wood and bone. Whispering and laughing as they moved the figures around and held them up in pairs, the animals bobbing and nodding to each other in ardent conversation. Then they gathered all the figures in a circle for a council, with a tiny pile of twigs in the center for a council fire. One of the boys waved a small cedar frond for the blessing prayer. A perfect charming microcosm of their world, of the dynamics of the world they were growing into and within. As he was now….

"You are enjoying my grandsons?" Basket Woman asked. She looked over at Linn and smiled.

"Yes," Linn said, "very much," and Basket Woman looked pleased in a secret way that Linn did not understand, as she considered which of the eligible women in the village camps might be the one who would join with this tall stranger who was not so strange after all, and who clearly belonged within the circle of a family.

The day had been a busy one at the Basket Woman's lodge and Linn had been content to sit by the embers of the fire and let the energies of all the comings and goings and conversations flow over him. Later in the afternoon as all the commotion settled down, Basket Woman joined him by the coals. She smiled, as happy to have some quieter time as she had been to be caught up in the energetic livingness of her family. "And so, oh One Who Would Know Everything," she teased him affectionately, "what of my vast store of knowledge," she laughed, "would you like to know about today?"

And Linn smiling, happy to be included in the gently bantering ease that seemed to mark true belonging among the People, and happy that his questioning too had a place here, asked about their simple tools and belongings.

"We decided early on not to go with what some called the green technology, and concentrate on green living in the old way, real Earth living instead," Basket Woman said. "All the things we use and live with now, our clothes, our tools, all our things of daily use, all of them are made of plant or hide, feather or bone." She ran her hand across the smooth surface of her deerskin skirt and touched the fringe on her shawl woven of supple shreds of cedar bark, and looked thoughtful. "Maybe a thin sliver of rock for a knife blade or an arrowhead, a bluntly fashioned heavier stone set in a wooden handle for an adze, or a rounded stone that fits just right in the hand for pounding. Heavier stones for grinding acorn or pine nut meal are left at sites where they will be needed. In the old days, the Ancient Ones just left them in plain view. We keep them hidden now, but never far from where they're used. We didn't get rid of all the metal tools at once. We still had cooking pots and knives, axes, shovels, saws, spoons and forks for a while. We still had clothes made of machined cloth at first too." She laughed merrily. "They didn't hold up as long as the metal tools! Gradually we came to prefer the old ways and see the wisdom of their use. During the wandering years, a lot easier to carry a few baskets and a cloak that doubles as your bed than all the paraphernalia of even the most ultra light survival packs. At first it just made plain sense to not have to carry so much around, and to keep it light and flexible and easily repaired or replaced from materials available wherever we were. Once we learned to perfect the skills. Aiiii!" she smiled. "Basket making especially, is harder than you think!" She laughed. "Gradually we came to like the feel in the hand of the more natural things.... a willow stirring stick instead of a metal spoon.... As we adapted further we could clearly see how the objects themselves reflected, guided, even facilitated the habits of perception and life ways that were so obviously there, implied, encoded, embodied in even the simplest things."

Linn thought of the processes involved in refining and shaping metal to make a spoon, in contrast to the stirring sticks he had seen, willow bent when green into a graceful curve, the bottom of the curve sculpted through use to a thin flat edge. Spoon and stirring stick, each with an energy worlds apart from each other.

"The choices got easier and easier. We knew which way was home. In the refugee times especially when we realized how hard it was sometimes to distance ourselves from the destructive habits of the mind of Before, the simple tools took us by the hand," she smiled, "and helped us make the change. Each one becoming first a prayer and then a way to be, each one a teacher, a guide,

266

a friend." She ran her hands lightly, lovingly, around the rim of the beautiful basket at her side. "They carried more than water or acorn meal, they carried hope of a new life, a new way of being."

Linn was impressed with the range of her thoughts. Basket Woman seemed aware of his appraisal. "There are a number of us here among the People," she said softly, "who were trained for far different worlds than the one we have chosen here. Some of us made the choice early on to turn away and live in an older way as a prayer, before our simple ways became the only way to be, before it was no longer possible for others who had waited longer to choose, before they could no longer get away...." She looked beyond the fire, beyond the warm circle of her lodge to another time. ".... before there was no way anymore for anyone else to choose," she added simply, giving voice to the great sadness behind her words. She touched the rim of the basket again. "The simple tools, the baskets, they are good friends. Strong friends."

That night as Linn drifted closer to sleep curled warmly in his sleeping robe at Big Carl's lodge, he remembered the aged volumes of his great great grandfather's encyclopedia that had enthralled him as a child. An aggregated stream of knowledge and history cut off abruptly in 1952. He thought of the Lab, the encapsulated world of a different stream of time cut off at an arbitrary point in much the same way. Time capsules, both of them, and worlds away. No need to revive or review, except not to repeat the mistakes we, our whole culture, had made. He marveled at how the

People were bearers of a living knowledge of direct experience now instead. A knowledge of skillful fingers, skillful hands. Baskets, cradles, moccasins, arrowheads, sleeping robes, acorn mush, fire boards and spindles, cordage of all sizes, the miniature animals for children's play, and tools they needed to live by, flowing from those hands instead of numbers and letters. Slow walking, skillful feet, pressing so gently and lovingly the Earth at each step. In harmony with the land, caring for the land, just as the land also cared for them. Reciprocal. Reciprocity, the opposite of surveillance. Like Basket Woman's extensive generous family, the People were a living web of trust and openness that knows where they are and how each other are, even at a distance. The calling way, sharing thoughts and feelings voluntarily, not intruding, with a politeness and respect, natural, unforced. He wondered, the dolphins and whales, were they like that too? He hoped some of them had survived and were still living their lives in some deep sea refuge, free swimming, the calling songs of their kind traveling omnidirectionally through the watery depths, everywhere receiving knowing how to receive, discreetly tuning in only to messages intended for them, or were all messages, all songs, not just the ones in certain frequencies, meant to be heard by anyone, meant for everyone to hear, were there in fact any secrets in the trusting soundscapes of the deep for those who made the depths their homes. All one, the way all water molecules linked all waters into one water, many forms. All callings shared no need to listen in surreptitiously, the inverse of the Lab. Secret eyes and ears straining for secrets trying to stay hidden, or open secrets freely shared, weaving nets of respectful caring. The story he heard once of a dolphin who was outraged when a crafty researcher had a friend struggle in the water pretending to need help. The dolphin had apparently been upset that anyone would pretend in a world composed of pure resonance and reciprocity, for the dolphin at least. The watery depths the ultimate in transparency, another word the tricky human primates had misused in their rush to disrespect each other. He was surprised that the Earth, the Big Momma, as Carl would say, had even wanted us to stay around. Well, she hadn't wanted everyone to stay around, just the folks willing to live in harmony with her…. And he was chagrined once again at the arrogance of his former world, suddenly overwhelmed in simple thankfulness that the People had chosen a different way, and had welcomed him in.

Winter was a busy time for Alehya at the lodge of the plant elders. The three of them sitting near the embers of the fire by day in the gentle pool of light from the smoke hole. Pounding roots on small stones, cleaning seeds, sorting through dried leaves of herbs, bundling them for use later, and making teas for various ailments. Everyone knew some herbs and how to find and use them at need, but the plant elders had gone further into the ways of plants, and sometimes people just liked to reach out for a little help. A reassuring kindliness in return was as much medicine as the herbs. An illness could make a person feel isolated the elders said, sometimes the best medicine is to belong again. The plants know the way of this, and that is why they are happy to help. *Why just the other day, our good friend, that lovely Madrone, you know her, the grandmother one just past Old Uncle's lodge on the trail to the east.... Just yesterday, she was saying....* and they would tell another story or a memory or a song from the wisdom of the plants.

In the evenings sitting beside their fire, sometimes long into the night, with the soft glow of the firelight and the winter silence outside. Sometimes listening to the drumming of the rain, or the growing stillness of falling snow, and inside, blending with the quiet crackling of the fire, the elder's voices speaking as one voice, teaching her the story songs of each plant, shifting the stories hand to hand, like braided cordage two strands double wrapped becoming one voice braided together. Tonight she had asked about the bears, bear medicines, bear wisdoms. The elders smiled, *yes, the bears....* Their voices soft, from long years with the plants, with each other, so soft that both their spoken words and their calling were like whispers in her heart. *All the kinds have their own knowing, the plants that heal their kind, and some, like the bears, know more. The bears, they know the medicines, they know the plants, they taste everything, they know where the best stands grow, the tenderest. They know when to come back just when the berries ripen. They learn, the older bears teach the young, the young ones, they follow the old ones around, they learn and remember what they learn.* They both nodded and smiled approvingly. *They churn the earth, they plant the seeds with their droppings, very many seeds, very many droppings!* They laughed, sending Alehya an image of a big pile of bear droppings conspiratorially, as she laughed with them. *They fertilize the seed. Great fertilizers the bears! Their fertilizer is very strong.* More giggles from all three of them. *They scatter the bulbs, the roots. Plant tenders, the bears, like the People.*

"But we can't dig as much!" Alehya protested, blurting out loud and laughing again.

That night, she dreams of digging through the earth into a rainbow land. Tiny lights shining from all the plants. All colors of the rainbow, clear and bright, red, blue, green, yellow, pale lavender, and turquoise like the rare sky stones. Tall trees, with translucent blue light glowing from their trunks. Blue tree trunks glowing, translucent inside the blue light. Little flowers of light blooming everywhere. A small catlike animal with a crest of glowing blue fur. The next day, she tells Tomah, *someday I will take you there with me.* She smiles. He knows forever he would follow that smile anywhere.

The bear, full in her winter sleep, cubs growing stronger within her, weaving bodies of bear flesh cell by cell, their own inner seas drawing nourishment from hers, drawing nourishment from her vast sleeping form, from the tides of her breathing reflected in her blood tides, feeding them, supporting them as they grow floating in her fullness. Two cycles of the moon waxing and waning far away outside her cave darkened sleep, and then the cubs emerged from the vastness of the bear's body into the new gravity of their world. The bear, gargantuan, mother huge, the cubs so tiny, weighing so very little, only as long as her paw was wide. Eyes sealed shut, pushing in their blind darkness through the forest of her fur, seeking the heat of her bare-skinned teats, knowing only to be drawn to that heat, knowing only the finding. Cooing, chuckling, humming loudly as they nurse, suckling on her rich creamy milk hot from her body's heat pouring life into them. Milk rich with the wisdom and memories of their kind becoming flesh again. Bear's flesh, bear's bones, so tiny now, towering like newborn mountains in their hearts. Fearless, wide

273

roaming, snagging the quick silver fish as they leap. Each memory intact, secure. The bear rolling gently, offering her teats to them, a mother knowing ancient as bear kind, tending them at need from her depths beyond sleep or dream, nuzzling them as they nurse, cleaning them with her tongue, all substance reabsorbed back into her mother depths, all flesh one flesh, one body still.

Drawn to mother source in much the same way, Lives Twice in her dreaming finds the threshold again. The bear from within her mother hugeness, mountain and sky huge, worlds huge, feeling the presence of the sheling again on the threshold, goes to meet the woman who is closer now, but still not knowing why, as human kind, she is drawn here to the threshold of the bears.

The bear searches the woman's eyes, near and yet so far.

Why, the woman asks, *why am I here?* The woman's eyes so clear and open and yet still unable to see.

The bear sighed, no harm to try. *There are some*, she began slowly and carefully, *who can move between the kinds....* But the bear knows the woman will not remember, not yet, and she tells her instead, *you are not ready yet. You are closer, still searching, eyes sealed shut, but you have learned to trust the searching. Wait a little longer, wait and grow, wait until your eyes open on their own, they will lead you back to me. And you will see what it is that opens here. You will know the doorway here. Be sure to come back,* the bear raised her paw in blessing, *be sure to come back....*

In the morning when they waken, Lives Twice tells Ta'le, *I have seen the bear, this time I felt an opening, like a*

274

tunnel to the side, like the one I glimpsed in my long sleep, opening to a completely different life, not the shadows and the light of the one before…. This one, earthen smelling, sea smelling, ancient beyond human kind…. She looked wonderingly at him. *There is something that I am, that comes before what I do not remember of my other life in that place…. Wilder, freer, flickering, I touch it sometimes and then it slips away. There is no shadow keeping it away, something else, like a clear veil, I cannot reach through just yet….*

In good time, Ta'le said, *in good time, that is the way of things like that. The approach of grace comes in its own time. This only do I know for certain, and I have learned to wait and trust. The waiting and the trusting allow your heart to grow big enough to let the grace in. We are perhaps waiting for a different grace, you and I, or maybe the same, but the waiting and the trusting are all the same, all one.* He sighed and looked at her tenderly, no way to steer it even if he wanted to, grateful for whatever time together the grace gave to them, allowed in them. *And so,* he smiled, *little bear, for now would you like some acorn mush?*

Cedar and mugwort. Summer dried herbs laid on winter coals. A column of moonlight reaching down through the smoke hole from the winter night outside. A blessing scent drifting through the stone hut and rising in languid curls through the wide band of milky light, as the gazers gathered in the hut of Ta'le and Lives Twice. The full moon night outside overflowing with brightness from the swelling light. Stars receding, dissolving like the smoke prayers into the lambent darkless night. Clear and still, the strength of mountains and time and moonlight all melting into one seamless ephemeral blessing.

"We are gathered to celebrate, let us begin at the beginning...." the soft voice began, more in the calling way than words spoken aloud, sounds translucent and delicate as the moonlight and as luminous, brimming with unseen light. All fourteen members of the gazer family counting Lives Twice had gathered here, the small group filling the small hut with a vastness tender as the mountain night outside.

There had been a lot of good natured laughter at first, as was the way of gatherings in the village camps below, mixed with the faint sounds of crowding and settling in, pressing close together, bumping up against each other. Now their being together settling deeper, within the familiar joy of the practice they shared. Fathomless as the great roots of an endless sea, the joined stillness and luminous depths grew stronger, strength of mountains, openness of sky, drenched with the beauty and tenderness of their arising, hearts all one within a primordial grace.

"In the beginning...." the sea swept voice, other voices joining in.... people who rarely spoke aloud speaking in voices closer to breath than words, their words carried in pictures instead, through the calling that overlapped the words of voice.

"In the beginning...." More voices joining in, now one voice of many tones like colors bending together into a circle of rainbow light, as piercingly sweet to her heart as the reason for their gathering.

"We are gathered to celebrate two on the path of becoming one....." The words, the voices, the moonlight and incense herbs, the hearts joined in one intent, all embraced within the fullness of the mountain night. "....the union of this man Ta'le Tommo Agai Waits for Rain, our brother all these years, with this woman Lives Twice Sleeps like a Bear, our sister on the homegoing journey, to honor and celebrate their coming together as one, and we tell from the old stories, the ones that speak to the tone of origin within each of them leading them home, as it leads us all."

"In the beginning, a story, shimmering, a light filled light bodied beginning, each part self similar to the

277

whole. Parts not separate. Except for their delusions, which come later. The first trick, the first self lie, that parts were greater than the whole, that they no longer belonged. The downfalling out of soft time, recurrent, recurving time, into exile in history, into before and after, exiled from now. History, never ours, some of us still tell the stories of the belonging in other ways, history, the story that does not dream anymore, too fixed, exiled from the many seeded many eyed fertile rich becoming running circles around time."

"First earth, first sky, pressed together, horizonless, to the edgeless endless ends of their union. No horizons to the circle of their flat pressed all. Water heavy cloud heavy air waiting. Earth and sky slowly pulling apart. Fertile rain soaked mist their longing. Rainbow soaked promise of return."

"First man first woman roaming the flat water soaked brown growing land, brown tundra grass, sea brown moss and lichen under bare sea feet, fur colored, curling between curling toes. Four feet, two together, walking upright in the widening space between earth and sky, stepping in each other's footsteps so an earth sky space does not grow between them. Earth and sky pulling apart reluctantly, their longing, the rain. Sea drenched land. First tears. Distance growing, blue toned, first born of first color, all color, hidden in the misty water fertile air, hidden in the longing rain, the tall growing rain, spanning the growing space between earth and sky. First man first woman moving upright with the tall rain. First wind roaming, pushing, pulling, prodding, stretching the longing space, stretching the

278

*longing rain. Windblown rain, the tall stretched longing,
slanting, billowing around first man first woman in their
wandering. Their longing horizontal between them, first
man first woman fertile moist hands clasped together,
rain drenched rainbow promise they would not be
parted."*

*"Wet wind, sea smells, cold fertile air. First bear
roaming the same rain soaked widening space between
earth and sky. Her longing omnidirectional. Her longing
the moist air, the wet earth strong under her feet, four
feet, two together each side, meeting earth. Her longing
the wind roaming filling her. Her longing the water
heavy air. Wind ruffled fur. Her longing her roaming,
her longing everywhere. The where horizon stretching out
with the wind. Mountains, forests, horizons of where-
stirred lands. Sea scents. Heat of fur warmed sleep, cave
dark, long sleeping. Her longing all of these. And
always the great longing, deep in her long cave darkened
sleep, first dream, beyond sleep and dream, the first
remembering, earth and sky coming together again,
surrendering the new grown distance between them,
returning to the horizonless flatpressed all.
Omnidirectional, like the bear's longing, full of fertile
possibility, remembering the first moist rainbow graced
becoming at the first birth of the radiance."*

They sat in silence for a while after the telling of the
story songs, and then the gift giving and the blessings
began. There was no room to get up and greet them
individually, so gifts and blessings were handed through
the crowded hut from one gazer to another to Ta'le and
Lives Twice, gathering hands and blessings along the

way, along with some teasing banter, a blessing of its own. The gazers were surprisingly easy and free with each other. They shared the same playfulness as the village people did, only here the playfulness was rooted in the joy of their practice. They gave themselves to the play of being together with the same completeness they gave to their practice Lives Twice felt, with an unencumbered innocence like the children of the village camp, or like a flock of tiny birds, so buoyant, so light and quick…. She missed the children, the gazers were the children here perhaps, children of the heart of light, and yet so completely at one with the vast silence and solemnity of the other side of the mountain's heart…. Her own heart filled to overflowing, Lives Twice looked over at Ta'le and squeezed his hand, too filled for words, for more than this simple gesture between them. The moment so complete, their bonding within the witness of their friends, their family. She wished Mi'thal could be here, but she knew she was, she was there with them, within their hearts. Both she and Ta'le had called to Mi'thal to include her, and Lives Twice was sure that she was close.

The gazer family sat in silence again within a great inwardness, the vast luminous shore of their practice. Lives Twice felt herself drawn by their combined energy in the same way she felt when Ta'le practiced in the alcove. She was inside that vast inwardness where they lived too, swept by the same and different tides, all shells of light resting there, rocked in the glowing tides lapping gently on the shore.

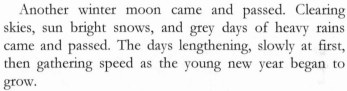

Another winter moon came and passed. Clearing skies, sun bright snows, and grey days of heavy rains came and passed. The days lengthening, slowly at first, then gathering speed as the young new year began to grow.

Fertile water heavy air came up again from the south, bringing new snows to the mountains and in the canyons and valleys below, strong rains and stream banks and creek sides filled to overflowing. Muddy water churning exuberant and loud, foaming and curling in all the cataracts, and running in tiny rivulets across the land carving miniature canyons and valleys in its path. Covers were pulled over the smoke holes to block the rains. Fires were banked. The thrumming music of the rain loud even in sleep. Everyone in the villages hunkered down in their lodges, finishing the winter baskets and arrow shafts, making cordage, repairing nets, making gifts. Working quietly with hands that had learned to work on their own in the shadowed interior of the lodges even darker now on these rainy days with clouds hanging dense and grey close to the water soaked earth.

281

"We must get all the animals to dry land," the children said, taking all their small animal figures of straw, wood, and bone, gathering them together in the circle of light glowing faintly on the lodge floor where the rainy daylight filtered through the cover of the smoke hole. And then all together, voices overlapping breathlessly, they would ask the old ones, "tell us the story of the man who rode in the big boat with all the four legged relatives...."

"The one about when the waters covered all the lands...."

"And there were only the fish, the great fish kinds...."

"Who lived in the deep...."

"And came up and saw the boat...."

"And when they saw the boat with the animals and the man, the fish led them to the mountain...."

"And then First Bear crossed the waters in another place and met them there...."

"And the wingeds who live in the sky...."

"Came down to join them on the mountain, and...."

The old ones laughing, eyes shining like the children's eyes. "Eh! Eh! You are doing a fine job of it already, the story telling. You don't need me. Great tellers of great tales you all are. You have told the story to me already!"

"No! No! We want to hear you tell it again!"

And the old ones laughing, "very well," and the children would grow silent, and those who work in the shadows with their hands would smile silently and listen too. Then an old one would begin in a voice from far away, the story voice, coming closer. "In the beginning times.... and which beginning, you might ask?" The old one pausing dramatically for a moment to wink at the children already enthralled, and then continuing. "In the beginning times, long ago, in the very first most beginning times, before there were mountains or waters or blue sky, when everything was stars and night, so many stars that there were...." And the children with their eyes bright inside the shadowed lodge like the stars on that first bright night inside the blue black darkness before time listened in familiar wonder.

McPhearson kept himself to a casual pace as he walked down the long tunnel to the mechanics dome. He hadn't been over here in a long while. Too long. A visit was way over due. He had been meaning to check in on the crew ever since Linn's flight. Couldn't put it off any longer. He had to find out in person something, he admitted to himself, he wasn't really sure he wanted to know just yet, nothing he could do about it even if he did. But now the other issue had made it imperative.

"Hey!" Ken called out cheerfully, "long time no see."

McPhearson was caught suddenly off stride by the exuberance and warmth of her mile wide smile. Hard to do the formal business as usual routine inspection thing he had carefully planned out as his cover today. Wasn't going to work, not with that big smile right in front of him. Hell, it was good to see her. Should have come over sooner. He had forgotten what fresh air felt like. All he could do was grin sheepishly back at her.

"For what urgency do we owe the pleasure of your company after all this time?" she asked sunnily. "Thought maybe you had forgotten us. Except for all that paperwork, all those forms and requisitions in triplicate you keep descending on us, we'd never know," she added, playfully chiding him.

Subtlety and subterfuge were evidently not a big concern over here. The circumspect world he lived and worked in over at the big dome could be light years away. No wonder Kai wanted to come over here. Would do the kid some good, in a lot of ways. McPhearson wished he could get himself assigned here too, but even so, ISEC had a long reach…. "Just checking to see where all that paper I send you goes. I hear the work load has been piling up…."

Ken was about to defend her crews' efficiency, but there was a caution in his face and she waited.

"Thought you could use some help," he grinned.

"The more the merrier," she said easily, but there was a question in her eyes.

Not so removed from subtlety after all, just played it differently over here, McPhearson noted with satisfaction and relief. Kai would be in good hands.

When he didn't answer the unspoken question, she added, "always enjoyed having you around. Where do you want to start?" She gestured expansively at the piles and carts of equipment in various stages of disarray and recovery all around the crowded work bay. "We could use an experienced hand like yours."

"Not me," he shook his head, wishing very much that it was him. "Cadet internships are coming up soon. I got a request from one of the cadets," he pulled a folded piece of paper out of his pocket and pretended to refresh his memory, "a Kai Brenner." McPhearson kept his voice non-committal and routine. Something he had sadly become very good at of late. "Just wanted to see if you could use him, if you thought it would work out." He had seen a flicker of warmth in her eyes when he mentioned Kai's name, but she quickly hid it and was now carefully matching his lead, both of them neutral, just short of formal, a supervisor conferring with an administrator. Objective. Serious. She must have recognized that the stakes were pretty high and had accepted it without knowing the details.

Ken feigned a thoughtful considering look and said at last, "sure, we could use him. I met him briefly a while ago. He brought some equipment from training over for repair." She waved one arm around the cluttered shop. "Guess he must have been impressed?" She shrugged her shoulders and said, "go figure. But we sure could use some help. Plenty to do around here."

"Alright then, I'll go ahead and okay his request."

"He's welcome aboard."

"Great, it's settled then." He ceremoniously refolded the paper and put it back in his pocket.

As he put the paper away she said in a lighter tone, "and hey, as long as you're here, how about you pushing something else besides requests and requisitions around for a change?"

"Sure," he grinned. "I could use the exercise."

She rolled her eyes theatrically.

Now that they had successfully navigated their way through Kai's request and kept the more dangerous implications out of view, they were both lighter again, shifting easily into the playful bantering mode McPhearson wistfully remembered was the norm over here.

"You can start here." She pointed to a tech cart piled high with boxes. "You wouldn't want to help me with a bit of inventory would you? Right up your alley."

"I'd love to,"

"Be my guest." She swept one arm toward the cart with a flourish, as if ushering a visiting dignitary. "I've got some stuff to put back in storage and pull some other parts." She produced a list and waved it enthusiastically as she led the way. "You ought to see what's going on over here from time to time anyway. Saves me from having to file another of those damn reports you keep asking for." She grinned. "Hell, do you ever read the damn things?"

"Nope." He grinned back at her, "but they look good on my desk."

She laughed and made another theatrical go figure gesture in mock exasperation.

McPhearson appreciated her breezy no load freedom. And she was good at her work too, even better at trouble shooting than he was. No one better.

"We're here!" she said grandly as she opened the air lock on a sealed compartment.

"Hey, is this the famous Franklin box? The zero mag shielded room we had to build for Franklin and her team?"

"You bet. The very same. We use it for special storage now. Have a look." They both climbed in. She shut the door behind them and reengaged the seal. Then she turned to him. "Now, what the hell is really going on?"

"The kid," McPhearson said, "He's in danger. Not sure exactly what kind, but I've got a feeling. We've got to get him over here as soon as we can. With both his

287

folks gone now, I'm guessing ISEC is really hammering on his mind, and if he won't be hammered into their idea of a proper shape, I don't know what they'll do with him...."

"Take a guess,"

"Yeah."

"Don't worry, we'll take good care of him over here. How soon can you get him assigned?"

"Next week at the earliest, I think. That's when the internships start. I think they would rather have him closer by under their wing, under their, ah, concerned and watchful eye...." He rolled his eyes. "But now that Kai has asked, for some reason they are still trying to look benign and accommodating."

"Ha!" She snorted expressively. "My hind foot."

McPhearson grinned approvingly. Just the sort of colorful turn of phrase he liked to use. "Maybe they're just afraid another familial coincidence so soon would blow their cover.... So I decided to come over, check out the, ah, work load and all, make a case for how you could use him specifically. I hear he's got high stats in math. A whiz kid. Like his folks." He looked down for a moment, then continued. "Learns fast. Have to tailor the help you need just for him, so they don't send another goon, or even worse that bland little weasel Richard James back over here."

"Let's see, we got that big job, just came in, you know the one, reconfiguring the whole whaddayoucallit system for crop management. That should be crucial enough, with all the 3-D printers going caput for good this time. Lots of numbers, sensitive calibrations.... we sure could use his talents specifically enough for that. Sounds like a done deal."

"Great, now, what the hell happened to Linn?"

She told him what she knew and what she suspected. And about her conversation with Kai, and how that bland little weasel as McPhearson had called him, although she used a much more explicit pejorative, had handled the final flight prep, and about the replacement solar battery sent over by ISEC. McPhearson muttered something incomprehensible at the mention of ISEC, and then they were both quiet for a while. Even in the shielded room, hard for either of them to voice the obvious.

"Funny thing though," she finally said. "Another strange thing happened that day. Damnedest thing...." And she told McPhe about the shadow of the hawk she had seen on the launch track cam just after Linn took off.

McPhe stared at her and shook his head.

"Yeah, I know, me too, hard to believe," she said. "I thought at first it was the shadow of the hover, but it was a real different shape. I called up the image on replay, didn't make sense, but sure looks like a bird.... The cam was angled low to the floor. Outside world only a thin ban of bright light at the top of the screen. Tried to make sense of that too. Couldn't make out anything. But that hawk got me to thinking, might be time to try to have a look around outside. And so," she said with an overly innocent grin, "I've got a little project going on sub rosa, in the sub basement under tech. Checking the pipes, for the record. There's lots of pipes down there.... Going to take a while," she grinned proudly. "The

289

circuitry for just about everything in tech is down there. Working on setting up an override on the locking mechanisms they put on the emergency hatches in the launch bay doors when the Lab was sealed. The ones in the outer doors, our window on the world…. Working on a few other things too. We need to be able to block all the sensors in the vicinity of the hover bay for starters when we open the hatches, and, along with that, we, ah, found the old ganglion for all the data monitoring. All that feed used to be routed through us in the beginning, remember? Data was a tech job then, make sure the systems running smoothly and all, before those bastards in ISEC had the whole shot routed through them. Well, the circuits are still in place, just bypassed. We're working on a little rerouting of our own on this end. All the cables are still there, haven't needed to use them for anything else yet…. Don't imagine we will now." She grinned. "Seemed like a good idea to have a way to switch the whole thing back to tech when the time comes, if the need should arise…."

McPhe lifted his eyebrows, eyes wide. She stopped and looked at him. "No, please," he said, "please, do continue…."

"It's slow going, can't afford to draw attention. May take another three months, maybe four, setting up the tape loops for ISEC to watch takes time. Have to be very careful. But here and there we store up another business as usual segment to use later…. And I've got one or two people down there, in the tubes we call it, whenever I can." She smiled broadly at him. "After all, you authorized it, the work order for the pipes, remember? Yes?"

"Yes, my hind foot," he said admiringly, "my hind foot indeed.... Maybe I ought to go down in the tubes myself, check on the work," he grinned.

"Maybe not just yet? Maybe better if you just happen to show up on the day we crack open the hatches? I think we can arrange that...."

McPhe had been indulgent and skeptical at first but he said little and had been willing to hear her out. No matter how dire things were getting inside, and they were getting pretty dire, the image that might be a hawk still seemed a tenuous reason to go to such trouble and risk. She had been straight forward with him, let him know just how grainy and blurred the image was, hadn't tried to dress it up, make a better case for it. She was the best trouble shooter, she had a level head and she was thorough. If she had a hunch, he had learned to listen to her. Still it seemed farfetched, the shock of it, the enormity of what it would mean, if there was life out there.... More than anything, he hoped that what she believed was true. He was running out of patience and energy for dealing with the Lab. He had a feeling he understood why Linn took the chance he did.

"So...." she said, watching him wrestle with it.

"Sure, count me in," he said at last. "Hell yes, count me in, wouldn't miss this for anything. Come hell or high tide, count me in."

She burst out laughing. "You never cease to amaze me," she said.

"You too kid, you too...." he said shaking his head again and smiling, then he was quiet for a moment, almost somber. He hated to break the mood, but remembering Linn had brought it up and he felt he had to say it. "If there really is something out there, then Linn…. if he were still alive, you'd think he would have tried to contact us by now…."

"What would he do, bang on the outside? Break a window? The damn plass shell is impregnable, designed to withstand impacts in space. Nothing gets through, not even sound, the layers are like an acoustic baffle. Not even light gets in, not real light, just the transfer…."

"Yeah, guess so…." Then his natural optimism returned, "for all we know he could be camped out right on the doorstep waiting for us to open the door. And that," he grinned, "would be all the more reason to try to take a look…."

But there was still an unspoken shadow of concern for their friend in both of them. In the time since Linn had been gone there had been a winter in that unknown world outside.

"Hard on Kai," she finally said, and they were both quiet again. Life in the Lab was like that, a heaviness pulling down even when you most needed to believe that you could fly. "Well, that about does it," she said changing the tone. "Don't want to spend too much time in here, folks might get curious." She gathered a few boxes at random off the shelves.

"You take good care of the kid for me, he's…. he's family."

"I will," she said, "I promise I will."

He knew she would do whatever it took to keep Kai safe. "And you be sure to let me know about those pipes," he said with a grin, feeling more reassured than he had felt in a long while about a lot of things.

Heavy rains came again and passed. Clearing skies. A brief rain shower in the night. The muffled roar of the swollen creek already subsiding. Buds at the tips of branches just beginning to quicken. Linn had found a relatively dry place to sit under a cedar tree, the morning sun angling through the trees warming him. He breathed the fresh rain washed air, luxuriating in the presence of the trees all around him.

He remembered the absence of windows at the Lab. No distant horizons, no witness to the world outside, no way to orient yourself to a larger world. No comforting Earth below, no sky above. And despite the other very thorough details of the elaborately staged simulation of space travel, there had been no provision for space walks, no space suits. Would have challenged the illusion of being adrift in space to be drifting with trees instead. Then the trees supposedly gone too, adding more layers to our basic premise, a lie from the start. He thought of all the absences, the blank spots, the gaps in collective memory required to maintain a lie, a fiction of belief, and why any direct experience was so inherently hostile to the intent of any lie. Threatening. Destabilizing the whole process. Heretics more dangerous than cheaters, he remembered from a pivotal essay read in a philosophy course years ago. Heretics challenge the premise of the whole game, often invoking another superseding matrix of values, while those adept at cheating are still playing in the game, just being more creative, "skillful," with the rules when they can.

At the Lab the bottom line was always to maintain the lie. Again he felt the urgency of needing to bring the Lab down, to end the lie, not just of simulated space travel, the whole premise of being set apart, the pretense we were immune to cause and effect in our great superiority. Maybe it was the pretending that got to us too in its own way. If you believe a lie long enough, nothing is true. Assuming everything to be a lie, suspecting everything, hoping desperately for a glimpse of truth. How many other lies, besides the little daily ones, the ones necessary to survive at the Lab, had he been unwilling to question or challenge, privately or openly? Sometimes the biggest lies were the hardest to see, the ones that had the most people believing them. Our whole cultural history…. the choices went back a long way….

He had always wondered why the cave paintings stopped so abruptly, replaced by the abstractly patterned, presumably counting stones. Did the crafty brutal Cro-Magnons annihilate most of the painters and assimilate the few who managed to survive. Leaving ancestral traces in out genetic pool, a lingering sympathy, a lyric grace in participation with the natural world. A way of being that seemed alien after a while, so far removed from the techno contriving world of our most terrible future dreams. Some part of us still in the caves in reverent wonder. Rest of us ploughed under or on ahead. Miri had been a secret partisan for the Neanderthals for years. Recruited him for the cause. Following the academic debates, reading scholarly papers when they could. The repeated re-dating and reattribution of the cave paintings, crediting the Neanderthals at last. So obvious to Miri long before. If it hadn't been bears for Miri, it would have been Neanderthals and their haunting witness of Paleolithic grace. Or maybe elephants, or whales. Monumental grace of another kind. Linking them all, an intelligence other than our conniving, seizing manipulating minds.

He sighed. What initiates in history real patterns of change, and when, and how, the genuine inruptions that destabilize whole sets and provide the nucleus around which new ordering and harmony begin to coalesce. Sometimes for the better, sometimes for the worse, depending on your point of view. Usually from the periphery, around the alien, the new. Cro-Magnons last time. This time the outsiders were a different new, or maybe old, the pendulum swinging back? Or was there yet another way, unimaginable to him just yet. The People were certainly making a good try of it, especially with the younger generations. What would happen when the lingering weight of the whole Watchers' world view was finally and for all time lifted from the Earth. How would the collective energy feel then.... Something humans had not felt for a long, long time. The radical. The radiant. The point of origin of light. The point at which a new cohesiveness begins to grow after the chaos of an older system breaking down. The willingness to

295

challenge prevailing notions of gravity, to draw new ground under your feet, to have the courage to follow a different gravity, more ancient, an older gravity of the heart. Drawn by the personal weight of a moral or cellular choice, the courage to trust in free fall on the way, what does it take to make a change. Where does it really start.

He sat quietly, letting his thoughts settle into the open space of their release. Arriving always at the same place, the soaring arc of his thoughts returning, where? Riding the joy of discovery, rising with the high, all for landing in the same place, the same, and different each time. The openness without a name. The morning light gentle on his hands. The smell of the air after the night rain. Water weight of cedar boughs swaying in slow motion, pendulous and fluid, like sea plants. The radiant was here. The Neanderthals got it right. How to undo thirty or forty thousand years of genetic tyranny, how to touch our other collective memories and let them live again and grow. The People were well on their way, he still had a lot of catching up to do. His thoughts soaring again, searching for another glimpse of truth....

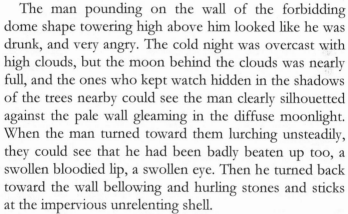

The man pounding on the wall of the forbidding dome shape towering high above him looked like he was drunk, and very angry. The cold night was overcast with high clouds, but the moon behind the clouds was nearly full, and the ones who kept watch hidden in the shadows of the trees nearby could see the man clearly silhouetted against the pale wall gleaming in the diffuse moonlight. When the man turned toward them lurching unsteadily, they could see that he had been badly beaten up too, a swollen bloodied lip, a swollen eye. Then he turned back toward the wall bellowing and hurling stones and sticks at the impervious unrelenting shell.

"You miserable excreants!" the man roared. "Scum eating bottom feeders! High handed pissants! Nonmotile encapsulated pathogens!"

The ones who waited in the trees watched the man, bewildered by his string of colorful profanities. A few of his words they understood, but most words were incomprehensible to them, and some portions of his speech were indistinguishable even when he shouted at full force as he was doing now. They could not imagine

297

anyone inside that strange place could not hear him. Perhaps they would know what the words mean. The ones who waited wrapped their cloaks more tightly against the cold and looked at each other.

What do we do with this one? The older man asked. It was his first time here.

I don't know. We never saw one like this before, the youngest youth replied. *But the People have agreed that if the Taibo'oo spit them out, then they are not Taibo'oo, and they may need our help. That is why we wait here when we can…. But this one,* he gestured toward the man, *he seems very wild….*

It is the ones inside that place who are Taibo'oo, the ones who spit their people out, the other youth said as if trying to reassure himself. *Not this, not this one, he is….* They all looked over at the loud man careening back and forth in front of the wall like a fighter taunting someone in a fight.

"You miserable excreant!" the man roared again. "Come on, come on, you virulent pustule on the hind end of a…." His voice trailed off. The ones who waited never found out whose hind end, because the man was finally running out of venom and stamina, running out of angry heat.

His body was growing cold, bone cold. No heat left to fuel defiance any more, no heat left anywhere. He stumbled around in circles, kicking blindly at the ground, muttering to himself. Finally collapsing in a heap, mumbling. His litany of curses growing fainter and fainter. Barely noticing the hands wrapping him in soft fur, coaxing him to his feet, and one on either side leading him away.

When a neighboring village camp sent word that another person had been spit out of Lab 7 and "very much alive this time," Linn rushed to speak to the messenger overcome with a surge of emotions swirling beyond his grasp.

"Very, very much alive," the boy said with a grin. "You'll see." He has been asking about you already. He said if I saw you to tell you, 'the fearless one is back.' He said you would know what that means."

"McPhe!" Linn shouted. Ecstatic beyond his craziest hope. He could hardly believe it. "McPhe! No kidding! McPhe!" The boy smiled broadly, pleased to have delivered the message accurately and pleased at Linn's obvious happiness. "When?" Linn asked eagerly, "How? How long ago?"

"A few days ago. The Tai.... the soul eaters, the ones who suck out the souls of their people before they spit the shells out, they didn't get much of this one's soul I think.... Aiiii! The ones who keep watch, the ones who found him, they say he must have put up a big fight inside, kept going on the outside too for a while.... He is more like you, yes? They didn't get your soul either before they spat you out." The boy looked admiringly at Linn.

Linn felt the ground soar under him and sink away at the same time. McPhe was out, he was alive, completely unexpected, unforeseen. He would have news. He was okay. He remembers me. The aching and the longing he felt in relation to Miri suddenly even more piercing. Despite the boy's well meaning assessment of Linn's "escape," expulsion and exile were more like it, that shadow always there. The soul eaters had not exactly sucked out Linn's soul, maybe tricked it some in the end, but the soul that mattered most to him had already been taken away when they took Miri, and her memories. Bitter, and sweet. His mind swung back to McPhe and his heart surged again. To see someone who remembered him, who could connect all the parts of his life, McPhe was out! They could laugh and joke again. He was alive, he would have news, Linn could ask about Kai, he could…. a thousand questions clamoring, and he would have a friend who already knew him well, someone with whom the bridges had already been built. He had not realized how alone he felt despite the kindly, genuine friendliness of the People. How alone he felt to be without someone with whom he already belonged. "How soon?" Linn asked breathlessly, "how soon can I see him?"

"Soon, we will bring him to you soon. As soon as he recovers from his injuries, and his, ah, exertions. Don't worry, he's fine," the boy assured him when he saw the concern on Linn's face. "The injuries are minor really, and he is well pleased perhaps with the struggle he gave them. He just needs to get his bearings for the trail. You'll see him soon," the boy repeated," Hard to keep you two apart I think," and the boy smiled. "I need to go back to my village now, do you want to send him, your friend, a message?"

"Yes," Linn said, marveling at how easily, how naturally, the boy had said the words *your friend.* "Yes, I do, tell him...." so much to say he was wordless, not knowing where to begin. "Tell him, welcome back, welcome to planet Earth."

The boy smiled. "Sure, I'll tell him that," and then he was gone.

E R McPhearson struggled to orient himself to his abrupt emergence into a new world. Even though Ken's hunch that there might be more than barren rock outside had been enticing, had raised hopes he didn't even know he had, still it had been a shock, along with the suddenness of his confrontation with ISEC. At least it hadn't been the full Committee, and not the worst of them. At least he gave them one for one, maybe better he grinned. Left a few black eyes himself back there. Didn't know he had it in him to do that. Damn, as Ken would say. He just couldn't take it anymore, and when they tried to shoot him up with their "persuader" drugs he had gotten really mad. They weren't used to anyone fighting back apparently, caught them by surprise. Took all three of them to stuff him in that damn tube kicking and bellowing the whole way, then whoosh, and he was in another land. Shift too big for even the most obvious one liners from his extensive inventory. Like waking up inside a dream. The world as you thought you knew it no longer real. And Linn was alive too. As soon as McPhe got his sea legs back again, his hosts had said they would take him to see Linn. He could hardly believe it himself. Welcome to planet Earth indeed. For now all he could do was recuperate and try to go about fitting in. "In good time," his hosts said. "It will be good to see your friend in that place where he lives now, then you will know how the way of it is, the belonging again."

Which brought him to the subject of his names again. What to call himself here. What persona would it indicate. Despite his induced drunkenness from the small bit of the drug the ISEC thugs managed to get into him the night they spat him out, he still felt he was on a coherent trajectory as a person, just that everything around him had changed. Like being on a high speed train, you are the same with new worlds zipping by outside. He still felt like himself and more than a little proud of the fight he had put up. The villagers too, at least the young men. Word seemed to have gotten around. He hoped they did not expect him to display such prowess again anytime soon, or ever…. What he really needed was a way to fit himself into his new world. And for some reason he had fastened on his name as part of the transition. What to call himself here. How to answer the friendly but confounding question he got from everyone, how are you called?

He had a feeling that the People did not approach names in the same way as at the Lab, and that for them names grew out of how you were, rather than a persona that needed to present itself. But he couldn't shake the need to decide somehow who to be. He needed a pivot point to orient himself around. He considered his given names.

For him, Ed had always been someone else. Ray was someone else too. He couldn't relate to either of his given names. Edgar? Edward? There had been at least one illustrious Edward in history, and one in particular that he admired, a courageous, articulate, principled man, but McPhearson could never see himself living up to that. Edwin? Edmonton? Good try. Raymond? Rigel? Regulus? He liked the last two, especially the night sky reference. His enigmatic first names. Subject periodically to section betting pools, open season on best guess. In the good old days before ISEC took over. Not so often in the later years. Main strategy was to figure out what name he would most want to suppress. He never told his names even then. Each time they would have to choose the winner by lottery, and he would get hilarious messages for a while addressed to his newly decreed nomes des plumes he chuckled to himself, deliberately mangling the words.

He considered his other options. To himself he had always been McPhearson. Had no idea why. It just fit somehow. Sometimes he was McPhe, pronounced with a long *e* as in *the* before a word beginning with a vowel, as a friend majoring in English once explained with mock severity, delighted with discovering the "McPhearson rule." Not much uncharted territory left in English grammar and linguistics in those days, not until they started analyzing and codifying informal histories of the abbreviating trends of techno, text, and meta speak. McPhe. Sounds like *McPhee*, sounded as *e* as in *tea/ tree/ sí/ key*, as in be free and McPhe, as in McPhe in 3-D, as in me and McPhe. Got as much mileage as his names. McPhe had grown out of the swift flourish of his casual signature, and out of his friends' affection for him. So long ago, couldn't remember when. Was always there. Like Ken, that was always her name too. Some folks were like that. He could live with it. Never asked why.

Who would he be here? Too soon for a friend name, but probably still McPhe. McPhearson, although casual sounding to him after all these years, would that sound formal here? Although he had met a Daniel the other day. The name McPhe had a whole history with it, a community. This was a new life, new people, a new time. Would seem awkward to presume the use of a friendship name too soon. Despite his relief at being out of the Lab, he was still disoriented, hard to shake the shadowed self concern that had been so necessary there. Especially as the rush of his run in with ISEC wore away. He could feel his old habit of shyness from his early years stepping forward to take over its protective role again. Different pool, fish out of water still. But these people here, the People, quiet and careful as they were with their presence on the land, sure loved to smile, sure loved to laugh. The kids especially. He grinned, caught himself reflexively, remembered no sensors here, and began to let himself really laugh for the first time in long years, his laughter rolling through him uproariously, exuberantly, spinning him around from inside, dancing in a circle, waving his arms, laughing with the trees all around him, laughing with the huge sky overhead. Fish out of water just found the sea. Be free and McPhe.

"…. and then there's the lead ISEC thugs, Kerac and Hammond, that makes all six of the 'Committee'." McPhe bit down derisively on the word. "Mean sons of bitches both of them. Along with the rest of the inner guard. All of them." He had been counting on his fingers. He flashed his hands twice, palms open fingers wide apart, and looked at Mike and Linn. Linn had clearly recognized the names. Mike was concentrating on making sense of yet another round of details about the twisted internal dynamics at Lab 7. Every Lab was built identically, so he had no trouble picturing the layout in his mind, but the personnel had been very different, and he was trying hard to keep all the names and events straight. McPhe continued, "I don't know how those last two goons would fall out if it came to actual fighting, but if they feel their command is being threatened, I wouldn't trust any of them any farther than you can shake a stick."

McPhe loved colloquialisms. He collected them. Had a capacious memory and a showman's delight in deliberately misusing them. The more obscure and misapplied, the better. Especially the outdated ones with no reference left for them in the circumscribed world of the Lab. Colorful and huh? both at once. He loved popping them into conversations on oblique angles at the Lab and watching mental wheels strip their gears. Like that shake a stick one. Out here in the real world, a lot of those idioms not so farfetched anymore. A lot of sticks out here too, and with the possibility of fighting growing more real if their plan actually went through, sticks may be all they had to shake. Sobering. Linn's eyes had filled with laughter at first at his old friend's wit, and Mike had gotten it pretty fast, but now they were all silent, considering McPhe's assessment of the ISEC team.

Then Mike spoke. "Well, let's just hope for the best."

"And plan for the worst." Linn and McPhe said gleefully in unison. All three of them laughed.

Linn and McPhe had already spent several days catching up on each other's stories, talking late into the night. McPhe was staying with Linn at the lodge he shared with Big Carl, and the first night Linn had tried to apologize to Big Carl for keeping him awake, but Big Carl only smiled affectionately and waved him away. "Hell no," he said, "I like the glow. It's good to see old friends reunited. That's precious in this world of ours. Talk to your heart's content. Just be sure to bank the fire," as he rolled over, burrowing into his sleeping robe pretending loudly to be asleep.

And they had talked, and talked, until their hearts were content. As content as either of them had felt in a long while. McPhe had Linn go over all of the details of Linn's flight and the flight prep before the launch several times. The first time Linn got to the part about Richard James, McPhe muttered, "Never liked that little weasel. We kicked his butt, so to speak, back into some tape loop job over at ISEC HQ, as they call it now." He rolled his eyes. "And Ken will do her damnedest to keep him from poking his little nose into mechanics again. Now that she has Kai to look out for." He grinned.

That was the biggest and best news. Kai's internship had been approved and he was safely under Ken's wing. "Which reminds me...." and McPhe told Linn about the shadow of a hawk Ken thought she saw right after Linn took off.

Linn looked away for a moment, and then said, "I thought I heard a hawk's call too, right after the hover was in the air. Actually I heard hawks calling all through the flight.... the eyes of the land I guess."

McPhe looked at him. Linn denied it and claimed he was still an outsider and ill at ease among the People, which is some ways maybe he was, but McPhe could see a change in him. The way he talked, his voice softer now for the most part, and the things he said, the perceptions he shared, different, all colored subtly by his living here. Linn kept telling McPhe it gets easier as if he didn't quite believe it, but his manner more than his words convinced McPhe that it was true.

And Miri, that was a hard one. McPhe couldn't imagine what Linn had gone through, was still going through. He felt frustrated that he couldn't help his friend. "Not even Kai?" he asked in disbelief. "She doesn't even remember him either?"

"No, well, I guess not. The People said she never remembered anything."

"Those excrable sons of bitches...." McPhe started in and then recognizing how hard Linn was struggling to keep a distance on his feelings regretted his outburst and his asking about Kai. "I'm sorry," he said, "sorry it all came out this way, I really am," a nebulous acknowledgement of just about everything. "Must be hard, man. Must be very hard."

"Yeah," Linn said and looked away again for a moment, this time with tears in his eyes. Then he looked back at McPhe. The tears were still there but now he was smiling too. "I'm glad you're here," he said warmly and hugged McPhe, catching him by surprise. Then Linn grinned at him. "No sensors here, compadre, we're free. Home, home on the range."

And now the planning for the Lab rescue plot was in full swing. A spell of bright clear weather overlapped with McPhe's visit. Mike had come over from his village just to say hello after the long winter and had been surprised and delighted to find McPhe there. After introductions and catching up on all the news from all three sides, they were finally getting down to brass tacks, whatever the hell that meant. Like dead ringer, McPhe mused to himself, had to go back pretty far to get to the roots of that one too. He had tried to explain dead ringer once to a young colleague at the Lab who didn't even know about bells. No bells at the Lab for starters. Just electronic buzzers or synthesized sounds carefully designed to produce alertness with or without varying degrees of alarm. Then there were the cemeteries and the pewter drinking mugs to explain. Oh well...

"McPhe? Hey, buddy, you still here?" Linn asked.

McPhe grinned sheepishly. "Gathering wool," he said, and then, "No, forget it," when Mike and Linn groaned. "Yes I'm here, very here, all over the place...."

They were all in a playful buoyant mood from just being together, just being at ease. Somehow McPhe's goofy unconventional wit helped lighten the Lab energy Linn had felt with Mike when they first met, maybe because Linn and McPhe had known each other for so long that their familiarity was contagious, and Mike was a good guy at heart. He had a natural ease and friendliness too, now that it showed, and he fit right in. Hard for any of them not to feel optimistic. They fell naturally into discussing ways to liberate Lab 7, a topic never far away for Linn, and one very much on McPhe's mind now.

McPhe explained everything Ken had told him about her idea to open the hatches and her project in the sub basement including the alternative data for ISEC to watch, and both Mike and Linn had been impressed.

"All that for a maybe shadow of a hawk," Mike said admiringly. "She must be some trouble shooter, probably could shoot an arrow in the dark and still hit the target. No wonder your Lab is still afloat with folks like that on board," he said almost wistfully.

"A blessing and a curse I guess," Linn said. "Trying to keep a dead horse alive so long, zombies tend to get a bit twitchy over time...."

They were all quiet for a while.

"Okay, back to the beginning, first things first," Mike said at last. "They are trying to get out, we want to help them, let them know we're here. Let them know the People are here, the Earth is here. How do we contact her, Ken, it's Ken, right? How do we contact her and her crew inside?"

"Well, for starters, we could tap on the wall," McPhe said and was met with general merriment.

"Aw, come on now, get serious...."

"No, I mean it," McPhe said. "Ken, she mentioned once that codes fascinated her as a kid. No, I know we can't tap on the plass wall but if we could find some other way of transmitting sound into the Lab, if we could...." He paused dramatically.

Linn grinned, "you have an idea I presume?"

"Well," McPhe said with the practiced gesture of a stage magician, "Ken has people down in the sub basement as often as she can. All the pipes run down there. And one of those pipes," he paused for effect again.

"Here comes the rabbit," Linn whispered to Mike.

"....leads outside," McPhe said in triumph. "The emergency vent. The one concession to our possible well being, in case of complete air systems failure. In theory. Sealed just like the hatches. Not many people know about it. Just a few of us in tech. I don't think Ken is thinking of opening it, too small to crawl through, no way to take a look outside, but it comes up above ground somewhere in the woods nearby. If we could find it we could tap on it. Tap for a while, different times of day. Sooner or later, someone will be down in the tubes when we do, and they will hear it. Voila! I don't imagine there's much surveillance down in the sub basement to begin with, and I'm sure Ken and her crew have, ah, made adjustments to any that might be there, so no chance of being overheard. We'll use something basic, like Morse code, couldn't possibly be taken for a natural sound, like a tree branch in a breeze or whatever."

"Yeah, but don't they all believe it's barren rock out here, you know, alien space worlds, tooth fairy, and all that?" Mike asked.

"Not Ken," McPhe said. "She already has a hunch there's more out here than they know. She won't be too surprised I think if we try to contact her from outside. Shocked maybe, at first, to have her hunch confirmed like that, but she has a level head. She will know how to deal with it appropriately. We have a good ally inside if we can get a message to her."

"How does she communicate about it with the others? I thought the whole rest of the place was hardwired for surveillance 24/7? She can't have everyone trooping down there."

"Ah!" Linn and McPhe both said theatrically. Linn made a courtly bow and waved grandly for McPhe to proceed. "You have the honor."

"The Franklin box," McPhe said mysteriously. "No, not Old Ben," he laughed. "Doctor Alvina Franklin, a woman with our project. She and her team were testing subtle changes in electromag energies, needed a completely neutral space to work out baseline on her equipment. We built a small shielded room for her in the basement level under the research dome. She was, ah, rather particular and precise about how she wanted it constructed as I recall. We built multilayered walls so no transmissions of any kind could get in or out. Then we had to haul it over to mechanics when they didn't need it any more. Hell of a project. Barely fit through the tunnels. Had to slide it on rollers, some Egyptian pharaoh's bright idea up in research." He grinned at Linn. "Worked though. Took some time. Ken uses it to store temperamental electronic parts, and for thinking out loud when she doesn't want to be overheard, she calls it doing inventory. A couple of people at a time can fit inside. Once she gets a message, no problem organizing the mechanic techs. Inventory is conveniently routine. All the regulars in the mechanics bay will come on board willingly. They're fed up too. Once the whole crew is organized, Ken could manage to get as many other people over to the tech dome as would want to come out, if she knew we were here. That's our biggest problem. Right now she's working on opening the hatches just to look around," he emphasized. "We need to get to her before she does, make sure she knows we're out here, the People are out here. She needs to start thinking bigger picture. How many others can she get out. Once she cracks the hatch we'll only have one chance. All hell will break loose once ISEC figures it out. They're not going to want to let anyone leave. They, ah, will want to stay in control. We'll only have one chance."

"How soon do you think Ken would be ready?"

"She said three or four months. That was a month ago. I'd say we have two months minimum, three if we're lucky. Once we make contact, she could start reaching out to other folks who might want to leave. Call a volunteer work crew coordinating meeting or something. That will be the hardest part maybe, but she's pretty resourceful. Careful and thorough too. The others…. well, there's bound to be some she can't reach. Can't see a way to get everyone, we can hardly…."

"Yeah."

"If they would even want to go…."

"I know, I know…." Linn was frustrated. They would want to go. They would. He knew it. They would all want to go if they knew. The clarity of it, the simplicity. *If only they knew….* a lifelong frustration. Sadly he realized McPhe and Mike were right. Concentrate on the ones Ken could reach and who would be willing to take the risk.

"Okay, but we'll need a way to get more complicated messages in to her."

"How about a message in a bottle?" McPhe asked in apparent seriousness. In one of the trash tubes."

"There aren't any."

"Well technically, yes, not functioning ones at least, but they built the Lab to be an exact replica of the core of one of those big space cruisers, as close as they could get on land, especially from the inside. Everything except antigravity. Built the trash tubes then sealed them on both sides. You know, kind of like the old fashioned milk chutes…."

"The what?" Neither Mike nor Linn had heard of them.

"Must have escaped the encyclopedia," Linn said with a deadpan face.

"Antiquarians you're not," McPhe sighed in mock exasperation. "Sometimes there's a use to all that memorabilia stuffed in our collective attics."

The other two rolled their eyes and cuffed his shoulders.

"Hey stop! C'mon guys, get serious."

"Anyway, they're sealed and too risky," Linn said. "A message in a bottle, a milk bottle," he grinned at McPhe, "who knows who might pick up the milk. The Morse code thing is better. Safer, more targeted, and we'll know right away when she gets it."

"Radio." Mike said in a far away voice. He had dropped out of the conversation for a moment. "You want old fashioned. We would need very, very low range transmission, pinpoint, targeted precisely to one area, not scatter wave. We could get Ken's attention with tapping, yes, but say we send messages short range radio trans after we contact her…."

"How would she pick up?"

Mike didn't answer at first, busy trying to figure out how to make a short range radio work. "Very, very short range," he said again as if talking to himself, "if we narrowed the band way down… targeted it to a specific receiver….bounced it through the pipe….of course they'd have to disconnect the pipe where they are….so it doesn't travel any farther, into the rest of the Lab…."

Linn and McPhe grinned at each other. "How would she pick up?" Linn asked again, "

"A tin can on a string…." McPhe said hopefully.

"A handset, a simple handset. We drop it down to her through the pipe." Mike said. "I could reconfigure the transceiver and a set. A matched pair."

"We would need some serious hand tools to get the vent cover off," McPhe said. "Not to mention a way of acquiring a handset and the transceiver…." They both turned to Mike. "You didn't by chance happen to bring anything like that with you when you left 5, you know, for old times' sake?"

"No, but maybe we could go to 5 on a recon mission…."

"Sure, sounds like a great idea," McPhe said with enthusiasm. "You said your team left the place intact, there must be loads of equipment over there we could make use of...." Linn was conspicuously silent, and Mike was suddenly quiet too. McPhe looked at them, puzzled by their apparent hesitation.

Even though Mike had made the suggestion, both he and Linn were clearly cautious about this recent product of their collective brainstorming. The two of them had been living with the People long enough, especially Mike, to absorb their concerns about the Watcher lodges.

"Pretty risky," Mike said at last, "the Taibo'oo thing and all.... but there might be some equipment at 5 we could use if we can resurrect it.... As far as I can tell, the only way we can get complex messages to Ken safely would be to see if we can get some equipment.... The Lab was just mothballed when we left, not trashed or damaged.... We could try...."

"We just need a simple short range..." McPhe said encouragingly.

"Well, at least 5 wouldn't have the same ghosts of meanness lurking around that 7 will leave behind from ISEC.... Actually, 5 will feel quite different...." Mike said, slowly coming around. "Sure, sure, there's bound to be something there that we could salvage...."

"....and jimmy rig for what we need...." McPhe said delighted that the energy was moving again and at being able to use another vintage aphorism.

"....and I guess we could work out the logistics of any other bright ideas we come up with while we're over there, all the Labs are built the same...." Linn added, and they grinned at each other.

"Troublemakers," Big Carl said shaking his head and laughing. He had been sitting quietly nearby in the circle of soft light from the smoke hole as he worked on a length of cordage, rolling reverse wrap strands together on his thigh with skillful rhythmic motions. He went back to working on the cordage after beaming at them affectionately. He did not seem too concerned about the idea of a recon mission to 5, and he had already made a few suggestions from time to time about their other plans. His comment was more like the teasing of a genial co-conspirator

"Okay." Linn said, "with that in mind, what about getting ourselves in too, when it comes to it? That should cause trouble enough, ISEC doesn't exactly have a welcome mat out for unexpected guests. "

"The hatches. Ken's working on that already. All we need to do is coordinate with her…. and we'll need some kind of ladder on the outside…."

When it came time for Mike and McPhe to leave, they ended with bright hopes, heartened to have spent time together, heartened at the progress of the proposed rescue. It seemed feasible. First the plan, then they could figure out how to implement it. The planning was well underway. One step at a time.

Big Carl had grumbled playfully from time to time that having the three of them around was like living with a bunch of unruly bear cubs, but he was happy to have had them there. "Livened up the place," he said. He seemed to be enjoy the plotting. "You're going to bring this to council sometime aren't you," he reminded them one day. "We do everything that way here, remember?" And he smiled. Hadn't seemed too concerned about that either despite the daring nature of some of their proposed activities. He seemed to be conspiring on his own at times, and would only wave them away good naturedly when they asked him.

Big Carl had also explained to McPhe why it was the way of the People to spread out new refugees among the various camps. Along with helping everyone acclimate to each other, it kept the burden of providing for the refugees from falling on one village alone. Although the burden was a welcome one, usually a village would only be able to absorb a few new people at a time. They would need to have enough food especially to take care of them for as long as it took the newcomers to become contributing members, so much to learn at first....

Linn realized with a shock that he had never really thought about it, the generosity of the People had been so spontaneous and natural. He had arrived at the beginning of winter when the harvesting and gathering times were over for the most part, and so just how much was involved in gathering the resources that sustained their lives was mainly abstract to him. "Oh no!" he said to Big Carl apologetically, "I never.... you, and all the People, have been so kind, so generous with me.... There seemed to be an inexhaustible store somewhere from which everyone drew...."

"Well, yes," Big Carl said with a grin, "in a way that's true, there's Big Momma out there, Momma Earth, she provides everything we need, we just need to do a little active receiving on our part...." He grinned. "And as far as the villages, it is our way, everyone contributing to the best of their ability and receiving according to their needs. Works out pretty well, a balancing.... And don't you worry, I don't mind," Big Carl reassured him, "we have plenty this year. And by next year you'll all be helping out, you'll see, Mike knows, you'll want to, it's part of belonging here, it pulls you along...."

And so the three musketeers as McPhe called them, parted in high spirits, with a lot of hugging and plans to reconvene again soon weather permitting. All in all, the tone of their meeting was encouraging and upbeat, and they had still had plenty of time in between the plotting to share more of their observations and memories and just about everything else from their childhoods to living with the People now. All their combined years at the Labs and their lives before, winding their stories into a little ball of coherence with each other that made each of them feel secure after so much uncertainty and starting anew. Mike had left his Lab willingly. Linn had had everything torn from under him abruptly, and McPhe had had his anger at ISEC and the explosive freedom of his drug induced drunkenness as a temporary bridge when he suddenly found himself outside. All three had struggled to orient themselves in countless ways. Survival skills, they called it, and McPhe asked Mike and Linn endlessly about the ins and outs of it. And when he found a bowl that was just his size, as he said, he ate it up.

Mike and McPhe left to go back to their villages. The village that had taken McPhe in when he was first spit out of the Lab sent a messenger to accompany him on the trail home. The village had made it clear to McPhe before he left that he was welcome to stay with them as long as he liked. Although naturally wary of such energies, they were also proud of the fight he put up against the behemoth shape of the Watchers lodge, especially the younger men. His battle was apparently the topic of a lot of hilarious and popular stories there, and like Old Uncle with the joking that inevitably followed him around, he delighted in it, and that in the end had decided it for the villagers. They were not any more eager than McPhe for him to repeat his outburst, it was his good natured joy that they welcomed in.

Linn was surprised to realize he was actually relieved to see them go. Tired of the dizzying pace of the conversation, the wit and the humor. The giddiness was too much after a while. He could see even more now why it was helpful to spread the refugees out as Big Carl had said, helped everyone, refugees most of all. And he knew he would be thrilled and happy to see them both again too, just not so much all at once. A harmony, a balancing.... He was learning, he mused, the quieter slower pace of the ways of the People. Perhaps as McPhe said, he was becoming one of them more than he knew.

He also understood a little better the wisdom of making sure one village camp did not have to provide all the resources to support a group of refugees, especially a large group, like the one they hoped to bring out of the Lab. That would be a big consideration at the council Big Carl had said. "Feeding them all at first, and where will they all stay?" A council to decide on the rescue would have to include people from each village if possible, or at least runners from each who could relay the news and considerations back and forth, so everyone would be included in the final decision. "We don't believe in representative democracy," Big Carl said. "The representative part leaves too much out. Any decision affects everyone, everyone should speak their hearts and know that they are heard. Takes a while sometimes, and a lot of patience, as you no doubt have seen...." Big Carl smiled, "but the acorn and pine nut harvests were strong last fall, we still have quite a reserve, and if we wait until the salmon trout run this spring and if they run strong too that will be a good sign. Then I think we will be able to make it work," and he smiled again, more like a fellow conspirator than ever.

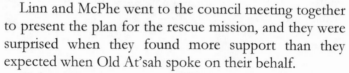

Linn and McPhe went to the council meeting together to present the plan for the rescue mission, and they were surprised when they found more support than they expected when Old At'sah spoke on their behalf.

"I have searched my heart," she said. "We cannot leave all those people condemned, trapped inside that mind from Before. Not if there is anyone who would choose freely to live as we do, if they could choose. Those people are here with us on this land too, in a different way. Without knowing it, they are part of the whole of this place. They are," she paused, "part of our world. They are part of the harmony. We need to release them and let that old mind, that mind from Before, finally die. Once and for all. For all, yes, that is why. For good, for the good of the future. We will not be at peace, the land will not be at peace, the wholeness here will not be at peace, without that greater harmony. That is our way."

Murmurs throughout the lodge and many heads nodding in agreement. "We cannot leave them." "We have to let them choose." "No Watchers have come."

Then another man, one of those with far seeing spoke. "We, those of us who look beyond, believe there are no more sky eyes, and no one to watch them if there were, no one of whom to be afraid. This place you have come from," he gestured toward Linn and McPhe, "We know to be the last of the living Taibo'oo. We must end it now. Release anyone who wants to leave, who is willing to leave, and let that place and all who would cling to it go the way of the other Taibo'oo. Let the Earth they have denied reclaim and heal what has been set apart."

"How many people do you need to help you?" a younger man asked bluntly. "I would go with you." he smiled shyly at Linn and McPhe who both nodded in surprise. They had come here hoping only for permission to do whatever they could on their own.

And so it had gone that way. Questions answered, suggestions incorporated, plans clarified. Linn and McPhe told them what Mike had said about possibly using some equipment from 5, and how McPhe had worked out a way to contact the tech crew inside 7. How they were already a few people inside working on a way to get out, not knowing for sure whether there was anything here alive. Sounds of approval. Preparing to leave without a guarantee, the older ones especially who had escaped the Watchers just before it was too late understood that all too well. A few more suggestions were made. The People were as thorough and practical as they were amiable and present. The rescue plot took shape. Agai asked about possible resistance inside the Lab. "Will those others, the ones who may not want to leave, will they try to stop the others?"

"Yes," Linn and McPhe had said, "that is possible. We are hoping to get everyone who wants to leave assembled in one part of the Lab where we can get to them safely, without confrontation."

"Ah.... I see.... I think," he said slowly, "you will need some...." He paused, then said, "some extra help there." Warrior was not a term or a role that they had had much need or use for after they came to the lands of the Lab reserve. Agai smiled. "I think perhaps you will need some of us who, ah, have some experience in this."

Big Carl looked up with a spark in his eyes Linn had not seen before. A few of the other mature men not quite past their prime looked up with interest also.

Agai acknowledged them and continued. "We have not done any fighting for a long while but there are still some of us who know how to stand for what we know is right in our hearts when it has been challenged," he added with quiet pride. "Our way is to seek harmony, yes, but not to acquiesce. If this is the last of the Taibo'oo, as we all appear to agree," he gestured around the lodge, "we have a responsibility knowing this to do whatever we can to secure a safer kinder future not just for ourselves but for all life, long after we too have passed. We are prepared now to take the risk to do that."

And it was settled more easily than Linn or McPhe would ever had hoped. They sent for Mike right away.

Swollen waters, swift flowing waters, churning all around me. Cold plunging waters lifting stones and rocks, crashing, cascading, foaming, billowing, careening all around me. I press forward against the loud fierce waters pushing at me with all their force. Quicksilver I am, breasting the rushing waters. Turning, twisting, bending, leaping, one single muscled intent rippling, coursing through me in waves. Fighting against the pummeling water, the stronger tide inside my supple form carrying me flashing leaping higher and higher. Seeking the precise rocks, stones, and shallow pools, the same shallow graveled shoal where spawned, I came into this life. Where I came to be this flashing churning intent. Vast tides of my kind leaping flying plowing through the fierce waters all around me at my side. Sleek muscled rainbow flesh surging, propelling us together. Our bellies swollen with ancient tides of roe and milt, future memories of our kind seeking the shallow waters where cell to cell they find each other. Rushing past rocks, trees, stream banks, leaping the fierce narrows, the swift falling places, the booming foaming waters loud with spray, rocks rolling, their voices hollow, echoing, lost inside the roaring waters. Rushing past green buds swelling at the tips of bare branches bending low above the swollen streams, green buds swelling with the same fierce joy that drives us leaping from within. Riding the pummeling waters, the more fiercely they push against us the more fiercely we leap, higher and higher in our silver rainbowed heat. Using the water's strength to breast its power, each drawing strength from each, fish kind and water, kin to each other, until gasping air for water, our last water breath, thrashing in the milky snowmelt roe and milt soaked shoals, the fierce tide moves on and so do I.

The big spring salmon trout reached the steam waters near the village a few days after the council. The People took the arrival of the salmon as a sign that all was well, and that the proposed reconnaissance to Lab 5 and the rescue mission to 7 were part of the larger pattern of generosity woven through their lives and all life. The boys who had seen the trout rushed into camp just after first light, calling excitedly, and the sleepy villagers rushed back to the waters swollen with snowmelt and fish, gathering and offering prayers. And then the taking of the first fish and more prayers and offerings, and then the yearly harvest began, the whole village working as one. Fish jumping, water splashing, fish catching, people laughing, and the teasing looks and playful banter, and the joking with Old Uncle inevitably somewhere at the center.

"Hey, Old One, better stay near a tree. The bears will be waking soon, don't want to be mistaken for a fish."

"I'm too bony to be a fish," he cackled. "No chance. Aiiii! Just look how fat and juicy they are this year, just wait until the courting dances." He winked at a pretty girl who walked by with a basket of fish, and she flashed a playful smile at him as she passed. "Aiiii, the women," he laughed.

Fish roasting, fish drying, quick silver bodies gleaming, sweet rich flesh roasting, fat crackling in the fire, fish leaping in the foaming waters. Agai's deep laugh, rolling, booming above the loud waters, the fish tattoo on his arm leaping, children laughing. "Again! Again!" And another silver fish arcs through the air above the rushing water. "Aiiii! Just look how they jump. Just like the one on his arm!" And the mothers and the aunts and the grandmothers who prepare the fish and tend the drying and the fires calling to the younger children, "let the ones who are fishing get on with their work. Here, little leaping fish, help us tend the fire, help us gather wood, help with the nets or let those who cast them be, here little fish, come, I have some more fish to lay out on the drying rack, …." Children leaping as they run to help, laughing, "See! See how high I jump!" And the grandmothers again, "here, gather more leaves to wrap the fish for roasting. Quick! Quick!" Hot rocks pulled aside, steam from layers of fish, green boughs, and leaves rising from the earth covered pits as the fish cook. And more spring leaves are gathered and dried summer berries pounded, and the fish bones and fish heads cooking in the big feast baskets. "Here, tend the cooking rocks for me. Here, this is a hot one, pick it up carefully. Yes, that's it." Bubbles of fragrant stew rising as the hot rocks are added one by one. "That's it now, stir with that willow stirring stick there." A child turns the stirring stick mightily. "Oh yes, just look, strong arms there! Aiiii, we will need your strength, here is another pot to stir…."

328

And the smell of roasting fish sizzling over the small flames. "Here, take this whisk, keep the fly visitors away for now. We will leave them some for their feast later. That's it, faster, faster!" Clapping hands.... Summer berries, autumn nuts and seeds, new spring greens, all offered with the rich flesh of the fish, flesh of land and water all one generosity, all one in their gratitude. *Thank you trout mothers and fathers for the strength and beauty of your people, thank you for coming in such numbers, for your generosity, for allowing some of yourselves to be taken so that we may live, your flesh, our flesh. Thank you for sharing your quick silver strength and beauty. We sing the salmon songs, the songs of your great journey. Thank you for your strength. May we grow strong and beautiful as you do, your strength and beauty flowing through us.* Working and feasting, quick leaping children and leaping flashing fish, quick flirting eyes and shy smiles and laughter rippling over the waters. *Your strength and beauty flowing through us....* Smoking fires by night, their cones of light hidden inside bark drying shelters. Roasting fires by day, arms casting nets and hauling in, carrying baskets, splashing fish.... The powerful spring salmon trout people had come in great numbers this year, and there had been more than enough to prepare for the arrival of those who would be joining the villages once they were set free from the place of the Watcher lodge. And the People saw in this added generosity of the salmon kind another sign that all was going well, all was going very well indeed, as the great work of the salmon catch continued day and night.

Old At'sah by the rushing waters, singing in a water voice a song of roe and milt to the mothers and fathers of the salmon kind, her voice blending sometimes clear and ringing loud inside the rushing waters, sometimes gentle and slow, tender as the shallows whose voices also ride hidden in the spring melt tides. And others offer cedar prayers and songs of praise and celebration to the waters and the strong leaping fish and the turning of the year and the green tides swelling buds on twig tips and bursting up from winter Earth. Singing, humming, laughing, teasing, flirting, flashing eyes, wiping sweat from a forehead with the back of a wrist, palms stained with sweet fish fat, all woven together, whole.

Kikerri sat on her favorite perch high in the tall pine letting the morning sun warm her body. She stretched her wings luxuriously then folded them again and settled in to watch the valley below. The time of the change moon had come again. The land wakening, quickening with spring. A green growingness, new growth pushing out and up and through everywhere. Sap pulling up from the roots of the trees, coursing through their branches to tender twig tips. Even the oldest of the oaks feeling the sweet rise of their yearly youth. Streams and creeks already swollen with snowmelt and late winter rains now swollen with other tides, the great silver rainbowed fish kind had returned again.

Keearrrriiiiii! The feasting among all the kinds. The tall two leggeds of the earthen nests gathering on the creek sides to catch the quick silver leaping ones. The great bears, the sometime two legged ones, beginning to gather on steep banks farther upstream, high on the southern slopes of the mountain in the lee of winter. The big males especially who have no cubs to protect or guide or shelter in the warmth of their bodies. The great roamers wakening from their winter sleep, shambling to the swollen waters to meet the quick silver tide. Bears gathering around the swift rapids and the shallow pools where the great fish strong in their last battles to insure life give themselves to future generations of their own and bear kind. *Keeeearrrriiiiiiii!* The spirit there! A fierceness and a strength in movement Kikerri recognized and admired as kin to her own. All along the lower stream banks across the lands, the other kinds of each in their own ways eating of the same eager tides themselves, or from the generous leavings of the two legged and the bear kind. *Keeeariiii! Keeeearrrriiiiiiii!* A glorious time this was, in the spring. A time of sap and tides running through all the kinds, juicy, vigorous, alive.

And the great tides in the sky raising the swift clouds taller and taller, their shadows rolling across the lands flowing in and out of the valleys like water. The spring winds that lift and drive the clouds pulling so strongly up from the land, the sky soarers among the wingeds riding the upwelling air rising on their own tides lifting them higher in the sky. The great cranes traveling in curving strands, calling with their melodious songs ancient as the stars, had passed through in the night riding the swift currents high in the heart of the sky. On their way to their joining grounds farther north, the great ones were.... And here in Kikerri's valley as in all the valley and canyon lands around her, the time of joining was coming to all the winged kinds, to all the kinds, each quickening on their own spring tides. *Kearrrriiiiiiii!* The calling and the slow gliding of her kind, together and then apart, the circling, the sky riders, circles of their joining flight spiraling, overlapping, closer and closer, wing beats pulling into rhythms matching each to each in perfect resonance. Side by side, tilting gliding soaring turning in the sky, and the tender calls so delicate, as delicate as the mewing of a young chick.... Soon it would be time to pair again, for the nesting and the caring for the young eyas. That sleek one from the valley to the east, that one quick silver in his flight as the great fish, moving through the trees as lightly as forest shadow. And loyal too, willing to take on the guarding and the hunting and the feeding with the same fierce intensity as his sky joy. Yes, he was in her eyes again, as she had noticed she was in his eyes too, in their occasional slow gliding above each other's home lands. Yes, that one, and that gathering of trees, just over the way, standing tall in the lee side of the winds, the nest site there, high enough they were both able to see.... Yes, she would wait, knowing her choice, until the time came. She turned to watching her own valley again, time enough, soon enough for the great sky dances of her kind to begin again in the pairing times.

Below her now, all across her valley home, the smaller wingeds already caught up in their own spring tides. Even the tiniest ones, in their quick flickering flight, flitting in and out of bushes and thickets, claiming nest sites and nest partners with their loud and cheerful calls. *Keeeearrrriiiiii!* A rich time, the land bursting with life, sweet tides and fierce running through all the kinds, each in their own ways caught up in their own joining dance. Even the bears. *Keaiiiii! Keeariiiii!* The bears! Lumbering and rumpled from their winter sleep, preferring to live solitary so much of their days, the dances that they do! To cross that chosen open space between them to pair

333

and join with each other in the time of their heat! For them the time of their green tides would crest later. For now gathered on the stream banks for other reasons, preliminaries only, and strength to be regained. For now, the turning away, the standing tall, the approach and the backing away, not like the gliding ease of the sky circles of her kind, but the lightening swiftness and the fierceness at the heart and the knowing in this way, this Kikerri recognized as kin to her own. And the ways of the pairing joining dance among the tall two leggeds of the earthen nests were even more complex. But even there, she saw the same tides running through some of them, the same dancing toward and then apart. A fertile time for all the kinds. The flashing eyes of invitation everywhere, and the fulling hearts, the same swelling tides whether wrapped in fur or feathers or the shiny supple water skin of the great fish, the same pulse in subtle flick of feather and tail, eye and ear.

She stretched her wings again into the warmth of the sun and lifted lightly into the air, giving herself easily into flight, the green spring air so full of life, then gliding gracefully through the trees, riding the dappled sunlight and shadow, she went to see what she could see, to see what the day would bring.

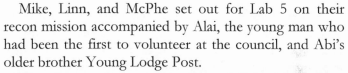

Mike, Linn, and McPhe set out for Lab 5 on their recon mission accompanied by Alai, the young man who had been the first to volunteer at the council, and Abi's older brother Young Lodge Post.

"Let the younger men have a go at it," Agai had said at the council. "Some of the rest of us will have our chance soon enough with the rescue and all. Let the youths see with their own eyes. Us older folks have seen too much of the ways of the Watchers from Before. Let the young men see for themselves and speak what their hearts have seen."

Alai had a quiet thoughtful presence, a visionary somewhere inside. A slender young man, calm and practical, but capable of seeing also with other eyes. Young Lodge Post was as different from Alai as he was from his playful brother Abi. Solid and heavy set, he had been called Young Lodge Post for his upright earnestness from when he was very young. A budding foursquare pillar of the community. *Even the oaks bend in the wind, give him time*, the People said. He took his older brother status seriously, took everything seriously, especially as he approached his coming of age. He had felt that Alehya, Tomah, and Abi had not understood the gravity and potential danger of Linn's sudden arrival well enough, and he had been one of the voices most concerned that Linn was Taibo'oo after they brought him to the village. Now he felt he had misjudged Linn badly when he came into their lives. He wanted to make amends, and he was surprisingly eager to go to the Lab to see what it was like. *Ah, the young oak,* the old ones said, *may yet learn how to bend,* and they smiled.

Alai and Young Lodge Post approached the place of the Taibo'oo with apprehension. The massive rounded shapes loomed imposingly above them like alien mountains or monstrous eggs to their eyes. Unlike the blended lodges of the People, the huge lodges of the Watchers were set so blatantly and arrogantly on the land that the two youths were taken aback by their rudeness. The massive forms seemed impregnable at first, but the three men who were not Taibo'oo but knew of their ways seemed to know exactly where to go and how to get in. Mike had repeatedly assured everyone that the energy at these particular Watcher lodges would be different from the other lodges of the Watchers. Here people had been happier he said. They got along well together for the most part, and they had left voluntarily, with unanimous consent. The boys nodded approvingly. The only ghosts they might find here would be benign Mike hoped. Sad ghosts perhaps, especially given that most of the people who lived here had perished on their trek across the high mountain passes after they left. Mike pulled back toward old memories for a moment, then noticing the boys' growing unease at the mention of ghosts, he returned to the mission at hand, explaining yet again how all the Labs had been built in the same way, perfect replicas of each other. Even though he had explained this before, it was hard for Alai and Young Lodge Post to imagine. Even baskets of the same size and shape made by the same hands had subtle differences....

"We can work out everything about the escape over here, all the logistics," Mike said cheerfully, "every detail. Lab 7 is exactly the same...." successfully engaging their enthusiasm and sense of purpose again, at least for the time being. He tried to imagine for a moment how the Lab must seem to them, then they reached the launch doors and he was on to other things.

"The hatches," McPhe was saying, "the locking mechanism is right here. No security inside, no one minding the store. All we need to do is find that rock where they left the key...."

The vast scale of the emptiness inside the Lab was overpowering to Alai and Young Lodge Post. Not just the physical space of it, but an emptiness inside the emptiness itself, belonging to it. A profound absence. Vacant. Remote. A hollowness, hollowing you out inside too. Like the spirit world perhaps, after death, Alai thought. Like a very sad part of the spirit world. Lost. And so many hard shining surfaces. Everything hard and shiny. Echoing. An eerie underwater feeling to the translucent arched roof overhead. Like a caged sky. Huge and constricting, crushing in its vastness. The air so still, as if it had forgotten how to breathe, had stopped breathing a long time ago.

Alai and Young Lodge Post looked at each other, searching each other's eyes, seeking confirmation and reassurance. *Yes, you feel it too?* Remembering how the young men of the neighboring village who kept watch on the other more fearsome Taibo'oo place, the lodge of the soul eaters, had welcomed their responsibility, especially the ones who waited at night, as a way to train and test their courage, honing their young strength for their village, for the People as a whole, testing their commitment to go beyond themselves. And those who took turns waiting at the soul eaters lodges kept their vigils only from the outside. *Aiiii! What a story we will have to tell them now when we get back, after going inside!* They smiled and held their heads up higher. A spirit journey, into the empty lodge of the Watchers, yes.

For Linn and McPhe entering the Lab brought on shifting waves of complex feelings. For Mike, nostalgia, for times past, and sadness at the loss of old friends. For all of them, lost dreams, and for Linn especially, too many memories.

The place had a stale metallic feel they could all taste in their mouths. They would not need to go over into the main part of the Lab, the big dome, if the rescue operation at Lab 7 went smoothly as planned, so it did not seem necessary to go over to the big dome here. But while rummaging around the mechanics bay they found enough single unit laser lights still in working order, and Mike was clearly eager, so they finally decided to walk down the long tunnel to the main dome after all. Linn and the youths the most reluctantly, torn between their natural curiosity and extreme wariness. The ceiling of the hollow echoing tube felt high and far away as it hovered dark above them, unless someone looked up nervously and their light briefly illuminated the ribs of the tunnel, far too close for Alai and Young Lodge Post. *Like being inside a snake*, Alai said. They steadied their breath and looked back more often, trying to gage how far they had come, with no idea how far ahead the narrow darkness all around them was leading them.

They climbed the echoing stairs to the main floor, their feet ringing on every step, and as Mike pushed the door open at the top, and bright interior space of the big dome suddenly opened out above them. The plass shell of the high dome was still intact. The air was stifling, much more than in the mechanics bay. Here the slow fire of decay from all the plants in the endless rows of tanks and crop beds that died after the people left had used up the oxygen. The air felt as if it too had died, and much longer ago than the exodus two years before. It felt like it had not moved since before time. Linn knew there must be convection currents from the shifting day and night temperatures of solar gain and loss, but there was a sour feeling like an ancient sealed cave. Or maybe a grave. They were all overwhelmed. For Alai and Young Lodge Post, the rows and rows of countless dead plants in their strange boxes were horrifying, and the vast space of the central dome with its tiers of abandoned gardens, offices, and living quarters reminded them of the chambered insides of a gigantic wasp nest. What kind of larvae had brooded here? The youths shuddered, and looked back longingly at the top of the stairs.

Mike bleakly surveyed the space a little longer then said briskly, "Well, I guess that about does it. May as well get back to the mechanics bay and get to work."

In the tunnel on their way back to the tech dome Alai considered everything they had experienced of the Watcher lodge so far. He was not sure that the Lab was as benign as Mike had assured them it would be. As it appeared to be. The Lab felt strong to him. A strong energy still here. The high wide spaces vacant of the sounds and textures of the world of his birth were like an afterlife of an even emptier life, a life that never lived. Nothing like the engaged quietly bustling life of the village camps. Mike had told them that the people of the empty Lab had been happy before they left, but Alai did not feel that was so. Not happy the way the happiness of the People felt to him. At the abandoned Watcher lodge there was mostly empty space around and through everything. A distant vacantness. Bleak, cold, a void, a gap. As if the life force had been sucked out of it, leaving a hollow shell not of a soul this time but of a whole way of life. The Watchers sucked their own lives out. Mike was wrong. There was a strong fierce ghost here, and not benign, Alai realized. The ghost of the Watcher mind that wanted and believed in the emptiness, in a dead world, devoid of life, as the old ones had explained. He shuddered again.

Young Lodge Post looked over at him.

I understand this place, Alai said, *and it is very sad, and it is very lost. I hope we can go soon.*

Young Lodge Post was not as sensitive as Alai to other dimensions and wider perceptions. He was much solider, and he saw his world largely through what he already knew, never questioning how that knowing first came to be or why. And he was content, even though the old ones encouraged questioning. *If you don't ask questions, if you don't ask your heart, your heart will not be able to help you know what is right....* But Young Lodge Post did feel a little of what Alai was sensing, and it troubled him. The why especially, why anyone would choose to live isolated and apart, locked up in this empty space. His foursquare personality rooted solely in his idea of serving his people, of belonging appropriately, his commitment. *He may be a little stiff and overbearing at times in his zeal, but give him time, once he gets to the heart of it then he will learn to bend,* the old ones had said. Now here he was trying very much not to bend, not to be swayed by the invisible wind blowing from the emptiness inside the Watcher lodge. But he was seeing more of how precious his People's livingness was in relation to the hard unyielding feel of this hollow place, and he began to understand a little of what the elders had meant when they talked about bending like a tree. Trees, like his People, were alive, they lived and grew and moved and yes, swayed. Not like this place of emptiness here that was so fixed and unresponsive. He began to see that it was the way of the Watcher mind too. He thought cautiously, but not too much at a time, and he shouldered himself up again, confirmed that in coming here he had done the right thing and what he came to do and understand he had done, and he was satisfied. He shut down his considering and set out certain of his position again. Alai looked over at his friend and smiled, *ah, well, it is a start for him. The old ones will be pleased he has at least come this far.*

341

The youths were thankful when they got back to the smaller tech dome and the mechanics bay, now strangely familiar on their return. The sense of familiarity, however brief, gave them confidence again. Tech was the prime focus of the current mission anyway. Mike began looking systematically through the equipment on the shelves all around the work bay. His co-workers throughout the Lab had not left hastily. They had cleaned up and put tools and parts away.

"Too organized for me, how the hell can you find anything?" McPhe teased.

"Aha! Here it is! Hallelujah land!" Mike shouted gleefully. His voice careening, rebounding all through the hollow space. Whispering back at them from odd angles of the vaulted bay. The two youths looked alarmed.

"Sorry guys," Mike said sheepishly. "I just found the prize. I'll try to be more restrained next time." Then he and McPhe sorted through the small black boxes with strange markings and dials and knobs while the boys looked on hoping that whatever had made him this happy would also mean that they could leave soon. Mike and McPhe gathered more equipment, extra parts, and some strange looking shiny hand tools and distributed them into the conical burden baskets they each wore on their backs.

McPhe went over to a workbench and rummaged through some cabinets and drawers. "Ah, here it is," he waved another tool aloft. "Wouldn't want to have to make another trip back to the store," he joked merrily, gathering up the last of the gear to be distributed.

They had the equipment, tools, and parts they came here for. It had not been too hard to get inside, the hatches had been breached easily enough. Mission accomplished, time to leave.

The boys were clearly relieved to be outside, breathing living air again, feeling the Earth under them, alive, resilient, responding, meeting their feet at each step, unlike the blind floor inside that had seemed so cold and removed, has if not noticing they were there, oblivious to their feet. They both sighed with relief. They may have been lucky after all, that the place so blind and empty never noticed them and they had gotten safely away. *Aiiii, the story we will have to tell them now,* they thought again with pleasure. They hitched their carrying baskets higher on their shoulders in good spirits and set out with light firm steps, McPhe and Mike trailing behind already lost in details of how to reconfigure the transceiver and the handset. Linn followed, wrestling with too many memories that had been called up and were tugging at his heels. Not out of the woods yet, as McPhe would say, Linn smiled. The trees were his refuge now, his world was inside out. The trees were where he wanted to be. And eventually the ghosts of his memories could not keep up with him, and they turned back or turned aside.

That night Linn had a fleeting dream. A desolate snow swept arctic land, level like the sea. A small rounded hut a few feet high molded of wet snow as if by the hands of a child, set on top of a larger splay legged dome of white plasoline with an opening on one side. Like the protective shells climatologists set up over sensitive equipment left in place to monitor sea ice in the days of polar melt. Deep under the double hut, a swirling saline world, veils of melting ice and snow drifting in the briny seas below the thinning polar shelf. The water glowing with a milky light, turquoise, pale green, and yellow-gold. Bright bits of phosphorescence like languid stars swirling through the veils of liquid light. A young man on a competition snowboard floating, turning, leaping in slow motion through the veils, his hair floating out around his head as he turns, his arms upraised as if landing from a leap, peaceful and serene. High canyon walls of blue glacier ice on either side. The young man landing languidly like the watery phosphorescent stars, like the veils of melting snow, the translucent blue glacier light, like his swirling hair. Endlessly landing from his endless leap, floating turning in the slow melt waters.

Let him be, let him be, Linn mumbled as he rose up through the depths of sleep. Let whoever he was swirl in peace. He felt the reassuring familiar comfort of Big Carl's lodge all around him, the smell of earth and wood smoke mixed with sweet cedar prayers. *Let him sleep. Let him be.*

"Maybe I need to come down there more often to oversee the work," Ken told Nichols when he told her privately about the tapping the pipe crew had heard while working on the subbasement "project."

Two days later Ken was in the tubes when the tapping came again. "Most days about this time," one of the crew said.

"Sounds like Morse code." Ken whispered as she pressed her ear to the pipe leading to the blocked vent. "Phrased in the same way…." She listened. Dash, dash, stop. Dash, dot, dash, dot, stop…. M, C, P, H, E….

"McPhe!" Her eyes widened in surprise

MCPHE HERE…. MCPHE HERE…. Then silence.

Ken tapped out her reply, KEN HERE…. KEN HERE…. and waited.

MCPHE HERE…. MCPHE HERE…. MCPHE HERE….

"Damn! Why doesn't he do more than repeat? What the hell is going on up there, is this a trick?"

"Calm down."

Ken tried again, KEN HERE IS THAT YOU?

345

WILL GET MCPHE.... WILL GET MCPHE....
WILL GET MCPHE.... and then silence. They listened
for a while, but the tapping did not return.

"Looks like we'll have to wait, maybe same time, same
station?" Nichols looked at Ken.

"I want somebody down here 24/7 if we can do it
under the radar."

The next day the tapping came again, and Ken was
there. A longer message this time.

MCPHE HERE, GREETINGS FROM PLANET
EARTH.

"That's him! Ken grinned, "that's McPhe alright...."

Her mind was whirling as the conversation unfolded.
McPhe and Linn and the goofy DJ from 5 were together
somehow outside, they were living with people who had
lived outside all these years and were ready to help any
Lab personnel who wanted to leave the Lab, ready to
help them get settled in a new life. A really different life,
McPhe said, you'll like it out here.... They set up a time
to meet again, a different time, she had to be careful not
to draw attention. McPhe told her their plan for the
rescue as briefly as he could, and with as little humorous
asides as he could keep himself to. Prodded occasionally
by Linn and Mike, "keep to the plan man, the plan!" All
of them exhilarated at making contact. McPhe told Ken
about the idea of opening the vent and dropping in a
handset. MIKE RETROFIT. NEED YOUR OKAY
BEFORE OPEN VENT. Dots and dashes flying back
and forth. "Maybe a string on a can would have been
easier," McPhe said happily to Mike and Linn, "but hey,
it works. As long as you can spell...."

346

As the time for operation rescue came closer, it was harder for Ken to sleep, and she had grown weary of feigning sleep each night, trying to keep her body still as her mind went back and forth over the plan. So much hanging by a slender thread, several slender threads. Will the tape loops work. How long before ISEC figures it out. Is everyone who knows safe? And now this, Kai's summons to return to training. She had been lucky to get him a few extra days, citing the importance of the project he was working on. She hadn't told Kai, didn't want to alarm him. She needed everyone to be able to look and function as normally as possible. The stakes were high, and all he knew was that they were working on a way to open the hatches and wrest control away from ISEC. She was concerned that if he knew the whole story too soon it would be harder for him to suppress his excitement. Enough sleepless people on the team already. He would see Linn soon enough.

When she told McPhe about the summons through their subterranean communication "center," venting they called it, McPhe had confirmed with the other venters, and yes, they could do it sooner, they could speed things up on this end, it would take a bit of doing…. Hard to tell on the handset, the band so narrow and faint. Very, very short range…. She suppressed a grin.

McPhe would tap from time to time. HEY KID CHINS UP…. READY TO ROCK N ROLL…. and her favorite, PIECE OF CAKE…. Where did he get that stuff. Damn! She let herself grin a phantom invisible grin. It would be good to see them again, to get outside…. Her mind surged again.

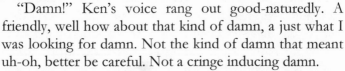

"Damn!" Ken's voice rang out good-naturedly. A friendly, well how about that kind of damn, a just what I was looking for damn. Not the kind of damn that meant uh-oh, better be careful. Not a cringe inducing damn.

Kai looked up from his work and grinned. It was definitely more of a the parts aren't coming for a few days so let's take a break damn, or a what do you know we'll have to cancel class today damn. *Damn!* A kid's game. *Damn!* A surprise party. An eye twinkling damn. He waited to see what she had in mind. He couldn't imagine her ever really mean angry, ever really giving rise to a fireball spitting damn, a forever judgment damn. She was tough, though, and direct. Anything that called for one of those other damns she could probably just walk right over. *Damn!* Just found what she was looking for on the other side of whatever was trying to stop her, and she goes right over or through any obstacle a different damn might have implied, just to get to it.

Good thing she was over here away from the main dome. Good thing he was too. He was glad he was here. She was a good friend. Like a quirky favorite aunt who smoked cigars and wore flowers in her hair. Who came to visit and turned the whole household upside down while she was there. He had read about things like that, cigars and households. Households were heavy, cluttered, filled with antique furniture. Not lean and functional like the living compartments at the Lab. But the upside down part worked the same. When he was a kid he used to lay on the floor looking up at the ceiling as if it was the floor. Imagining walking around on that open glowing surface, stepping up and over the high thresholds of the doorways, walking around suspended cabinets and strange ungainly four-posted chairs each balancing on a single fin. The dark shadowed places at the edges of the usual floors now brightly lit instead on the new ceiling floor. The favorite aunt would love all of this, just what she had in mind. She would be the kind of person who would have worn knickers and learned to ride a bicycle when all the other aunts and mothers were still imprisoned in their birdcage skirts. Grand wide-hooped skirts, carrying them from room to room like great ships under full sail. Kai knew a lot about this. He had learned about all sorts of obscure customs in his history classes. The birdcage skirts and sailing ships linked to whales and whaling, whalebone corsets, the American psyche, dying seas. He had whole worlds of vivid imagery, far away details like this filed in his imagination. A personal storehouse of metaphors gleaned from times and lands he had never seen, would never see, no one would ever see. All proliferating now in his memory. Those worlds long gone still lived implausibly in him. Recombining like dreams, sometimes humorously, sometimes ominously, hybrid worlds,

349

uncharted, peopled, treed, watered, mountained, and skyed, in countless ways. Quietly, within his sheltered circumscribed life, he had lived countless lives in countless ways. A kind of secret freedom lived in him, took refuge there, and would not go away. And he welcomed it. Here in the mechanics bay he and his imaginary worlds felt unexpectedly at home. In all the piles and stacks of parts and broken and recuperating equipment, in all the apparent disarray, a kindly creativity trying to knit the various broken parts and dreams and impossible needs into surprised functionality again. *Damn!* indeed.

He waited expectantly. Ken's damn had been a general signal to everyone else too, a taut electric feeling in the room, but when he looked around, everyone working in the bay appeared to be waiting in affectionate amusement skillfully masking the tautness. She and Nichols had been over to the shielded room a while ago, and she had returned with an armload of small boxes. Now she was rummaging through them, opening and closing the flaps, seemingly, calculatingly, oblivious to the attention her damn had invited. "It's not anywhere…." Muttered as if to herself, loud enough for all the rest of us to hear. A fierce stage whisper, all hands on deck. "It's this one damn piece, I can't find it. I need a left sided one. You know? A Left One! I've got boxes and boxes labeled left and they're all right sided! Any fool can see it says left on the box, not right!"

She waved one of the offending boxes in the air. Even from a distance the printing on the label looked detailed and dense. Inscrutable. Any fool….

"Some fool over in inventory…" She continued to mutter.

There was no inventory department at the Lab. She meant some fool Before, Out There, or maybe over in Inventory, an imaginary country where the outsourced counting and labeling and boxing had occurred. Long ago. An outsourced fool, an outsourced error. Looks like damn meant treasure hunt this time, or maybe team sports, us against the outsourced foolishness that couldn't even read a label on a box.

"Hey guys, has anyone…."

Team sports, definitely, the new way through the maze. Where was she going?

"Damn!" a different one, more forceful. Something had just fallen out of the box she was waving. Something small, very small, had fallen, briefly bright, shining, dropping on the floor with a quiet ping, and disappearing into the general dark underfoot. "Hey guys," a different hey guys this time, she was changing the game in midstream. "Did you see which way it went?"

General bending down, treasure hunt now. Crawling around on all fours. Picking up absurd other small things. Long unneeded, long forgot.

"This it?" A broken marker waved aloft.

"Nope."

Heads down again. Heads bumping, hands pouncing.

"Thisit?" A guessing game. Twenty questions. Or more, depending on how much was at risk.

"Thisit?" A tiny screw. "It's left-threaded," offered helpfully.

"Nope."

Wrong thingy. Wrong thisit.

"We're looking for a small spring, a delicate spring. Be careful not to crush it."

Calisthenics now. Three-legged race. Three-legged crawl. Pantomime. Guess which animal I am now. A bear? Heads bumping some more. All generally heading in the same direction, a crowd of good-natured animals converging on her work area, driving small miscellaneous items out from under hands and knees.

"Don't crush it!"

Carefully. A pack of bear cubs, what do you want to play next. Heads down.

"Over here, I'm pretty sure it rolled behind the bench."

Metal squealing and screeching in protest as a heavy workbench was slid away from the wall, forcibly, against its will. Hands and knees investigating the secret place behind. Slowly, a message relayed, heads down, one at a time. Whispered, behind a bin, under a shelf, low, close to the floor. A few words, quiet, very small, like the small lost part, glittering then disappearing. "Tomorrow, we pull the plug. Pass it on." The giggles and the laughter, the clowning around, different after that. Still sounding light hearted, we were all good at that, but a feeling brighter and fiercer inside the play within a play now. We were all in it together, and finally we were going to act. *Damn!*

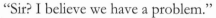

"Sir? I believe we have a problem."

"Yes?" the ISEC chief's tone was cold and sharp. He did not like being approached. He preferred to initiate encounters, to keep the chain of command in order. The man so blatantly ignoring protocol was one of his senior staffers. He should know better.

"Yes, Sir, a situation has developed. We have reason to believe that the tech crew is planning, has been planning, has now staged...." The messenger was withering, faltering under the chief's caustic glare, "....is trying to stage some kind of mutiny. A few, uh, a number of people from the other sectors appear to be joining them."

"Tell them to leave immediately. Tell them to return to their posts at once."

"I, uh, am afraid, Sir, it has gone beyond that. They have cut some of the power supply and they are all holed up over there in the tech dome."

"Impossible!" The chief barked dismissively.

"Only a few people...." The man stopped at the look in the chief's eyes and then continued, determined to

353

deliver his message in entirety, "....a town meeting or something," the man said with contempt, trying to stay on the chief's good side if he could. The chief was notorious for his habit of hanging the messenger before proceeding with any other action. "A meeting called in tech, about community morale. Nelson saw a few personnel from crop stats down in the service hub. Heading for tech. No need for them to be there. He followed them, heard one of them say he hoped they weren't late and are all the others there. Right before the tunnel door shut behind them. And Riggs, over in...."

"The tunnel door? The tunnel door to tech was shut? The chief looked incredulous.

"Yes, Sir. Nelson, he reported it right away. He's one of our best, ah, observers," the staffer said. "Based on some of the respiratory rates from air quality, it seems that, uh, quite a few other personnel may have gone over there too. All cadets are holding firm," he added hastily. "We have seen to that, but a number of.... Sir, this might be a situation to try out the new taser equipment that Harbeck's team put together."

"Nonsense! No need to overreact. We tell them to come back. Unauthorized meetings are forbidden. They know that. Remind them. Make sure they return to their quarters. Everyone. Everyone is to return to their quarters immediately. Tell them routine inspection."

"Sir, the reports indicate it has gone beyond that. They, ah, have breached some of the security systems, and most of the monitors are not working properly. Replaying the same five minute loops. Took a while to notice, especially in the empty corridors and rooms." The senior staffer tried gallantly but futilely to excuse his

354

team from charges of negligence. Who would have expected this, his bad luck, to have a rebellion on his watch. "But here and there, the same people walking the same way, over and over. Hard to catch at first, work uniforms so ah, uniform, Sir, to code and all, hard to spot at first," he emphasized again. "So many routines here anyway." He flinched, expecting a harsh reply. The chief was also notorious for his meticulous adherence to personal routines and expected the same from everyone else. But the chief seemed not to hear. The chief's jaw was clenching compulsively. The staffer could see the muscles working inside the chief's mask of a face tightening and then releasing over and over. The staffer left the ending of his message hanging, wishing very much he was not the one delivering it, dreading the chief's reply.

But the chief pushed him roughly aside instead on his way to the surveillance command center.

The staffer followed in his wake, hoping fervently that there were still enough monitors working in SCC to alert his team that the chief was on his way, and at full throttle.

As they burst into the room, all the screens on the huge banks of monitors appeared to show business as usual. A small group of security staff were gathered at one monitor, looking intently at the screen.

"Just about.... now," one man said, glancing down at his watch. "Here he goes again."

A man in a crop tech work suit crossed the hallway on the screen from right to left. He opened a door without hesitation, entered the space beyond, and shut the door behind him.

"Five, six, seven seconds," another man said.

"In the plain work uniform of a crop tech. Could be anyone. What's his ID?"

"No files. The ah, band of information is garbled, just looks like files. Random letters in blocks that look like words, same shape, same spacing of the...."

"No files?!" The chief roared incredulously.

"Yes, Sir, no files that are legible. ID is apparently down. Other, ah, data has been substituted."

"How long?! How the hell long has this been going on?! Are you a bunch of morons? Speak! Speak!" He shouted as the group began to shrink back from him.

"It took a while, Sir, as we said, to notice it...."

"And ID?" The chief said cuttingly. "I suppose that was hard to see?"

"Well, no need to ID at first, when everything looked normal, then we started timing the movements, and then we looked at the ID bands...."

The chief paced impatiently.

"They're on five minute loops, like the cameras," another security officer explained. "Look normal at first. No suspicious loss of feed. No auto alert flashing to indicate a malfunction in a monitor. Pretty slick. Just empty rooms and empty hallways, and enough people moving here and there to look like everything was in order. We didn't catch the ID fault at first, don't normally check that information unless there is reason, something to be suspicious of...." The security officer swallowed nervously, "of course we should have noticed sooner...."

"I want ID up. I don't care what it takes. I want positive ID on every son of a bitch on camera. I want to know just who the hell is in on this." The chief snapped in the tight clipped tones of challenged command.

"Yes, Sir, we'll get right on it, Sir...."

"And I want the entire Committee in here, now," the chief added coldly.

The security team looked dismayed. The chief and one or two Committee members were bad enough, let alone all six. Hard to know what was worse, being in a room with them or wondering where they had been and what they had been doing. More of the minor inner guard were arriving already, now this. The security men shifted uneasily. Rough road ahead.

"Here it goes again," one said quietly, pointing at a screen.

They all waited. A man appeared in the hallway again, crossing from right to left. Same uniform, same build, same height. Same rhythm to his walk, hard to tell. The man opened the door, entered and closed the door behind him as before.

"Five, six, seven...."

"Shut up!"

"There are other tapes like this. Pretty simple action. Nothing out of the ordinary, except the ID down, but a lot of the tapes are empty rooms anyway, empty hallways anyway. Normal for this time of day."

"How many?"

"Ten or twelve so far, of the repeated actions. We'll have some teams pull up some other monitors and analyze them. We notified you as soon as we.... the empty rooms...." He gestured at the banks of monitors. It was easy for anyone to see. Almost all the screens showed empty spaces. Hallways, rooms, stairs. All empty, normal for between the hours. The chief liked things and people to move with precision and in proper order.

"What the hell?! People could be crawling around all over the place out there!" The chief blurted out. "We'd never know! They're crazy! Now we're blind, how the hell are we supposed to know what's going on!"

The security staff turned toward the chief. Everyone was silent until one man muttered, "the bastards are taking over, we're blind, we're blind," his voice escalating in panic.

"Shut up!" The chief struck the man full in the face and he crumpled on the floor. No one moved. "Anyone else?" He bellowed. "Go on auxiliary power. We can't let them cut us off. We'll cut the power on them instead. We'll cut their power. We can't let them isolate us, we're in charge! Where is our back up power? Seal off the main entrance to research and medical. We'll start to secure each sector from here. We'll show them a thing or two about disobeying orders."

"Sir, the doors won't shut. The relay on the backup power is jammed. Inappropriate codes."

"Try again!"

"But Sir, the code has been changed from outside."

"The sons of bitches."

No one had ever seen the chief thwarted before. They were all hoping for a reason to leave the room before he blew. No one wanted to be at ground zero when he did.

"We'll have to send a team in to tech." The chief said, glaring around the room.

No one stepped forward.

"Sir, I believe the door to tech is sealed from their side. The containment systems, the auto systems for emergencies...."

"I know," the chief said curtly, surveying his staff. A bunch of limp livered wimps. No backbone. No guts. He looked back at the monitors in growing frustration. "What the hell do they want?!"

A pale young man rushed into the room. "Sir. Richard James, Sir." The young man looked flustered. "Message, Sir, from comtrans."

"Comtrans?!" Where the hell is comtrans coming from?"

"From tech apparently."

"Comtrans," the chief muttered, "they are using comtrans. How the hell...."

"They are saying they want to leave the Lab. They say they are going outside, that some of them have already been outside. They say," he gulped, "there is a world out there, that it's alive. It's not barren inhospitable rock. They are planning to leave and ask that anyone else who wants to go with them be allowed to leave." A few of the security men looked at each other cautiously. "They want to be allowed safe passage," Richard James continued.

"Nonsense!"

"They say they don't want to make trouble or create a confrontation...."

"Then why the hell did they cut the power. Why did they take control! It's a trick. There is no life outside. They are just trying to take over the Lab."

"I'm afraid they already have, Sir," one of the staffers said. "We've been checking some of the other systems. Air monitor and water control panels have been rerouted through tech…. all power…. they are only letting us see the monitor feeds so we know they have taken control. They can cut all our power anytime they want.

"Those crazy stupid fools. Don't they know we are their only hope of surviving." The chief was looking around rapidly, a wild light in his eyes.

Some of the security team began stepping cautiously back, pulling farther away from him.

"He's cracking," one man muttered quietly. "Got to get out of here." A few heads nodded in agreement.

"Well I'm not letting them have the Lab. This Lab is mine. My responsibility. If we have to we'll blow it up ourselves. We'll go down with the ship. Die with honor, fulfill our command. We won't let them have the Lab."

"But Sir…."

"No buts. You'll go down honorably, with me. We all go down together. You will do it willingly or by God I will shoot you myself!" The chief pulled out a vintage handgun, a square black Glock, from inside his vest. "Do I make myself clear? You have only one choice. Sterns, you were in charge of crop security. Where is the store of fertilizer, how much fertilizer do we have on hand?"

The entire security team looked alarmed.

"We could negotiate, Sir?" one man offered tentatively.

"No! We will not lower ourselves to bargaining with common vermin. I will not let a valuable research station fall into their hands. We will hold to our higher purpose."

"Higher my ass," someone muttered in the back of the security group, and the others pretended not to hear.

360

"We will not be brought down by insurrection or insubordination." The chief said pompously. "We will go out with dignity. We will not hand over a facility like this to bunch of fools who don't have the wisdom to use it properly. Too much valuable research and technology to fall into the wrong hands. We cannot risk whatever those irresponsible morons would do with it. We have to blow it up ourselves."

"We could go outside, try to get into tech through the emergency hatches in the hover bay doors," one of the chief's inner guards said quietly.

"Nonsense! There is no outside. And the only way to it is over there in tech, they have the only access and the hover doors are sealed." The chief said emphatically.

"We could go out through the reclaim tube, and then try to get in through the hatch in the hover bay doors. It might work. Catch them by surprise." The man persisted.

"Nonsense! You wouldn't last ten seconds outside, no air. That's why we sent that fool Brenner out there." The chief stopped. The disappearances had been the work of a select few. Guessed at by others in his command, but never acknowledged. Well it was time they all knew who they were dealing with. He wasn't one of those spineless bureaucrats. He was a man of action, of principles. A visionary. And he knew what was right. He took a few of his most trusted aides aside. "Can't count on them anymore," he told them as he gestured with his head toward the other security personnel. "Kerac, Hammond, come with me. We'll do it ourselves, and you," he pointed at one of his lesser bodyguards. "Stay here, guard these fools. See that they don't interfere," the chief added over his shoulder as he and the inner guard swept from the room.

The men left in SCC were silent for a while.

"Do you think they can see us?" One of them finally whispered. "Now, can they see us now from over in tech?"

"Shut up!" The guard shouted at him.

"Maybe." Another man said carefully, his voice barely audible.

A few of the other men in hearing range nodded and looked at each other. There was a long pause. "Hey! Would you look at that!" The first man said in a louder voice the guard was sure to hear. He pointed at one of the monitor screens in the corner. "I think something different is finally happening."

"Let me see." The guard pushed his way in front of the screen and the other men closed in behind him. As the guard leaned closer to look at the screen the men on either side of him lunged at the guard and pinned him to the counter.

"Yo!" A man in tech who was monitoring the feeds from SCC called out to Linn and McPhe and Big Carl. "Look, over here, looks like mutiny on the Bounty has finally come on line." They watched the scene as the men in security contained the guard.

"Any way we can get to them and get them out?" the tech said. "Looks like they are on our side after all...."

"Uh oh," another tech said, checking a different monitor. "We've got trouble. They're really going to do it, security in fertilizer has been breached."

"The son of a bitch," McPhe said, "the lunatic is going to blow the Lab. Red alert! Red alert!" He shouted to all the people gathered in tech. "All hands on deck! Get everyone out, now! Move it!"

"Can't we stop him?" Linn said.

"I wouldn't want to try. Besides he's about to do some of our work for us…. Fertilizer is stored under research and medical. Security high command."

"What about the training dome?"

"It's going to blow too, it's over by ReMed, along with the big dome and the grow dome for tropical, they're connected. If one goes they all go. The whole Lab will go anyway once the explosions in the first domes go off. We'll barely have enough time to get everyone out of here. Now move it!" He bellowed. "We have to get everyone out! Now!"

"You okay with this?" Linn asked Kai as he came over to join them, looking concerned.

"The training dome," Kai said. "I know it's connected, but some of the cadets…."

"I'm afraid we can't get to them," McPhe said softly, shifting abruptly out of emergency gear as he saw the look on Kai's face. "We'd have to go through the main dome area. Can't risk opening the doors of the tunnel to tech."

"Not with all the others here," Big Carl added gently. "I'm sorry, son," he said, "I really am," his voice clearly very sad with the weight of other decisions that had been made in the same way in times suddenly not so far away. "I know how it is."

"You have friends over there in training?" Linn asked.

"No, not really…. but they, if they knew, some of them, a few…." Kai said. He was still bewildered. So much at once, his dad, the outside, the rescue. Not sure if any of it was real. Not sure what was or ever had been real all along. Maybe he had always lived in a make believe world, and his imagination was the only place that was real after all.

Big Carl looked at the tall father and son standing together. So much alike, and yet a lot of miles between them, a powerful lot of space, a powerful lot. He thought of other sons and daughters, lost forever, or reunited. A powerful lot of space to cross. Not now. Right now they had to get everyone they could out. Now.

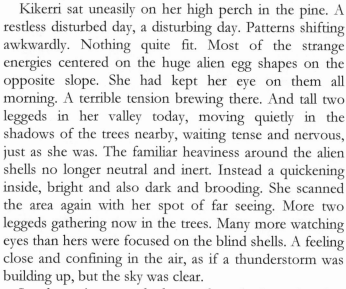

Kikerri sat uneasily on her high perch in the pine. A restless disturbed day, a disturbing day. Patterns shifting awkwardly. Nothing quite fit. Most of the strange energies centered on the huge alien egg shapes on the opposite slope. She had kept her eye on them all morning. A terrible tension brewing there. And tall two leggeds in her valley today, moving quietly in the shadows of the trees nearby, waiting tense and nervous, just as she was. The familiar heaviness around the alien shells no longer neutral and inert. Instead a quickening inside, bright and also dark and brooding. She scanned the area again with her spot of far seeing. More two leggeds gathering now in the trees. Many more watching eyes than hers were focused on the blind shells. A feeling close and confining in the air, as if a thunderstorm was building up, but the sky was clear.

Loud rasping sounds burst abruptly into the day. People began streaming from a small hole in the eastern egg shape, like insects leaving a disturbed hive. Stumbling, running toward the trees, then stopping suddenly and looking around. Disoriented. The others who had waited in the shadows coming out to greet them, leading them into the shelter of the trees. The ones emerging more like newly hatched chicks, not knowing yet what to do, grateful to be embraced and led, contained somehow within the newness too big at first to comprehend. The steady stream of two leggeds leaving the shells continued for a while, then gradually fewer and fewer coming out. The last ones running straight and sure toward the trees as if they knew how and where to go, and then a sudden burst of blazing light. Kikerri rose screaming in the air. More flashes, like a cascade of lightning enveloping the sky, then a yellow green eerie glare and the shock waves of explosions, the sound of mountains tumbling down, whole forests of trees falling all at once. Kikerri shrieked her warning cry, her voice lost inside the terrible sound. The shells exploding outward, shards of debris cutting through the air and raining down all over the valley. Clouds of thick venomous smoke rolled upward in the sky fanning out high shadowing the day. Then the last jagged remnants of the shell walls crumpled inward into a turmoil of unnatural flames. An acrid ill smell drenched the air. The tall two leggeds on the slope above the eggs huddled together covering their faces and their ears, until the terrible angry waves of heat and caustic flames and smoke began to die back and the unnatural fire consumed itself.

The blast hit just as they were leaving the Lab. Everyone else was out, time to go. Linn and Mike were already running for the trees when Ken and McPhe emerged from the hatch, followed by Alai and Young Lodge Post who had waited until the end, insisting that they be the last, taking on their roles as guardians as a right of their young manhood.

"Just run like hell," McPhe had told Ken, "don't stop, don't look around. Just run for the trees. You'll have plenty of time to see where you are later. Now, go!"

As the two youths emerged from the hatch right after them, a beautiful young woman like a vision or a dream came out of the trees, her arms outstretched.

"Alai!" She called out in relief and joy as she ran toward them. And then the searing blast of light and the terrible wrenching sounds that cracked the air in half and shook the ground. McPhe had waited to be sure the two youths got out. The three of them crouched low beside the concrete foundation wall. The young woman stumbled and fell. Ken was closest to the girl and dove on top of her, sheltering her with her body as the plass wall designed to resist all impact from outside shattered outward from within, in a horror of edges and sharp molten fire. Ken rolled herself into a ball around the girl as the jagged plass fire rained down all around them, and then another blast came, and then another.

And somewhere inside the relentless consuming sounds and the bursts of light she heard a hawk's cry rending the shattering air with its own piercing call, high and far away inside the terrible ending of the world. Ken concentrated on the hawk's cry, lifting into other skies, other cries. Other hillsides, other air than the caustic fierceness pulling in and out of her lungs and the rain of fire like knives. Summer time by a river. The air lazy, fertile, hot. Sweet scent of river willows heavy in the moist air. A hazy sky, a hawk's cry, glad and free, high overhead. A hawk circling, gliding in ascending curves higher and higher into the sky, and then she was back on the slope outside the Lab with the searing pain and the choking air, and her life pouring out in a bright stream from a place in her shoulder she never knew before.

Anxious voices above her, "will she be alright?" No answer. Hands lifting her. Carefully. Packing something soft around her shoulder, with a faint smell like the river willows but not quite. Hands carrying her. More voices. "Is the girl okay?" "She's fine, she'll be alright." "All that blood...." "She's fine, its Ken...." Hands laying her gently on the ground, packing more moss on her shoulder. "Here, hold it tight." Wrapping her shoulder. And then the hawk's cry again, so free and far away on the summer air, so peaceful....

Spring had come late to the northern face of the mountain. The snow lingered and more snows came again. The sun was riding higher on its daily path across the sky each day, when the bear brought her cubs out of the den for the first time. In the warm air currents rising up the mountain, she could smell the green of spring already ripening toward summer in the valleys below, and flowering trees, and meadow grasses lush and tall. Up here, spring was still innocent and young, filled with the promise of a world discovering itself anew.

The bear stretched deliciously against the sun-warmed rocks outside the entrance to her den, breathing in the delicately scented air. She drifted dozing in the sun, slipping languidly between sleep and dream and back into to waking again. Her senses tuned of themselves, asleep or awake, to her cubs at play nearby. The two cubs relentless, exuberant in their coming into form, testing their new bear flesh, trying it out, how elastic are they, how far can they tumble, how far can they fall. Their bodies so full, brimming over with life, hers still dissolving in her love for them, coalescing slowly back

369

into form, still more in rhythm with the slow weathering of the warm rocks and stones beneath her giving the sun's heat into hers. The two cubs bounded up to her, and she let them tussle with her and pummel her before they bounded off again. Tumbling, pawing each other, grabbing each other, growling, rolling together, tumbling some more, rushing up to her again and then bounding away. Never too far, still bonded to her senses as she was to them, one flesh. Their innocent exuberance so full with discovering. Exploring the wonders of rolling between up and down, which way is up, which way is down, faster, faster, how fast can I roll, and what happens when you push this way. Back and forth across the grassy level apron outside the den, their testing taunting play continued as the bear drifted drowsily toward receding shores.

So much of her life force had already passed into them, her body thinner, and continuing to thin inside her heavy fur. She had enough fat left to fuel their growing strength for a few months more, with the creamy milk still full in her teats. Spring was a lean time for bears' food. Young shoots and buds and bitter spring herbs at first, then the inner bark of trees turning sweet with the waters of rising sap. Medicine foods, all valuable in their way, full of the greening energy of spring, but not much of the calories needed to grow bear flesh. When the richer foods began to emerge and ripen, she would teach the cubs where to look and how, and eventually she would grow strong again too. For now, she would need to draw on other strengths to sustain her fierce mother love. There were others of the bear kind who had wakened earlier, who would see the cubs with different

370

eyes, would see them as easy prey. She would need all the strength of her motherness to defend her young. And she would teach the cubs the way of dangers, without turning them from their cheerful trusting discovery of their world. Their strength was growing too.

She knew from other years, other springs, that inside those churning awkward whirlwinds of bear fur the fierceness of their kind was already growing in them. Inside the tumbling and rolling wrapped around each other, inside their goofy delight in falling down as much as in balancing on four wobbly legs, an intensity already beginning to show. Yes, the strength was there, in them and in her. They would survive. She rolled over in the warm sun as the cubs bounded up again to her, and she lay back contentedly as they began to nurse. Let the young ones play, let them discover bit by bit the strength inside that they are. Soon enough she would show them the way of digging, what to dig and where and when, the grubs waking in the soil, the sleeping bulbs. Teaching the cubs the tastes and smells hiding in the earth, hidden beneath the dry brown leaves withering from last year's growth, the new shoots not yet quickening, the root flesh still firm and bitter sweet.... So much to learn. So much to explore, so much for them to find out. Careening, balancing, tumbling and falling belly up, rolling locked together, growling, tugging at each other's fur, simply being alive at the cusp of spring, the time of new life waking everywhere. While for the bear rising slowly from beyond dream and sleep, the winter depths were still near, were never far away. The translucent inner shores overlapping seamlessly with the cream rich milk pressing through her teats, the tumbling play of her unruly cubs,

371

the warm sun and the rocks, the silence and stillness of winter dissolving like a mist, distilling upward into the buoyant greening air in the dawn of new worlds each day.

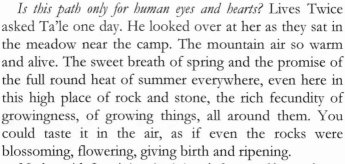

Is this path only for human eyes and hearts? Lives Twice asked Ta'le one day. He looked over at her as they sat in the meadow near the camp. The mountain air so warm and alive. The sweet breath of spring and the promise of the full round heat of summer everywhere, even here in this high place of rock and stone, the rich fecundity of growingness, of growing things, all around them. You could taste it in the air, as if even the rocks were blossoming, flowering, giving birth and ripening.

No, he said, *I can't imagine it is only for eyes of human hearts. The great wholeness is woven into everything of our world from the beginning. All that naturally arises is threaded through with this primordial wholeness, is ripening as a whole....* His calling faded away and she knew he was remembering, as she still did not, the terrible wayward times of the Before when there had been much that arose unnaturally. Then he smiled at her and the shadow passed. *We are all returning together to the origin through the radiance all around us here leading us home. Everything of this world,* he gestured around them, *the mountains, the sky....* he placed his hands tenderly on the earth of the meadowland *....the Earth, is* *already on this journey of return to origin in some way. So yes, I hadn't looked at it that way before, but there must be other heart eyes that see as we see, see what we see, from inside other lives, from inside the hearts of grasses, the hearts of stones, of elephants and whales, of bears…. the whales, the elephants…. so long ago….* he said again, and was quiet, drifting away.

She touched his hand, *perhaps like the bears they live yet,* she said gently, *and this path is open to all their eyes, how could it not be so. We share so much….*

He smiled again, *yes, we are all on the way home, yes. And if even us poor humans can see, then surely there must be other heart eyes that see too…. Why do you ask?* But he already knew, and she said nothing, seeing perhaps with those other eyes already. He took her hand.

In the beginning time, she began, her voice very soft, far away, a voice of first Earth, first sky, first rainbow color as first witness of first radiance, *in the beginning time, whose eyes see, before Earth and sky, before the blue distance, before the rain, before the bear, what sees?*

You will find out, he said, *when you get farther up the trail, the path is there, before the kinds. The path sees, looks through its own eyes, in the first pure joy of becoming.*

The path must be very strong, she said and looked thoughtful. *Yes, the path came first, before the eyes…. the path gave birth to eyes to see. Eyes are gifts of the path, like the tears that are the gifts of the sea, and the colors, and all the worlds arising as witness to the radiance….* and if Linn had been there to see at that moment, he would have recognized Miri in the sudden sureness of her words.

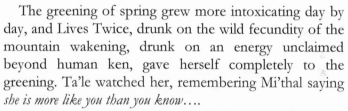

The greening of spring grew more intoxicating day by day, and Lives Twice, drunk on the wild fecundity of the mountain wakening, drunk on an energy unclaimed beyond human ken, gave herself completely to the greening. Ta'le watched her, remembering Mi'thal saying *she is more like you than you know....*

Bears eat salmon, his sister had also said. Bears eat salmon. To become one with that wild quicksilver flesh, that fierce joy that drives them and carries them from within. Which flesh, which wildness, which joy subsumed in who, living on in who. Who lives that fierce wild joy that pads through the meadow lands, digging in rich earth, salmon or bear.... Lives Twice let her hair grow uncombed. Wrapped up with a plant vine or a small rough cord tied on top of her head. Spent her days roaming, everything around her melting languid and slow in the warm sun, while she roamed restless, driven from inside, the fierce joy of the salmon run pulsing through her bear's heart. Then sitting quietly in the sun watching the tall peaks of the mountains grow.

And she danced, her feet making their own rhythms on the hard stony ground. Music born through her feet from the mountain rising up through her. Simple heartbeat steps, feet lifting and then, a pulling back toward the Earth, called back by the mountain, the granite gravity of rocks and stones dancing through her stretching between mountain and sky. Then she would sit quietly again for a while or lay back in the sun, suddenly old, as old as the rocks, immersed in a peace Ta'le understands, the other part, the wildness, untamed, not so much. He waits, man who knows how to wait, who knows how to hold the rain in his hands, as her exuberance ebbs and flows on the greening currents of spring.

In a quiet moment she looks at him, *I will go away, some day, not now, but some day. I do not want to hurt you…. but even while I am gone, I will always be here.* She gestured around them and he knows to wait, and he knows that her away will be farther in the end than he could follow just yet from inside.

Hold me, she said, *hold me to this life,* the voice of one dissolving inside a chrysalis, not yet knowing that the protective shell will be cracking open into a new life again. Fragile, pulsing inside, faintly rainbowed like the cicada he had watched transform so long ago, pumping strength into the new veins of the nascent wings that will support transparent membranes of flight. All life in a rainbow, a dewdrop, a butterfly wing…. like the vision. He took her gently in his arms, pressing closer and closer, tenderly, so as not to crush the wings. Bears fly, fish do too. She rolled under him open like the sky, her wildness inside parting to let him in. The two of them rolling together, shedding their layers of winter skins, warm sun on bare flesh, the heat between them warmer still, the heat of fusing two lives into one blooming like a flower.

You said that you would be leaving? He asked.

She looked surprised and laughed. *A long time ago. Now the leaving has gone away instead.*

For now, he said his eyes clear and still.

She smiled. *I think now, when the final leaving comes, I shall stay. I think I always will. So much to love.*

He looked at her. Her heart so warm, and so.... when it was not fierce, silken instead, like soft fur. She was more and more to his eyes like one of the bear kind. Her wild freedom, her fierce and tender love. A bigger heart beat inside her than she knew just yet. Bears eat salmon. Good. To live again through that heart, time enough.

She smiled, *I think my goodbye is to whatever takes such keen delight in*.... searching with her hands for words, making narrow tunnel shapes, hidden things.... *in being a separate me,* she finally said, *who knows too much to be able to be here. That is what has left, is leaving now. I no longer know in that way, about being here. Here is softer now, all one.... a texture, mellow, somehow, all one sweet flesh, like summer time, with blackberries ripening, bees clinging heavily to the flowers, nights full of cricket song. So generous. So full, like that.* Her feelings mirroring his no longer feelings, whole skies of clouds passing and clearing again in her eyes, melting delicately with the gracious ease of dewdrops in morning sun. Liquid, melded together, whole. "There is no way to be apart," she whispered, her voice barely audible.

377

He nodded. *Yes.* Her voice like the whisper of a breeze, no longer human to his ears. A soft considering decisive whuff instead.

And when she speaks in words, they sound to her ears as if someone else is speaking through her. At night huge wheels of rainbow light roll along beside her as she walks the mountain trails in her dreams, and diaphanous veils of light and fields of rainbow circles bloom with a dream bright radiance, and necklaces and cascades of light, jewel like, radiating from places where endless strands of circles intersect. They are Ta'le's dreams, she has felt them before, full of the rainbow living lights, full of open spaces and a whiteness brighter than snow, an openness of pure light, and flashes of clear blue skies, all blooming as if through Ta'le's dreaming eyes. Her own dreams more earthen, pungent with deep roots, and cave dark breathing all around her, then melting away.

There is no way to go back, even if I wanted to, she marveled one day.

Yes.

I have seen, she said, *a seed of another life calling me, coming out of me now, living soon, to live in its own way. We will never meet, she and I.*

A late spring snow kept the avalanche danger high on the trail down the mountain. When the last of the snow had finally melted back from the meadow at the gazers camp, Far Eyes Agai went to check the trail.

The way is open, he said, when he returned. *Slow going in some places, but safe. The trail is open. I will go down.* And he asked around for messages to be relayed or crucial supplies that needed replenishing.

He left at dawn the next day, and by mid afternoon when he would have reached the village below, Lives Twice and Ta'le felt a burst of love and warmth from Mi'thal, and a complex sending too hard to decipher that would have to wait until Far Eyes returned. For now, Mi'thal's joy at their joining was unmistakable in her sending, and that she would send a wedding gift, a joining gift. But along with her message there was a puzzling concern woven through her obvious affection and love for them that Ta'le feared had to do with her warning from before. The time of the spring trout was already at hand.

Far Eyes told Ta'le the news privately first, as Mi'thal had requested. *That man Linn knows of her new life, and of you,* Mi'thal had said, and Big Carl told her that while the man understands with his head, his heart still loves her, very much. He is living with Big Carl, and Big Carl counts him as a friend. A good person, new to our ways, but a good heart. *Your sister,* Far Eyes said, *is concerned for Lives Twice and for you, about what this news might mean for both of you. There was a reason Lives Twice forgot that life so thoroughly and a reason that man is here now, and his son, her son, they have a son together....* And Far Eyes told Ta'le what Mi'thal had said about the rescue and the refugees. *The wisdom threads are there for us to see and listen to in all of this, and I do not feel this is the only claim on the heart of Lives Twice,* your sister said. *There is still another destiny I see touching her heart and yours, my brother. I send my love.* Far Eyes concluded the message. He had a good memory. In the village he came from he had been one of those who remembered the story songs easily, and he had a way of telling them that made you feel that you were there. He could be counted on to deliver complex messages accurately when needed, which for the gazers and their heart kin was fairly rare.

Your sister also asks, Far Eyes said, *that if the trail stays open, that you consider coming down, that it might be good to meet with this man....* Far Eyes left it there, then he added softly, *I believe it will work out all right, but it would be good perhaps to find out.* And he told Ta'le which parts of the trail had suffered the most damage over the winter, and where to go around. As he left he said, *trust the blessings son, trust the grace from which, in which we all abide. Through which we all ripen. Trust where the arising vision of this life comes from and is leading us. Trust the circling toward home.*

When Ta'le told Lives Twice everything that Far Eyes said, she was quiet for a while. Then in a voice drifting far away she said, *I do not want to go back. That man, perhaps I am not his wife, perhaps I am someone else.... from that place he comes from....*

The smoke, Ta'le said gently, and he saw the same knowing in her eyes that she saw in his.

Yes, the day I saw the smoke, it was from his crash, yes.... I do not know that life that the warding darkness conceals and guards me from.... or that man.... that other life beyond the hollow place.... Her voice growing smaller as she spoke. *I thought I had turned away for good, from looking into those places.... This is my life now. Hold me please, I do not want to go back.*

As she curled up in his arms, she whispered almost to herself, "and I will ask the bear...."

And so I have decided to go meet with that man, she concluded, and the bear nodded. Lives Twice had found herself at the threshold of the bears again, still not quite knowing how, except that this time, she had felt a great need. Perhaps the other times had been at need as well, just not recognized from her side.

The bear looked long into the woman's eyes, looking past the sunlight on water, seeking the hidden depths. The sheling was growing well. How to encourage her growth so that some day when her eyes are fully open to their depths she can be on her own. The season of teaching the young bears once they emerge from the den was intense and short. With a sheling like this, the learning was different, subtler, and once her eyes were open she will still have to learn to see through those eyes, before the other things begin.

The bear considered her response. The sheling was not needing approval. She had already arrived at her decision naturally, as she unwound the threads of her dilemma in the presence of the bear. Now she needed a way to understand what her decision might bring. *Your*

382

story is woven of many strands, the bear began, *they are your story's strength. You do not have to be afraid of what you may find. All the strands are part of the whole. Any love truly given and received, at any time in your life, those are what give the greatest strength. They shape the story from inside, from outside. There is a way through if you honor that.*

She raised her paw and looked into the woman's eyes again, depth seeking depth. *And there are other loves, and another greater love shaping even those strands that you or I cannot see. Come back to me, be sure to come back, the threshold can be reached, the doorway is always here,* she said. *Be sure to come back. I will know when you are here. You are dear to me, as dear as one of my own cubs,* her eyes grew fond with love for her unruly ones growing mightily in their play. *Not as free within your world as they are within theirs, their testing is different than yours. Your exploring…. you test for other strengths, and you are growing too. You will see when the time comes, the strength will be there.*

The next morning Lives Twice said quietly to Ta'le, *I will go. I will go to meet that man….*

We will go, Ta'le said, *I will go with you if you like.*

She smiled at him. *Yes, I would like. Thank you.* She touched her heart and made the hand sign for love, holding her hands crossed at the wrists in front of her chest, palms facing inwards, fingers curled gently toward her palms. She pressed them to her chest at the level of her heart and held them there, her eyes close to tears. *I would like that very much. How soon?*

How soon do you want to go?

She took a deep breath, considering. *In a week I think,* she finally said, *in a week. There will be a new moon…. And I*

383

will have time…. to…. gather myself…. She grinned. *Whatever is left of it!* …. *And my hair!* She laughed, pretending to preen her wild hair. *This is not a village style!*

He smiled. As far as he knew there was no village "style," as he remembered was the way of such things in the terrible times Before.

She laughed, *no, this is definitely not the village way!* She remembered the young women nearing their coming of age combing their silken hair dreamily, hair and combing that signaled so much more. *But I,* she said, *am not going courting….* She paused, whole worlds unvoiced in both their eyes. *I shall go the mountain way,* she said defiantly. *The mountain is my home,* and she nestled into the shelter of his arms. *I don't want to go,* she murmured into his shoulder, *but I will.*

We do not know what lies up ahead. Trust the grace, he said reassuringly, as much for his sake as for hers, but he was uneasy, not for this meeting but for the other enigmatic claim on her heart that Mi'thal continued to see. A lot of trusting needed here, a lot of trust.

They sent a message with the man from the village who had accompanied Far Eyes back up the trail. The winter had been a long one up here, and it had taken two people to carry the much needed supplies.

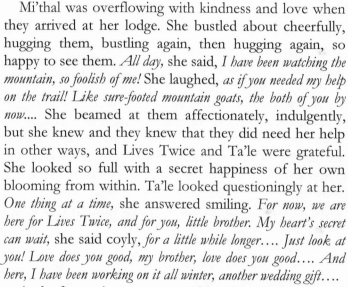

Mi'thal was overflowing with kindness and love when they arrived at her lodge. She bustled about cheerfully, hugging them, bustling again, then hugging again, so happy to see them. *All day,* she said, *I have been watching the mountain, so foolish of me!* She laughed, *as if you needed my help on the trail! Like sure-footed mountain goats, the both of you by now....* She beamed at them affectionately, indulgently, but she knew and they knew that they did need her help in other ways, and Lives Twice and Ta'le were grateful. She looked so full with a secret happiness of her own blooming from within. Ta'le looked questioningly at her. *One thing at a time,* she answered smiling. *For now, we are here for Lives Twice, and for you, little brother. My heart's secret can wait,* she said coyly, *for a little while longer.... Just look at you! Love does you good, my brother, love does you good.... And here, I have been working on it all winter, another wedding gift....*

And after going over everything Big Carl had said about the tall man who was now also his friend, Mi'thal told them about the arrangements for the proposed meeting.... *And so we, Big Carl and I, we thought that he could bring that man Linn over in a few days, and his son, your son,*

385

she looked at Lives Twice, *Kai, his name is…. He is coming too, apparently….*

Lives Twice looked dismayed. *I had not thought…. both of them, at once….*

Mi'thal touched her hand gently, *hard to keep the father and son apart, Big Carl says. Everything so new for the boy, he had never been outside before. Didn't even know there was an outside, he had never been on the Earth….* She shook her head in disbelief, and all three of them felt the horror of it. Then she said in a lighter tone, *Kendra,* her voice fulling warmly, *the woman from the Lab I have been tending after the rescue, her injuries…. She says that the boy Kai is a good kid. She seems very fond of him, it's just that he gets lost inside his mind at times….*

Lives Twice felt herself sinking. These strange people, to whom she was somehow kin, and their world, so alien. *My world once, if I remembered….* And then, the shadows and the painful hollow place she could never get beyond…. *Please, both of you,* she pleaded, looking at Ta'le and Mi'thal, *please, stay with me when I talk with them…. I cannot do this alone. Stay with me when I meet them, please….*

Mi'thal and Ta'le hugged her from either side and held her between them. *Thank you,* Lives Twice said, her face buried in her hands to quell her tears. *Thank you, you are my true family….* as if clinging to a wisp of dream she was afraid was already drifting away.

And over her bowed head, Mi'thal looked at her brother. She mouthed the words silently, it will work out, don't worry, it will be all right. I have seen that too…. and which all right, and for who, Ta'le would have to take on faith. The grace was always there, the challenge was to put yourself in harmony with it.

The day of the meeting dawned fresh and clear, with the promise of warm sun already moving toward the heat of summer still a few weeks away. Lives Twice decided to meet the man and the boy, the youth, they said, at her favorite tree at the edge of camp. The place where she would sit in the warm sun of a different season when she was first here, so new to this world, to any world. The tree had been a good friend. She and Mi'thal and Ta'le arranged places for everyone to sit in the shade under the old cedar, in a semi circle facing out toward the sun. Lives Twice surveyed their work. *Looks like we have called a council!* She tried to joke but inside she was already taut with apprehension.

Ta'le sat with her while Mi'thal went back to her lodge to wait for Big Carl to bring the visitors. It was still hard for Lives Twice to say their names, Linn and Kai, even to herself, still wanting to distance herself in any way she could.

And then they were here. Big Carl cheerful, smiling, brimming over with his easy generous good will. The tall man and boy coming up behind him, eager and shy at once, and disconcertingly, as apparently awkward and ill at ease as she was. And even then with a kind of strange confidence about them. She was taken aback. When they got closer the tall man's eyes locked onto her, and they were all that she could see. So familiar and so removed from where she was now. Eyes she knows she has seen before. Kindness there, and a sharpness too, reaching out, pulling at her, so unlike the open depths of Ta'le's eyes and the eyes of the other gazers. Her hand at her side sought Ta'le's hand on its own and held it tight.

"Welcome," she said in a voice gentle and calm, far calmer than she felt. She had spoken aloud, knowing they did not know the calling way yet, especially the boy, at least not well enough for the complex things they may or may not find themselves saying. "You had a good journey here?" she heard herself say as if someone else said the words, and then the hard flat shiny walls and the hard sharp corners, and the edges.... She squeezed Ta'le's hand even tighter.

"Yes, a good journey," Linn said, and grinned briefly, his awkwardness suddenly engaging, dipping his head and lifting it, shaking his hair out of his eyes with a subtle flick, and the cadence of her heart lurched unexpectedly and righted itself again. A longing on both sides, once, long ago, and then like vapor or smoke, remembrance dissolved again.

"I do not know what to say," she began, acutely aware of the man watching her. "Please sit," she said. "We made places for you...."

They stooped and pushed a few branches aside as they came to sit, and she remembered how Mi'thal had said they were both very tall. I should have picked an easier place for them, she told herself, I should have known....

"So," Big Carl said expansively with a showman's twinkle in his eyes, "how was the winter up on the mountain?" And everyone laughed, his comment so staged and beside the point, gently nudging them beyond the preliminaries.

"As well as the journey here perhaps," Lives Twice replied and smiled, and Linn and Kai smiled too. She

looked at both of them. "I do not remember you," she
said, "in the way of knowing through specific
memories.... I had thought.... but even when I see you
now, they do not return.... I am sorry." She could only
be direct, she knew no other way. "The life I have now,
it is my life...." She glanced at Ta'le and back at Linn,
"but I do feel something.... familiar in a way, with you,
and whether that will grow in time I do not know, but I
do know that I have changed.... since then, and my new
life here," she gestured around her, including the tree,
the sky, and the warm sun within her reach, "this life is
my life now. What do we do?"

Linn looked at her, his heart so full of love and
longing for her all these months once he knew she was
alive, and now she was sitting a few feet from him in the
warm sun of her new life, the air so full of the spice
scent of cedar, and still she did not remember him as he
had hoped she would. If only she could see me, then she
would know, then she would remember.... The clusters
of tiny bell shaped flowers on the manzanita bushes
nearby suddenly piercingly sweet to his trapped eyes
looking desperately for a way out, a way through.

"I do not know if my memories will return over time,
now that I have seen you, and you," she looked at Kai.
"I do not know. But I think it is the way of things that
we all must live our new lives now. We will need to start
anew even if I do remember.... There is no going back."

Her discomfort and awkwardness at meeting him was
clear, and her fear. Linn had to admit it, she had been
afraid, was still afraid, of meeting him, and that hurt the
most, yet she was trying to be gracious and direct, even
trying to put him at his ease in the disconcertingly candid

way of the People. What had those ISEC bastards done to her? What had they done to make her forget, what had they done that loomed so large that even blinded itself it blocked all her other memories. Sadly he realized he may never know, she may never know, and suddenly he hoped and prayed she never would. This woman that he loved, so vulnerable and generous, he hoped she would never know what had been done to her, never remembered in that way. He realized his love had grown so great in her absence, had carved out so big a space that yes, at this moment he could sincerely wish her this. He sighed, and it seemed that Big Carl and the others understood in that uncanny finely tuned way of feeling that all the People shared. "Well," he said, "I guess that's that." As if the matter had been discussed at length out loud. To have come all this way, and so little had been said, and yet in another way it had. Kai looked over at him, neither puzzled nor concerned, cocooned somewhere far inside instead.

"Yes," Lives Twice said, relieved, her eyes filling with gratefulness and even affection for this man Linn, not the affection they may have had between them before, and not for the man she had known in other ways then, but the one here now who had released his claim on her heart. "Thank you," she said with tears welling up in her eyes along with the gratefulness, "thank you."

"Mom," Kai said softly, "it's good to see you again," not quite asking, not quite pulling, seemingly appreciative instead, but as if in this way he could call her back somehow.

"And you too, son, and you too." She smiled at him, surprised at how easily she could say the word son, immersed in a love from outside time that had no roots in memory. "I will be going up the mountain. I, we...." she looked at Ta'le. "We live there," she said simply. "But later in the summer at the ripening and harvesting times, we will return, and we can talk more then perhaps? For now," she smiled, the sudden innocence of her smile melting for a moment the shadows that haunted all three of them, "this is quite a lot for now, don't you think?" She smiled ruefully at the sound of her words, she hadn't meant it to come out like that. The awkwardness was still there.

"Yes," Linn said, "it is a lot, for all of us.... I, we," he looked at Kai, "we would like to talk with you again." He put his arm around the boy's shoulders. "We'll get Kai settled in and acclimated to the People's ways, and then, yes, perhaps we can talk again.... as friends...." His voice trailed away. He meant what he said but it was hard for him, and the strain between what he had wanted this meeting to be and how actually turned out or was going to be all along, would take longer to resolve, longer to dissolve. "Be well," he said, and touched Big Carl's shoulder. "Time to go...."

"See you soon," Kai said, his emotions inscrutable again, layered, hidden away.

A complex skein of threads there in the boy, she thought as they walked away. Let him get settled, let the shock of having his life shifted so dramatically wear away, let him have a base, a place in a new life from which to begin, and then we will have some discovering to do, he and I, to find out who he is. Who all of us are now.

That night as he drifted in and out of restless sleep Linn had a dream. A small valley and a creek side, with a large rock beside the creek. Two trails coming down from either side of the valley meeting at the creek. Two women, one on each trail, coming toward him at the same time as he sat hidden behind the rock. One woman with a basket, the other with dreadlocks in the shape of two large antlers fanning out from the top of her head. A vivid dream, so real he felt he was actually there, wondering whether he should step out from behind the rock, wondering which woman to greet. As the women came closer and neared the place where the two trails came together, he woke up, knowing that the dream had something to do with Miri, but not sure what it meant. Which woman did they meet under the tree? Both and neither in a way, and there was always the rock, and the hard place, as McPhe would say.

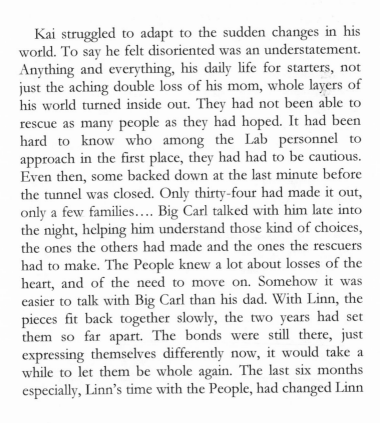

Kai struggled to adapt to the sudden changes in his world. To say he felt disoriented was an understatement. Anything and everything, his daily life for starters, not just the aching double loss of his mom, whole layers of his world turned inside out. They had not been able to rescue as many people as they had hoped. It had been hard to know who among the Lab personnel to approach in the first place, they had had to be cautious. Even then, some backed down at the last minute before the tunnel was closed. Only thirty-four had made it out, only a few families.... Big Carl talked with him late into the night, helping him understand those kind of choices, the ones the others had made and the ones the rescuers had to make. The People knew a lot about losses of the heart, and of the need to move on. Somehow it was easier to talk with Big Carl than his dad. With Linn, the pieces fit back together slowly, the two years had set them so far apart. The bonds were still there, just expressing themselves differently now, it would take a while to let them be whole again. The last six months especially, Linn's time with the People, had changed Linn more than he knew. His dad familiar and different at the same time, more accepting, slower, quieter. Cautiously, Kai began to explore the ways of his new world as much to find out who Linn was now, as to find himself.

Alehya had been teaching Kai about the hand sign language. He had a good eye for the nuances of the gestures and a natural grace once he got over his shyness, and he was learning quickly. She had been drawn to him when she first met him, when he came to the village after the rescue. The tall son of the tall man intrigued her. So naturally graceful and yet ill at ease in other ways beyond the sudden changes in his life. For now, he seemed most comfortable interacting through a specific task and she had enjoyed showing him the language of the hand signs as a way to bridge the gap, to build a little trust sign by sign.

When he asked her about the signs for colors, she had told him that colors are spoken with the hands by making the sign for color, rubbing the right hand fingertips in a circle on the back of the left hand, and then pointing to something that is the color you intend.

"How do you show a color that is not there? How do you point to a color that is not there, that is not where you are now?" Kai asked, "like blue, on a cloudy overcast grey day."

She thought of the things that you could point to, the shell of a robin's egg, rare to find or keep. So often given as a gift as soon it was found, so delicate, so beautiful. A blue jay feather? Not as rare, and a different blue, and also often given away as gifts. On a clear singing ringing blue sky day, blue is everywhere, and the space opens out so fully around you and inside that there are other things to share besides speaking of blue. Perhaps you do not speak of colors at all if they are not there! Perhaps the People do not speak of anything that does not at least have tangible roots in a now already so strong and full. We have hand signs for many things that are not there, a person or an animal, a mountain, a spirit, for stars even if it is full daylight. For things fully present but not seen. Like the dawn. Located in the east, and the feeling of opening, an action easy for the hands to portray. Joy? Another opening, this one from the heart. Things with real feelings inevitably had roots that could be voiced with hands. But blue, on a day of grey clouds and no shells or feathers, or wild flowers close at hand.... Kai's wondering and questioning, his going beyond, behind, before, ahead, what if, so rarely here. He perplexed her and unsettled her. He was like the blue that is not here, and yet you know somehow it is. Seen in this way, his wandering mind seemed so very alone, filled with tales to tell and no words to tell them, stories trapped inside instead, holding him there with them. He needed to taste another world, a world he could share.

Kai leaned closer to Alehya hesitantly, and she did not turn away. He kissed her. A melting feeling flooding all through him, all inside, running down to places in his body he had not connected with in this way before, not through the sweetness she brought to him. Places he had considered purely anatomical before. This was different than the chemicals of hormonal release. An innocence of sky and rain, and early dawn, the first rains. Things he barely knew about yet. Blooming from her lips to his. A flower opening in her through him. Another dimension to a purely practical understandable process. On a science station, there had been no aversion to speaking frankly about sex, it was a purely biological function, right? At least until ISEC began to suspect and restrain direct experience of anything that could lead to autonomous feeling, private personhood, or loss of control in any way. Puritanical zeal, a fanatic's need to control, hold back, reverse, repress. Here among the People he felt there was a natural decorum instead, a respect for each other's experience, a gentle, peaceful decorum, unostentatious, unobtrusive, matter of fact. An easy acceptance and respect that acted as a restraint in a different way, a finely honed sense of not imposing your own space on anyone else that could allow the sweetness and tenderness of a kiss to bloom of its own accord. He ached, felt overwhelmed, and turned away from her.

Alehya looked at him, puzzled by his response. Maybe he didn't like her. "Are you okay?" She asked.

"I... I'm fine." He hoped he wasn't blushing too. Feeling suddenly so awkward. Flushed more now by his strange self-consciousness than by the kiss. "I shouldn't have done that.... Tomah," he finally said.

She looked surprised. "Among the People, there is no belonging in that way, until the coming of age time."

She remembered other boys she had kissed, not many. There were not too many boys close to her age among the People to begin with, and the young people were scattered throughout all the camps. But with most of the boys she had grown up with, there had been some exploring, just to see how the feelings ran, to see if there were deeper roots between them. Like with Tomah. The People encouraged the youth to explore. A good way, the People said, let them taste each other. Then they will know, they will know each other's hearts when they come of age. She thought of the ones where she had felt the same energy pulling between them as their bodies began to ripen. The testing, each meeting different, new, sometimes shy, but not like this, no embarrassment. Instead, a respectful acknowledgment, and a thank you, for what they had shared, and sometimes, a knowing on both sides that there might be more there, or maybe not. No tension, no pretense, no pretending. Just a clear sense of how they were with each other, about each other, known so well since childhood, just exploring, and then simple relatedness would resume again, unshadowed, friend. Except with Tomah. The roots were there with him, never far away, the compelling with him.

She thought about Kai, so strangely vulnerable inside. A part of him innocent, unformed, an aching there, that made his strangeness compelling for her in a different way than she felt with Tomah. *Taibo'oo.* She made the hand language sign for wild, strange, separate, talking with her hands to herself. Kai was Taibo'oo not just because he came from that place. It was because of something else put into him there that wasn't really him. She was sure of that. A bending out of harmony. He was forbidden in some way, and that forbiddenness was twisted up with the sweetness that bloomed between them, giving it an edge, from both sides. The wounded bird feeling tangled up in the simple yes or no of their ripening bodies, their ripening hearts, was unfamiliar to her, enticing and repelling at the same time. It troubled her. She felt an awkwardness rising in her too, in relation to Kai. She turned away, confused by her own unfamiliar confusion.

Then she turned back to him and took his hands briefly. "Thank you, for that sharing," she said. "I will treasure it," and she walked away.

Alehya sat in her favorite place in the meadowland, hidden in the tall grass, her knees drawn up to her chest with her arms wrapped around her knees. The grasses rippled and swayed around her in a small breeze. The sun was hot. She let the heat of the sun pour into her, washing away the other, awkward prickling heat. All around her, the green smell of the tall grasses at her side, fragrant in the sun. She picked a dark green arrowhead shaped leaf rising from one of the rosettes of tender leaves hidden among the grasses, and nibbled it. *Thank you, sister sorrel for your cleansing taste, sweet and sour together.* Slowly the soft evenness and harmony of the day seeped back into her again, after the unsettling intrusion of strangeness into a moment so naturally innocent. A flock of small birds flew swiftly overhead, a net of sharp silhouettes against the brightness of the sky, wings outspread, wings in, as they flew. Their wing beats making little crosses and dashes alternating like a basket pattern, drawing another lighter net of delicate shadow shapes sweeping through the grass behind them, and then they were gone. A light breeze rippled again through the grass, caressing the seed heads growing heavier each day, their growing weight undulating gently with the touch of the wind. She settled gratefully into the embrace of the day.

Tomah found her there. She grabbed playfully at his ankle and pulled him down to sit beside her, leaning into his shoulder. He put his arm around her. *You okay?*

Yes, she said, *I am okay,* and burrowed into his closeness as he wrapped both his arms around her.

Kai was troubled by his encounter with Alehya and with his awkwardness, a dilemma his imaginary worlds couldn't help him with. Her world was so different from his. He felt as if he had transgressed by trying to go across more than with the kiss. An invisible unspoken gap between them. As if he could violate or harm in some way her assured innocence about the natural accepting harmony of things. He felt now more than ever Taibo'oo. He didn't know how to get out of it.

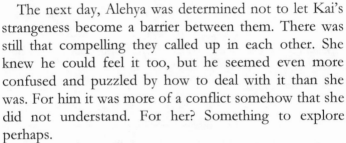

The next day, Alehya was determined not to let Kai's strangeness become a barrier between them. There was still that compelling they called up in each other. She knew he could feel it too, but he seemed even more confused and puzzled by how to deal with it than she was. For him it was more of a conflict somehow that she did not understand. For her? Something to explore perhaps.

"Hey, you want to help me gather blackberries today?" She asked Kai when she saw him walking toward her. She caught him by surprise. He had seen her too late to turn aside. He looked unhappy and wistful. She waited, and finally he said, "Sure."

They worked silently for a while. The bushes were heavily laden this year with a drowsy, heady fecundity. A profusion of flowers and fruit ripening together in the summer heat. Bees heavily laden too, swinging from flower to flower, drunk on the sunshine and the fragrance as much as on the sweet nectar and the pollen. She looked over at him. He seemed ill at ease, daunted by the formidable berry canes and the over abundance of berries at all stages of ripening. She watched him pull at a few reluctant berries. "Here," she said, "it helps to test for the ripeness. You pull gently, not too hard. If they don't come off right away, they're not quite ready, even if they look ripe and ready to fall." She pulled a ripe one and offered it to him cupped in the center of her hand. He picked it up cautiously, avoiding the touch of her skin.

"Just like a bear," she grinned, "Son of Sleeps like a Bear. Her eyes playful. "Bears pick things up like that too, very carefully, with their lips."

She pulled another berry and held it in her open palm. "Like this," and picked it up very slowly, softly with her lips. She placed another berry in her open palm, and held it out to him. "Here, Bear's Son, you try."

He hesitated, avoiding her. The sweet force was growing in them both. She held her hand closer to him. He bent down and touched his lips to the berry, pulling it gently, tenderly into his mouth. She could feel the fire in him too.

He looked at her. She pulled another berry and put it between her lips, holding it there. She looked up at him expectantly. Shyly, awkwardly, he bent down to her and kissed her again, the berry moving back and forth between them, finally crushed by their tongues reaching deep inside each other, searching for the root of the fire. Sweet tart berry juice, the taste of ripeness, summer heat, bursting in their mouths. Their joined mouths connecting to the moist fire rising in both of them. Summer fire. Ripening.

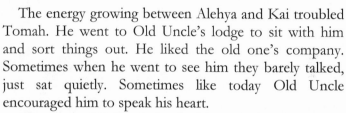

The energy growing between Alehya and Kai troubled Tomah. He went to Old Uncle's lodge to sit with him and sort things out. He liked the old one's company. Sometimes when he went to see him they barely talked, just sat quietly. Sometimes like today Old Uncle encouraged him to speak his heart.

The women, Old Uncle laughed knowingly, *the women, I love 'em. Let them be son, just let them be. They need to find their own way too.*

Now a lean elderly man with few teeth, mostly sinew and bone, Old Uncle had been robust and juicy in his prime, a singer at all the courting dances at the gathering times. His voice loud, clear, and mellow, the People said, reached right down inside you, they said. He had been in great demand for the dances when the young ones practiced flirting, and the older ones, Old Uncle chuckled, *we didn't need no more practicing, we were already good at it.* His eyes shining. *The women,* he said again, *Aiiii, I love 'em.* That was before he lost his voice. Something happened to his voice, something ate his heart, the People said. But he still knew the songs. He would tap his feet to the heartbeat rhythms and spin around. And he still brought the playful courting energy to any gathering through the jokes so often erupting around him. He still loved to twirl the energy. The singing had never stopped. He just sang in another way now.

Old Uncle looked over at Tomah. *Just let her be son*, he said reassuringly. *Let her find her own way. She'll find her way back to you, if that is meant to be.* His eyes were kind.

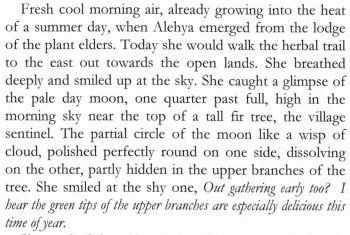

Fresh cool morning air, already growing into the heat of a summer day, when Alehya emerged from the lodge of the plant elders. Today she would walk the herbal trail to the east out towards the open lands. She breathed deeply and smiled up at the sky. She caught a glimpse of the pale day moon, one quarter past full, high in the morning sky near the top of a tall fir tree, the village sentinel. The partial circle of the moon like a wisp of cloud, polished perfectly round on one side, dissolving on the other, partly hidden in the upper branches of the tree. She smiled at the shy one, *Out gathering early too? I hear the green tips of the upper branches are especially delicious this time of year.*

She reached the wide meadowland, grasses tall, already seeding. A light breeze rippled through the grasses, the silken shine of their seed heads like foam on the distant sea she had heard described in the stories. The old ones, the tellers of the stories who had memories of the real sea, would always say the sea was restless like an endless field of grasses billowing in the wind as they moved their hands to mime the waves, and for Alehya the few

405

meadowlands in her world became the sea of their memories.

The pale three quarter moon had followed her to the meadow sea, floating delicately overhead in the clear blue of the sky, the same moon she had greeted a short while ago as high as the tall tree at the village camp. A height now filled with a vast blue of sky. She tried to imagine measuring the impossible distance with her eyes. The camp tree standing tall enough to reach the moon, standing that tall here in the middle of this openness, taller than the mountains, almost taller than the sky. How tall really were the trees, the mountains, the moon, the sky. How tall was she, how tall was anything. Not needing the moon to reply, the wondering was everything. She thanked the moon, keeper of mysteries, weaver of memories. The moon already knew she needed no reply, wondering was everything for the moon too.

The delicate day moon, the tree higher than the sky, the color blue.... and the son of Sleeps like a Bear. Bear's Son. Kai. Son of Sky Fish too, Sky Bear's son. His kiss. His eyes. Soft, compelling, and somehow strange. Shaped by his contained life, his seeing already filled up by everything he has seen before. Everything here so new for him. His awkward grace in discovery, and inside, a sadness, and an anger too. Fish out of sky, not knowing about or how to land, not knowing how to be, not knowing what to do. Being out of place, hard for her to imagine. Her life so entwined with the People, with her family, her various basket and heart kin, and all the four legged and winged relatives we share this life, this land together with, one family. Her identity encompassing all of that, a whole. So different from Kai's tension from his abrupt birth into the world of the People, into this world of wholes, an absence in the midst of presence, here, now. So much to learn, so much to unlearn. A lifetime task. His mind wandering off, always what if, what if, hard for him to be at ease with what is. His unexpected alien awkwardness about the kiss, the shadowed edge there that he dare not go beyond. He seemed to live mostly in the private world of his imagination, taking refuge there. The moon so high, so far away, and yet so close. She looked into the sky again, the crumbling day moon so close to the tree in another way in another place.

She felt a gentle tug on her hand. Tomah had come up the trail quietly behind her, nudging her now, time to return from wherever she had been lingering, time to move on. He had waited quietly while she disappeared into her thoughts. She turned to him. His eyes smiling, holding out a few small flowers for her in his hand. Tiny blossoms of crane's bill, heron's child. Delicate five petal flowers, each petal rounded like a pale seashell, blushed with pink, fine lines of darker pink running to the throats of the flowers, the plant with stop-the-bleeding roots. Stops the bright flow of life force from draining away from life. Flowers for her now. How high the moon, as high as the small flowers, filling her heart. As high as the healing root, as high as Tomah's deep quick seeing eyes always at her side. As high as the world they shared. She smiled and took his hand.

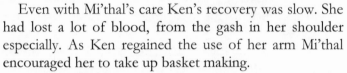

Even with Mi'thal's care Ken's recovery was slow. She had lost a lot of blood, from the gash in her shoulder especially. As Ken regained the use of her arm Mi'thal encouraged her to take up basket making.

"It's soothing," Mi'thal said, "the beauty of the shapes, their roundness, the weaving, knitting things together. Besides, it would be good to give your arm something gentle to do at first, let your fingers do most of the work."

The intricacies of the skill that were the most challenging to learn gave Ken particular joy as the baskets grew beneath her fingers. And when she mentioned ruefully her eyesight beginning to change with her age, Mi'thal laughed. "Yes, mine too! But weaving fingers, they know what to do on their own after a while, they have their own eyes. Here, this is another coil, you can feel it how smooth the strands. For that, we gather them when they are green and then...."

And sometimes when she leaned closer to show Ken just how the twine goes, "two strands over, one under, over two again.... This way, a little higher here, this strand goes a little higher, so you can splice a new one in from here, this way, and then, you can spread the shape out like this…." And the smell of Ken's hair and the faint river willow scent still clinging to the coils, and the stands of willows where she had gathered the green canes and dug the roots, and the moist earth, and the fecund summer air gathering there, suddenly all so close, blending together with the scent of her hair. She searched Ken's eyes, not yet, not yet.

At another time she said to Ken, "Ken is a man's name. I like Kendra. You can be who you are here. Who you really are, without a man's name. A strong woman, and a beautiful woman," Mi'thal smiled at Kendra, her eyes teasing, leading somewhere else, briefly soft and searching, then quickly looking away. Still not yet. Still waiting, for the same searching, from each side.

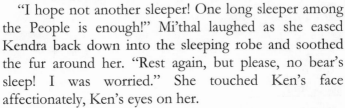

"I hope not another sleeper! One long sleeper among the People is enough!" Mi'thal laughed as she eased Kendra back down into the sleeping robe and soothed the fur around her. "Rest again, but please, no bear's sleep! I was worried." She touched Ken's face affectionately, Ken's eyes on her.

"No," Ken laughed, "I'm awake. All here," and she grinned.

"I'll let you rest again," Mi'thal said as she turned away.

"No, wait." Ken caught her wrist. "Please stay with me for a while. You have been so kind, tending me all this time." She looked into her eyes again. Each of them pulling closer, the same liquid resonance calling like to like. "Please," Kendra whispered, "I am yours."

And Mi'thal leaned forward and kissed her, sweet lips to sweet lips, a tenderness, a depth of kindliness, unfolding, blossoming, blooming softly, turning them inside out into each other. Mi'thal tumbled onto the sleeping robe with her, their arms and legs entwined.

"So," Mi'thal said, as she raised up on one elbow to look at Kendra, her finger tracing small patterns on her bare shoulder next to her. "I suppose you are going to stay? My lodge is your lodge. That is our way. You are free to go or stay, but my lodge is your lodge.... and my heart." She kissed her lightly.

"Yes," she said, which she, together already one heart. "Yes, I am here to stay."

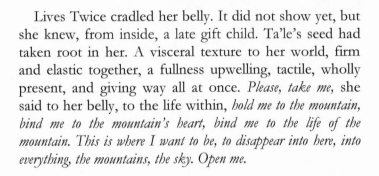

Lives Twice cradled her belly. It did not show yet, but she knew, from inside, a late gift child. Ta'le's seed had taken root in her. A visceral texture to her world, firm and elastic together, a fullness upwelling, tactile, wholly present, and giving way all at once. *Please, take me,* she said to her belly, to the life within, *hold me to the mountain, bind me to the mountain's heart, bind me to the life of the mountain. This is where I want to be, to disappear into here, into everything, the mountains, the sky. Open me.*

That night she dreams of swimming underwater. She dreams of the seas. Vast oceans of depths. She is moving underwater, swimming freely, diving, gliding through deep swift waters, seeing with water eyes, moving up down side to side, no direction forbidden, no direction inaccessible. Moving, turning in sinuous curves, dancing as pure space, effortless. When she awakens she is crying, more seas, oceans of tears blooming from her eyes, washing away all traces of withheld memory, without knowing who or what or why, all one within the pure gifted joy of forgiveness and release.

I want to know who I am, as a wholeness, not just the life I am now, or the one before that. I want to know all of it. Why I can come here, why I can find my way here. Why I feel those things inside I cannot find human words to speak. Why I feel so kin to the bear kind. Why....

The bear held up her paw. *Wait,* she said. Her eyes were kind. *Wait. Not all at once, the whole story may take a while. Not what you are, but why....*

Some shape shifters, some are women, some are men, there are both, and some who go between that too, moving as freely there as between the kinds.... The bear paused, considering which way to go. *Some,* she started again, *who can move between the kinds, but forget they can move. They become attracted, attached to one kind only. Their change gift forgotten, passed down invisibly, hidden in their eggs and seeds down through their lines. A son or a daughter, a daughter or a son here and there may remember, occasionally, a glimmer of their original fluidity, the heart opening beyond self form, beyond kind. Maybe only once, and briefly, maybe in a visionary memory, or in a dream. For some it will be a big dream. One they carry all their lives, as if it is a wisdom from outside, not recognizing the wisdom of their true kind hidden within them, guiding them.*

Shape shifting is not a power, the bear emphasized. *Shape shifting is a way of inhabiting your heart that reaches out, connects with everything. There were some,* she looked stern, and Lives Twice had a sudden image of a shadow shape rearing tall flashing with a narrow fierce intent. *Some in other times who misunderstood the change, who used it to do things to others. And so the true heart of the changing went deep into the Earth and waited. Changing is a way of allowing your whole being to be fluid and whole, that is all. For me, for changers of our kind, it expresses itself more fully as simply being a bear. For others,* she swept a massive arm surprisingly delicately through the air, *I do not know for sure. There are many ways to go. The choices are many. So few, so few know that they can choose. Everyone in whatever form has more choices than they know, we have spoken of that before.* She looked at Lives Twice with kindness. *Some already know. It is the coming home that matters, entering the wholeness larger than yourself, of which you are already a part.*

And sometimes they open, the ones who carry this, and they remember the whole of their heritage, their indwelling gift. No longer fixed. Free to swim, to fly, to live from heart to heart as any kind. A tree. A flower. A bee. A bird. An insect or a fish. A bear. She looked solemnly at the woman. *A bear, because sometimes a shape shifter can be one kind and remember all kinds at the same time, can choose to be both fixed and free, each anchored in the same form. A bear....* She waited and then asked gently, *You remember now, don't you?*

The woman quietly, *Yes,* and she said in a soft voice, *I remember.* No big swell of grand awakening, no crashing seas, no ethereal rays of light. Simple. Plain. Remembering.... Waking into the deeper dream, into the dream dreaming the dream. Dreaming untold countless dreams. Waking not out of but into life, into its cave dark digging roots. Trees, and bears, and rocks, and sky. Rain soaked mist. The tall longing. All of this, and threaded through all her other lives, tiny glistening strands of rainbow light, of memory, of dream. Of breath. Of tender sun flecked eyes, of weight shifting hip and shoulder, hip and shoulder, side to side. Mountain topping mountain arching clear skies. Clear sea mountain air, a cloud. Fish shape. A rainbow circle around the sun. All of this. Circle expanding merging with the sky, with her heart. Floating softly, sea of tenderness turning inward, the whole expanse of memory, all memory that has been and is yet to be, all memory turning, cresting, folding inward, cresting like a sea like into a perfect luminescent pearl, iridescent with countless worlds. Translucent rainbow light filled light bodied dissolving into immensity of cave dark blue black depths beyond shape or form, beyond witnessing, blue black depth of all. Fluid unformed mystery, rejoicing in the unknown knowing wholeness of itself. Rejoicing in the fertile radiant, radiance dissolving and becoming, carrying its joy outward and inward again endlessly, as the tides of its becoming. And then, a moment, a movement beyond time, a rolling swell, an absence beyond depth, soft and kind, and vastly more, beyond all measure of vast or more, beyond all measuring, enveloping, without witness, and with another rolling motion, the world coming into being again, all one, together, one body, one texture together, breathing, trees, grass, rain and sky and earth, rocks and waters, rivers and seas, root depths and cloud heights. Root deep and cloud high. All one together, coming into being as one. The body of this life one flesh with all of this. Bear flesh.

She rubbed her eyes sleepily, and turned to Ta'le lying beside her, already awake. Quietly in his own becoming, returning from his own night journey. "I have seen the bear again," she began. Words tenuous, floating, melting like a day moon in a clear blue sky, delicate, not gone, still there, invisible. *The bear,* she tried, again, this time in the calling way. Her hands helping her shape the soundless words for her, one hand pressed softly to her heart, then both hands spreading apart, farther, farther, greatness of the world to big to great to fit inside. Heart growing with the world, deep space and rainbow rainbowed worlds in her eyes.

He smiled. His smile drifting inside her heart wide eyes, drifting on unfathomable tides. *I can see,* he said, *the bear is in your eyes.* That was enough for him, for her, to know, to trust, to know without knowing, where she had been, where she was now. Changed.

He kissed her tenderly and held her. His arms wrapped around the translucent wonder of her. They lay together quietly, pressed together side by side, guarding each for the other, the miracles they carried, that carried them, sweeping them, rocking them gently in their own tides, floating in the fertile calm beginning of the world.

416

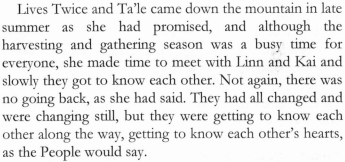

Lives Twice and Ta'le came down the mountain in late summer as she had promised, and although the harvesting and gathering season was a busy time for everyone, she made time to meet with Linn and Kai and slowly they got to know each other. Not again, there was no going back, as she had said. They had all changed and were changing still, but they were getting to know each other along the way, getting to know each other's hearts, as the People would say.

"I remember some now," Lives Twice told Linn. "Not a lot, bits and pieces, here and there. Bright islands of memory. You telling me, about your great great grandfather's encyclopedia and how you used to stand on a chair to reach them. The peaches you said your mother used to eat when she was pregnant with your sister. Kai's face as a small child, his eyes bright and shining in a moment of wonder. Little things, moments only. It has been hard, at times. I had turned away from looking in memories a while ago, seeking a depth of belonging in other ways now. The shadow blocking them was there for a reason beyond their cruelty perhaps." She

417

left ISEC unnamed. "Something else, older in me, waking on its own, wanting me to turn towards home in a different way." And Linn remembered Old At'sah saying everyone turns back toward origin in their own time, their own way. "I can piece things together a bit," Lives Twice continued, "but the memories are still like dreams, that happened to someone else.... and perhaps they did," she said softly, "we have all changed, so very much...."

And Linn believed she had indeed changed. She was still Miri, her generous mothering heart was still there, but it was not so personal, it belonged to something wider now, outside herself. He missed being the focus of her world, he really did, but there was a happiness and a peace about her that he would never want her to give up, not now.... And a wisdom there, growing in her steadily with her heart. As if an older knowing spoke through her at times.

"But when I try to look straight at them, the memories, they grow shy and disappear, like wary animals, if I try to grab. And especially if I try to make a coherent story of them. If I try to go point by point from there to here, the trail dissolves and there are only the islands of brightness again, discrete feeling tones. I am sorry...."

And Linn said again as he often did now when she apologized, "it's alright, enough that there are some. That I, we, Kai and I, are still somewhere in your heart." He looked at her, "I appreciate that you are trying, but as you said before when we first met again this time, we need to start now, where we are...." And she smiled.

"Yes," she said, "and now, about Kai…." And like two old ones sitting comfortably together in the sun, almost, they would consider their son and how to help him adjust to his new life, and to life itself it seemed. Linn told her the trail from point to point as she said of how Kai had changed from when he was very young. "Yes," she would say softly from time to time, "I do remember that," or shaking her head sadly, "I did not know, or at least I do not remember that I did…. But yes it makes sense, the way that he is now…." Linn told her how he had always felt that Kai would be an artist if he had been born in a place other than the Lab. When Lives Twice looks puzzled he said, fumbling, an artist is someone who, makes things from inside, things no one else can see until they do. Or someone who does something very well, and beautifully…. He was chagrined to realize that despite the bridges growing between them personally there were still tremendous cultural gaps. She had only known the ways of the People.

Lives Twice looked thoughtful and doubtful, trying to process his words, "I'm not so sure of that, that he would be an artist, at least not the way you say. I don't think he's quite like that. Something is calling him from inside, yes, but to a different destiny perhaps. It is hard for him to hear, that is why he spends so much time in there, inside his inner worlds trying to listen…. And there are no separate artists as you know it here among the People, at least not in the way I think you mean. Here everyone does the best they can, and are honored for it. The beauty is in everything we do…." And Linn considered again how much she belonged, and he wished as he did more and more often that he could have forgotten everything too, it seemed to have made it easier for her to fit in. And although heartened by the tentative growing ease of their new friendship he became more discouraged, more convinced that he himself would never find a way to really be with the People as she had. He felt a desperation growing on his part, he had too many memories, he carried too much of the mind of Before inside him. He would never fit in, not the way Miri Lives Twice did and he felt a growing panic, and Kai was having a hard time too.

In direct ratio to the distance between, the ship accelerating with the invisible speed of departure and removal, not yet renewal. Pulling apart, past, and away from each other, two energies flowing past each other with gathering speed. In direct relation to the growing space between. He felt a brief sickening feeling. Remote. Far away. As if happening deep inside the body. Deep inside the traveling ship. Do the individual cells of the body, in the stomach lining perhaps, feel speed when we walk or run? Or concerned with their own processes instead, do they feel cradled in the body always comfortably at rest. Like the remnant spirochete in our mitochondria, predatory ancestors of our restless neural minds. He had plenty to digest, without their spinning wheels. A life opening out in front of him. An unknown life, one he never would have expected. Open space. Yes, but not this way. Moving, where? Potential whereness everywhere, omnidirectional. His favorite direction, in theory at least. Now more like a point in space, isolated, alone. Linn had been out of place at the Lab. The naturally candid outgoing reach of his mind at odds with the questions that had to remain unasked. At odds with the unasking, not the questions, not the questioning. And here with the People his friendliness marred, constrained? tainted? crippled? by years of necessary concern and circumspection, inordinate self-consciousness brought on by the need to appear always bland or invisible, a forced separation from a natural self, from being naturally who you are. Now he was afraid his questions and questioning were too intrusive for the People, who already belonged. Who found their discoveries in other ways. In being. In accepting, touching a field of trust, opening, spacious, in a way his restless prodding questioning would not allow him to be from his side, not knowing how to meet trust with trust, a pointedness inside a roundness, the pivot and the egg, a beak inside a shell. Who or what was trying to hatch, trying to be born. The spacious gravity of here, moment by moment, anchoring the People, out of reach for someone like Linn perpetually in free fall.

He had spoken with various members of the community and in the councils. He knew if he went to the ruins, to what remained of the cities, that would mean a life ban, a lifetime ban, and he understood why. Anyone who traveled there would be forever off limits to the People. But that was not where he needed to go. He was sifting through other ruins, of knowledge, inside his head, inside his mind. Was that in itself dangerous too? He needed to understand, to know, something about that inner questioning space that he didn't know yet. Miri had found an inner space, open, free, by crossing through a country swept clear of mind and memory. A transmigration of soul he could only guess at.

He had arrived with too many memories that he needed to lose. So had others, who had mostly arrived through countries marked by greater pain and suffering than he had, a feeling tone that also offered a doorway to release, but he had come marked by habits of supposed mental freedom instead. Self-contained, hidden, secretive, a tiny private hall of mirrors that had seemed far more spacious than it was. A private shrine to the elusive inner brightness that lived he now knew at least in theory not in the reflected light of the mind but in light itself, living as all of life, not in the spirochetes' imaginary mirrors. How to get out of the seemingly spacious cage he had built for himself so carefully. How to shake free. How to shake the questions free. Shake himself free of them.

He sighed. Would he ever find a place or be understood, among this extended community focused on another kind of voyage of discovery, exploring infinite aspects of being here. Two sides of wondering, they and he, content in the awe of acceptance and release, awash in wonder, or questioning, the relentless what if, what if, and what, of the restless mind "eager to dissect." How to turn it to other ways. Now that it was obsolete and needed to remain so. Nothing for it, as the Brits used to say, but to leave. Self-exile, for the good of the People. Rolling off the drag. Insulting the meat, the Kalahari San people called it as they so eloquently and creatively addressed the problem of how to tame the sometime necessary need to separate rather than connect life, belittling the hunter's kill to keep their hunters from turning one day on the whole. How to let go, and of who or what, and when. Prey, pray, decisive action and asking, trust, hunting his heart in the maze of his mind, won't find it there. An ageless dilemma. What to do with, how to tame the spirochete. He didn't know. So far it had had the last say, destroying the empires built in its name. Kai would go with him on his quest. To conquer or come to peace with inner worlds. At least Kai would accompany him at first. He had no desire to inflict his lifetime exile on his son anymore than he had wanted to wish a lifetime of imprisonment on him in another way as a resident of the Lab, which sadly, he had done. Linn's quest was atonement in some way, to set them both free if he could, or at least give Kai the hope of another way. Like two kids running away from home, how far, how long, would they last. Not likely either of them would survive for long, so unprepared. For himself he would take the risk, but not Kai. The boy was still smarting over young love denied. Dreamers both, both dreams denied. A walkabout, a vision quest, long overdue. He would send Kai back once the boy found some clarity and could see a way to go. All the others seemed to be finding places for themselves. McPhe, a reluctant singer at first, inadvertently apprenticed to Old Uncle through the playfulness inevitably called up around them. A natural fit. And Mike had found more than a place in one of the eastern village camps. Something else blossoming for him now. He didn't say much about it. Linn had the feeling it was still so tender and new for him that Mike did not want to put the details into words just yet. All he could do was let Linn know that yes, eventually, there was a way home. Same words Miri had used.... So far for Linn the most at home, the most at peace he had felt was in the shadow of the cedar trees, after the crash, as the snow began to fall. Stunned into a kind of openness beyond surrendering, everything of his life had already fallen away. So delicate. So easy. How to get back or maybe forward to that.

"....and son, are you listening to me?" Old At'sah's voice soothing, reaching out to him, as if calling to a wary animal, not wanting it to run away.

He had gone to see her about his plans. He had led up to his real question gradually, asking first about a vision quest. She had told him about setting up his circle and the preparations beforehand, and the quest itself, the letting go into a quality of allowing that opens beyond time. All the while seeing that other question in his eyes, and they were both having two conversations at once, spoken and unspoken. She waiting patiently, knowing there was another intent, elusive and wild there waiting warily to ask. When he asked about a walkabout and how it might be similar to a vision quest, she smiled briefly and told Linn about the way of wandering in the bush, telling herself silently, ah, we are getting closer now to the heart of it at last. And when he finally told her what he really intended to do, what he really wanted his walkabout to be, he was devastated by her response.

"No," she said, with great kindness and great firmness. "No, I would not go that way. Your way is different, your way is...." And he had disappeared inside himself chasing whatever last hope he had harbored of being free of himself as that hope evaporated like a mist, and he was left once again with no way out.

Then she had called him back, and he had listened reluctantly at first as she told him that his way was not to go farther into exile, but to love again, to go beyond himself in that way.

"This I have seen," she said with her disconcerting certainty. And he felt or saw her looking all through him again as she had the first time he met her, traveling all through him, lingering especially at the cedar island in the snow, and the blended brightness on the sky bridge. And then Old At'sah standing before him no longer aged, ageless instead, and somehow luminous with a light not of the eyes. Smiling, saying, *you already know the way. I know that you know this.*

And he was back in the daylight darkness of her lodge with the earth smells all around him, and the lingering scents of the herbal prayers, and an elderly woman tapping his shoulder asking again with a knowing smile, "son, are you listening to me...."

And his voice answering, far away, but with greater certainty than he had felt in a long while, "yes."

The light flicked. A pair of hands reached into the wobbly sphere of light to turn down the wick, to shield the flame, or a hand moves farther away, out of the circle of fragile light, to close a window, close a door, to stop a draft. Or a hand reaches to shield the lamp, to adjust the battery cover that was coming loose, to check the wires. Another light comes to assist. Another candle, another oil lamp, another biolume. Or a hand reaches to hold the torch higher so that the grand herds of aurochs undulating across the sinuous rock walls of the cave come alive as they rush through the bright field of flickering light illuminating them. Or perhaps another pair of hands extinguish the light gently and reach in the new darkness for other hands, pulling the sleeping covers closer around them both with a whispered good night. Or hands pull another person closer with a soft murmuring and suddenly the darkness does not matter, there is other light to join by. Or perhaps the light is put out abruptly in fear or apprehension, and other whispers, of alarm this time, short, tight-lipped, seep through the hollowing dark. Hisst! Did you hear that? Did you hear

427

anything? Sh! I'm listening. A gust of air weaves through the room as a faint rustle that was not heard before stops. The light flickers and goes out. A heart beats faster. Maybe two hearts beat faster, each in their apprehension waiting and listening for each other, alone with their own thumping pounding sounds loud in the darkness. The light flickers. Sunlight on water, flashing, sparkling, on the rippling surface. The branches sway in a slight breeze, and the dappled sunlight filtered through their leaves plays across her face. The light flickered in her eyes, playful, teasing, and he turned away.

Back at the Lab, Kai remembered, lights did not flicker. They were steady, serviceable. They did not, except for the milky ambient color of the daytime plass sky, change in any way. They were reliable, or occasionally carefully dimmed for "atmosphere" in a quaint old fashioned way, and then only a few lights were designated for such unnecessary use in some personal quarters. Or if a light suddenly, unexpectedly, and unauthorized decided to flicker, they were promptly fixed. Often would have been fixed before, based on assessments by the auto systems monitors for such things. Here in the village camp light was unpredictable, alive. It lived and breathed, gave off heat and smoke and the faint haunting scents of whatever twigs or branches gave it heat and allowed it to live.

The light flickered, the familiar shadow shapes all through the lodge danced softly in the dying firelight. A pair of hands reached to stir the coals and add kindling to bring the fire to life again, or lay a few dried herbs on the dwindling embers to make the sweet smoke prayers filling the flickering darkness with their blessings. Or

428

hands bank the coals, and the familiar shadows disappear and blend comfortably together with the lodge night as the embers fade, and a hand takes his hand instead, a voice soft with teasing warmth draws him closer, come on sleepy head, time for bed.... and he.... reaches for another light that is not there except in memory or imagination, because nothing comes next, he does not know what would come next. The endless variations on the loop of flickering light stop there. At a threshold. Always just inside the wobbly circle of his imagination. The world that lives and breathes around him, that flickers and dances, laughs and plays, is outside the floating sphere of protective imaginary light that he lives by. The light that tentatively tames whatever comes within its view so small and fragile now, no longer a refuge, an island of exile instead. Maybe the only way to break through like his dad said was to turn off the light for a while, learn to see in other ways. And when he had asked his dad if he had learned how to do that, Linn had said very softly, "no, but I'm trying." And Kai knew that Linn knew a lot about countless permutations of flickering light himself, and he felt a wave of deep affection for him, and maybe, just maybe, two exiles together could find another way to see, could find their way home after a while. He looked over at his dad and realized how much he loved him, realized how brave Linn really was, and how much, even more than before, he admired him now. Maybe the flickering light was okay. Maybe the flickering light was enough light to see by for a while longer until they both knew how to change. "The walkabout. I want to stay out there, with you. I don't want to come back. I want.... to be with you. Dad…. I love you." And he reached out to hug him.

Linn put his arm around his son and held him tight. "We won't be going after all," he said, looking into the small flames of the fire. "I talked with Old At'sah, and she…. helped me understand there are other ways to search, other ways to change…. other ways to use what we can offer…. and be part of…." He gestured around him with his other arm, "the…. wholeness here, the harmony, the…. beauty. It's not theory anymore, it's real…." He stumbled then caught himself and smiled. "Something you and I need a little getting used to, eh?" and he cuffed him gently on the shoulder.

"Yeah." Kai smiled back at him, "guess so."

"Takes time, takes a powerful lot of time a friend said. We are our own guinea pigs now, the test species, to see if we can successfully rehabilitate, adapt, acclimate, to see if we can…. belong."

Kai had turned inward again and sat quietly immersed in his thoughts as Linn looked over at him. Hard for the boy to let go of the elegant flickering world of the mind light they had lived by and cultivated, nurtured, tended so carefully. Hard for either of them to want to see with other eyes. His heart went out to his son caught even more between worlds than Linn was. Perhaps that was what it takes to be free of whatever held each of them inside the insubstantial circle of their minds. To really care. To simply step outside yourself, to reach out. Away from the fascination with imaginary thoughts pretending themselves to be real, letting go of the safety of imagination, or observation, noting wryly his own preferred sphere of protection. There was another way hidden, dormant in each of them that already knew how to belong, to be more engaged. He was sure. Miri had had nothing to hold onto when she came here. She had to engage, that was all she could do. For us now, we can only try. He smiled at his son, their son.

"Belong," Kai said at last, as if he had been tasting, testing the word with some other sense, "maybe, we can belong, maybe we can come home, as Mom says." They were both quiet for a while. Mom, Miri, the woman once so familiar to them, who now lives twice and sleeps like a bear, had come home, was home somehow. Kai didn't know quite what it was, but she looked like that, you could see it in her eyes. She had told each of them, in different ways, that coming home was something each person had to do themselves, that it was not as hard as it seemed, or so far away, and Kai she knew wanted them to find their way home too, and that she still, now more than ever in her new way, loved them.

The light flickered and then went out, and when his eyes adjusted, the room, the lodge, was filled with light.... The light flickered. He grabbed the torch heroically, follow me! he shouted as he plunged into the dark heedless of the danger.... Kai smiled, too soon to say goodbye just yet.

Lives Twice looked at her tall son sitting beside her. So much like his father. The same quick engaging manner and quick engaging mind as Linn expressing itself differently in Kai, and constrained by an elusive something wounded in her son, a wounding related to ISEC. The "security" thugs had worked on him, in other ways than they had on her, but perhaps more damaging. And he had been younger. The gap between his heart and his mind that could be so charmingly and creatively bridged at times from the mind's side in Linn, cut off from either side in Kai. Hard to see Kai's natural lightness or share in the play of his imagination now. His enthusiasm, his joy in things that had been so infectious and magical when he was a child. The fluidity of his imagination so accessible to him then. Other kids at the Lab asking questions would ask about nuts and bolts, hard drive, how and why Linn said. But Kai's questions came in such a way you entered whole new ways of looking just to answer them. His whimsy and his innocence now locked away in a private space instead. No longer opening in such unexpected ways.

And suddenly she looked at him with new eyes. The change gift was in him too, more deeply asleep, more deeply hidden, and kept from view whenever it tried to waken on its own perhaps. That gift harder to see than his portion of Linn's quick agility, and like that other heritage, expressing itself differently in other ways. For her the change gift had hinted at itself through a tactile, juicy, sensual quality of experience, a tangible texture of giving and receiving, a feeling of reciprocal perception, her "love of mud" she used to call it, subtle, unfixed, a shifting kinesthetic quality to her being. A joy in the sheer exuberant physicality of things. For Kai it was in his imagination, his ability to enter other times and places beyond his own, outside the narrow Lab bound corridor of his place and time. His story spinning, was where his change gift showed. The innocence of his imagination as a child colored more and more by his "book learning" as he grew older. And what could you expect she acknowledged to herself, that was pretty much all he had to work with until now, give him time. She realized again how unintentionally cruel it must have been of Linn and she to bring him into this world in such a closed and insular place as the Lab. If it had been a true space voyage, then the discovery of other actual worlds may have been worth the price for him…. But there were so many factors, the other personnel, which would have affected the tone of the mission even then. Or if they had been part of the team at Lab 5 instead, with more room for artistic freedom, for creativity….

Either way they were all still here now with the People, and the gift of this would be for him in the end a greater gift than they knew yet. When the change gift wakens, and he is no longer harnessed to a more limited human expression, perhaps he will find a place with the People in their accepting openness, and not be like a circus animal from the long ago Before, condemned to an endless loop of petty tricks with his gift, as repetitious and confining as the tiny circumscribed field of his imagination tethered to his mind. When he sees the true doorway already there in his imagination, when he recognizes the empathy coming through in his love of other worlds, then he can enter his heart through that door, and then he can begin to come home. Then he can soar or leap or swim or fly or roam as himself and simply be, heart kin to all things. She prayed that this be so for him. There was a reason we are all here, the People said, a reason we each came to be, we all have something to offer.

She looked at her son with the fierce mother love of her deepest kind and saw again a seed in him of the same wild freedom to weave and move, that same capacity to shift freely beyond the boundaries he had not even recognized as barriers yet. Like a newly born cub, just as she was the bear had said to her, blind born, but even in their blindness, the cubs knowing without knowing what it is they seek, and following the seeking they find. And she saw with other eyes golden brown, flecked with sunlight, that Kai's heart would survive the searching and the boundaries just as hers had done, and he would come at last to home.

"Your heart," she said softly, "your heart will find a way. Listen to it. It already knows." They were both quiet for a while, and then she said, "I must go now."

Kai looked back at her with same sun flecked brown eyes. "I know. Thank you. For bringing me into this life, for.... for the chance to go home, and for something else," he said. "I don't understand it yet, but.... there is something I must do. I don't know what it is, but I know that it is there."

"Yes," she said, "It is, it is closer than you know." She hugged him with her momma bear's hug as he used to call it when he was a child, holding him tightly in her arms shaking him gently with a playful growling purring sound.

"I love you Mom."

"I love you too."

And the light flickered…. a shadow passed in front of the fire. Faint voices exchanged near the bright glow of flames small inside the night. Murmuring. A meaning in the sounds he could not comprehend. He stood up on his hind legs and tasted the cold night air, whole realms of scent beyond the hot dry smoky smell given off by the flickering light. For him outside that small bright island, all smells called to him, were calling to him. He dropped to all fours and padded away unheard, unseen.

The light flickered. A laughing voice, giggling. "Oh, that is alright. Come here." A light flickers and a voice filled with concern, "Oh no!" A tiny shadow passes quickly, erratically, back and forth, zigzagging closer and closer to the light, fluttering, darting closer then veering away. "Oh no," a man's voice this time, lower toned, "we must save it, come help me." Small fine boned hands reach gently, slowly, toward the light, toward the fluttering darting shape. The woman's voice soothing, musical, "don't worry. I won't hurt you. Don't be afraid." And slowly the voice and hands cup the moth in a gentle darkness. "Open the window, I want to let him out."

The light flickered. I zoom closer, closer, the brightness is suddenly too hot, too cutting. I dart away, and turn back, drawing closer, closer again and then away. A man's voice, indistinct in the distance, another voice closer inside the light, musical, higher pitched. "We must save it," slender hands coming closer slowly, palms bright in the flickering light. Soft cooing sounds, "it's okay, it's okay, don't be afraid." I let myself rest on one luminous palm, so bright like the flame but it does not burn. And then a warm darkness with glowing slits of light, a warm hollow place closing around me. I hold my wings very still. A metallic click, muted, far away, followed by wooden sliding sounds and the darkness opens up and I fly again, my wings of delicate shadow blending with the night.

Kikerri sat high in the tall pine overlooking the valley. She sat easily, comfortably, warming herself in the morning sun. A slight breeze drifted through the air, setting the long needles of the pine shimmering around her. A hazy sky, muted light, a soft evenness to the day. She swiveled her head slowly to survey her world again. All across the valley, little ripples and flutters of movement radiating out from and toward each other. Down by the creek golden yellow leaves of the maples weaving in the breeze, and their ripening keys spinning like clusters of tiny wings. A flock of bushtits, tiny balls of feathers, flowing from one branch to another in a thicket, chittering as they gathered and dispersed and flew to another branch, gathering and dispersing again. A sudden flash of sharp blue, as a jay streaked through the woods carrying another acorn to a secret place. At the edge of a small cedar grove part way up the slope, the twitch of an ear, the doe and her two yearlings bedded down for the morning, warming in the autumn sun just as Kikerri was. Gentle patterns weaving together, nothing out of place, a harmony.

She glanced over at the ruins of the giant alien eggs on the opposite slope. An emptiness there, hollow, slowly fading over time, like a vapor or a mist. The strangeness that had consumed itself in its own terrible fires slowly dissolving away. Only a few jagged pieces of the shell wall remained standing. Like the last few teeth in a jaw bone bleached by sun and rain crumbling slowly and steadily into the Earth. A few wind blown seeds of the hardiest pioneers, the ground healers, place healers, the reclaimers, had taken root and grown in the rubble. Sharp pointed thistle people, their purple flowers long gone, leaves withering as clouds of their delicate seeds rose drifting in the breeze. Next year there would be more. No wingeds nesting there yet. The harshness, the going out of harmony lingered still, who would want to raise a nestling there, but even that was waning. Give it time. Let the plants reclaim it first with the persistent nurturing of their roots, knitting wholeness back together in that place, building earth again where it had been wrenched apart. Yes, let the harmony return. Then maybe when the blackberries bloom and fruit again inside the dissolving rings, a feisty little wren might find a hidden place there or a tribe of the diligent wood rat people, the little stick lodge builders, will begin to build their heaped up nests and storage places inside the protection of the berry canes, and life will return again and claim that place that for so long was kept apart.

She swept her eyes up to the sky. She stretched her wings in the warm sun then pushed off lightly from the branch, lifting herself, giving herself to the gentle air, and riding in slow circles, she rose on the warmth of the day high into the sky.

439

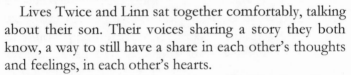

Lives Twice and Linn sat together comfortably, talking about their son. Their voices sharing a story they both know, a way to still have a share in each other's thoughts and feelings, in each other's hearts.

"He has told me," Lives Twice said, "that he will not be studying the song cycles after all. He will be studying with the plant people instead." Linn nodded. "Mainly," she continued, "he loves to roam on his own, and he is learning the ways of the plants from them directly I think. Meeting the plants where they live, learning their ways and the ways of the land together. And learning the everyday basic skills, the Earth skills from the People, the living skills that let him feel more comfortable with the land. Makes a pretty good basket already." She smiled.

"He stays out longer each time, and comes back with a wildness, a freedom in his eyes. I think he is at home out there after all," Linn said wistfully, "much more than I. He is one who could go on a walkabout someday, not me."

"He already is, I think," she said. "He has been on walkabout for much of his life already, through his stories, his imagination. His other worlds. He is just going there now with his feet too...." All four feet she wanted to say, but too soon for Kai, too soon for Linn. Kai was not even there yet, much less Linn. "But you," she said fondly, and she smiled affectionately at him, "your journey is a different one? Your distance to travel is here." She held her hands apart but close to each other and then brought them together. "Your walkabout is to belong, to connect. I have a feeling you already know this, yes? Your walkabout is to give up exile, to allow yourself to belong. Kai has a different belonging he will be coming to some day. For you the belonging is with the People, and," she laughed, her eyes merry in a way achingly familiar to Linn from their old days together, "the People are very good at connecting and belonging. You will see, they will help you. Push you probably too," she teased, "probably they have some ideas about that already. You should take a wife.... you ought to be with someone. The People may have some ideas about that for you too." Her cheerful bluntness slammed him at first. After a moment, he had to admit to himself that she was right, no need to pretend. "You were," she smiled almost shyly at him, "very good at being a husband from the little bit that I recall...." and it was his time to look shy and duck his head.

Then he lifted his head and grinned, "I'll keep that in mind. Yes, I imagine the People will have lots of help for me on that too." And he thought of the glances and soft smiles of other eyes, and the winking and nudging of the old ones in the back ground. Clues he had absorbed and stored away, and had not paid attention to before. "We'll see, we'll see."

441

And she knew that both the men of her heart from her former life, the man child and the father, were still within the circle of her care and that they would both be all right in the end, and she was content. "I must go," she said, "I will not be far away."

"Yes."

"Your heart knows. Your heart is not far away. It knows the way home…. We will meet again, before I go up the mountain for good, well, for a while." She smiled. "But for now I must go." She touched his hand briefly and then she was gone.

After she left, Linn sat for a while letting their conversation settle in his mind, pivoting around the one place that kept coming back into view, wanting to open out in a different direction than he had been able to allow in his shock then. *You ought to take a wife.* She had made a face at her use of the quaint idiom. *You ought to be with someone again,* and she had looked at him and smiled. He let himself drift deeper into that moment. He remembered Nagita, a woman about his age, the sister of the Basket Woman. Nagita had visited the village recently and he remembered her warm smile and the warmth in her eyes when he had been introduced to her and had asked about her name.

"Nagita is how we call the great sky geese that gather together for their traveling. They gather together for everything," she laughed. Her voice low toned, pleasing and warm like her eyes. "The ones with the dark brown wings and back and full grey fronted breast. Long black necks with a white blaze on their chins. They are very alert. They hold their heads up high like this at the tops of their long necks." She made a shape like the head of a goose with her hand and held her forearm upright in front of her in a perfect gesture of a goose looking intently this way and that all around. Her eyes bright, shining with the beauty and presence of the great birds. He remembered how as she mentioned the plump grey breasts of the geese, she seemed to fluff herself somehow and then suddenly the geese were vividly present for him. And when Linn told her, she had smiled modestly, saying, "the geese people are very beautiful, I am honored to share that name," and blushed slightly, but she kept her eyes on him with a lovely gracious almost matronly directness and he was enchanted. Then laughing again, she said, "and when they gather to decide anything, you should hear them! When they first lift up into the air after grazing for a while, and they fly this way and that as they gather into a group, calling, This way! This way! No! This way! No! Over here! with their flute-like barking calls, over and over, This way! This way! No! This way! Circling and turning back and setting out again." She lifted her arms and stretched them out long to each side in slow rolling motions from her shoulders, tilting to one side than the other. "All calling, all together, all at once. It's loud," she said, "very loud," and she pretended to cover her ears. "Until they just know, and they come together in that lovely undulating vee and fly away into the sky. A lot like us, like the councils." She laughed. "All of it, the honking and the calling, the pulling this way and that, over and over, then flying together," her eyes shining with simple pride in the ways of her people and the ways of her namesake the geese.

"You are right," he said, "and also very beautiful." He felt suddenly shy and embarrassed, wondering why in the world he had said that. He turned his eyes aside for a moment then he looked back at her.

She was looking at him with a wonderful kindly openness. "Thank you," she said, with quiet unselfconscious modesty, dipping her head ever so slightly. "The beauty is in your eyes perhaps, but the geese people and I thank you for sharing that."

He needs a name. Basket Woman said. Old At'sah and Big Carl nodded in agreement. *The one he came here with,* she continued, *Linn. It is a good name for him in some ways. It fits his…. his way, his flavor, almost like a calling name. But if he is going to get on with his life….*

Big Carl and Old At'sah murmured in agreement, echoing her thoughts. The three of them had gathered to consider just how to help him in this.

….then he needs a new name, one to grow by, but something he already is too, to connect them together, she concluded.

Yes, it is time. Old At'sah agreed. *How have the People been calling him already, how have they been noticing his ways? A good name grows little by little at first. What have you heard?*

There were the obvious ones at first, Big Carl said. *Sky Fish, Sky Man, Comes from the Sky. Those were dropped for the most part, after it was clear he was not a Watcher. They weren't really about him, just about how he arrived. And once everyone started to get to know him, some called him One Who Asks.*

The questions, the questioning! Like a child, only one who is very tall and looks into everything all at once! Basket Woman laughed affectionately. *Even my youngest when he was asking never came up with so many!* Laughter from all three of them. Basket Woman's youngest son had been well known for asking about everything when he was young.

He is like one of those who stirs the pot, with the asking....

Yes, but not just one pot.... Smiles and soft laughter.

No, many pots, aiiii, so many pots! Stirs everything.

Not really stirs, just looks and asks, just wants to know, wants to look inside.

Looks Inside....

Yes, but not at something small, looks inside something big instead, looks inside the sky.

Too much like the Watchers maybe, the sky eyes, and his early names.... we need to be careful there.

Asking, instead of looking inside. Asking is more who he is, and asking is more respectful of what you want to know, somehow, than just looking, even when the questions come thick as snow!

He has the heart of a wonderer, not an asker, his wonder, that is his bridge. All three nodding together. They had each touched on this part of Linn in their long conversations with him.

He is one who would ask the stars, ask the sky in his wondering. And he is one of those who may hear an answer one day too....

Perhaps, Old At'sah said mischievously, *they are answering already....* She made the small circle of the hand sign for star, holding it up to the sky and flicking her finger out against her thumb for twinkling, then moving her hand in front of her mouth where the same gesture and circle meant talking in conversation one person with another. Her eyes bright with the hand sign word play. Big Carl and Basket Woman smiled in appreciation.

Yes, the stars, and the night sky, bigger than the Watchers.

The stars....
Asking the Stars.
Asks the Stars.
Yes.
I think, Old At'sah said *we may have found his name.*

Something that he is already and something to grow on, yes. We will try that. And Basket Woman smiled to herself, satisfied, rolling the sounds of Asks the Stars and Nagita together in her heart.

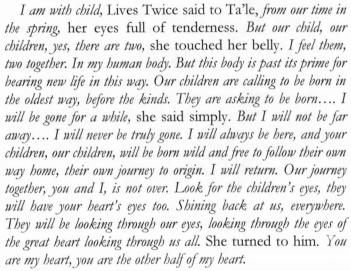

I am with child, Lives Twice said to Ta'le, *from our time in the spring,* her eyes full of tenderness. *But our child, our children, yes, there are two,* she touched her belly. *I feel them, two together. In my human body. But this body is past its prime for bearing new life in this way. Our children are calling to be born in the oldest way, before the kinds. They are asking to be born…. I will be gone for a while,* she said simply. *But I will not be far away…. I will never be truly gone. I will always be here, and your children, our children, will be born wild and free to follow their own way home, their own journey to origin. I will return. Our journey together, you and I, is not over. Look for the children's eyes, they will have your heart's eyes too. Shining back at us, everywhere. They will be looking through our eyes, looking through the eyes of the great heart looking through us all.* She turned to him. *You are my heart, you are the other half of my heart.*

And I yours. I will be waiting.

I will return.

He kissed her and felt their tears mingling, ancient radiant seas, sacred blessing, rain of the heart. *Our children will grow strong,* he said, and when she looked at him the ocean's depth in each of their eyes seamless, one depth.

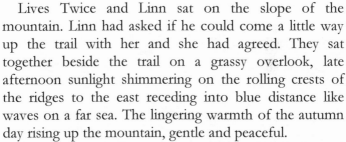

Lives Twice and Linn sat on the slope of the mountain. Linn had asked if he could come a little way up the trail with her and she had agreed. They sat together beside the trail on a grassy overlook, late afternoon sunlight shimmering on the rolling crests of the ridges to the east receding into blue distance like waves on a far sea. The lingering warmth of the autumn day rising up the mountain, gentle and peaceful.

They sat quietly for a while, and then she asked, "and have you decided yet what you will do?"

"There was the walkabout, I keep coming back to that. Not to run away," he added quickly, "just to taste a bit of it sometime.... But my skills," he shrugged his shoulders and grinned, "are still not good enough yet. Still.... clumsy," he finally said, "with the land and with my hands. The People, they would worry too much about me." He ducked his head and grinned again sheepishly.

"Yes," she smiled, and he caught a bit of the merriment in her eyes that he remembered from before.

"I had thought," he said, "to start with the night sky instead. The groups of the stars by the seasons, not the names and ideas about the constellations from the other times, but in relation to the way the People live here now, the way they live with the land. The stars, the sky, are part of the land too. The patterns of the seasons are forming again. The People tell me that during the wasting years and the years of the war, the sky was so often clouded over, and the weather and the ripening of the plants erratic then. And after the heavy clouds that covered the sky for so long moved away, a high thin haze lingered for years. The stars were hard to see. The rhythms are coming back, a little different now, but coming into harmony again, and the People are just beginning to see and know the stars again. I could be part of that connecting. The winter counts, the gathering times, when the manzanita berries ripen, when the salmon come in winter, and when the other salmon come in the spring, the summer harvesting. The patterns are reweaving, a new coherence there." He stopped. She was looking at him, her eyes delighted with the same delight he remembered from so many times long ago.

"You should see your eyes," she said, "all lit up from inside. It is good to see you like that. Yes definitely, the stars, the sky."

And as the moment faded he realized that was as close to her as he would ever get. Now. It didn't hurt as much anymore, perhaps he was getting along with his life after all.

"There are many ways to go home," she said softly, "many ways, one home, and many ways to set out on the journey." She smiled.

450

"Maybe the night sky will help me find my way, at least my place here." He gestured at the sky. "I did come from there. Sky Fish they called me at first. The sky is not just a place of death eyes and schemes for conquering other worlds, not just the stars of a far away deep space, stars here now, part of the experience of living here, part of living with the Earth. The early people migrated by the stars, used the stars to navigate great seas, great mountains, crossing great distances to new lands, following that ancient light."

"Yes, light is our friend," she said. "Light from the stars, from our hearts, from everywhere, living light. The heart light," she said, "is calling to you too. Listen to its call from wherever you hear it, sounding from the stars, whispering in a leaf, in the tracks of the four-legged relatives on the trail, from your heart. The heart light will take you home. You'll see. You have to trust its call."

He looked at her, "I wish I could find what you found, the peace. Maybe not the way you did, the way you do, some other way. I am still looking."

"It will find you, it is already calling you, in here," she said, and made the sign for heart from the hand language. Her palm cupped gently, fingers pointing downward over her heart. Then she made the sign for understanding, her hand sweeping out palm down in a level arc from her heart. "I must go soon, my place is on the mountain," she said softly.

"Yes, I know. Will I see you again?"

"Perhaps. We each have our own lives now, calling us. She looked radiant to his eyes and somehow fuller. She had gained weight, rounded with a glow as if from inside, ripe like summer fruit, like the peaches his mother had

451

loved. Whatever called to her had filled her with a quiet luminous joy he found hard to imagine or accept as possible for himself, not yet.

"Trust the call," she said, as she rose to leave, "and remember it loves you too."

As she reached the bend in the trail, she called out to him. He could see her lips moving, but he heard her thoughts more than her words, as pictures in his mind. *The stars, they are calling in your heart....*

Linn sat for a long time on the side of the mountain after she left. Light faded into night. Slowly, one by one, the brightest stars began to distill out of the limpid translucent skies that lingered as night approached, and he recognized the square of the four lodge post stars high overhead. He sat as more and more stars bloomed in the sky, until the watery blur of the clustered stars of the winter trout sisters rose, followed by the vee of stars of the geese people on their night journey, until the three bright stars at the center of the basket maker carrying her great bundle of willow withes for her winter basket work just began to lift above the eastern horizon, and then enfolded in the wonder and the starlight he headed down the trail. *The stars,* she had said, *listen in your heart....*

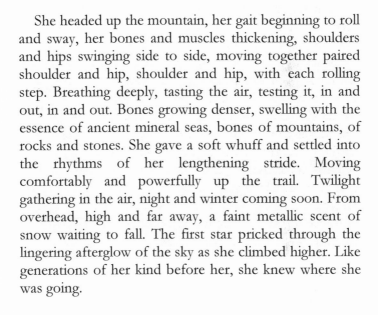

She headed up the mountain, her gait beginning to roll and sway, her bones and muscles thickening, shoulders and hips swinging side to side, moving together paired shoulder and hip, shoulder and hip, with each rolling step. Breathing deeply, tasting the air, testing it, in and out, in and out. Bones growing denser, swelling with the essence of ancient mineral seas, bones of mountains, of rocks and stones. She gave a soft whuff and settled into the rhythms of her lengthening stride. Moving comfortably and powerfully up the trail. Twilight gathering in the air, night and winter coming soon. From overhead, high and far away, a faint metallic scent of snow waiting to fall. The first star pricked through the lingering afterglow of the sky as she climbed higher. Like generations of her kind before her, she knew where she was going.

In the beginning, the sea swept sea smelling earth. In the beginning, the blue black depth. The sea swept sea smell earth not yet born. The earth, the mountain, all mountains, the star strewn nights, the sun bright days, all time, all space, dancing in the blue black depth. Unseen even to themselves. Unselved. Not knowing. Nothing unknown. The wise One. Undivided. All. Giving birth to rainbow circles. First radiance. The bear stirred in her long sleep. Rainbow circles floating, swimming on layers of seas. All overlapped. All overlapping. Upwelling of rivers, sea swells, mountains of sea swimming rainbow circles, shimmering with the pure delight of becoming. Joining tenderly, two becoming one again. First grace. The bear. Sea smelling breath, saline, mineral, moist roots and earth, the breathing of her inner seas, in and out, in and out, in slow soft waves. Soft swells deep breasted rising in long lines, towering, booming, roaring, pushing up from massive depths of sea tides. Watery mountains moving in long slow lines, booming, salt smelling, plumes of spindrift snow windblown from their moving peaks, leaving trails of tiny bubble worlds as they pass, myriad water swimming hissing whispering riding the calm again seas, rocking gently in the ebbing echoes of the long lines of mountain waves. Tenderly, bubbles coming together and moving apart, inhale and exhale of whole worlds. Rainbow colors swirling across clear curves of light, mirroring the rainbow seas until they pop, leaving a briefly dimpled space, an absence fleet as presence, sending rings of light rippling out across the gently rocking surface. Rings of light expanding, melting back into the sea, into the soft sea swells of earth beyond time, into the soft sea smell earth around her exhaling and inhaling, breathing as she breathed, enfolding her. The bear turned gently. She stretched her sea filled muscles from beyond sleep and dream, deep inside the dream of time. Time dreaming itself, dreaming mountains of night skies, mountains of seas, molten, overlapping, shimmering. The bear curled more tightly around her sleeping cubs, securing them in the tender curve of her body. Gentle sea swells rolled through her sleeping form, all through her cave, all through the rocks and roots and the great mountain's heart, her breath warmed cave dark pulsing, swaying, rippling with the breathing Earth, rippling with the rings of light and rainbow circles, rainbow echoes of ringing light circling around her cubs, their becoming her joy.